MANIFEST DESTINY

Rebecca O'Donnell

Manifest Destiny
by Rebecca O'Donnell

No part of this publication may be reproduced, distributed, or transmitted in any form or by any means, electronic or mechanical, including photocopy, recording or any information storage and retrieval system, currently available or yet to be invented, without prior permission in writing from the publisher.

The story, all names, characters, and incidents portrayed in this production are fictitious. No identification with actual persons, living or deceased, places, buildings, and products is intended, or should be inferred.

Story by Rebecca O'Donnell
Book Cover and Artwork by Rebecca O'Donnell
Copyright © 2024 Rebecca O'Donnell. All rights reserved.

Published by talcMedia Press
411 Walnut Street #7720
Green Cove Springs, FL 32043 USA
www.talcMedia.com

ISBN: 978-0-945031-13-0 Hard Cover Edition
ISBN: 978-0-945031-14-7 Soft Cover Edition
ISBN: 978-0-945031-15-4 Digital Edition

First Edition 2024

For Cristina & Rhianna

1

It is our manifest destiny to take this new world and build with it a new heaven. And that heaven, with everything in it, shall be ours, and ours alone.

There was no pleasure regarding the sex. It didn't matter if her partner was male or female, ugly or beautiful, young or old. Fucking was just a job, and they both did it automatically.

Willow sat astride her fat balding businessman on the other bed. Dolly rode her own flabby john with rapid jerks of her pelvis, circling her hips and offhandedly noting how the ripples on his belly resembled a thumped gelatin. She was tired and wanted to finish quickly so she could go home and put her feet up.

Dolly glanced up at Willow, who grinned back and picked up the pace as well. They often worked together. Willow, with her lithe and pale Asian beauty, and Dolly, with her athletic but curvy Swiss heritage, were perfect foils for each other. This hotel was a favorite spot for the high-end clientele the women favored. Spoiled businessmen and shy, midlife crisis husbands were their main moneymakers. The businessmen were usually sharp and abrupt, all bluster and authoritarian in their mannerisms and language. Those, like the two johns the women were working tonight, were normally fast and easy once they got their clothes off. "Get off and get out" was the asshole motto.

The shy, middle-aged husbands were tender and fumbling, and always wanted to talk afterward. Dolly enjoyed them with an almost motherly instinct, often listening well into the night as they unburdened all their fears and timid gratitude to her. They paid as much for that time as for the fucking, which made it even better.

But it had been a long week, and she was glad that they only had these two assholes for the last gig of the night. Functioning on autopilot, she looked around the spacious hotel suite, glad of the cleanliness and regal appearance of the room. The whores had a deal worked out with the hotel manager, who took a small cut and sometimes even solicited clients for them. As long as they wore upscale outfits or concealing coats, he let them be.

Dolly's partner was close to finishing and, from the sound of it, so was Willow's. *Willow's really hamming it up tonight,* Dolly thought, smiling softly. She'd tease her about all that moaning and gasping when they went for breakfast later. Dolly glanced over in cynical amusement, but the smile froze on her face when she looked at her friend.

Willow wasn't moving like a high-class whore finishing up her john; she was locked in place atop him, arms rigid, body trembling. Her breath was wheezing in and out in painful gasps, and she stared straight ahead, eyes wide.

"Willow? Honey, you okay?" Dolly asked.

"Doll…something's wrong," Willow gasped through clenched teeth. "I'm…I'm burning…"

"What do you mean?" Dolly forgot about the man beneath her, twisting to look at her friend. "Willow? Baby, answer me!"

Her only reply was a guttural hiss. Willow began to jerk as if in a seizure, her legs still locked around the man as he tried to squirm free.

"Get this bitch off me! Get her off me!"

Dolly scrambled off her own client and ran to Willow, jerking her hand back when she touched her. Willow's skin was burning hot.

"Baby, what is it? Let go," Dolly said frantically, trying to pull the woman away. "Let go, Willow. Let go."

"Get her off me! Get her off me! Oh, God, it's burning! It's burning me! Help me!"

Dolly's john was scrambling into his pants. "Jesus. What the fuck?"

He grabbed his wallet and the rest of his clothes and ran out. Dolly yelled for him to call an ambulance, but he never turned around. She raced to the phone and tried to dial out, but punched the wrong number.

"Shit! What's the fucking call out number?"

Willow began to scream.

As Dolly watched in horror, Willow's smooth skin turned grainy and thick. Then sections of it began to pour off of her like sand from a bucket, exposing muscle and black bone. Her eyes swelled, pushing out of their sockets, then ruptured from the pressure, spraying Dolly with hemorrhaged tissue. Willow's midnight hair was smoking from the intense heat, drifting up and around her as if she were caught in an updraft. The grainy flesh continued to pour off of her, spreading across the bed and the sobbing man underneath, cascading to the floor and rippling out across the carpet like mercury on a glass surface. Then the exposed muscles of her shoulders and arms seemed to liquefy, pouring down across her body, enveloped in a steaming gray cloud. Dolly could see her friend's blackened skeleton grow red-hot. Willow's waist-length hair caught fire, swirling in an inferno around her head and back. She never moved from that terrible locked position. The frantic man beneath her clawed at her thighs, his skin crackled and black as it ruptured, spilling liquefied fat across the bed, his voice choked and sobbing as he tried to get away.

It all happened in seconds.

Then Dolly snapped out of her frozen shock, dragged a blanket from her bed and ran toward them, just as Willow exploded.

*   *   *

Dolly jerked awake with a shriek, arm raised against the force of the explosion. She was sitting up in her own bed, panting and disoriented, tears streaming down her face, hair wet with sweat. Looking around her tiny room, illuminated by the streetlight that had just come on, Dolly shuddered, running her hands through her soaking hair.

"Goddammit. These fucking nightmares…"

The clock read seven pm. Time to go to work. Dolly threw back the blanket and padded to the bathroom, shaking off the nightmare. She'd been having them for months now. Strange exploding women were not her only dream; some were from memories of her fucked-up childhood.

But most were scenarios that had never happened—gang rape, violence, being trapped in a tiny, claustrophobic box, bloody miscarriages, dead babies, pedophiles tearing her tiny womb apart, being stabbed while strapped to a bed. These were common horrors every time she closed her eyes. She figured the miscarriage and baby ones were her subconscious dealing with her infertility. Before she was ten years old, Dolly's own father had made sure her womb was too damaged to ever get pregnant.

She wished she could have her other reoccurring dream more often, where she was floating, weightless and relaxed in a garden, her body drifting over green grass and summer flowers. She always felt well rested after that one. Kyle, the limo driver for her and the other women, said the nightmares were most likely inspired by her profession. Being a whore could be a dangerous, ugly job. Maybe all this shit was just the past bubbling up to fuck with her head.

After a quick shower, Dolly squeezed into her uniform—black stockings, impossibly high stiletto heels, miniskirt, and embroidered corset. The shoes added to her already considerable height; she was six feet two inches tall when she wore them.

Her thoughts drifted back to the dream hotel with its beautiful rooms. *Too bad we don't have a regular gig with a five-star hotel*, she thought. *It'd be nice to have a classy place to work from. Oh, well. Three stars is good enough. Better than working the streets every night.*

She finished her makeup and hair quickly, then reached for a small crystal decanter of perfume. Lifting the delicately cut stopper, she dabbed multiple areas of her skin with it. Neck, wrists, breasts, knees, and ankles. Dolly luxuriated in the scent. It was real perfume, blended especially for her, and had cost three months' pay. It was worth the money. The perfume lasted all night and the scent was gorgeous. Johns were always telling her how much they loved the way she smelled.

Stepping back, Dolly took one last look in the mirror. Her makeup was heavy, her white blond hair smooth and shining, jewelry gaudy and noisy. She looked like a whore. Perfect.

Slinging a beaded purse over one shoulder, Dolly checked to make sure it held her phone and enough condoms, tucked in a handful of bills to make change in case of cash payments, and counted one lipstick, one pack of breath mints, dental floss, and three douches in the bottom. She slid a small knife into a hidden seam on the corset, grabbed her keys, and walked out.

Her friends were already out on their curb, hustling cars and showing leg as the traffic passed by. They worked the street if bookings were slow or in between dates, which usually were scheduled later in the evening. Tanja was just sixteen, barely the legal age for prostitution. She was a pretty blond wearing a metallic bustier over a low-slung sequined skirt, her bare hips showing the straps of a beaded thong. Dolly smiled at the sight, finding the teenager's apparel endearing in its youthful garishness. Keisha was a tiny Black woman, twenty-six, with elaborate cornrowed hair glittering with gold-plated and rhinestone clips. She wore a skin-tight green minidress with a halter top that plunged to her navel, a thick Byzantine-inspired necklace, gold bangles on her wrists, and stiletto heels she'd used more than once as a weapon against overzealous johns. Dolly admired Keisha's ability to carry it all off. She looked like a tiny warrior goddess.

"Hey, bitches," Dolly called out.

"Hey, bitch," Keisha responded.

"Hiya, Doll," Tanja smiled shyly, obviously pleased to see her. Dolly had taken Tanja under her wing in very much the same way Keisha had with Dolly when she first began hustling. These women were all close friends, and they protected each other.

The Los Angeles streets were normally busy, but tonight was slow. Self-driven cars rolled by, their passengers never looking up from their devices, faces cast in blue light from the electronic screens.

Dolly and her friends preferred a human driver to the cost of renting an automate, plus the added bonus of another human being to watch over them. Kyle, their driver, wasn't due with the limo for another two hours. So they waved and flirted and whistled at the traffic, to no avail. Car after car passed without even slowing down.

Half an hour into their night, a cop car honked and slid up to the curb. The women waved a greeting. Ever since prostitution became legal a decade ago, the police were usually a welcome sight.

The driver rolled his window down and grinned at them all. It was Officer Ramirez. He was a friendly man whom Dolly had done a couple times, but he had a real soft spot for Keisha. He'd even overseen their getting tracker chips implanted in their arms, a standard safety precaution for prostitutes. They trusted him enough to take care of them if anything happened.

With a welcoming smile, Keisha bent over and leaned against the frame of the car's open window. Ramirez grinned back, looking at all three.

"You ladies have a permit for this corner?"

Keisha laughed. "Fuck you, Ramirez. What you got for me tonight?"

He lifted a tray with three lidded cups and handed it to Keisha. "Hot chocolate for this chilly night."

"It's eight-five degrees out, idiot," Dolly yelled with a grin.

"That's cool for LA, Doll."

Keisha moved aside so Dolly could take the tray, then leaned back into the window. "That's sweet," she said, her voice low, one long fingernail tracing the man's forearm. "But I was thinking about you giving me some more of that golden brown exercise I'm so fond of."

Ramirez laughed. "You're so full of shit, Keisha."

"Maybe. But you love it."

"Yeah. I do."

"How about it, then?"

He shook his head. "Can't. We're running cover for a group of bigwigs at the Waldorf tonight. Me and ten other cars as backup security."

"Wow. Who's coming in?" Dolly asked, sipping her chocolate.

"Off-limits, Doll. Even we don't know. Some bigwigs from corporate, probably."

"Ah. Maybe we'll get some business later on. I love the Waldorf."

Keisha reached in and stroked his cheek. "How about a quickie, Ramirez? You look good tonight."

"No can do, and I'm sorrier than you are about it." He pressed a hand fondly over Keisha's arm and groaned. "Gotta go. See you later. Stay safe, ladies." He pulled away and drove off.

Keisha took the cup Dolly handed her, watching as the police car vanished around the corner. "Goddammit. Ramirez is always a lot of fun. I like his wife, too."

"You've met her?" Tanja asked, amazed.

"Oh, yeah. Sometimes we pull a three-way together. They're a great couple. Good parents, too. Got four kids and every damn one of them is happy."

10

"No shit?"

"Yeah." Keisha turned back toward the two women. "I just love that guy. He reminds me that good men exist." She gestured toward the corner where his car had turned.

"Too true," Dolly replied, tucking Keisha under her chin for a hug. "Most men I've known are only interested in their dicks and their wallets."

"Not necessarily in that order, either," Keisha scoffed.

"Yeah, well," Dolly said, looking where Keisha had gestured. "I'll agree with you there. There are a few good males out there, and Ramirez definitely is one. Me, I love my shy little nerds. They're adorable and they pay well."

Keisha took a drink and immediately scalded her mouth.

"Goddammit, this shit is hot!"

"Thus the name 'hot chocolate.'"

"Fuck you, Dolly. I burned my damn mouth."

"You're insured. Get a Band-Aid."

"You can get a Band-Aid for the inside of your mouth?" Tanja asked the question in all seriousness.

Keisha and Dolly looked at each other, then started laughing. Dolly swung a long arm around Tanja's shoulders and kissed the top of her head.

"I like how stupid you are, kid. Makes you very lovable."

"I'm not a kid."

"Yeah, you are. Stay that way for a while, hey? Don't get all tough and rough like Keisha and me."

"Speak for yourself, bitch," Keisha said. "I'm smooth as silk and soft as a fucking kitten."

Dolly snorted her derision. "A kitten with tiger claws, maybe."

"I ain't arguing."

They stood quietly after that, sipping their hot chocolate. Tanja looked down the street, watching for the limo that would take them to their evening gigs.

"Kyle's a good one."

"What?" Keisha looked at her.

"Kyle's a good man," Tanja replied.

"You fucked Kyle?"

"No."

"You don't know if a guy's a good man unless you fuck him."

"Who says?"

"I do."

"She's right, Tanja," Dolly said. "A man will show you everything when his dick is hard and even more after he comes. You can see into his soul if you pay attention."

Keisha snorted. "Yeah, but it's mostly some monster in there, and the fucker looks back, right into your eyes."

Dolly nodded. "If you gaze long into an abyss, the abyss also gazes into you."

"I knew you'd have some damn weird quote, Doll. But at least johns are still in the market for real pussy and not hardware."

"Why do you hate the synthetics so much, Keisha?" Dolly asked, finishing her hot chocolate.

"Because they cut into our business. Every high-class hotel has a set of fake pussies nowadays."

"Their eyes scare me," Tanja said. "They don't light up like people's."

"Just my point. Who wants to fuck that?" Keisha sneered. "Too goddamn creepy for me. Ever have a conversation with an AI?"

"Artificial intelligence? Yeah, every time I go eat."

"I'm not talking about robo-staff at a restaurant, Dolly. I'm talking about those advanced AI droids. They don't feel anything. What if they decide we're a lousy species and start a war or something?"

"Oh, yeah, humanity has such a good track record at preventing war," Dolly replied. "We've been at war since before I was born. Mass murder, all in the name of peace."

"But people have souls," Tanja said quietly. "Those things don't."

Dolly smiled at her young friend's innocence.

"I hope you're right, kid. But don't try to tell me the Profit mob have souls. They don't give a flying fuck about anything but money."

"Oh, yeah. The Profit Fanatics are the worst," Keisha said. "Those cunts are crazy."

Dolly agreed. "Remember that one john who wanted me to pray to a pile of gold coins before sex? Son of a bitch tried to beat me up after."

"Yeah, and you put him in the hospital."

"Not before he kicked the shit out of me." Dolly's voice grew fierce. "Fuck every one of those greedy motherfuckers. For that matter, fuck humanity. Bunch of lowlife backstabbing assholes."

Tanja and Keisha gaped at their friend, startled by her sudden bitter vehemence. Dolly was usually the most optimistic of the bunch.

"Now, you know you don't believe that, Doll," Keisha said. "What about all your books and art museums? Somebody made all that shit."

"Yeah, and most genius artists led tortured lives because of the rest of humanity, Keisha."

The trio grew uncomfortably silent. Then Keisha squared her shoulders.

"Damn, girl. What's the matter with you? You're more cynical than I am tonight."

Suddenly self-conscious, Dolly shook herself and laughed. "Nobody's more cynical than you are."

"Must be from hanging out with you."

They turned as a car slowed down. All three women offered the passenger suggestive smiles and provocative stances as he looked them over. Then the car pulled away without a word.

"Son of a bitch," Keisha said. "There's no action tonight."

"I know I'd rather be home with a book right now." Dolly sighed. "Good thing we've got gigs later or tonight would be a total bust."

Keisha and Tanja finished their drinks while Dolly half-heartedly watched the traffic. She told them about her latest nightmare, striving to sound flippant, but the memory was still too fresh. Her voice trembled as she recalled the fire.

"You've had that one before," Tanja said. "With the lady who blows up."

"Yeah, but I've never known her name before."

"Nobody names their kid Willow," Keisha said.

"Yeah they do. Remember that little girl whose uncle raped her, chopped her up, stuffed the parts into two garbage bags, and threw her into a culvert?"

"That was in the South, right? Couple months ago?"

"Yeah. It was all over the news. Her name was Willow."

"I don't watch the news," Tanja frowned. "Too depressing."

"I like to stay on top of the madness," Dolly said. "I watch the news before I go to bed."

"Wouldn't that give you nightmares right there?" Keisha chimed in. "Maybe that's where you got the name Willow, Doll."

"I don't know. I just wish I'd stop having these goddamn nightmares. They're starting to get to me."

"Dream about being the happy housewife and mom again," Tanja said. "That one's nice."

"I like the one where she's floating and it's really quiet. Worst one's where she's chained inside a fucking trunk. I'm too claustrophobic for that shit. But floating over a field of flowers is nice."

Dolly clicked her tongue in annoyance. "I can't pick which dream to dream."

"Do you still dream about your dad?" Tanja asked. "Mine got me, too. I don't know what I'd do if I started dreaming about him. Probably kill myself."

"Don't say that!" Dolly snapped, making both Keisha and Tanja blink in surprise. She grabbed Tanja's arms and hauled her close, snarling into her shocked face. "Don't ever say that again. You hear me? Never say that again!"

"Dolly, calm the fuck down. Let her go."

"I didn't mean anything," Tanja replied, eyes tearing up. "I just think it's so awful, you having these dreams every night."

Dolly softened, stroking Tanja's frightened face before letting her go. "Every day, you mean. We sleep during the day, remember?"

"WE sleep, Dolly. You have nightmares."

"Don't you start having them. One of us being a basket case is enough."

Keisha shook her head. "Yeah, but you are fucked-up, woman. I think you should study these damn things. Something is trying to tell you something. Figure that shit out and clean it up. You're never gonna stop screaming in your sleep if you don't."

"Don't go all meta-fuzzy with me, Keisha."

"Fuck you. You're a goddamn coward if you don't look this shit straight in the eye and figure it out."

"Thanks, bitch. That's really helpful."

"Truth, whore. Nothing but the truth."

"Here's Kyle!" Tanja cheered.

The limo pulled up to the curb and a young man jumped out. Kyle Holmes was in his early twenties, thin and gangly, with large brown eyes and a shock of thick russet hair that stood out all over. One small glittering stud adorned his right ear. It was his only adornment. A college student studying computer programming, psychology, and forensic memory patterns, he hoped to work for one of the big tech companies someday in their android and AI departments. It was way over most people's heads, but he liked to talk about it anyway. Dolly thought he was interesting but had a hard time deciphering it. Keisha and Tanja found it humorous but nothing more. Kyle worked the night shift with the limo company because he could study in between the women's gigs. He smiled now as he skipped around to the passenger side and opened the door.

"Good evening, ladies."

"Good evening, meat," Keisha replied, smirking. "Grown any hair down there yet?"

Kyle laughed politely. Dolly took pity on him.

"Leave the kid alone, Keish. I can see his blush in the dark."

The women piled into the backseat without hesitation. Kyle was a man they trusted. In the two years Dolly had been working this area, he'd never solicited or hurt any of them. The women assumed he was gay or asexual, but he never talked about his personal life. Kyle was interested in his studies and the intricacies of the human psyche. Dolly suspected he found her and her two friends all fascinating cases. He was always asking questions, trying to analyze them. They found his curiosity endearing.

"Hey, Kyle," Keisha immediately launched into gossip. "Dolly had another one of her fucked-up dreams."

"Shut up, Keisha. Kyle doesn't want to hear about my shit."

"On the contrary, I'm very interested," Kyle replied. "Are you okay? What happened?"

"I'll tell you later."

"Just another exploding whore dream," Keisha said. "She doesn't want us hassling her about it."

"Keisha, I will bitch-slap you," Dolly warned.

"Oh, I better shut up then. Your limber ass is likely to reach over and kick me from way over there."

Kyle dropped Keisha and Tanja off at one of their usual hotels, then invited Dolly to sit up front with him. She declined, stretching out across the back with a sigh.

"Just drive around a bit before you drop me. My date won't be ready for an hour."

"You got it. So what about this latest dream? Was it another rape? Did you see your father again?"

Dolly shook her head. "No. No, this was much worse than any of my daddy fuck nightmares. Those were memories, and it was just me. This dream, this woman—I loved her. She felt real to me. But it never happened. The damn thing is…it's like she was my best friend. I feel like I'm grieving for her, for Chrissake."

Kyle hesitated before speaking. "Are you sure you don't want to go see a psychiatrist, Doll? You could get in with a pro bono shrink. I know some really good ones."

Dolly sneered at the idea but Kyle continued.

"I know, you hate that shit. But I'm worried about you. You come from a terrible childhood and a pretty bad adulthood so far. What are you? Twenty-three? There's a lot of wounds in there for somebody so young. You joke about it, but that sort of thing can't just be shrugged away with humor. I study this, remember. I wouldn't suggest it unless I truly believed therapy could help you."

Dolly sighed and stretched along the seat, staring silently out the window. Kyle watched her in the rearview mirror. She smiled tenderly at him and went back to watching the traffic.

"I know, kid. And I thank you. But there's no fucking way." She suddenly turned to stare at him. "If telling you my shit bothers you, I don't have to talk about it. No need for us both to be batshit crazy."

"I don't think you're crazy, Dolly. I just see your pain. I want to help."

"I know."

"And you can tell me anything. Please don't think I ever want you to shut up. You're my friend. I'd do anything for you."

Dolly laughed, pushing her foot against the passenger window. "So I'll keep telling you my dreams. Maybe you'll write a chapter about me someday."

"More like a trilogy of books."

"I get a cut of your royalties."

"Deal."

The mood lifted, and they continued to discuss Dolly's nightmares as they drove through the city. She wore a slight smile as Kyle tried to fit those images to reality, cynically enjoying his naivete and legitimate concern. It was useful as well; although she loathed the idea of going to see some shrink who'd probably try to fuck her (been there, done that), maybe Kyle's obsession with untangling her mind might bear fruit. Anything to help her get some sleep. She didn't drink, and she didn't do drugs; a family of addicts had shown her what that road led to. Dolly trusted Kyle, and she didn't trust men as a rule. He also didn't treat her like she was stupid. Just because she was a whore didn't mean she was a moron. Kyle recognized her current occupation as the result of tragedy and abuse. He didn't blame her. That was rare. Men always blamed a whore.

It was a long night—over a dozen men, some in groups, plus a last-minute request from the corporate shindig Ramirez was working. Dolly finished with the final ones just as the sun was rising. Exhausted, she walked out of the Waldorf, sagging with relief when she saw the limo immediately pull up. Tanja and Keisha were already inside, equally tired and sore. Dolly collapsed beside them.

"Rough night?" Kyle asked.

"Her last gig was here, for fuck's sake," Keisha said wearily, stretched out across the back. "Dolly's turning tricks at the Waldorf while Tanja and me work a convention at a goddamn Ramada. How bad could it have been?"

Dolly lifted the half-asleep Tanja and repositioned her. "What a night. Slow on the street, madhouse at the hotels. All I want is a hot shower and my own bed."

"I gotta eat," Keisha said. "Take us through a drive-through, Kyle. I want pancakes."

"Yeah, that sounds good," Tanja sighed drowsily. "I want some, too."

Tanja and Keisha shared an apartment, so Kyle dropped them off first. He thanked them shyly for the money they shoved into his hand and warned them to eat their pancakes before they got cold.

"Yes, Daddy," Keisha rolled her eyes, swinging her take-out bag. "See you two later."

"Bye, Kyle. Bye, Doll." Almost asleep on her feet, Tanja's words were no more than a wisp of sound. Dolly waved silently as they drove away, too tired for banter.

She laid down across the back seat with a sigh, long legs stretched out over the upholstery. Glancing up, she saw Kyle worriedly watching her in the rearview mirror. She smiled.

"I can practically hear your thoughts," she sighed. "Go ahead and ask your questions. I know you're dying to pick my brain apart."

"I think you should take a break from watching the news for a while," he began. That one threw Dolly. She wasn't expecting such a strange conversation starter.

"I know you watch the news before you go to bed. It's probably been triggering these nightmares. After I dropped you off at the hotel, I did some poking around on my laptop. A news story ran three nights ago about the thirty-year anniversary of the Waldorf fire in Los Angeles. It was started, so the story went, by an Asian prostitute who died of spontaneous combustion. The explosion set fire to the bed and curtains, killed the john she was with, and burned through three stories before they could put it out. Fourteen people were killed."

"I don't remember seeing that."

"Maybe not. But even overhearing a conversation about it could lodge the story in your subconscious. You're sensitive enough for your mind to connect you with an image of the woman who died."

"Was her name Willow?"

"I couldn't find a name."

"Then where'd the name Willow come from?"

"Probably the little girl from that story you told me about last week."

"She wasn't Asian."

"The spontaneous combustion prostitute was. You were sexually abused as a child. So was the girl Willow, who was murdered and dismembered. There's a good possibility the woman who combusted was abused as well. Statistically, most prostitutes are. Instinctively, you recognize that. Your brain simply mashed them all together. The human mind doesn't care about making sense of these details. It throws everything into the mix. That's what comes out as nightmares. And it happened thirty years ago, Doll. Before you or I were even born."

Dolly ran a hand through her hair, lost in thought. Kyle always made some sort of sense when it came to mindfuck problems. He had a gift for it.

They pulled up in front of her apartment building. Kyle started to get out, but Dolly told him to stay where he was. Twisting in her seat with a grimace, sore and grimy, she opened the door.

"Yeah, well, thanks for trying to dig this shit out of my brain, Kyle. You're a good kid."

"No problem. Get some rest. Make sure you eat first."

"Yeah, yeah. I'll see you later."

"You should have gotten pancakes, too."

"Too tired to saw them apart."

Kyle smiled, his eyes tender. "Night."

"Day. Sun's coming up."

"Sleep well whatever the sky's doing."

Dolly laughed wearily. "I will. Go get some breakfast yourself."

He drove off with a wave.

Unlocking the door to her apartment, Dolly entered and threw the keys on a nearby wooden side table gleaming with polish. She'd restored the piece herself. Dolly saved carefully for decent furniture, haunting thrift stores, estate liquidations, and garage sales for anything she could find or turn into something beautiful. As a result, her small apartment had an old-world elegance. No chrome or plastic anywhere.

She kicked off her shoes with a groan of relief, then walked into the kitchen to make herself a cup of coffee. Humming a tune, she slapped a few pieces of bread into the toaster and got jam and butter out of the fridge as the coffee brewed. Hand shaking with exhaustion, Dolly spilled a drop on her hand as she poured, too tired to aim well.

Instantly, the burning sensation brought the nightmare back, and she saw Willow explode into flames. Again, the woman screamed her name as the fire consumed her.

Dolly knocked over the mug of coffee as she grabbed the counter, the scalding liquid cascading everywhere. Yanking her hands up from the spill, she leaned her body forward and pulled the wet corset away from her skin, gasping with pain.

It was too much. Overwhelmed with emotion and exhaustion, Dolly started crying.

"What the fuck is happening to me?"

2

"This sleep deprivation shit is gonna kill me."

Impatient with her own weeping, Dolly shook her head and angrily dashed the tears from her cheeks. Leaving the mess, she began to strip on her way to the bathroom, throwing her dirty clothes into a wicker hamper. She stepped into the shower cubicle, letting the hot water wash away her tears and all traces of the night.

The shower calmed her down. Rubbing herself dry with an enormous towel, she slipped a nightgown over her head and padded barefoot back into the kitchen to clean up the mess. Cold toast and coffee, but she was too tired to care.

Flopping down on the couch, Dolly turned on the TV, randomly flipping channels. There was a commercial for growing your own genius babies outside the womb (protect your girlish figure), followed by a mini-documentary about the Yellowstone Caldera Project, where engineers were drilling thousands of holes in the area to relieve pressure and prevent a catastrophic eruption.

"Yeah, that'll work," Dolly scoffed.

She finished her toast, put the dishes in the sink, and went to bed, falling asleep immediately. Her mind was full of dreams; her father first putting his hands on her as a toddler, a smiling man kissing her in the kitchen before going off to work, a beautiful little girl showing her a whirligig toy as they sat in the park, a doctor digging impacted wax out of her ear. These all drifted through her mind like whispers, fleeting and out of focus. Then came Willow, the fire, and the screaming.

Dolly jerked awake. Someone was pounding on the apartment wall, yelling for her to shut up. The screaming was hers. Still bleary, Dolly yelled, "Sorry!" at the wall. The pounding stopped. She felt something wet on her hands. It was blood. Bloody scratches oozed down her forearms, and her fingernails were crammed with skin she'd torn off during the nightmare. She'd clawed herself in her sleep.

It wasn't the first time. Dolly fumbled through the nightstand drawer for a tissue, dabbing the already congealing blood and surveying the damage. The skin was torn from elbow to wrist on both arms, but it wasn't deep and she healed quickly. She hadn't done anything like that since she was a teenager.

"Fuck…"

She started crying again. This time she didn't try to stop it. Sitting on the side of the bed, head in her hands, Dolly allowed herself to grieve for all the stress and many tragedies in her young life. From birth, life had been nothing but hard and cruel to her, and she felt as if the end was coming—that all this might kill her. If she could just get some sleep, maybe she could regain her strength. But the nightmares were all the time now, even intruding into her waking hours. This she hadn't shared with anybody, even Keisha. Glimpses of abusers seemed to follow her all the time now, ever present but never quite seen; corner-of-the-eye ghosts, forever haunting her.

"I can't take much more of this shit," she murmured, eyes swollen and wet with tears.

The clock read three in the afternoon. It was still hours before dark. Claustrophobic from the atmosphere of stagnant nightmares, Dolly pulled on a pair of jeans and a T-shirt, shrugged into her jacket, and went for a walk.

It helped immediately. The weather was sunny and bright, the air balmy. She wandered past the bistros and bodegas, butcher shops and smoke rooms, stopping only to look at the display window in the corner library. Her glance lit briefly on every title in the window, noting the names and jacket covers. She'd read them all and could recite the text of every page. It was just something she could do, remembering like that. Her mother had been a reader and highly intelligent, even after Dad had beaten most of her character out of her. Her mouth twisting, Dolly remembered her father beating and raping them both. She knew, without question, that she never would have become a whore if Daddy hadn't started hurting her when she was five years old. She remembered how much it hurt and how long she bled afterwards. *That fucker destroyed everything he touched. Even my childhood.*

Trying to escape her morbid thoughts, Dolly wandered down to the park. She bought a packet of breadcrumbs from an old homeless lady who looked like a character from Dickens. She knew all of Dickens's work but couldn't remember when she'd read them. Probably in school.

Dolly began tossing breadcrumbs to the pigeons as she walked toward the beach. She felt unusually morose today. *Keish was right. I'm usually the chipper one.* But the constant dreams upset her more than she wanted to admit. Even the happy ones, with the smiling husband and whirligig little girl. were cruel fantasies that showed her a life she would never experience. It left an ache Dolly couldn't get rid of.

She reached Venice Beach and sat down on a bench. Watching the people go by, Dolly listened to the hum of bicycle tires and random bits of conversation. The sand was glittering in the sunshine and the water was a blue streak filling the horizon. Seagulls wailed overhead and a gentle breeze lifted her hair. Dolly closed her eyes and drank it in, a soothing cocktail of footsteps and happy nonsense as the world passed by.

"I couldn't stand the sight of it," a woman's voice laughingly exclaimed. Someone chortled a reply.

"You don't know what you're talking about," another woman chastised. Older. Maybe mid-forties.

"Mom, why can't I go? Everybody else is going. It's not fair!" A kid. The word "fair" was drawn out in a high-pitched whine. The sound made Dolly wince, then smile at the mother's response as they walked past.

"I'm not listening to you."

"Rugby is just now coming into fashion. Good time to invest." A man. Late fifties. Heavyset.

"Rugby? Get serious." Younger man replied. Early thirties.

"Hold it! Hold it!" Another man on the water. Whirring metal sound, like cranks or a bicycle chain.

Water splashed. It was a fish jumping. Mackerel. Another one. The fish were racing the boat. The sound was like belly flops in a pool, impossibly magnified. Dolly looked up, startled. It sounded so close. Her eyes scanned the water. There was a sailboat far out on the horizon, but she could hear each word the crew was shouting.

Suddenly, every sound for a quarter mile in all directions bore down on Dolly simultaneously. No longer separate conversations or random noises, it was a screaming, unbearable cacophony of everything at once. She jerked her hands over her ears and squeezed her eyes shut, but it made no difference. The noise was a tidal wave of sensation that spilled her out of her seat and tumbled her to the ground. Curled up in the fetal position, Dolly groaned when a passerby asked if she was all right. That voice was so monstrously loud, she felt as if her eardrums would burst.

Then as quickly as it began, it was over. Sound no longer hurt, noise retreated to normal.

"Miss, are you okay?"

Dolly opened her eyes, confused. A middle-aged woman with a curious little boy stood over her.

"Let me help you." The woman took her hand and helped her to her feet, guiding her down onto the bench again. Dolly assured them that she was okay.

"Sweetheart, you look pale as milk. Do you want me to call 911?"

"No," Dolly shook her head. "I'm okay. Probably just hungry."

She endured the kindly woman's fussing for a few minutes. After they were satisfied that she was all right, the woman turned away, pulling the little boy with her. He kept looking at her and Dolly stared back, frozen to the bench. She wanted to go after him. The feeling was intense, primal, devastating. *He's MINE*. She started to rise from the bench to go after them but then sank back down, stunned by her fierce, possessive rage. *What the fuck is this?* Dolly thought. *I never saw this kid in my life.* But the emotion kept flooding through her.

She gripped the edge of the bench, trying to get herself together. She'd read about biological clocks going nuts in women and wondered miserably if that's what was happening now. But she'd never wanted children and couldn't have them anyway. With that thought, she began to cry again.

"Oh, goddammit," she whispered, angry with herself. "Stop being such a fucking baby." But the tears kept coming. Jamming her sunglasses on to hide her distress, Dolly sat there and wept, angrily wiping tears away.

That's how Kyle found her. Brown-bag sandwich and chips in hand, Kyle was walking by with his earbuds in, listening to Bach. He glanced over, saw the long legs encased in tight jeans, and slowed his pace so his eyes could surreptitiously admire. When he saw it was Dolly, he stopped in his tracks.

"Dolly? What's wrong? What happened? Why are you crying?"

Dolly groaned and turned her head away.

"It's nothing. Just these stupid dreams."

"Did you have another nightmare?"

She snorted in derision. "When do I not have these nightmares, Kyle? Huh? When was the last time I had a decent sleep? Because I don't remember!"

"I think I should drive you to the hospital. This is getting ridiculous."

"I don't need a doctor, Kyle." She sighed. "I'm probably just hungry."

"Here." Kyle unwrapped his sandwich from the bag. "Eat this."

"I'm not eating your goddamn sandwich, kid."

"Why do you always call me 'kid?' I'm twenty-four, about the same age as you."

Dolly laughed weakly. "You're a baby, kid. I'm ancient."

"No, you're not. Here." He broke the sandwich in half.

"Share it with me. Then you're not eating my goddamn sandwich. You're just sharing my goddamn sandwich."

She laughed again, this time with more strength.

"Here." He handed her half. "Pastrami on rye with pickles. It's delicious."

"Your New York roots are showing, kid."

"Yeah. My food choices give me away."

She bit into the sandwich and pulled a pickle halfway out of the bread. That got them both giggling. Kyle took a napkin out of the bag and handed it to her. She wiped her mouth, cheeks bulging. He unscrewed the top off a bottle of pineapple juice, and she drank from it gratefully.

They sat back on the bench and finished their meal in silence. Dolly was grateful he wasn't plying her with questions. It was soothing to simply sit together and eat.

They rested quietly for a while, but Dolly knew he was waiting for her to speak. She sighed.

"It's not just the nightmares that bother me. They're bad enough, but there's a whole jumble of stupid shit all mixed together and fighting for who's loudest. Good shit, bad shit, really fucking awful shit, all running at the same time in my head. I feel so angry, then sad, then fucking happier than I've ever been in my life. Those are the really bad ones. They're like memories of something nice that's never happened to me. They're not my memories. They're wishes I know can never come true."

Dolly began describing what had been happening to her for weeks. Kyle watched her carefully, his face blank, knowing she'd immediately shut up if she saw his concern. When she finished talking, he turned his head to watch the seagulls drifting over the water.

"I couldn't sleep either. I kept thinking about that awful dream you had, with the woman blowing up, fire everywhere. I kept imagining I was the guy underneath, burning up with that poor woman. My dick was actually on fire. That's when I woke up." Dolly laughed at his description, and he smiled ruefully. "I'm just no good with visual stuff like that. Got too much imagination. Had to get out of the house."

"Yeah, that's a fairly new one, the woman blowing up. I've only been dreaming that one for a couple of months. But it keeps changing. Sometimes we're in a different hotel room, sometimes we're at some guy's house, sometimes it's in a lab and scientists are filming us. But it always ends the same, with her on fire. It's so fucking real, Kyle. I can smell her burning. I wake up and I can still smell her."

"That's fucked-up."

"Yeah, you think?" Dolly asked wryly. "And kids are starting to freak me out. I always liked other people's kids, but now, every time I see one, it makes me sad. I'm sterile, so I'll never have any of my own. It never bothered me before. I never wanted any. But it's been making me sad. That's why I was crying just now. This little boy smiled at me, and I lost it. It's just so goddamn stupid."

"You keep saying that."

"Fuck you, mind cop. Get out of my head."

"Force of habit. I'm always interested in your head."

Dolly took a deep breath and held it, letting the pressure loosen the knot in her chest. Kyle watched the tension in her slowly relax.

"Why can't you have kids? If you don't mind my asking."

"I'm sterile. Happened when I was a kid. Fucked-up uterus."

"From your dad?"

"Probably."

"I'm so sorry, Doll."

"Yeah, what're you gonna do? It happened. Can't fix it."

Kyle put his hand over hers.

"You know what I think? Professionally, as a mind cop?"

She smiled indulgently. "What?"

"I think you'd make a great mom."

She dropped the smile. "Don't fuck with me, Kyle. I'm not in the mood to be fucked with."

"I'm not fucking with you. I'm just stating an observation."

"So you think a two-bit whore with daddy issues would make a great mom? You're never gonna get your license with that kind of thinking."

"You're a lot more than a two-bit whore, Doll. But yeah, you do have daddy issues. Small wonder. He was a prick. I shouldn't tell you this, but I tried to find his grave a few months back. Thought I'd dig him up and piss on him. Just a fanciful thought. You're not the only one with dreams."

Dolly looked at him, trying to blend this quiet thoughtful kid with what he'd just said. He stared back, eyes wide, sheepish grin on his face. She shook her head and laughed.

"You are a crazy motherfucker, Kyle. Must be why I can talk to you without thinking you're going to hurt me."

"Damn, I hope I never hurt you. It would all be involuntary if I did."

"I should worry about you hurting me. You want to dig up dead pedophiles and piss on them."

"That's a healthy fantasy. I have no problem with it."

Mood lifted, Dolly playfully nudged him. She was glad Kyle had shown up. She always felt a little lighter after talking to him. He was going to make a brilliant psychiatrist. Even now, she could see a question forming in his mind, making her grin. He was so transparent. He'd have to work on that or his patients would eat him alive.

"Go ahead, Doc. Ask away. I can see you're dying to analyze me."

Kyle looked sheepish. "I've known you awhile…"

"Yeah?"

"You're such a nice person, Dolly. You're also obviously very smart. Your vocabulary is impressive, I've heard you quote classic literature from time to time—in between the 'fuck you' and 'cocksucker' rants—so I'm asking, why do you, uh, stroll?"

"Rent. Why do you drive whores around all night?"

"Also rent. But I requested the night shift. I like to keep an eye on you all, you know."

"I remember when you went and found Marie when she didn't show up for her next date. That motherfucker beat the shit out of her."

"Yeah, he did. Then I beat the shit out of him."

"It's hard to imagine a skinny kid like you able to beat anybody up."

"I'm stronger than I look."

"Marie told me you gave her his teeth as a keepsake."

"Probably not a good trait in a psychiatrist."

"You're wrong there, darlin'," Dolly said. "Girls like Marie, me, Keisha, and Tanja? There's nothing more powerful than a man who will fight to keep us safe. You became our man then. We trust you. And whores don't trust anybody."

Kyle seemed shyly pleased. "Yeah?"

"Yeah." Dolly heaved a sigh and stood up. "Now stop fucking around with all this soul bearing and get to class." She started to walk away. "See ya later."

"See you."

Eyes intent, Kyle watched as Dolly tossed her napkin in the garbage and began walking back the way she came. When she vanished into the crowd on the sidewalk, he stood up and walked quickly in the opposite direction. Just before he crossed the street, his cell phone rang.

"Holmes."

He snapped his last name as an answer and then began talking, still moving fast.

Dolly stopped, her back to him, confused. She could hear the phone vibrate in his pocket, hear him answer, hear the voice on the other end say, "Pick up now." The sound was isolated just to Kyle, unlike the shrieking noise from before. She turned to look. He was already halfway across the park. It was impossible that she could hear him, let alone the voice on the other end. But she did. *God, it's happening again*, she thought. *Don't let it happen again.* Dolly put her hand up to her ear defensively, then turned and ran back to her apartment.

Unaware, Kyle crossed the street and turned a corner, where a black town car was waiting. He got in and said, "Get me to Bannick."

*   *   *

Three weeks went by with little change. Dolly turned tricks with her friends, Kyle drove them around, scribbling by hand in his old-fashioned little notepad as they described their customers with ribald humor. Tanja had a fleeting fear of being pregnant, hopping with gleeful relief when her period began. Dolly felt a strange melancholy about it. She would have liked to have helped sweet Tanja with her child. They all went for their monthly physicals, a requirement to keep their sex worker permits. Although Dolly's examination took longer than her friends' did, they were each given a stamp of approval on their IDs. They celebrated by having an enormous lunch together and then went home for a night off.

Dolly spent her free time reading in her own apartment, content to be alone. She sat beneath an Art Nouveau–inspired lamp in her living room, a pile of new library books beside her.

Dolly always had a theme when it came to books. She picked a subject that interested her and then read everything she could get her hands on about it. Photography, the study of viruses, the development of sentient organics, art from around the world, wars throughout history, classic literature, poetry, biographies, science fiction, insect extinction, bird migration patterns—Dolly devoured information of any kind. She was currently obsessed with medieval hygiene, stories of bathing and parasite problems in thirteenth-century Europe. Tanja was particularly horrified by the descriptions of chastity belts during menstruation. Keisha usually yelled for Dolly to shut up.

"As long as reading about this nasty shit stops your fucked-up nightmares, I'm glad," Keisha told her. "But I don't want to hear about all that gross shit."

"Come on, Keish. Imagine if our regular customers only bathed once a year."

"Bitch, we've all fucked assholes who haven't bathed in a year."

"Not like the good old Dark Age days, we haven't."

"Have you really stopped having bad dreams, Doll?"

Tanja dropped the question in the middle of their banter, her face lit with hope. Dolly looked at the teenager, nodded, and smiled. Tanja hugged her. Then Kyle pulled up in the limo, and they all went to work.

Despite these moments of levity, Dolly was still having nightmares. But she no longer had the heart to describe them to her friends. The dreams were now a constant in her life, melding into each other. She sometimes had difficulty discerning dreams from reality after she woke up. Her hearing seemed more sensitive than normal, but there had been no repeat of the shrieking cacophony in the park. Dolly was grateful for that. She now distanced herself from her friends, playfully teasing and joking with them, but keeping her mounting anxiety to herself.

There was a new dream she wasn't prepared to talk about with anyone. It began with Dolly in a nursery room she'd decorated herself, cooing over a newborn baby in her arms. The child was beautiful, happily gurgling back at her. A nurse came and took the baby away, which made Dolly inconsolably sad.

Hearing the sound of crying, she opened the door and stepped out into a darkened warehouse corridor. The nurse with her child was nowhere in sight. The noise grew louder as she moved forward, and Dolly realized it was more than just her own baby. Multiple cries issued from behind a set of double doors at the end of the hall. Running now, she reached them and burst through into an enormous room the size of an airplane hangar. She froze with horror, mouth agape at what she saw. The floor was covered with naked babies scattered across the cold cement. They were all screaming. Hundreds of them.

Suddenly, with a gush, her own bladder seemed to let go. But when she looked down, her belly was swollen and pregnant again. She hadn't pissed herself; it was amniotic fluid. Her water had broken.

Crippling contractions hit, one after the other, until she couldn't stand upright anymore. She dropped down to lie among the screaming babies. Within seconds, she could feel the child's head crowning.

A man in scrubs and a mask came in and pulled the baby out of her before it was time. Unable to move, Dolly's screams mingled with those of the other infants as he walked away with her child. A group of nurses came in and began shoveling the babies into large canvas-covered carts, ignoring their cries. Dolly tried to stand up and stop them, but she couldn't move.

The nurses emptied a circle of the floor around her, the canvas in each cart bulging with tiny infant bodies. Then they wheeled them over to a mortician's table at the far end of the room, where they dumped them into large bins by the doctor's side. The surgeon stood over the steel dissection table, a single overhead bulb casting him in a pool of light.

The nurse who'd taken her first baby walked in from another door and handed it, now naked, to the surgeon. The doctor grabbed the child dispassionately by the ankle and slapped it, still crying, onto the table. With a single stroke, he gutted the infant from clavicle to genitals.

Still unable to move, Dolly tried to scream but her voice was suddenly gone. She could only watch in silent horror as the doctor kept vivisecting the crying child. Behind him stretched a field of tiny bloody corpses. He disemboweled Dolly's baby and removed each organ, sliding them into separate lab bags. He took out the eyes and cracked open the skull to reach the brain, which he removed with minimal strokes of the scalpel, dropping it into a specimen jar a nurse brought him. Dolly's beautiful child, newly born, was now a hollow shell, umbilical cord drooping from its flaccid skin. Then he tossed it on the pile behind him and grabbed another.

That's when she woke up screaming. For the past five days, every time she fell asleep, it was this same nightmare.

This dream was far worse than the nightmare of Willow burning. Despite the strange love she had for this friend she'd never met, there was a far more poignant heartbreak regarding the babies. She felt a powerful maternal instinct, a fierce need to save them. But she couldn't. They wouldn't let her. That's a question that puzzled her. Who the hell were "they?"

Something was changing inside her. Dolly could feel it. A mixture of anger, confusion, sorrow, and fear was brewing in her mind, and her body was beginning to follow that chaos. Her muscles hurt and joints protested against her daily exercise, which she usually enjoyed. Even yoga and visualization practices couldn't curb the feeling of being stretched to the limits, of something rising within her. Something that would change her life forever.

3

It was a crystal clear night, washed fresh by an afternoon rain shower. Keisha and Tanja were working an office party, and Kyle was driving Dolly to the Waldorf Hotel where she was to meet a client. Her makeup was more exotic than usual—heavy black metallic eyeliner, iridescent green eye shadow, olive blush, and black lipstick. Her skin was speckled with small, glittering silicone scales she'd spent an hour applying, and she wore bright golden contact lenses, giving her a reptilian look. Her hair was upswept in a knot secured by a jade Kanzashi stick. She'd saved for a year to buy it. Keisha was always bitching about her spending money on "all that stupid fancy shit," but Dolly didn't mind. She was frugal in everything else. Kyle studied her in the rear-view mirror.

"Wow, Doll. You look amazing."

Dolly laughed. "I've got a request tonight. Thought this look would be appropriate."

"You're always gorgeous but this is just…wow. You look like you're in a movie about an alien seductress who eats her victims."

Dolly grinned. "Spoken like the oddball nerd that you are."

The hotel was an upper-class establishment, high-end but not elite. Her client would be in the lounge, reading a biography of Carl Sagan. He'd also given her a code—a set of sentences she was to recite—which made her laugh. She suspected some sci-fi role-playing was imminent. Kyle pulled up in front, watching as she donned a floor-length coat, dark glasses, and a whisper-thin black scarf around her head and neck.

"How do I look?"

"Like a spy."

Dolly laughed. "Are the scales hidden enough? I don't want some asshole manager stopping me at the door."

"Let's get out and see."

Kyle climbed from the driver's seat and opened her door with a flourish. Taking her cue from his theatrics, she smiled regally and took the hand he offered, sliding out with a flash of graceful thigh. A pedestrian stumbled as he saw the scales along her leg, which quickly disappeared beneath the coat as she stood up. She looked at him disdainfully, and he hurried past, head lowered. Dolly grinned at Kyle.

"Wonder what he'll describe that as."

"That he once saw a real live alien seductress as she climbed from a stretch limo. This'll be a story told for years to his buddies."

"Is my alien seductress paraphernalia properly hidden?"

Kyle looked her over. "All a mystery."

"Soon to be revealed."

"Lucky bastard. I'm going to pull into the underground parking lot until you're finished. I'll be there reading if you need anything. Got your phone?"

Dolly tapped her tiny handbag. "Right here. Wish me luck. I'm hoping for a big tip. This guy said he wants the works."

"Stay safe."

"Look at this place. Worst thing that can happen is if room service brings the wrong champagne."

"Your Willow dream was in the Waldorf. I don't want you getting triggered by how fancy this place is."

Dolly's smile disappeared. "Well, thanks for triggering me beforehand!"

Kyle looked horrified. "I…I just meant for you to not worry. I'm not leaving here until you're back in the car."

He looked so dejected Dolly forgave him.

"It's okay, kid. I know you mean well." She reached over and kissed him briefly on the mouth.

Even in the dim light coming from the lobby, Dolly could see the blush seep upward from his neck and vanish into his hairline, black lipstick residue on his mouth. Dolly tapped a finger against his bottom lip.

"You've got my mark on you," she whispered, enjoying his fluster.

Kyle stared, sucking in his lips to hide them. She smiled.

"See you in an hour or so, kid. Get something to eat while you study."

Dolly walked through the gilded entrance and into the lounge, looking around the room. She spotted her john immediately. The man was sitting in the corner, reading the Sagan book. Good-looking guy. Seemed pretty clean-cut, wearing a nice suit. Dolly walked over and recited the prepared, adorably cheesy opening line.

"Do you like looking at the stars?"

"I'm looking at one right now."

"You need somewhere dark to see a star properly."

"I know of a place."

"Then let's go."

They began walking to the elevator, the man careful not to touch. *He's probably married*, Dolly thought to herself. As long as it didn't get too gross, she enjoyed role-playing. There was something charmingly childish about it, like cosplaying. One client had had her dress up as a purple furry while he donned an orange pelt. Both costumes had been strategically cut for anatomical necessity. She'd sweated like a pig in that costume, but the man had been thrilled. Tipped well, too. Another night, she'd spent the whole evening with a john who looked very similar to this guy. He spray-painted her green and had her do some sort of striptease slave dance. Paid her three thousand dollars for that one night. It had actually been fun. Maybe this guy was the same. He looked like he could afford it.

"What's your name?" she asked.

He paused.

"John. What's yours?"

"Dolly."

"Seriously?"

"Seriously."

"Oh. That's fascinating. Dolly was the name of the first cloned sheep."

"Really? My mom just named me after a snack cake company. Are you a scientist?"

"I...I like to keep up with things."

"A patron of knowledge, huh?"

"Knowledge is power."

"Yes, it is."

They got to the room. John held his watch in front of the sensor, and the door clicked open. He gestured for her to go first. Dolly entered the suite. John shut the door and locked it.

"What do you have for me under that coat?"

She turned around, untied the belt and slid the coat off, letting it drop to the floor. She'd dressed for the part, wearing a sleeveless, iridescent gown, slit to the waist and open on both sides, held only by two golden clasps. A metallic serpent with jeweled eyes encircled her right forearm, another around her ankle, and a replica Georgian gold necklace draped her throat. The man swallowed with difficulty.

"So," she said, "what shall we do?"

He stared at her, absorbing every detail from her feet to her forehead, gasping softly when he saw the scales.

"Please undress."

She smiled and reached behind her, undoing the clasp at her neck. The gown peeled off slowly, revealing her beautiful body in stages. She wore no undergarments, and a gem glittered in her navel. John watched, marveling at how beautiful she was. She pulled the Kanzashi stick out of the bun atop her head, and her pale hair tumbled past her shoulders.

He shed his own jacket and unbuttoned his shirt halfway, stopping to watch as she walked gracefully toward him. She paused less than a foot away, with only the jewelry against her bare skin.

John stared at her for so long Dolly began to feel self-conscious. His eyes were oddly cold, almost analytical. She ran her hands over her body, hoping to galvanize him into action, but he just stood there and stared.

"You're very beautiful."

Dolly relaxed. This conversation she knew.

"Thank you. Will you show me how beautiful you are? Your skin looks so warm. I want to touch it."

He reached into his pocket and pulled out a metallic tube, rounded at the tip.

"Oh, what a tangled web we weave…"

Dolly immediately recoiled.

"I don't do dildos, hon. You don't need it."

"It won't hurt."

"That's not going in me. Not gonna happen."

He walked toward her. "Look, it's not a dildo. See?"

He held it up to her face and a light went on. Dolly immediately looked down and backed away as it flashed. She knew to avoid that light. She didn't know why, but she knew to not look into that light.

34

"Come on. What's the matter with you? I just want to play. I won't hurt you."

Dolly didn't believe him. Suddenly it wasn't a cute game anymore. Bristling with unexplained rage and fear, she was grabbing up her clothes before she even understood why that toy upset her.

"Sorry, babe. I've changed my mind. I'm out of here."

He stepped in front of the door as she rehooked her dress. Dolly groaned.

"Look, don't be an ass."

Shrugging into her coat, she marched toward him. He didn't move, just stood there holding the weird dildo thing up before him, pointing it toward her face. She looked down, avoiding its light. Dolly didn't know why it bothered her so much or why she was afraid of it. That thing seemed a threat, which made no sense. It had no sharp edges, wasn't a gun as far as she could tell, and wasn't big enough to hit her with. No matter the reason, she wanted no part of it.

"Come on, baby," she said softly, trying to keep the situation light. "Get out of the way."

"Just look at it. That's all. I brought it just for you."

She'd heard of electronic roofies used by rapists and suspected that might be what this thing was. Dolly tried to step around him, but he wouldn't let her. When she pushed him, he suddenly lunged, shoving her against the wall and trying to force her to look at the thing. Dolly fought back, kicking and twisting away. John threw her against the windowsill, and Dolly flailed against the glass until she shattered it with her left hand, trying to grab a piece as a weapon. Her bloody hand raked against his face, clawing strips out of his cheek. He cursed in pain and stumbled back. She almost got past him but he grabbed her again, angry, jabbing that damn device up against her face. Dolly struck him with her elbow, grabbed the thing out of his hand and ran to the door.

He was hot on her heels as she raced down the hallway, trembling with relief as she heard the elevator ding. Shoving her way past the emerging guests, Dolly pushed through into the elevator and stood in the back, gasping.

John stopped short in front of the open doors, his shirt hanging open with her bloody handprint against the shoulder and blood running down his jaw from her scratches.

An older man, mid-fifties, had started to depart the elevator but stopped as he gauged the situation. He looked at John's face, then at Dolly.

Then he stepped back in and stood protectively in front of her. Dolly gave John the finger as the doors closed. The older gentleman turned to her.

"Are you all right, miss? Shall I call the police?"

Limp with relief, Dolly shook her head and smiled slightly. "No, thanks anyway. My boyfriend got drunk and tried to get rough. It's okay."

"It's not, you know. You're a person, not a punching bag."

She looked up at him, startled. "Yeah. You're right. Thanks for your help back there. I think you scared him."

"I would have done a lot more than scare him if he'd tried to get to you."

Dolly felt oddly tearful at his kindness. Uncomfortable with the sensation, she gave a shaky laugh and pulled her coat closer around her neck.

"You're my hero for the day."

The elevator doors opened and closed as it descended, people entering and emptying out onto various floors until they reached the lobby. The man stayed at her side as she stepped out and then touched her arm gently. Dolly looked at the other elevator's numbers as it descended, knowing her john was probably in it.

"Are you sure you're okay?" He followed her eyes and looked at the second elevator, understanding her tension.

"Yeah, I'm all right. It just got intense in there."

They began to walk through the lobby to the front door.

"Have you come from a party or convention?"

"No. Why?"

"Because you're a very beautiful woman and quite exotic at the moment." He gestured toward her golden eyes and glittering scales. In her haste, she'd forgotten to drape the scarf around her head and neck or put on the tinted glasses.

"Still," he continued, "that's no excuse for anyone to lose themselves to violence. I am disgusted."

"Yeah, well. I took his toy away from him. That'll make him think twice."

The gentleman looked at the cylinder she held up, his gaze curious. "What is it?"

"No idea. But he kept trying to get me to stare at it."

His face hardened. "I've heard of this sort of thing. You should take it to the police. He should be reported."

"I like to not bother the cops unless strictly necessary."

Dawning comprehension slid across his face. "Ah. But he really should be reported, my dear. It will prevent it from happening again to someone else."

"I got his toy. He won't use it on anybody again."

"Then I shall report him. What room is he in?"

About to step out onto the sidewalk, Dolly stopped and looked at him. He was determined, his expression deadly serious. She thought about all the women she'd known, beaten and brutalized, and realized he was right.

"You need not get involved. Hotel security cameras have all the information they need, and I will tell them what has occurred. Don't be afraid."

Dolly looked at him in wonder. *I'll have to tell Keish and Tanja*, she thought. *Here's another good man right here.* She told him the room number and turned to leave.

"Shall I take you home?"

"No, thanks. My driver is here." Dolly fished her phone out of her purse and called Kyle. The man listened to the exchange, reached into his jacket, and withdrew a slim gold case.

"Very well. Here's my card if you need anything. Please don't hesitate to call."

Dolly smiled at the name on it. "Jester?"

"My 'handle,' as it were."

She turned it over to look at the back. "There's just your phone number on it."

"Yes. That's my direct line."

Dolly heard the second elevator ding and nodded silently, shoving the card in her pocket and quickly walking out the door as John emerged.

The man watched as the limo pulled up, watched as Kyle, looking confused, got out to open the door. Dolly gave a quick wave and slid into the back. Kyle climbed into the driver's seat, and they pulled away. The man's eyes followed them until they disappeared into the traffic, his forehead creased in a frown.

John came up behind him, his cheek still oozing from where she'd clawed him. The man turned to look at him in disgust.

"Idiot."

"I'm sorry, sir. It won't happen again."

"That is a certainty."

The man turned and strode back inside, coldly angry. John followed silently, wiping his bloody face.

Kyle turned the limo onto a side street, clearly agitated and bursting with questions. He began to pull over, but Dolly waved him on.

"No, don't stop, Kyle. I'm okay. Just a freak who liked to be rough. I shoved him and ran for the elevator."

Kyle was visibly angry. "I'm turning around."

"What? No! Hell no. I just want to forget it."

"I'm going to kick that cocksucker's ass."

Dolly laughed weakly as she removed the contact lenses. "He's twice your size, darlin'."

"I don't give a damn. I'm fast. Come on, Doll. You can't just shrug it off and not tell me. What happened? Did he hit you? Are you okay?"

"I'm fine. He just wanted to use some weird toy on me, and I said no. You know my policy for what gets shoved inside me. It just wasn't going to happen, and he was...disappointed."

Kyle glowered, hands flexing on the wheel. "Nobody hurts you. He's gotta pay for it."

Dolly laughed weakly. "He already has." She reached into her coat and pulled out the metal device. "I got his toy. Messed up his pretty face, too."

"Good. This shit happens too often to prostitutes. You all need to unionize."

"That'd be one hell of a picket line."

Kyle laughed, slowly relaxing.

"Come on. I'll take you home."

"No. Got to make rent."

"No way. You don't need to be strolling tonight after all that's happened. I can give you money for the rest of the evening."

Dolly was cleaning off her makeup with the wipes in her bag. She looked at Kyle for a moment, reading real concern and righteous anger. It was kind of sweet. But business was business.

"Thanks, sweetheart. But no. Just drop me off at my next stop."

Kyle grudgingly drove her to the hotel where she was to meet her next john. He turned on the interior light so she could redo her makeup and remove the scales, staying reluctantly silent after a glare from her.

Dolly slid the strange sex toy back into her coat pocket and climbed out of the limo. Kyle was already out of the vehicle, fingers drumming on the hood.

"Why don't we go get something to eat? I'll buy you a burger. What do you say? Just...just don't go up there tonight."

Dolly studied him silently, and he glared back, trembling with nervous energy.

"Want me to wait here for you?"

"No. He's a regular. I'll be fine. Go on."

She smiled as she shut the door. Kyle watched as she walked into the hotel, resisting the urge to go after her. Then he got back in the limo and drove off.

Parking two blocks away, he pulled out his phone and dialed a number.

"Come on, come on. Pick up."

The phone clicked and a voice answered. "Yes?"

"Sir, Dolly was attacked by a stranger tonight. She's okay, but he flashed a device at her. Possibly a roofie module. She didn't look at it and had to run when he tried to stop her."

"I have already been informed. He was one of ours. Bungled the palliate we were to run tonight. Jester smoothed the situation, but I'm afraid they lost the device. Retrieve it for us."

"Jester? Why is security here?"

"Where is the device?"

"She took it with her to her next john. I feel like I should go up there and make sure she's okay."

"Hathaway is her next appointment, is he not?"

"I'm not sure, sir. She said he was a regular."

"Hathaway is an important source of income and nonviolent. Under no circumstances are you to disturb them."

"I think the nightmares are beginning to get to her, sir. She's stopped talking about them, but I can see she's starting to break. Isn't there some way to stop them? Or at least slow them down?"

"Holmes, I chose you for this project to monitor and record everything. Your reports on her nightmares have been extremely useful. This goes far beyond anything we've ever seen. But do not get sentimental about this creature. Record and report. That is all you do. I have no interest in your feelings or theories. Do I make myself clear?"

Kyle stared blindly out the windshield for a moment. Then he cast his eyes down. "Yes, Professor Bannick."

"Retrieve the device." The line went dead.

Kyle glared at his phone and tossed it contemptuously onto the dash. Breathing an angry "fuck," he drove off.

4

In a large, seemingly dilapidated industrial warehouse seven miles away, a balding, middle-aged man with thick glasses and a frown sat in his underground office, rewinding video feeds on a nine-screen monitor on the wall.

"Stop. Play."

The video began again, and he sat back in his chair, watching. On the large center screen was Dolly having a conversation with Kyle in the limo. Bannick watched her pull the device from her pocket and clicked his tongue in irritation.

"Live feed. Follow her."

The screens flashed to live stream. While Bannick typed notes at the keyboard on his desk, the computer linked to different surveillance units as Dolly moved about inside the hotel. Some feeds were the hotel's own security cameras, but most were top secret Aquinas micro cameras, each smaller than a lentil. They followed her into the lobby of the hotel, tracking her movements throughout the building, even into the bathroom where she checked her makeup. Her watch dinged, alerting her that her next client was there.

She rode the elevator up to Room 412 on the fourth floor and knocked on the door. A soft little man opened it, flushing with pleasure at the sight of her. Dolly smiled.

Bannick searched his screens to confirm the little man's identity. Facial and voice recognition confirmed it as Martin Hathaway.

"Wow! Dolly, you look incredible."

"Hello, Martin. Good to see you."

The little man beamed. "I'm so happy you're here, Dolly. Come in, come in."

Bannick sneered. Hathaway was nothing in himself—a nobody who worked at a bank. But he had his uses. Aquinas often hacked the bank's client list using Martin's computer. The man was of low-level importance—just one of the many cogs they used as eyes, ears, and funding for this project.

Bannick watched as Dolly began to strip for Martin, then snorted with contempt and switched off the screens. He had a whole crew watching her. Let them monitor this smutty nonsense.

He shrugged into the jacket draped over a side chair and marched out of his office with the quick, impatient steps of a man dissatisfied with everything and everyone around him. Highly intelligent, he had never been able to find common ground with anybody he'd ever met, and he didn't care. They were all just stupid, predictable apes, throwing their feces around and squabbling over the best fruit or the most fucks. He had no patience for any of them.

Entering a cavernous warehouse, Bannick passed rows and rows of horizontal coffinlike pods set up in various laboratories, where dozens of scientists and staff were working. Whenever they looked up and saw him, they nervously doubled their activity. The man showed no emotion other than a curl of his lip at their absurdity.

A woman in a lab coat approached him, brandishing a tablet.

"Professor Bannick."

She pulled a digital pen from her lab coat pocket and held it over the tablet. He kept walking, forcing her to match his step. "Here are the results of last night's tests. Three of the subjects are responding to the negative environment; two are not. The other seven are resisting the new emotional stimuli."

Bannick signed his name on the spots she indicated. "What's the timetable on full indoctrination?"

"Another six weeks."

"Double the stimuli. I want it done in four. Get more trainers here if you have to. But four. You understand?"

"Yes, sir." She studied his face. It was rare to see Bannick visibly angry. "Sir, is there another problem I need to address?"

"One of my past ovens is panicking."

Startled, she replied, "Panicking?"

"Never mind that now. Get on this schedule right away. We're behind as it is."

"Yes, sir."

Bannick pulled a smartphone out of his jacket and spoke into it. "Call Jester. I want his report in half an hour. We need to get a handle on this. And fire that idiot from security."

He and the woman entered an elevator together, Bannick still talking as she scribbled instructions. He swiped his ID card against the side wall, and a metal shield slid down, revealing a set of numbered buttons. He punched the number twenty-two, and the elevator began to descend.

"Jester will be calling. Patch him through immediately."

"Yes, sir."

"And pull up the history on Kyle Holmes. I want intel on his childhood. He's already been vetted, but he might be becoming emotionally involved. I want to see if that's going to be a problem."

The elevator slowed to a stop and the doors opened. Bannick stepped out.

"And the idiot is coming sometime today. Didn't give me a specific time. If he arrives and I'm still in the Womb, put him in the Green Room. Not my office. Last time the little creep stole my nineteenth-century letter opener. Let me know when he comes. By a phone ping, not a call. He can wait."

The doors slid closed.

Bannick went on to a set of large steel double doors, endured a retina scan, a fingerprint ID, and a ten-digit punched code before the doors opened. The interior was massive, far bigger than the shabby dilapidated warehouse front. That was just camouflage. They sometimes even harvested unsuspecting bums who squatted there.

The entire facility was the size of an aircraft carrier. The dilapidated warehouse and its surrounding lots, all above ground, hid entrances to the labs and chambers beneath. Twenty-two floors and a series of connecting tunnels were below ground. Excavation had first begun two decades ago in Wilmut National Park, eight miles from the city. Bannick had been in charge of the project from the beginning. Using state-of-the-art technology, robotics, and subway tunnel boring machines, they'd dug a tunnel four miles from Los Angeles to this site and then bore upward and outward to create the top secret facility. Another four miles were dug the remaining distance to LA for access from the city. The Wilmut entrance, called Persephone, had an enormous horizontal entryway, like a gigantic trap door, hidden beneath living foliage and natural rock that matched the surrounding area. It rotated to open, revealing a steel platform big enough to hold four fully loaded semitrucks. Large equipment and vehicles used this entrance. The platform lowered the cargo two floors down for unloading. The engines and cabs went back up to ground level, while the cargo containers were either shipped lower or unloaded there and distributed throughout the facility. The Los Angeles site entrance was inside the broken-down warehouse, hidden beneath a pile of scrapped moving equipment in the south corner. The sliding doors in the floor opened to a platform big enough to hold a golf cart with four people.

Bannick walked the quarter mile to the labs, passing swaths of construction workers and electricians as they worked on the perpetual upkeep of machinery and other maintenance. He reached another set of steel doors; repeated the retinal, fingerprint, and code requirements for entry; and progressed to a set of wide corridors separated by soundproofed walls. He entered the corridor labeled "Level A."

Level A was lined with rows of glass-fronted rooms on one side, each with three soundproofed outer walls and a reinforced floor-to-ceiling glass observation front. Groups of researchers stood on the opposite side of the corridor, watching and taking notes. Each room was twelve by fourteen feet with eight-foot ceilings, and even with the soundproofing, you could hear the muffled screams from inside. Every cubicle was fitted up like a room in a normal house—basement, bedroom, living room, kitchen, even bathrooms. Some bedrooms were furnished for a toddler, some for a third grader, some for adolescents, but all of them had one woman inside being raped by a single man. The women were in their teens to early twenties, but all were semi-dressed in childish clothing befitting the age of the room's decor. The rapists were slobbering brutes with stained shirts and snarling decadence, all obviously drunk. They were all "professional trainers," hired specifically by Bannick and his team for their sociopathic tendencies, a necessary requirement for such heinous work.

Some victims were sobbing and fighting, some grimacing and enduring, some blank faced with dead expressions. All of them had been beaten severely. There was blood on the walls, blood on the sheets, blood on the torn jeans or ruffled pink nightdresses and panties lying on the floor. In rooms where the victims were totally naked, there was a twisted set of childish pajamas or play clothes crumpled on the carpet.

Bannick passed the bedroom stalls and approached a set of basement decor ones, complete with faux staircases. One woman struck vainly at her rapist, the way a small child would glance futile blows off a grown man. He slapped her into silence. Bannick watched for a few minutes.

"How long has this one been in treatment?"

The team leader handed him a computer readout. "Just under three weeks."

"Her age program?"

"Eleven."

"How long does her memory go for the abuse?"

"Molestation since four years, rape cycle under six months."

"When did she stop screaming?"

"Two days ago."

Bannick nodded. "Good. Monitor any throwback gestures, and let me know when her pupils stop Injustice Dilating. Then she'll be primed to move."

"Yes, sir."

Bannick moved past five basement scenarios and into a set of bathrooms in various cheerful colors. The women being raped in these were dressed more maturely, young teenager attire. They had expressions of disdain and grim acceptance. None were fighting, but they still had bruises and cuts from being beaten. Bannick silently took the report from this room's team leader, glanced at it for a few moments, and then looked again into the room.

"Is the new crop ready for fieldwork?"

"The conditioning is premature, and we've discovered several glitches, but they're well within indicated parameters."

"What age group are these?"

"Eleven to thirteen years old."

"Their dress looks older."

"It's common for the age dates of indoctrination. The suggestive dress helps form the self-hatred and shame. A sort of 'you asked for it' garb. This is reinforced by the trainer's accusations of sexual teasing."

Bannick shook his head. "Girls are trying to be women younger and younger nowadays. It's appalling."

"Don't I know it. My daughter wants to get a tattoo. It's ludicrous."

"How old is she?"

"Ten. Can you imagine a tattoo at ten years old? I told her absolutely not."

"Children are becoming sexually active at nine now. Federal regulations lowered age of consent to fourteen, but these kids just keep pushing it."

"That's what kids do. Give their parents gray hair."

Bannick watched as the man pulled the victim's hair, biting her hard in the shoulder, drawing blood. He made an irritated sound.

"Tell your slob to refrain from marking the flesh with biting. I've warned you about that before. We want the flesh to heal, not scar. If he does it again, wipe his memory and get rid of him."

"Yes, Professor Bannick."

Bannick moved down the line, stopping at different booths, getting didactic reports from each team leader, observing the horrific crimes in every room with the analytical interest of a concentration camp official. At the far end of the corridor, in a large separate segment, a woman was resisting being gang-raped and beaten in a darkened alley. Her back was to the glass, blond hair bloody and matted, but she was fighting back. Bannick watched this one for a while. The woman was fiercely resisting five men. Clothes torn, she was dressed as an adult in a ripped pencil skirt and bra, tattered blouse hanging from her shoulders, pocketbook on the ground, its contents spilled across the asphalt, cell phone smashed beside it. The men got ahold of her at last, and she bit and scratched as they threw her against a pile of garbage bags, four of them holding her down as one climbed on and pried her legs open. He reared back long enough for Bannick to see her face for a moment.

It was Dolly.

Bannick watched as she gave a soul-wrenching scream of defiance. Then the man punched her in the mouth, stunning her. He held her face sideways, avoiding her teeth, and began the rape. Her eyes rolled in her head as she struggled to stay awake. For a moment, she seemed to look directly at Bannick. Then her eyes crossed and rolled half shut as she lost consciousness.

"Has this model shown any other unusual tendencies? Any memory glitches?"

"No, sir. She is more aggressive than her programming suggests, but it's still within the normal range."

"From earth mother to whore."

"Sir?"

He ignored the question, staring at the unconscious woman, clicking his tongue in annoyance.

"She isn't responding correctly. She shows more rage than fear. Make sure the abuse backgrounds are fully engaged and imprinted with physical backup. This defiance must be eradicated. Fear is the goal. You understand?"

"Yes, sir."

Bannick left the corridor and walked through a simulated skywalk to the next set of prepared conditioning rooms. Despite the same number of scientists studying the interactions inside, these were very different. Women played with small children and babies, their faces lit with joy and security. Husbands and wives interacted with them, all loving and happy, each cubicle holding an ideal family within. Some were in kitchens, some in nurseries or bedrooms, some in living rooms where the couples sat and watched television, a baby nestled in the mother's arms. Bannick walked past these with little interest, signing the occasional order, until he came to a new section where he had to don a paper hospital gown and pass through a hygiene room before entering.

The layout was the same as before, with happy homes and spouses within calm interior decorating, but the subjects inside the rooms were all pregnant women. Bannick stayed here for over an hour. He questioned each scientist, looked at their notes, gauged the expressions of the pregnant women inside. He looked for any sign of stress or anxiety, noting two women who seemed worried.

"Are these the two test subjects from Level A?" he asked the man with the tablet.

"Yes, sir."

"What age group for their abuse memories?"

The man indicated side-by-side rooms. "Four to eight years here, six to twelve in the gold room. They were fitted with Child Services Rescue memories, followed by adolescent psychiatric sessions. After Level A conditioning and the rescue scenarios, we matched them up with loving actors and safe homes to see how they progress."

"When was the in vitro?"

"Four months ago."

"Level of fetal development in that time?"

"Approximately six and a half natural months."

"Any difference in fetal behavior from the non-abused hosts?"

"More agitated. High incidence of curling and thrashing."

"What about diet?"

"All the hosts consume healthy diets, but the two fetuses from the test subjects show signs of hunger motions far more often than nonabused hosts. Up to forty percent more. They receive the same amount of nourishment, but it does not satisfy like the others."

Bannick took the tablet from him, punching in code for accessing fetal movement. He studied it for a few minutes and then shoved the tablet back at the man.

"Try protein-only diets for a few days. See how the fetuses react."

"Sir."

Bannick walked on, checking his watch as it dinged. He sighed in exasperation. The idiot was here. He'd have to head upstairs.

Bannick left the sterile area, walking fast to the skywalk, retracing his steps. Halfway across the skywalk, he paused briefly to watch a large truck enter, the words "Nurturing Genius" printed in large block letters on its side. It backed into a bay where workmen were waiting to unload. Bannick walked away as they opened the truck's cargo doors. Inside were over a hundred naked, unconscious women, stacked like wood, all the same age as the women in the rape corridor. The men began loading them into roll bins, ten at a time, wheeling them into the facility. A supervisor marked each count with a color code, barking orders to the carriers.

"Come on, come on. Get the meat in the bins and let's go! Don't make me miss my dinner. Move it."

They stacked the women on their sides to maximize space in the bins. As a worker turned a raven-haired woman's head to fit more snugly against the neck of the body before her, her face showed for a brief moment. It was Willow.

5

The Hammer Museum on Wilshire Boulevard was one of the most revered museums in Los Angeles, displaying both classical and modern art, as well as showcasing young and emerging talent. The restaurants were affordable, the art was inspiring, and the tickets were cheap. Weekends were packed with visitors, but Mondays through Thursdays were low enough volume for patrons to stroll comfortably from room to room.

It was Tuesday, Dolly's day off and the beginning of her own "weekend." She was spending it alone, as she often did, in the museum. Having a passion for culture, Dolly had tried to cultivate the same passion in Tanja and Keisha, but they had little interest. She'd once coaxed both of them to come to an exhibit on classic Chuck Close portraits, but they'd gotten bored within half an hour, complaining like children about how long they had to stay. Dolly never asked them after that. Knowing that they felt no connection to any of the glorious art around them would have ruined her own joy and wonder. She didn't resent their disinterest. It would have been as ridiculous to resent a blind person for not being able to see. They were simply blind to culture, and Dolly didn't hold it against them.

Strolling through the rooms, she came upon an exhibit of Egon Schiele, pausing before a portrait of a battered woman with velvety bruised eyes, her limbs twisted and disjointed, her legs spread and lax with despair. It was a haunting portrait, and one Dolly knew well, feeling her own body clench at the sight. *This is truth*, she thought. *Beautiful, heartbreaking, horrible truth.* She shook her head briefly and blinked the tears away. *This is way too real for me to deal with on my day off.*

She turned and walked out of the exhibit, searching for lighter fare.

She found it in a wing of classical work—Rembrandt, Rubens, glorious Vermeer, da Vinci, and Caravaggio. Another room housed a delightful array of children's book illustrations—Sendak and Silverstein, Dulac and Rackham, gentle Cassatt, hopeful Chaudhri, wise Seuss, incomparable Beatrix Potter. This was all balm for a troubled soul. Dolly drank it all in, feeling herself relax into the grace and beauty of a happy child's world. Her eyes wandered over the artwork, memorizing each beautiful detail in much the same way her mind absorbed words on a page. These paintings would be part of her memories now, and she could visit them in her mind whenever the nightmares descended. Art would be her comfort and road back from madness. A whore's life was a hard one, and Dolly recognized that she needed these new memories. She needed to build up a library of good thoughts to escape to. They would be her shield.

A man coughed nervously from across the room, and Dolly looked up to see him with his family. He was a client. The look of horror on his face as he hurried his three children and soft dumpling of a wife out the door made Dolly smile. *The absurdity of man*, she thought. *The goddamn absurdity of them all.*

She got a salad and iced tea at the café, carrying her tray to the museum courtyard where quaint tables had been set up. Statues and stained glass fed her spirit as she ate. There were a handful of other patrons in the courtyard, all talking about what they had seen that day. Pleasant discussions regarding color and style drifted about the room, and Dolly enjoyed listening to the gentle passion of fellow art lovers.

Finishing her meal, she sat back and stared up at an enormous La Farge stained glass depicting a smiling woman beckoning a welcome. Tendrils of flowers and vines surrounded her, the whole scene aglow in the late afternoon light. Dolly got up to study it more closely, hovering near a couple who were doing the same. The woman gestured toward the glass.

"She has a kind face."

Dolly silently agreed with her.

Slowly becoming aware of another man staring at her, Dolly shifted and approached the glass, hoping to break the unwelcome attention. Being stared at was nothing new, but she felt uneasy, as if it was John the roofie guy watching her. Glancing over, she saw a tall, studious-looking man staring intently, not dropping his eyes even when she stared back.

She didn't recognize him—medium build, dark hair, glasses, late thirties, early forties. He looked like a nerdy professor.

The man wasn't a client, and he wasn't with anyone who was a client. But something about him made Dolly uncomfortable. She turned and left the room. Hurrying through several galleries, she glanced surreptitiously over her shoulder. He was following her. She turned and almost ran up the Deco staircase nearby, emerging into an exhibit of contemporary art.

He followed.

With memories of the Waldorf attack, Dolly kept moving away, but he kept coming closer.

"Grace? Is that you? Grace, it's me."

Dolly turned and looked at him. His expression was earnest, unbelieving. It wasn't a pickup line. He really did think she was this "Grace."

"I'm sorry. I'm not Grace. I don't know you." She walked away, but he continued to follow.

"Grace, what's the matter with you? It's me."

"Get lost, jerk. I'm not interested."

"Did you get work done? You look amazing," he said breathlessly. Then his face grew serious. "I thought you were dead. Where the hell have you been?"

Dolly just kept walking.

"Grace..." He took her arm, and she whirled around, furious.

"Get your hands off me!"

Startled by her own vehemence, Dolly turned and quickly walked away. The man continued to watch her, puzzled.

She left the museum. The strange little scene had ruined the day for her anyway. Running down the steps, she looked back to see if he was following her, and froze. Dozens of men were staring at her from the large museum windows, shoved together like cattle, their faces pressed up against the glass. Some were in suits, some casual wear, some even had lab coats on. They were all strangers. She shook her head and looked again. The rows of men were gone.

"I'm going fucking crazy," she muttered to herself as she hurried down the steps to the street. Hailing a taxi, she looked back as the cab slid up next to her. The men in rows were there again, watching her from behind the windows. She opened the cab door, pausing to look at the mob. They were terrifying.

"Grace?"

The stranger with the glasses had come out of the building and was standing on the steps, watching her. The crowd at the window didn't vanish, even when she tried to blink them away. They were as real as the stranger coming toward her.

"Grace!"

She got into the taxi, scrambling in her bag for her ID card and swiping it against the payment screen, waiting in agony as it ran her credit. The monitor turned green. She gave her address to the driver, hearing the name "Grace" called out one more time.

The taxi pulled away just as the man reached the bottom of the museum steps, his arm up and waving. She took a deep, shaky breath of relief, close to tears as they left him behind.

"You okay, lady?" the driver asked.

Dolly nodded shakily. "I'm fine." She took a deep breath. "I'm fine. Thanks."

*　　*　　*

Dolly dreamt of her father that night. He was savagely tearing into her, the way he often did when he was drunk, and she felt her flesh rip, his weight suffocating to her little eight-year-old body. Memory dreams were always horrible, and she often dreamt about this one. But there were variations this time. As he held her down, his hand gripped her breast so hard the flesh bled where his nails scratched her. Dolly didn't have breasts at that age. He heaved on top of her, grunting like the drunken animal he was, face jammed down against her neck as he bit her. Dolly yelped in pain, and he jerked up to yell at her.

It was the man from the museum.

"I told you to keep your fucking mouth shut." He punched her in the temple, and Dolly's vision went black.

She woke with a gasp, hand raised defensively, skin and hair again soaked with sweat. Body memory assailed her, and she clenched her legs against the pain. Hand pressed against her belly, she could still feel her tiny womb tear as he hurt her. It was because of that bastard that she could never have children. He had shattered her womb before she'd even reached kindergarten. Dolly remembered the painful limping, first in private at the house and then in public, the other schoolchildren making fun of her. She remembered the loneliness and playground jeers, the broken ribs and cigarette burns on her scalp, the wetting the bed and fainting at her schoolroom desk.

Worst of all was how no adult would help her. Her mom blamed her, called her a slut who was trying to steal her man. The teachers ignored her wounds, her disheveled and dirty appearance, uncomfortably yet hurriedly allowing her to leave the class for the many trips to the bathroom, where she pissed blood and laid wet paper towels on the finger bruises all over her inner thighs, desperately trying to cool the burning pain that seemed to be everywhere.

Childhood memories flooded over Dolly, and she leaped out of bed, barely making it to the toilet, where she vomited until the past faded and she was back in the present. She lay on the bathroom floor, exhausted, watching as the daylight faded. Time to go to work. Time to let other filthy men fuck me, squirm over me, bitch about the price. *I can't do it*, she thought. *I can't fucking do it.*

She dragged herself up and went into the bedroom to fetch her cell phone. Tapping out a swift message to Kyle, she tossed the phone down and fell back against the covers. They were damp with sweat. For a moment, Dolly thought she'd wet the bed again, something she hadn't done since she was sixteen. But it was just sweat, cold and clammy against her overheated skin. She reared up, tearing the bed clothes off the mattress and throwing them in the small washing machine. Tossing in a detergent pod, she slammed the lid closed and started sobbing as the automatic wash began to tumble.

"I can't take this shit anymore," she said aloud, voice choking. "I can't fucking take any more of this!"

Dolly slid down the side of the machine, spent and exhausted. She let go of all the cynicism and humor she normally cloaked herself in and allowed herself to cry. She grabbed a handful of folded laundry and screamed into it as the room faded into twilight. Then she rolled onto her side, the scattered clothing pulled tight against her shoulder and chin in a sad, damp pillow, and fell asleep.

The neighbor's alarm clock went off, easily heard through the tissue-thin walls. The noise jerked her awake. Dolly looked at her watch and cursed softly in amazement. She had slept fourteen dreamless hours.

Morning was breaking. The buzzing noise sounded again. She stumbled up from the floor and looked around. It wasn't the neighbor's alarm clock. It was her front door.

Dolly tentatively moved to the living room, uncertain. She looked up at the monitor beside the door and sighed with relief. It was Kyle, looking worried, armed with a brown paper bag from the bakery. She opened the door.

It was Kyle's turn to sigh with relief.

"God, Dolly. I thought you were dead or something."

She laughed weakly and gestured for him to come in. "Nah. I was asleep, actually."

"Why didn't you answer my messages? I've been texting you all night!"

"What part of 'asleep' did you not understand?"

"Why didn't you work last night? Are you sick?"

Dolly ran a hand through her hair and sighed.

"Sick of life, kid. Sleep deprivation does that to me."

"That's not funny, Doll. Don't joke about that. I thought the nightmares had made you blow your brains out or something."

She pointed at the bag. "Is that for me?"

"Yeah. In case you were still breathing."

"You could have eaten it if I wasn't." She grabbed the bag and pulled out a huge Danish. "Mmm. I need this after the crazy fucking day I had." Dolly padded to the kitchen and turned on the coffee maker, shoving the Danish in her mouth while she took two mugs out of the cabinet. Kyle glared impatiently.

"So you gonna tell me or not?"

She waved her arm dismissively. "Oh, you know. Daddy-fucking-daughter shit."

"Jesus, Dolly. I'm so sorry. I wish he was still alive so I could kill him."

"There's that healthy mindset for a budding psychiatrist."

"I'm not kidding," he said, deadly serious. "I'd kill him."

"I know. I wish I'd killed him myself, actually. I even tried once."

"What happened?"

"Hit him with the bat he used to beat me with. Just glanced off his head enough to make him mad. He put me in the hospital that time. He even had to move out for almost a year because it got reported."

"What happened then?"

"Child Services stopped coming, so he moved back in."

"And your mom let him?"

"I think she was too drunk to notice."

Kyle took the coffee she handed him, and they sat down on the couch. Dolly devoured her breakfast with relish, but Kyle simply held the bag with his own Danish. Relaxed by his company and refreshed from her unusually long sleep, Dolly watched him nonchalantly as she drank her coffee.

"Oh, that's right. I almost forgot." Kyle set the bag down on the coffee table and fished into his jacket pocket. "I found something when I was cleaning the limo out the other night. I think you dropped it." He pulled out the device the john had tried to use on her and held it out.

"Oh, God, that thing." Dolly curled her legs up under her on the cushion and sneered. "Don't go ruining my breakfast."

Kyle pointed it at her face and then pulled it back and sniffed it.

"Don't! Gross!"

He laughed and cupped it in his hand, examining it. "It's not a dildo. There's no switch or anything."

"It lights up though. Who knows where it's been. I've never seen one like it. I think it's one of those roofie things from the news. Who knows what the hell that asshole had planned for me. Men get crazy when it comes to their hard-ons."

Kyle was still studying the device, turning it in his hands. "I just had a classroom discussion about that."

"Sex toys and roofies?"

"Men and their hard-ons."

"Oh, that. Yeah. My bread and butter."

"It doesn't always have to be."

"Tell that to my bank account."

Kyle kept looking at the device, running his thumbnail down the sides.

"I told you I can give you money. You don't have to do this."

"And have you slow down your studies until you can pay tuition? No way, Kyle. I'll live vicariously through your success. You go get famous and write a book about me. Then I can retire."

Kyle smiled, still examining the device. "Deal. Ah! There's some sort of switch here." He held it up triumphantly. "Look!"

54

Dolly leaned forward indulgently, and a light flashed from the device. Her face went slack and expressionless and she sat up straight, frozen. Kyle looked up, noticing her silence and rigidity.

"Dolly?" He put the device back in his pocket, concerned. "Dolly? Can you hear me? Dolly?"

He tried to get a response from her for a few minutes, but she never moved. Satisfied, Kyle took the mug from her hand and placed it on the table. Then he pulled out his phone and punched in a coded message. The phone immediately rang.

"Yes, sir. She's under. What do you want me to do?"

$$* \quad * \quad *$$

Bannick ended the call, taking a moment to look out the huge picture window with its view of Los Angeles. He was in his office at Aquinas corporate headquarters, surrounded by priceless antiques and art. Two walls had floor-to-ceiling mahogany shelves filled with books and small statuary. A Persian carpet lay spread across the floor, and his enormous, hand-carved marquetry desk had once belonged to a king. Bannick sighed and turned his eyes to the man impatiently drumming his fingers on the seventeenth-century settee in the corner.

Struggling to keep the contempt off his face, Bannick waited for Fogetti to speak. Every CEO he had ever met lived only for money. Greed was literally a religion to these people. Their credo was "'The bottom line is God, and God is all." Bannick always felt tainted whenever he had to deal with them. Fogetti, this latest Aquinas idiot, was particularly virulent. He sat there in his tailored suit, unoriginally following the latest trends in male fashion. His black hair was slicked tight against his scalp, rigidly controlled by pomade and gel until not a strand moved against his pampered skin, which looked plastic from all the chemical peels and eyebrow threading. Fogetti was handsome in a sharp, predatory way. He was also very angry.

"Was that your pet dog in our intern program?"

"Kyle Holmes, yes. You chose him, remember?"

"So what's happening with the meat?"

"He's going ahead with the linkup we've arranged to lessen the extreme emotional reaction the subject's been experiencing. Which is completely against my wishes, as you know."

"The only reason we even consider your wishes, Professor, is because your toys make us money. If she can't work, she doesn't make money. And let me point out, she was making a lot more for us at the Waldorf until you decided to make her your pet project. Why you want to turn this beautiful piece of machinery into a two-bit whore, I'll never understand."

Bannick watched him coldly. "I am aware you will never understand."

Fogetti lit a cigarette deliberately, drawing the smoke into his lungs and blowing it out against the settee fabric. Bannick clenched his fist for control.

"Mister Fogetti, this android is unique among all other recorded units, both as a womb and now as a sex droid. It is imperative that we find out why. This android, and only this one, from literally millions of others, goes far beyond any emotions we've programmed her to feel. Her unprecedented dreams might even be accessing wiped memory. This has never before occurred. Ever. The creature's extremity began while in zero gravity but has continued since she returned to the surface here, despite being loaded with new memory parameters. She is showing signs of independent thought. It is fascinating. She is dreaming. Actually dreaming. We might be looking at the next phase in AI evolution. This subject is worth far more than money."

"Don't blaspheme, Professor."

Bannick clicked his tongue in exasperation. "There is the possibility that we can learn about both the human brain and the synthetics by studying this particular unit. Allowing it to evolve. That could result in riches beyond your dreams. But I need time to see how this progresses."

"I don't give a shit about your theories, Bannick. This project costs a lot of money, and this piece of meat needs to bring more in. There were six clients lined up for last night, all important, powerful men, all of value in either connections or dollars."

"Mr. Fogetti, I can assure you…"

Fogetti cut him off. "I won't have all this undermined because one glitchy bitch decides to grow a mood. Fix it. Don't study it. Fix it."

Bannick looked away in contempt, his eyes gliding over the books on his shelves.

"I believe the company receives daily deposits, including extra income from unscheduled meetings, on a regular basis," he began. "There is a readout of imprinted purchases with each deposit. We make provisions for unforeseen moments like this—a pool of emergency profits to cover the loss. The company gets its revenue and contacts, which are consistently above the allotted requirements. This is to cover the unexpected. Everything, including this 'glitch,' as you call it, is standard and up to par."

"It's not standard and up to par when I have to spend an hour calming down blue-balled assholes we need connections with." He stood up and buttoned his suit jacket. "I don't want to see another fuckup, Bannick. Do you hear me? The bottom line is God, and God is all."

Inwardly reluctant, Bannick answered, "God is all."

6

Dolly jerked awake with a gasp. Looking around in confusion, she saw Kyle next to her, their hands entwined.

"What happened?"

"Are you all right? I've been trying to wake you up for two hours! You just sat there, frozen. I couldn't get you to hear me or even move!" He leaned forward and touched her cheek. "You and your stupid fear of doctors is the only thing that stopped me from calling an ambulance. I told you something was really wrong! Next time, I'm calling 911. You're just going to have to deal with it."

Dolly slumped forward, holding her head. "Definitely some kind of new roofie." She groaned and flopped back against the cushion. "Who knows what that sick fuck had planned for me."

"He knew you were a prostitute. He knew you would be up for any of the regular requests. So it looks like you had a narrow escape."

She shut her eyes with a sigh.

"Are you okay, Doll?"

Dolly shook him off and stood up, dizzy. Kyle steadied her.

"Be careful."

"What happened? I don't remember anything."

"We were eating Danish and I was playing around with this fucking thing. I found a switch on the side, it flashed, and you were gone." Kyle looked anxious. "It was almost like some kind of catatonic fixed seizure or something. Nothing could stir you. I even tried to bend your arm, but it was like solid steel. Couldn't budge it. I wanted to call the hospital."

"Hell, no, don't call the hospital. Fuck them. They charge an arm and a leg every month for my checkup."

"Are you sure you're all right? I can stay if you want."

"No, get out of here. Get some sleep."

He stood up reluctantly. "Okay. But only if you're sure you're all right."

"I am. Thanks for breakfast and watching over me."

"Any time, Doll. You need me, I'm here. I hope you know that."

"Yeah, I do. Thanks, Kyle. See you tonight."

After he left, Dolly leaned against the closed door and groaned. She saw the two empty mugs on the coffee table, picked them up and washed them. Pacing around the apartment, it felt as if the walls were closing in on her. Claustrophobic, head pounding, she had to get outside. Get fresh air and space.

Dolly changed into her sweats, yanked on a pair of running shoes, grabbed her keys, and left the apartment. On the street, she stood for a moment, eyes closed, listening to the sounds of the neighborhood. Then she opened her eyes and started hesitantly moving toward the West End. After a few blocks, she began to jog.

Five miles later, she began to notice her surroundings. It was a seedy part of town she'd never been to—run-down bodegas, tattered convenience stores, and elderly laundromats. She felt herself drawn farther and farther west, away from home. Shops gave way to abandoned factories, warehouses, and automated industrial buildings. Dolly grimaced at the ugly structures, noting garbage in all the lots. The city's ablution robots apparently didn't go this far. She slowed to a walk, feeling a strange sort of déjà vu. There was something familiar about this area.

She kept moving forward, no longer wandering but walking with a purpose, her eyes searching. An old sign for snack cakes hung drunkenly from the side of an abandoned building, and her eyes narrowed. It was advertising the cupcakes her mom said she was named after. Dolly stared at the sign for a long time. Then she turned slowly toward an old warehouse across the lot. The windows were shattered, the steel siding speckled with old graffiti. Even the gangs had abandoned this place. The warehouse was surrounded by a sagging chain link fence, its gate chained.

Dolly approached the fence and scanned the area. Nothing but weeds and cracked cement, scraggly with age. She walked the fence line until she came to a soggy wooden board on the ground, lying along the edge of the sidewalk. Dropping to her haunches, she picked it up. It was too faded and weather damaged to read. Turning it over, she noticed a metal strip attached to the upper right corner. The strip was obviously new.

"May I help you, miss?"

Dolly jerked her head around, dropping the sign and standing up. An armed security guard was walking toward her along the outer fence line, a strong young man with a military haircut. Though it was clean and well pressed, she could see that his uniform was old. Something about him made her wary.

"Miss? Can I help you?"

She wiped her dirty hands against her sweatpants, nervous.

"No. Just walking around."

She backed away but hit a solid object behind her. It was another security guard, almost a twin to the one in front of her. She looked around. Where had they come from?

The second man spoke more sharply.

"Why are you here?"

An image flashed before Dolly's eyes, and she stumbled. In it, the second security guard had her bound and gagged across a table and was fucking her as she screamed into the gag. She covered her face in her hands and groaned. *I'm going nuts*, she thought. *I'm going out of my fucking mind!*

The first guard smiled at his companion, slinging his rifle.

"It's okay. She was scheduled. Just got the call."

Dolly started to back away.

The first guard spread his hands and looked at her, grinning. "Oh, what a tangled web we weave."

"What?"

The two guards looked at each other, startled. Then the first guard stepped closer and looked directly into her eyes. He repeated the line, more slowly. "Oh, what a tangled web we weave."

Dolly responded, "'When first we practice to deceive.' Sir Walter Scott." She stuck a smile on her face and started to slide past him. "Glad to find a fellow reader. I've got to be getting back. See you later, fellas."

Both men gaped at her with an odd astonishment. She waved nervously and began jogging away. The two men muttered between them, one speaking into his headset. *Just let me get away*, she thought to herself, heart racing. She got twenty feet before they started yelling at her.

"Hey miss!"

She kept jogging.

"Halt! Halt or I'll shoot!"

What the fuck? Shoot? Are they kidding me?

Dolly began running in earnest. Then a bullet pierced the asphalt beside her, and she stopped, almost weeping with fear. They were bad men. She knew they were bad. She had felt them before. She had been here before.

"Turn around!"

She turned to see them both walking toward her, weapons aimed and ready. Trembling, her hands automatically raised.

"She had to have been flashed. Why the hell else would she be here?"

"Yeah, but why isn't it responding to prompts?"

"Forget it. Let Bannick figure it out."

The second security guard caught her arm, running his thumb across her skin. Dolly looked at him nervously, steeling herself. She knew that look.

"Hey, guys," she said jauntily, hiding her fear. "I was just jogging and lost my way. No need to go all commando on me."

He smiled but didn't let go of her arm. "Come on. We'll give you a tour of the premises."

Dolly tried to laugh it off. "No, that's okay. I need to get home."

The first guard was speaking into his headset again. He nodded and stood in front of Dolly again, his face intent.

"Oh, what a tangled web we weave…"

"Why do you keep saying that?"

His head tilted slightly, concentrating on the person talking on the other line. Dolly could hear someone speaking through the headset, but she couldn't make out any words.

The men looked at each other. The first guard took her other arm. "Come on. You're coming with us." He gestured toward the warehouse and began to pull her. "It'll be fine. Come on."

Dolly resisted, planting her feet, but they kept pulling her in. As they passed through the open gate, an overwhelming fear engulfed her. She couldn't go back in there. They couldn't make her go back in there.

Dolly began to fight in earnest. The second guard pulled out his billy club and struck her on the head with enough force to flatten a grown man, but Dolly kept fighting. The first guard tased her, making the second man yelp and jump back.

"Fucking warn me, asshole!"

With a scream, Dolly dropped to her knees, the Taser leads embedded in her skin above the neck of her sweatshirt. The pain changed everything. She wasn't afraid anymore. She was angry. Yanking the leads off her skin, Dolly threw them aside and stood up.

She knocked the first guard to the ground effortlessly, too fast for him to react. She straddled his chest and jammed both thumbs against pressure points in his throat, watching his panicked face as he struggled and passed out. The second guard pulled out his knife and stabbed her as she leaned over his companion. Feeling the blade penetrate, she twisted and grabbed his wrist, pulling him to the ground. He dropped with a heavy thud, and she was on him instantly.

It was over in seconds. Panting, Dolly stood over them both, braced for more violence. But they were no longer any threat. A fierce satisfaction gripped her. They weren't dead, although she knew killing them would have been effortless. She looked down at the two puncture wounds on her chest where the prongs had sunk in, then reached around to feel the blood pumping from the back wound she didn't even feel yet. Her fingers came back with what looked like oil streaked with blood.

As quickly as it came, her aggression collapsed, and she staggered.

"I almost killed them," she muttered, stunned by her own actions, "I could have killed them. It was…it was easy."

She looked back at the warehouse. The building itself seemed to be watching her. She tensed, half expecting an army to come pouring out.

Nothing happened. The building stayed silent, the rusted frames of its shattered windows feeling like eyes to her. Dolly turned away and began to run as fast as she could. The men lay where she'd dropped them.

After a mile, she came to a dilapidated old gas station/convenience store. It was an odd place for a station—off the beaten path and ragged with age. She went inside and grabbed a bottle of water. A bored-looking cashier glanced up briefly as she paid and then went back to her video game.

Dolly walked outside to the locked bathroom. Waving her card against the reader, the door clicked open. She hurried inside, locking it behind her.

She pulled off her sweatshirt and pants, standing in her underwear as she examined her wounds. The Taser marks were small, and there wasn't much blood, but the wound on her back had to be bad. She'd felt the knife split the skin, felt the blood soaking her back as she ran. Grabbing a fistful of paper towels out of the dispenser, Dolly dabbed at the base of her spine, grimacing as she felt the towels soak up the blood. There was a lot of it.

She pulled the towels back to look at them, startled by what she saw. There was very little blood; the wetness was mostly some sort of golden liquid, similar in color to olive oil.

"What the hell?"

She wiped again at the wound, twisting to try and see what was happening behind her. More of the olive oil shit. She sniffed it. It had a mild, almost clinical odor, like the corridors of a sterile hospital. Dolly touched it curiously, rubbing it between thumb and forefinger.

What the fuck is this stuff?

She quickly washed her face and hands, standing over the sink and staring at her reflection. The pain from her wounds barely registered. Her vision was skewed, probably a concussion. It seemed as if there were two images of herself superimposed over each other, as if she was reaching out to another version of herself. Alice through the looking glass, existing in a world upside down from the one she knew.

Suddenly the bathroom doorknob rattled, making her jump. Somebody banged on the door and yelled for her to hurry up. Dolly automatically began to answer but then stopped, listening. There were multiple muffled voices outside. The doorknob began to twist back and forth.

She scrambled back into her clothes.

"Hurry up, lady! I gotta go!"

Lady? How does he know it's a woman in here? The bathroom is unisex.

Instinctively, Dolly knew it was because of what had happened at the warehouse. There were armed men outside that door, she was certain. She looked around wildly, searching for another exit.

There was a ceiling vent just big enough to maybe climb through. Quick as a flash, Dolly was standing on the sink, removing the vent cover. The pounding on the door grew louder.

Dolly pushed the cover up into the opening and hoisted herself into the ceiling. Sliding the cover back into place, she began crawling through

63

the narrow space until she reached the air conditioning vent on the flat roof of the gas station.

Cautiously pulling herself out onto the roof, she heard a crash as the bathroom door flew open. Lying flat, she didn't dare crawl to the edge to see who was down there. But she could hear them. If the roof had been pitched instead of flat, they would have already seen her.

In the parking lot below, a squad of soldiers, all in black, were exiting what looked like an unobtrusive refrigerated truck. They fanned out, weapons drawn, and deployed around the station's lot. A restructured six-wheeler, obviously military, was at the other end. Three men, also in black and carrying weapons, climbed out of it, while one stayed in the driver's seat with the engine running.

A large black van pulled into the back entrance carrying another group of four men. They were the tech crew. One was already out and bent over his tablet, tapping on the keyboard. He pulled up the station's surveillance video, which showed Dolly entering and leaving the store. An older man, slim and sharp faced, scanned the area with alert, piercing eyes. He glanced at the screen the computer analyst showed him and then back at the store. Two of his men were already inside questioning the cashier. Two others had broken down the bathroom door.

"That feed was less than six minutes ago," the older man said. "Her ID tracked her here. Show me the outdoor surveillance."

The man's voice was as sharp as his features, the words snapped out in a manner that was used to being obeyed. More tapping as the laptop logged into the outdoor surveillance camera feed, which showed her going into the bathroom. The security cameras weren't placed high enough to record the roof.

"Her card was last used at the outdoor bathroom," the tech said. He looked around and pointed at the broken door. "There."

Two armed men were already coming out. "Clear, sir. She's not in there."

The sharp man spoke into his com. "Ask if this place has a basement."

Dolly heard the muffled, tinny reply. "That's a negative, sir."

"Fredricks. Dawson." Two men halfway across the parking lot looked up. "Check the roof."

The men jogged over to the building and began to search for a way up.

"Where are my drones?"

64

The sharp man stood in front of the broken bathroom door, barking orders, when the computer man called him back.

"Sir, look!"

"What've you got?"

"The parking lot surveillance. See?" He pointed at the screen. It showed Dolly running across the parking lot just before the refrigerated truck pulled in. "We just missed her. You can see our truck pulling in at the south entrance right as she ran down the west."

"West? Heading toward the hub? What the hell is she doing? Is she going back there?"

"The feed only extends to the edge of the lot, sir."

"Tap into the street feed."

"There isn't one. Most of this area is abandoned."

"Then access her vision."

"The monitor is in the truck, sir."

"Are you fucking kidding me, Leland? Go get it. How the fuck can I find her if I can't see what she sees?" He spoke into his com. "Fredricks, Dawson. She exited the area. Get back here." He turned to four other men. "I want eyes on her right now. She can't be far. If she's responding to programming, she'll be heading back to the hub. Follow her until she arrives but don't approach unless she changes course. Keep me informed live. Go!"

The men ran to the refrigerated truck and drove off, back toward where she'd just come from. Leland ran toward the black van, vanishing inside. Lying on her back, Dolly could just see the van and the refrigerated truck when she turned her head sideways. She watched both vehicles pull out and drive back toward the warehouse. *Why did the surveillance show me running back there?*

She exhaled silently, focusing. She could think about that later. Slowly turning over, Dolly crawled to the other end of the roof, where another delivery truck was parked. This one looked legit; the driver was unloading cases of beer onto his hand truck. One of the soldiers yelled at him to get the hell out of there, brandishing a rifle. The driver dropped what he was doing and jumped into the cab of the truck, fumbling for his keys. *Good,* Dolly thought. *They'll leave soon. Then I can get out of here.*

Voices came over the sharp man's com. Dolly could hear them. It was the four soldiers who'd driven after the phantom her.

"We've canvassed the area, sir—a full two klicks down Weston. No sign of the target, Lieutenant Wendell."

"Hold up!" the sharp man yelled at the beer truck. He gestured for Fredricks and Dawson to search it and turned to the com.

"Why the hell don't you have her vision yet?"

"I don't know, sir. It's not responding."

"Goddammit. You got drones flying?"

"Loading them now, sir."

"Find her."

Dolly cringed. She had to get out of here.

Dawson stopped the beer truck, ordering the driver to get out of the cab and open the back. They went around together, and the nervous trucker opened the rig. Dawson went inside to search, emerging a few minutes later with a can of beer in his hand. Fredricks scanned the truck roof and undercarriage with a mirror extension and then gave a thumbs-up to the man holding the beer. He spoke into his com.

"The truck's clean, sir."

Lieutenant Wendell barked an affirmative.

The soldiers waved the man on. "Now get this thing out of here."

The driver nodded, climbed back into the truck, and fired up the engine. Dawson popped the can and took a swig, watching the truck idle as the trucker clicked himself into his seat belt. He threw the can in the nearby trash as Lieutenant Wendell walked toward him.

"No sign of her, sir."

Leland returned with a different tablet, tapping rapidly.

"Two minutes and the drones are up, Lieutenant."

Wendell looked around, his face hard. "She's not on Weston. That's the only road for half a mile. Could she have hacked the surveillance cameras with a false image?"

"Doubtful, sir. She isn't equipped for that sort of parameter."

The lieutenant looked around, irritated. Then his eyes narrowed on the gas station again.

"Check the roof."

"There's no way she could have gotten up there without our seeing it."

"Get a drone up to canvas the area."

"Yes, sir."

Wendell gestured toward the military vehicle and said, "Conley, this Hummer stands out like a sore thumb in civilian traffic. Get it back to Aquinas, double time."

"Yes, sir."

In the idling beer truck, the driver was patiently waiting for the mercenaries to move so he could leave. Not daring to honk, he gently revved the engine, catching their attention. They stepped back, allowing the truck to move forward.

Dolly braced herself for a leap. They'd have a drone on her in seconds if she stayed here. She had to get on that truck.

As the men turned away and the beer truck began to move, she jumped the short distance from the station roof to the top of the truck's cargo hold, rolling twice before lying flat in the middle, arms straight out at her sides. She slid slightly from the oil still oozing from her back, soaking her top. Even now, there was no pain. She lay there, mind racing over all she had heard. Why? What the hell did the military want with her? Was it because she defended herself against their men? Was it because she was some sort of intel threat because the warehouse's cover was blown? What the fuck was in that place?

One other sentence from the conversation stood out. *See what she sees? What does that mean?*

She looked up at the sky, uncertain. Her hearing grew sharp and clear, like it had that day in the park, and she could suddenly hear everything— the subordinate rifling through the cab of the van in search of codes to launch the drones, the sound of his feet shuffling across the floor, his labored breathing as he searched. There was a clarity to the noise this time; the sounds weren't crashing together in that unbearable cacophony. She could hear each man walking around the parking lot, hear one soldier questioning the bored cashier, who obviously had no idea what was happening. She heard two of them scraping the vent lid, musing as to whether she could fit through it or not. She heard the sink give way under one man's weight as he climbed up to see, the gush of spray as the plumbing broke open, the cursing as the men got soaked. All of this in just a few seconds. Then the subordinate found the code he was looking for, and she heard him run it to the team leader.

How can I see what she sees?

On a hunch, Dolly suddenly closed her eyes as the beer truck left the parking lot, the gentle hum of the engines and the vibration of movement comforting. She methodically moved her fingers against the roof of the truck as she thought. Her fingers tapped out how many men were in the group, as if somehow tracking each of them. One of the men turned to look at the beer truck as it pulled out onto the street, and she moved with him, sliding out of view.

"Goddammit, the screen is blank!" She heard Wendell snarl. "Do your goddamn job, you idiot! And where're my drones?"

The subordinate tapped at the monitor.

"There's nothing wrong with it, sir. It's working."

"How can it be working if I can't see anything?"

"Maybe…maybe she has her eyes closed."

Wendell snorted in anger. "Get me her GPS. And get those goddamn drones in the air."

The beer truck lumbered forward half a block, moving far too slowly for Dolly. She could hear the men climbing to the roof of the gas station, the crunch of their boots on the rough shingles as they looked around. Knowing they'd see her from that height, she rolled to the far side of the vehicle, dropping down against the side of the truck and hanging on by her hands, out of sight of the men now on top of the gas station.

"Sir, this model doesn't have standard GPS."

"What the fuck are you telling me? You have this multibillion-dollar investment and you don't install a goddamn GPS?"

"It has a more sophisticated tracking system that requires a coded entry and vocal or fingerprint ID. I don't have either."

"Oh, for fuck's sake. Get me Bannick."

Another tech approached them. "Drones are launched, sir."

"Show me."

The beer truck was now three blocks away. Eyes still closed, Dolly heard the strident hum as six baseball-sized drones lifted into the air. Military drones followed a grid pattern. She should have about thirty seconds before they spotted her. Dolly slid down the side of the truck, out of view of the driver's mirrors, and curled underneath the moving vehicle, bracing herself against the undercarriage. She didn't question how she was able to do this with so little effort, how she knew what kind of search pattern military drones used, how she knew where to find hand

and foot grips beneath this six-wheeler. Something in her memory was triggered, and she just knew. The heightened sense of hearing was not a torture now. It was a survival mode blessing.

Dolly listened to the wind as it whirled around signposts and stop signs, bouncing off buildings. She also knew, without seeing, exactly where they were logistically—less than four miles from her apartment. But it wasn't safe on this truck. It wouldn't take long for them to figure out that she'd probably hitched a ride on it. They'd be after her soon.

The truck was a mile from the gas station now, entering sporadic traffic. A semitrailer pulled up beside the beer truck at a stoplight and Dolly, still without opening her eyes, slipped out from the truck's undercarriage and effortlessly rolled beneath the trailer. She listened to the wheels of the beer truck move forward as the vehicle she now hid under turned left toward the highway.

Then she heard it. As clearly as if she was plugged into the com system, she could hear the sharp man's voice.

"All units! Subject is possibly hiding in a refrigerated beer truck, last seen on the corner of Hindley and Soundview, heading north. Visual tracking impaired but audio confirms it. Follow that rig. Find her. Drones are in pursuit."

Dolly moved to the edge of the trailer and swung over onto a gas truck traveling in the opposite direction. Scrambling onto the undercarriage, she rode for another three miles until the truck stopped at a stoplight underneath an overpass.

Sheltered by the temporary gloom, Dolly climbed off the truck and ran to the inner concrete wall of the overpass, vanishing into the shadows there. She stayed motionless, back pressed flat against the concrete, until the truck began to move forward. Then she bolted across the lanes to a copse of trees on the other side. City cameras were common here, but she had to take the chance. Her eyes were open now, but she kept them focused on the ground beneath her feet, careful to not look up at any buildings which could give them a clue as to where she was.

Dolly didn't know what was in that warehouse, but she was certain this team was from there and had been scrambled specifically to find her. Not only had she trespassed on what was obviously some secret government base or some such, she'd assaulted two of their men when they tried to detain her.

Her stride evened out into a steady run. She didn't know what their range was to track her, but surely it wasn't more than a few miles. She needed to find a quiet, safe place to think it all through. *Keisha,* she thought. *I'll go to see Keisha and Tanja. Get a change of clothes, gather my thoughts.* Dolly turned and began running west toward the apartment complex her friends lived at.

She didn't stop until she reached their building. Sprinting up the steps, through the entrance, and down the hall, she banged on their door.

"Keisha! Let me in. It's Dolly! Keisha!"

Muffled crashing noises came from inside the apartment. She heard Keisha climb out of bed, bitching a blue streak.

"I'm coming, I'm coming. Shit. Fucking cat, get out of the way!"

Latches clicked and the door chain slid away. Not waiting, Dolly pushed it open, making Keisha stumble backward. Dolly closed the door and locked it, hands shaking as she pushed the chain back into place. Keisha continued to grumble sleepily.

"Doll, what the fuck are you doing? You know it's my night to sleep in, goddammit…"

Dolly turned and Keisha's attitude dropped away.

"Babe…. Babe, what's wrong? What's the matter?"

"Tanja. Where's Tanja?"

"Probably at aerobics. You want to tell me what the hell is going on? What's the matter with you? Why are you so damn filthy? You been mud wrestling or some weird shit with a john?"

"Listen to me, Keisha. Some awful shit has been happening. Men are after me. Military, maybe mercenaries. They almost got me."

Keisha visibly relaxed and rubbed her eyes, still bleary with sleep. "Oh. This another one of your nightmares?"

Dolly went to the kitchen and poured a glass of water, drinking thirstily. Keisha shuffled impatiently behind her. Dolly yanked a wad of paper towels off a roll and began to wipe the sweat and dirt from her face. She turned the sink faucet on, splashing her cheeks and throat, showering droplets across the counter.

"Watch the mess! What the hell's all over your back? What is that greasy shit?" Keisha grabbed a towel off the stove handle and swiped it over the counter as Dolly paced the room.

70

"Keish, things have been happening to me, shit I haven't told you about because they're just too damn weird."

Keisha finished mopping up the mess and turned a skeptical eye on her friend.

"Yeah? I'm listening."

"My hearing has become really acute. I heard Kyle on his cell phone the other day from a block away! And these dreams, these nightmares…I'm not sure they're just dreams. They feel like memories, Keisha. I think they're memories. Then today, I went for a jog, took a different route and ended up at this abandoned warehouse on the edge of town. I was scared of the building. Actually scared of it. It felt familiar but really bad. Then these two military types appear out of nowhere and start quoting Scott to me, over and over. I tried to leave, and they actually fired a shot at my feet! Something's at that warehouse, Keisha. Something bad is going on there."

Keisha turned on the coffee maker. "Did you get any sleep at all?"

"Keish, I'm trying to tell you, this is serious. I think they want to kill me." Her voice dropped to a whisper and she leaned closer to her friend. "What if…what if I've been there before? What if they did something to me there, put something in me? Like an experiment or something? Remember the dildo thing? I think it's some sort of electronic coma roofie or something. That john kept trying to get me to look at it. Kyle accidentally flashed it at me, and he said I didn't move for two hours. I don't remember any of that. Then I go jogging to a place I've never gone before, like I was drawn there. Two guards shoot at me, one stabs me, and Keish, I took them down like a fucking ninja. Now there's this posse of soldiers trying to find me. I jumped on a beer truck and got away. But they're probably still after me."

Dolly pressed her hand against her forehead, willing herself to calm down. "I needed to tell you to be on the lookout. Can I borrow some of Tanja's clothes? I don't know if it's safe to go home. Facial recognition software would have already identified me if they don't know my address already."

Keisha stood silently, her eyes assessing, pondering how to begin. She sighed, running a hand through her hair. Dolly was obviously sleep-deprived and at a breaking point.

"Go take a shower."

"What?"

"You're nothing but filth right now. You know I can't stand dirt."

"Keisha…"

"And I sure as hell can't concentrate on anything you're saying when you're so grubby. And you stink."

"Keisha, this is serious. They can track me through my eyes. What if they come here? What if they know what you look like because I'm looking at you right now?"

"Then I'll blame you for leading them straight to me," Keisha answered sarcastically. She waved Dolly toward the bathroom. "Go take a shower. And give me those goddamn nasty clothes so I can throw them in the washer."

"I can't stay here. There's no time. I just needed to let you know what's happening. Maybe rest a little. Catch my breath."

"Well, you're not resting on my couch with your greasy ass. Get in the shower. Then we'll talk."

Dolly reluctantly padded into the bathroom, handed her clothes to Keisha and stepped into the shower. Keisha took the clothes between thumb and forefinger with obvious loathing and dropped them into the washer.

Dolly came out refreshed and a little calmer, wearing Tanja's pink kitten robe. Keisha handed her a glass of red wine.

"Here. You need something stronger than coffee. Your clothes'll be ready in ten minutes."

"Thanks. I don't want to drink right now. Got to stay clear."

"Drink it. I'll watch for the bounty hunters."

"I'm serious, Keisha. I think they were mercenaries. Maybe hired by Aquinas. They mentioned Aquinas."

Keisha sighed and shook her head. "Doll, you gotta go see a shrink about this, for real. Things are getting just too fucking weird with you. I've never seen you like this. Listen to your voice. Why you talking like that?"

"Like what?"

"Like you were born with a silver spoon up your ass."

Dolly stopped short, her mind racing.

"I…I'm not talking different."

"'I'm not talking different.'" Keisha mimicked, snorting in derision. "Just fucking listen. Are you trying to tell me you always talked with that hoity-toity bullshit accent? Come on now."

Dolly ticked over the last twenty minutes, staring at Keisha with dawning realization. Keisha stared back, face a mask of cynicism, arms crossed over her chest.

"Oh, my God."

"Mm-hmm. The penny has dropped."

Dolly really was speaking with a different accent. Cultured, more rounded tones, almost aristocratic.

"You said you had a British accent in the mommy dreams," Keisha said softly. "I think all that shit is spilling over into real life now."

"But I…it happened, Keish. It just happened, just now."

"Woman, you fell asleep in the hotel under a john the other night. You're practically walking in your sleep now. Why the fuck else would you have that accent?"

Dolly grabbed her head, hands curling into fists against her temples. "I'm going crazy, Keisha. I'm going fucking crazy!"

"Yeah, no wonder. When's the last time you slept without getting gang-fucked by monsters inside your head? It makes sense that you'd finally break down. Look at you. You're vibrating, you're so tense. Relax, take a breath, and calm the fuck down."

She led Dolly to a living room awash with purple furniture and striped rugs, walls hung with tiny colored lights. Keisha shoved her down onto the couch and covered her with a violet lap blanket. Dolly curled up against the cushions, trying not to cry.

"It wasn't a dream. I know it wasn't a dream."

"When's the last time you slept more than an hour?"

"I slept fourteen hours yesterday on the bathroom floor."

Keisha gave her a look, got up and rooted around the refrigerator, pulling out a plastic tub of turkey meat. She brought it over to Dolly and handed her an enormous turkey leg. Dolly looked at it, hiccuping through her tears, and Keisha waved the leg menacingly.

"Go on. You need some protein, and turkey helps you sleep."

"Keisha, this is serious. I'm not kidding. I got attacked."

"So what's new? You're okay now, aren't you? What whore do you know who hasn't been attacked by some cocksucker?"

"It wasn't like that. They weren't johns. Look, I can't stay long. I know it sounds crazy, but I think they can track me by what I see. I heard them say it. I have to leave. But I wanted to warn you, and I don't trust our phones."

"Will you listen to yourself? So you didn't call because they're tracking your cell phone and contact lenses?"

"I don't wear contact lenses."

"Then how are they tracking you from what you see? You sure this isn't another nightmare? 'Cause it sounds just like one of your dreams."

"No." Dolly's voice grew firm. "No, this really happened. You saw me when I first got here. You think I did that to myself?"

"You're not bleeding, kid. But you did have a shitload of some kind of grease all over you. Did you fall in something? Smelled bizarre."

"That's from where they hit me with their baton. And one of them cut me in the back, but I can't reach it. It wasn't too deep, but it dripped olive oil all over. But I think it's stopped now."

"You wouldn't be sitting here talking like this if they split your scalp open with a baton or stabbed you in the fucking back."

"It happened!"

The dryer buzzed. Keisha stood up and shushed her to silence. "I'm gonna get your clothes and I'll get my med kit in case you do have some kind of hurt. In the meantime, get that food in you."

Dolly gaped at her friend. Standing like a regimental mother, Keisha pointedly looked at the food and crossed her arms. Exasperated, Dolly took the leg and obediently bit into it. Satisfied, her friend went to the bathroom closet to get her emergency med kit.

To her surprise, Dolly found that she was ravenously hungry. Keisha came back with the kit, the bottle of red wine, and another glass. By the time she poured herself one and laid the folded clothes down, Dolly had eaten the whole leg and a hunk of turkey breast.

"Goddamn, girl. When's the last time you ate?"

Licking her fingers and wiping them on the paper towel Keisha tossed at her, Dolly sighed and took a swig of wine. Her friend was right. The food did make her feel better. She pulled on the clean clothes and stretched.

"Okay," Keisha said, "Now that you've calmed down some, tell me again. What the hell has got you so wound up and weird voiced?"

Dolly recounted the entire story, from the museum to taking down the guards to escaping the search party. Keisha listened silently, wrestling with disbelief. No matter what had actually happened, Dolly believed it completely. Keisha could see that.

"I felt my scalp when I was washing my hair."

"And?"

"And there's nothing there."

"Mm-hmm."

"But a lot of that greasy shit came out of my back. There was some blood in it, but it was mostly that olive oil stuff."

"It better not have clogged up my washer. I'm running another cycle just to make sure."

"Keisha, stop making fun of me. This is serious. One of the guards stabbed me, but I can't find where."

"Fine. But give me a general direction. Where'd he stab you?"

Dolly twisted, pointing at her spine under the sweatshirt.

"Back here. Stabbed me around the kidney. I'm scared, Keisha. I felt the blade go in, but it doesn't hurt. It didn't hurt when he stabbed me. I'm afraid he hit my spine or something."

"Just as long as you don't bleed all over my couch. Turn around. Let me see."

Dolly shifted, lifting her shirt. "It's not bleeding much now, just a lot of that greasy shit. Could it…could it be spinal fluid?"

Keisha snorted, pulling the sweatshirt higher and pushing Dolly around until she could look at the small of her back.

"Goddamn, Dolly. There is a cut."

"I told you. Is it deep? I don't feel anything."

Keisha bent down to examine the wound more closely. It was small but deep. She prodded it gently with her fingers.

"What the hell…"

Keisha pulled her hand away, looking at her fingers. They were glistening with the oily substance. She bent again and slowly pulled the wound wider. A tiny line of blood rimmed the outer skin, but only the oil seeped from the interior. She jerked her hand away.

"What?" Dolly asked, alarmed. She looked at Keisha's face. "What do you see? Is it bad?"

Keisha yanked the shirt down and gave Dolly a shove.

"Keish, what? What is it?"

Keisha jumped to her feet and backed away. Her face was rigid, raging.

"You lying sack of shit! How long have you been fucking with me? With Tanja? You made me care about you, goddammit!"

Dolly stared as Keisha stumbled back, wiping her hand on a towel in disgust.

"Get the fuck outta my house!"

"But…but he stabbed me. I felt it."

"If he stabbed you and you were a woman, you damn well would have felt it, bitch."

"If I was a woman? What the fuck else am I?"

"I'm not fooling around. Get OUT."

Dolly just gaped as Keisha jabbed a finger toward the door.

"You heard me, you toaster piece of shit! I don't deal with fake pussy. See this?" She pointed at her own crotch. "This here is real pussy. Now get the fuck out before I throw you in the scrapyard. Get out!"

"What are you talking about? What's the matter with you?"

"Telling us all that bullshit about your daddy and your nightmares. Are you recording this? Fuck you and fuck all you cunts watching! Do you get off on this? Is that what this is? Do you double-team johns with me or Tanja so they can watch? Is this the latest rich man's game?"

Dolly stood up and took a step toward her. Keisha stomped her foot in rage and screamed, "Get the fuck out!"

"Keisha, you're not making any sense. Please. These people really are after me."

"Yeah, and I hope they get your ass, hardware. If I find video of Tanja or me on the internet, I'm suing whatever goddamn company set you up to study us."

"Are you serious?"

"As a heart attack. Get out."

"Keisha…"

"Don't call me by my name! Don't you ever call me anything, ever again. Get out! Get the fuck out!" Eyes full of tears, Keisha ran to the kitchen, grabbed a knife, and went to the door, jerking it open.

Dolly gaped at her friend, bewildered and horrified, unable to process what was happening. She had never seen Keisha cry before. They had been best friends for years. Now, in an instant, it was over. This hurt far more that the guards' brutality or the wounds they'd inflicted; this was a new fear, one she couldn't look at yet.

"Out."

"Why are you calling me hardware?" The question was just a whisper of sound.

Keisha just pointed at the door with the knife, refusing to answer.

Dolly looked at her, sick at heart. She knew, suddenly, that she could take that knife away easily, that the sight of Keisha brandishing it was as threatening as an arch-backed kitten hissing a warning.

She went to the door, giving one last look at her best friend, hoping that maybe Keisha would come to her senses, realize that they loved each other.

"I would never hurt you, Keish. Never."

"Don't ever talk to me again, you lying sack of fake shit."

Dolly's eyes welled with tears and her face crumpled.

"I…I love you, Keish. You're my best friend."

Keisha faltered for a moment as she watched Dolly's wretched, dejected weeping, but then her gaze hardened, and she raised the knife higher.

Brokenhearted and spent, Dolly stepped out into the corridor.

Tanja was walking toward them, fishing her key out of her pocket.

"Doll!" She said in delight, her face lighting up. Then she took in the expressions of the two women—Dolly's dejected and weary, and Keisha furious with a knife in her hand. The smile faded.

"What's going on? What happened?"

"Tanja, get in here," Keisha snarled. "Don't talk to it."

"Don't talk to what? Dolly, are you okay?"

Dolly smiled sadly, reaching out to brush a strand of hair off Tanja's forehead.

Keisha exploded.

"Don't touch her!"

She yanked Tanja away, the teenager stumbling as she practically threw her in the apartment, slamming the door behind them. Dolly heard all the dead bolts snap back into place, heard Tanja's muffled questions mixed with Keisha's yelling. She stood in front of the door for a moment, placing her hand against its surface, noting the childish, delightful paint job Tanja had proudly done on the apartment number. Then she turned away and left the building.

Standing on the sidewalk once more, she nervously looked right, left, and up, listening for the hum of a drone. Nothing. She began walking away hesitantly and then quickened her pace until she was running again.

Images began to run with her, quicksilver flashes of painful memories eating her alive as she ran. Past rapes, both real and imagined, babies, the little boy at the museum, the man who thought she was Grace, herself going into labor, masculine hands groping and grabbing, the stench of rancid breath and grunting, hairy flesh, all smothering her. And throughout all the noise was a cacophony of crying and childish screams. Her own, yes, but many others, hundreds of others, all mixed together with a sea of strangers staring at her as she was torn apart. It was the men at the museum again, staring at her through the glass, but there were hundreds of them. Thousands.

Dolly stopped in mid run. Keisha's fear and rage had triggered a possibility she could scarce give credence to. And the men at the gas station. All of them there for her.

See through her eyes.

See through her eyes.

Do they know where I am right now?

Dolly placed her hands over her eyes, then off again, trying to sense if there was something unusual about her vision. She saw things the way she'd always seen them. She closed her eyes and started to jog slowly, but soon tripped on a break in the sidewalk. That didn't work. She stared down at the concrete. If they really could see through her eyes, track her that way, then she wouldn't give them any landmarks to find her with. She also needed to get rid of the tracker in her arm that Ramirez had urged them all to get. They could hack into her medical history and find her that way, if they hadn't already.

First things first. She fixed her gaze on the sidewalk, looking neither right nor left, and began to run again. *Find me now, fuckers*, she thought. *Let's see if you have a map of the concrete.* She knew where she had to go.

*   *   *

Bannick sat at his massive desk, a cup of lemongrass tea curling steam into the air beside his right hand. He leaned back, steepling his fingers together as he watched Dolly run down the block.

Lieutenant Wendell's voice came over the speaker. "Professor Bannick, the subject is moving again. Shall we pursue?"

"No. Let's see where she goes."

"What about the two in the apartment?"

"Leave them. Send a letter tomorrow, stating that it's from lawyers who represent some sex doll company or the like. Make it a veiled threat. If they attempt a lawsuit, it'll go badly for them, etc. It's perfectly legal for research and development to send their property out for educational and enrichment training." He thought for a moment. "Include a line or two about Dolly's personality being programmed to blend in with this Keisha woman specifically. That it was a parasite phishing exercise to mimic a real-life mid- to low-end prostitute. Say it's data for a more affordable line coming out."

"Sir?"

"It will cut these two off from ever being a haven for the subject again. That bitter little whore will never forgive Dolly after she reads it. We've learned all we need to about the subject's interaction with them. Now let's see what happens when they are lost to her."

"The target is half a mile away already. She's running while looking straight down at the sidewalk. Our team is following via GPS and street surveillance cameras."

"Patch all the feeds to me live."

"Yes, sir."

7

As storefronts go, it was deplorably unimpressive. Peeling yellow paint framed an old-fashioned pull-open glass door covered with faded posters depicting alien spaceships and buxom warrior women with scant clothing and thigh-high boots. The display window was crammed full of old computer towers, laptops, satellite dishes, and miles of color-coded wires in no discernible order—just a jumble tumble of electronic parts stacked haphazardly to the ceiling. Equally seedy, the name "Techno Tidbits" was scrawled across the glass in bright red laser tag lettering. A soggy-looking deli framed one side of the computer tech store, with a grayish blue laundromat on the right.

Inside Techno Tidbits was a hugely fat man sitting behind the counter, discarded candy and chip wrappers and a crumpled sandwich littering the glass surface. The man was wearing a set of wraparound glasses that blocked out any outside light, his hands resting on the dirty counter, fingers moving softly as if he were typing. Staged moans and grunts could be heard faintly from the headset. The man was watching porn.

Dolly banged on the locked front door, and he yanked the headset off, startled. Checking the security camera screen, he saw who it was and buzzed her in. It was Dolly, obviously agitated. He instinctively smoothed his hair at the sight of her.

"Hey, Doll. What's up?" He looked at her sweat suit, disappointed at the absence of her sexy work wear. "And why the fuck are you here at this time of day? Not strolling tonight?"

Dolly launched right into it. "Jabba, can you scan me for a bugging device?"

"One of your johns slip one in while you weren't looking?"

"We all got chipped awhile back. Officer Ramirez recommended it. I think I'm being followed, maybe by my tracking chip. I want it gone."

He looked at her for a moment and shrugged.

"Ten credits. Up front. You think maybe one of your johns is tracking you?"

Dolly didn't answer, just pulled out her ID badge. She started to hand it to him but then pulled it back.

"Is there a way to scan this without it being traced?"

He looked concerned. "Sure, no problem. Hey, I was joking about the john. I've heard of this kind of shit with obsessed fuckers stalking beautiful women, even beautiful kids. And you are definitely something to stalk, Doll."

Dolly had no patience for Jabba's usual sexual innuendo. He fixed her computer for her when she needed it and set up her entertainment system years ago, but he was also the best source for antique magazines and comic books, something which she enjoyed, loving the stories of outcast heroes and their struggles with nobility. That was the main reason she put up with Jabba's nonsense. But not today. She waved the badge at him impatiently.

"Can you do it or not?"

"Sure." He tapped instructions into a keyboard, holding out his hand for the badge. She gave it to him, and he scanned it over a code reader. The ten credits were deposited. Heaving himself up from his chair, he lumbered over to a steel door in the back.

"Come on, then."

She followed him through the door, flinching when it automatically locked behind them. The room was set up like a library, with rows of heavy metal shelves crammed with mountains of electronic junk in seemingly endless bundles. Even the ceiling had large steel overhead racks loaded with heavier equipment. Jabba went over to a bank of computers on a wide L-shaped desk against the wall and began to press buttons.

"So what's my favorite cruise lady gotten herself into?"

"You don't want to know."

Jabba glanced over his shoulders with raised eyebrows.

"Okay."

81

He sat down at the desk and typed some more, the chair creaking alarmingly under his weight. He hit another switch and waved her toward the machine in the corner as it hummed to life. It looked like an airport security scanner. A small basket sat on the table in front of the scanner, and he told her to take off any and all metals. Dolly took off her earrings and a necklace Keisha had given her, looked at it sadly, and dropped it into the basket. She walked through the scanner.

It immediately beeped.

"You've got a tracker, all right. Sounds like more than one. Look." He pointed at the computer screen, which showed five spots on her torso and upper arms. "Those are all trackers. Heat signature, GPS tracking, pulse monitor. This is weird." He typed some more. "There's something weird with your bones too. What the hell…"

Jabba turned off the alarm, marked the spots on the screen that lit up, and tapped on the keyboard a few times, frowning. He told her to walk through again. The same results happened with the five points, but now her entire skeletal structure glowed green on the monitor. Jabba stared at the screen, dumbfounded, looked up at her, and then ran his hand over his mouth.

"Fuck me sideways. You're a breeder."

"A what?"

He tapped furiously at the keyboard, face bluish green from the screen readout, then sat back in amazement. Dolly walked over to where he sat and saw an image of her own silhouette on the monitor. It was alight with bright red and blue spots, green-glowing skeleton, and bluish white sexual organs. Even her eyes seemed rimmed in red and blue light.

"You're a fucking breeder! This is incredible." He tapped some more. "An old breeder. Look at that."

"Jabba, just tell me what the hell all that means."

He turned to her and grinned like a kid in a candy store. "You ain't human, Doll. Well, not completely. See this?" He pointed at the screen. "That's your uterus. It's human tissue, that's why it doesn't light up with any electronic signature. It's a mass of scar tissue. A human uterus is usually about two by three inches and shaped like an upside-down pear. That…" He circled the area. "That is about six by nine inches and looks like a fucking puked-up hair ball. All that filament shit? That's scarring. This uterus went through some real trauma. See this here? You don't have ovaries. Your whole skeletal structure is knit artificially, probably by a set of 3D printers. Your eyes seem partially organic, but these red ring and blue dots? Those are cameras. They track you by a simple remote camera. Your retinas act as their lenses. They see whatever you see." His face grew stern and tense. "Good thing I've got scramblers in place, or they'd be looking at my damn face right now, probably recording every sound, too. Fuck." He leaned back with a heavy sigh. "The other ones are simple GPS trackers like you'd put in your dog. Maybe a bit more sophisticated but basically the same idea. I can fry the sublingual ones and physically remove them with a simple walk through, but your eyes…gonna have to use lasers on your eyes."

Dolly was reeling. Jabba typed furiously, scribbling down codes and numbers as she sank weakly into a chair. *How can this be?* Her mind raced over the events of the last few months—the nightmares, the anxiety, Keisha's rage and fear, the whole Willow dream. And the babies. *Oh, God, the babies. Were they dreams or memories? Had any of those awful things actually happened?*

Jabba continued. "See this?"

He pointed at the screen on a second monitor, showing what looked like a bunch of rippling fiber optics jumbled in a ball. "This is from one of the first models of android mechanics. That's the AI brain. That's you, Doll." He grinned. "You're really old. This is so fucking cool."

Jabba started hauling components off the steel shelves surrounding them, arranging them on a large steel table. Dolly sat in the chair opposite, trying to take in what he was telling her. He saw her expression and stopped.

"You really didn't know?"

She shook her head, dazed.

He shrugged. "Don't feel bad. I had no fucking idea either. Whoever made you is good. Really good. I can usually spot synthetics."

He reached over and took her hand, turning it over and stroking her wrist.

"That's real skin. You're a fucking android! Wow." He drew the word out, clearly in awe. "Real uterus and real skin, organic components throughout. I'll bet you a million dollars you're just exactly to code ratios."

"This can't be," Dolly said. "I have memories. I had a childhood. I remember my parents, my school."

He began hauling electronics around again, hooking them up.

"I don't know. You might be a cyborg, which is an enhanced human. But with all the shit in you, I doubt it. Why the fuck are you a whore? I mean a street one. Most sex dolls are super high-end because they're so goddamn expensive. Exclusive. And you are definitely beautiful enough to work any five-star hotel or billionaire property. So what the hell?"

"Stop talking about me like I'm a fucking toaster, Jabba."

"More like a toaster you fuck."

"Shut up!"

"I don't mean nothing, Doll. This is a first for me and it's…it's pretty damn great." He laughed, obviously delighted.

"Can you help me or not? Without the snappy patter, please."

He was bent over a table, adjusting one last thing, and straightened with a loud groaning sigh.

"Now I don't think they can track you in here. Not with all the dampers I've got in this place, but they know you're here from GPS. And there's two surveillance cameras outside on the street, each a block away. So if it's any sort of high tech, they've most likely hacked into those, too."

"I don't have GPS tracking," she said, hands to her temples. "I heard them. Their tech guy said I don't have GPS. They need a special code."

"Every model has GPS, ever since they started rolling them out. They're right there on the screen, Doll. You have to have it, special code or no."

"I don't."

Jabba's lips twisted, skeptical. "Well, whatever is in you, it'll cost fifty credits to countermand them. Up front." He paused. "What do you mean, their tech guy?"

Dolly sighed and told him about the men at the gas station. Jabba's face went from the gleeful thrill of meeting a real android to stone-cold sober.

"You heard them say 'Aquinas?' And it was a whole team of military personnel?"

"Yeah. They chased off a guy delivering beer to the gas station. I jumped on top of his truck to get away after I climbed through the air vent in the bathroom."

Jabba snapped at her, deadly serious. "If a team like that was scrambled to come get you, there's something important about you. Aquinas is all bottom line. Bottom line is God to them. What the fuck are you, Doll?"

He shook his head and leaned back.

"Well, this changes things. This is a whole new fucking ball game. You can't use your badge after this. At all." He rifled through a drawer and pulled out a new badge. "I'll use this to transfer a couple grand from your account. They won't be able to trace this because it's not registered to you and I'll erase all traces of the transfer. And I'm gonna need those payment credits now. Right now. Then forget you ever knew me. I love ya, Doll, but I'm not risking my neck for you."

She gaped at him.

"Come on. Right now."

"What are you talking about? I thought you said they can't trace anything here. Why would you be in danger?"

"I'm small potatoes, Doll!" He yelled, startling her. "If Aquinas is looking for you, I don't want them finding you here or even that I've had anything to do with you. They'll burn my place to the ground. If I'm lucky, that's all they'll do."

He yanked the badge out of her hand and scanned it, shoved it back into her palm and began furiously typing on the keyboard. Dolly watched him access her account as easily as if it were his own, and her entire savings was gone in the blink of an eye. He typed some more, and it reappeared in the bank records as untouched. Then he scanned the new badge, typed some more, and the money reappeared in a new account.

He changed initiation dates on the new badge so that the account seemed to be six years old. Her photo ID portrayed the name "Janice Olson," and her address was eighty miles away. He scanned the badge again, added phony fingerprints, placed a retinal scanner over her head, added the retinal ID, and then handed it to her. Dolly took it reluctantly.

"Jabba, are you sure you haven't made a mistake? That I'm not what you think I am?"

"We don't have time to discuss it, Doll. Walk through the machine."

Dolly moved forward, still talking. "How can I not know I'm a goddamn android? It's impossible!"

"Remember that old movie *Blade Runner*? That's the film that inspired your creation. Aquinas's president said that in an interview. He was bragging about their surrogate mother program and how they'd fixed the glitches that created all the fucking sociopaths in the early 2030s. No more shrink-wrap wombs, no more maniacs. What was the tagline? 'All the love you'd have yourself with none of the hassle.' Fucking bullshit, but they sold it. Their research into human brain synapses regarding correlations with memory helped them grow their bleeding machines."

"Bleeding machines?"

"Yeah. Like you. They eat, shit, sweat, even bleed like humans because of the synthetic circulatory system that feeds your skin. But their personalities can be changed anytime a client or owner is dissatisfied."

"But I didn't bleed when that asshole stabbed me in the kidney. I just kind of…oozed this olive oil shit."

"Lubricant. You have a simplified arterial system that has blood, but it's not as pervasive as in a living organism because it doesn't have to be. All you need is enough to appear human but not actually be human. Those are the strictures needed to stay within the legal guidelines. Anything more detailed would be classified as cloning and lose the nonhuman immunity clause."

"What the fuck is that?"

"About sixty years ago, the Aquinas Corporation paid a fortune to have the government declare all androids and AI robots property, thus declaring you immune to any human rights. You're a toy or a gun, Doll. That's it. That's what all of you are. Outwardly human, inwardly synthetic, with organically grown nonhuman organs."

"Fuck that. I'm alive."

He turned and looked at her.

"After the law passed, Aquinas's PR company began a media blitz, describing how their research had led to this so-called breakthrough and they'd begun to write code for human emotions in a host breeder. Far better than the old sociopath shake-and-bakes, these breeder units would instill whatever kind of love and learning the human parents desire. They simply load your mind up with whatever memories they want, like a menu at a restaurant. I don't know what they're doing with you, but it's obviously important enough for them to break cover like this. Aquinas is notoriously private about the ins and outs of their 'research.'"

Jabba rubbed his chin thoughtfully. "You're probably an experiment. You know these android units are being used for espionage, sleeper cells, covert stuff. Probably assassination plants, too. Lot of conspiracy buzz about that. But that's kept strictly under wraps and the corporations deny it all anyway. Robotics is not just fucking, housekeeping, and yard work, you know. You're big business." He gestured toward the machine, agitated. "Enough of this bullshit. Stand there until I tell you to move. Go on, go on!"

Dolly moved forward and stood under the arched dome of the machine, which now bathed her in a soft blue light. She felt small ticks of pain under the skin of her elbows, wrists, ribs, hips, and inner thighs as the radiation disabled the trackers. Suddenly, there was substantial pain in both her temples. Dolly groaned out loud. It felt like hot needles were driving into her skull.

"Keep still."

"This really fucking hurts, Jabba."

"Just keep still. It's almost over."

The pain faded to a dull throb and Dolly closed her eyes in relief.

Jabba kept talking as he tapped on the keyboard.

"What I don't get is why they let you out on such a long leash. If they have a big investment in you, why let you out at all? And why make you a whore? What kind of clientele do you get? Politicians, billionaires?"

Dolly's head began to clear. "No. Small-minded men in business suits, mostly."

"Doesn't make sense. Christ, you could be a goddamn bomb for all I know. There, that's done." He heaved his bulky frame up and moved to the table with the helmet device.

"What about your money from whoring? Do you keep it, or is it controlled?"

"I keep it."

He shook his head. "I'm liking this less and less the more you tell me. It's got to be something covert. As soon as we're done here, forget you know me." He saw Dolly's expression and grimaced. "Sorry, Doll. It's got to be this way."

He got up and headed toward the steel door.

"Stay here and don't look at anything else. Just in case. Be back in a minute."

Dolly was immediately paranoid. "Where are you going?"

"Up front to sequence my security systems with the emergency protocol. Then I want you out of here."

"You said that already."

"Then act like you heard it."

Dolly watched as the steel door clanged shut behind him. First Keisha, now Jabba. By this time, probably Tanja as well.

Jabba came back in the room and handed her a bottled water and a wrapped sandwich from his fridge. The small gesture brought her to tears, and he quickly turned away. He began assembling the parts on the table and sighed with frustration. "Goddammit, I'm gonna have to realign my accounts again."

"What do you mean? What's happening?"

"If they've got a tracker on you they damn well are tracing your money. I don't want it traced back to here."

"Jabba, how can I be what you say I am? Couldn't I have been a human that they've…they've altered somehow, put those trackers into?"

Jabba shook his head as he screwed a segment into place on the motorcycle helmet. "I told you. From the way you lit up on the screen, there's no way."

"You don't know that."

"You told me you got fucking stabbed in the kidney by some mercenary type and ran all the way here from the West End. If you're human, how's that possible?"

"I am human. I remember being a little kid. I remember growing up."

"I doubt you were ever a little kid, Doll. Ever."

He set up a tripod with a brace on it and gestured for her to sit in the chair he placed directly in front of it.

"Now hold still."

He lifted the helmet apparatus and placed it over her head, aligning two segmented discs to both of her eyes. To these, he attached two long cylinders that looked like a pair of jerry-rigged binoculars. These he attached to the tripod brace.

"Look straight ahead. Don't blink, don't move your eyes." He peered into the binoculars. "Ah. There they are. Hold your breath and don't move."

A red light flashed as small lasers were activated. Dolly felt a strange stinging sensation but stayed motionless as they burned the tiny devices inside her eyes. It lasted only seconds. Then Jabba pulled back, checked the pupils and stepped away.

"Can you see okay?"

Dolly blinked repeatedly, looking around.

"Yeah. I don't see any difference."

"Right. Done. Get out now."

"Wait a minute! You've got to give me some answers. I don't even know what a breeder is. What would my function be? Do I live like a normal person? Do they keep me in a lab while the baby grows? What does it mean to be a breeder?"

"Pretty self-explanatory, Doll."

"But I can't have children."

He shook his head. "They can wipe your memory, remember? You've probably had hundreds. I know the early lab-grown wombs wear out after one hundred fifty kids. I read about those. All the babies were sociopaths or worse. Theory is, fetuses absorb emotions as well as nutrients from the umbilicals. 'Maniacs in a can,' I think they called them back then. Euthanized every one of the crazy little fucks by the time they were ten years old. Aquinas had to figure out another way to tap into that almighty dollar. So they made you and probably thousands like you, programmed you with human emotions, and fertilized you with the clients' sperm and ovum. All so rich brats can keep their girlish figures, and the parents still get their heirs. And since you're mostly synthetic, you have no rights. You're legal property, nothing more, and the corporations can do whatever the fuck they want with you. But I'll tell you one thing: you, all of you, are a big investment, and they'll squeeze every single penny out of you for as long as your body holds out. Nobody knew what they did with these breeders once the wombs go bad. I guess now we know."

They left the back room and Jabba waved her toward the front door.

"Come on. Time to go."

"I don't know what to do now. I don't know where to go."

Jabba shook his head, mouth stretched in a grimace.

"Figure it out, hardware. Can't help you. Come on. Out, out, out!"

"Jabba, what if you're right? What if they're following me right now? Do you really want them to see me exiting your store?"

Jabba pulled the door shut, his face slack. Dolly could see him thinking.

"Hell no, I don't. Come on." He started to walk back into the shop. "I've got a back way."

They went through the locked room they'd just been in, passing the desk and rows of steel shelves piled high with electronics, until they came to the back of the storeroom. Jabba rolled a large shelf out of the way, revealing an old canvas movie promo display that had to be ten feet tall.

He pulled it away to reveal a blank cinder block wall. To her amazement, Jabba tapped a command into his watch and rolled a section of wall up like a window shade, revealing another steel door behind. He shrugged at her look.

"Escape route. Lead-lined cinder block facade in case anybody comes sniffing around."

"Jabba, what the fuck do you do in here?"

He raised an eyebrow and pulled out his keys again.

"This and that."

Bending, he unlocked the door, pushed it open and gestured for Dolly to go through. She stepped into a long corridor that smelled of pizza and old carpet.

"Go to the end of the hallway and turn right. You'll come to a stairway. Go up to the top floor. You'll see a skywalk that'll take you into the next building. The code for that first door is 1298C; the second door is A677T. Go down to the basement, where there's an old steam tunnel. You can take that for six blocks before you hit a wall. Go up the ladder, and it'll take you back up to the street."

Dolly pressed his hand. It was sweaty with nerves.

"Thank you, Jabba."

"Yeah. I'll change the code in ten minutes, so hurry up." He shut the door with a clang. Dolly looked around and began to run down the corridor.

8

The large six-wheeled refrigerator truck lumbered down the street adjacent to Jabba's store. It was a shocking shade of pink and blue, its sides painted with a manically grinning toddler holding a large ice cream bar under the banner "Everybody Loves Feynman's Ice Cream!" The driver, clad in a blue uniform and baseball cap bearing a Feynman logo, grinned and waved to a mother and her delighted toddler as he drove past. Inside the truck, monitors blinked, and tech soldiers stared at screens. Leland suddenly spoke out.

"Sir! We've lost the signal."

Wendell stood over him, staring at the blank screen. "What do you mean, you've lost the signal?"

"It just went dead. I think it's been deactivated."

"Goddammit. She can't be far from here. Find her!"

Dolly hit the code into the first door, and it unlocked. She pulled it open, relieved that Jabba hadn't lied just to get her to leave. The skywalk was deserted, with thick waist-high opaque walls beneath the glass dome. She bent low and ran the entire length, punching in the code to the second door so as to enter the neighboring building. She used the stairs to get down to the basement to avoid elevator cameras, hoping that there were no security ones in the stairwells. There weren't. Most older buildings like these were able to skirt the codes of more modern structures, which required cameras in both. She found the entrance to the steam tunnels and climbed down.

The tunnels were eerily silent, lit with a faint yellow glow from sparsely hung bulbs in cages on the walls. Dolly hadn't seen those since she was a little girl. She shook her head. *Who knows if I ever was a little girl?* Still trying to absorb the shock of the last few hours, Dolly began to move down the tunnel, her breathing deafening in the silence.

She came out six blocks away, just as Jabba had said. Cautiously, she lifted the grate and peered out onto the street. It was around dinnertime, so there were only a few people about, most of them in too much of a hurry to notice her. She slid out onto the sidewalk and looked around to get her bearings. She was near the park. That would be a good place to rest and think. Try to get her thoughts together.

She wandered through the park until she found a homeless woman sitting on the ground under a tree, dozing. The woman was wearing clean clothes. Dolly could smell the detergent. She knew about the shower and laundry buses for the poor, which the city had commissioned years ago. Dolly had donated to their fundraisers several times. She nudged the woman with her toe, waking her with a groan of protest.

"What? I ain't hurting nobody. Leave me alone!"

"How'd you like to switch clothes with me?"

The woman squinted. She eyed Dolly's sweat suit, chic and comfortable. Her own clothes were worn and, although clean, threadbare and cheap.

The switch took less than three minutes. Dolly shrugged into the baggy T-shirt, man's denim jacket, and old camouflage pants, while the homeless woman slipped into her tank top and sweat suit.

"Thanks."

The woman looked up for a moment then back down, too absorbed in her new outfit to ask any questions. Dolly walked away as the woman was checking the pockets.

She found a bench in a secluded spot, scanning the area for possible drone surveillance. It seemed as good a place as any. She crawled under the ornamental bushes, making sure she was completely hidden, curled up and closed her eyes, exhausted. She still didn't know if Jabba's story was accurate. Why would a machine get tired? It was more likely that she was some sort of enhanced human. *I'm a person*, she thought. *Even if all this is true, I have feelings. I have memories that are mine, regardless of what they injected into my head. I remember them as mine.*

She fell asleep thinking about it.

Jabba finished breaking the helmet apart and wiping his computers of any evidence that Dolly had been in the back room. He used an infrared light to show any heat signature from where she had been, and the room lit up with her foot and handprints, as well as where she'd sat in the chair. Jabba's own showed up as well. He wiped them down and cooled them with another one of his gadgets, then checked the room again. Heat signatures only lasted for half an hour. Now it looked as if only he had been back there. He then created a fake transaction of her buying a small retinal scan and laser pointer, loaded the new account minus her actual transaction, and doctored the security camera footage. Finished, he sat back in his storefront chair, one eye on the surveillance cameras flanking the block. Hopefully, he had done enough to keep himself safe.

A Feynman's refrigerated truck pulled around the corner, driving too slowly to be a normal delivery vehicle. It parked across the street. Jabba felt his stomach clench. Grabbing a box of tissues and a vial of lubricant, he slid the waistband of his pants down, exposing a large swath of belly. He swabbed the lubricant over his hand and smeared it on his stomach, surreptitiously watching the men emerge from not only the truck but also a van from the other corner. Dolly hadn't been lying. They were obviously military.

He put his wraparound glasses back on, unable to focus on the porn that continued inside the lens. One hand slid down into his pants while the other began shoveling beef jerky into his mouth. Swilling great gulps from the now tepid soda beside him, Jabba forced himself to calm down and wait. He muttered erotically to himself, blindly watching the porn while inwardly terrified.

It didn't take long. Wendell walked into the store with two of his men. They split up and began searching while Wendell went up and rapped on the counter. Jabba grimaced and paused the video, lifting the glasses with apparent impatience.

Wendell struggled to keep the disgust off his face. This pig reeked of body odor, jerky, and lubricant, and he didn't even have the grace to look embarrassed at what he was obviously doing.

"Yeah?" Jabba asked impatiently.

Wendell flashed his corporate badge, which made Jabba hurriedly take off the glasses and try to look innocent.

"How can I help you?"

The lieutenant held up a photo of Dolly. "Have you seen this woman?"

Jabba took the photo. "Yeah, she was just in here. She's a regular customer. Nice lady. Really good-looking. High-class whore."

"Why was she in here?"

"She bought a laser pointer for her cat and a retinal scanner."

"She doesn't have a cat."

"How should I know that? What do you want from me?"

"Why the retinal scanner?"

"Hey, I don't ask her questions."

"Why not?"

"She likes to keep to herself."

"Why's that?"

"Like I said, I don't ask questions. She had the money, I had the product, she was in and out of here in half an hour."

Wendell picked up the glasses and toyed with them. "Half an hour seems a long time without any conversation."

"It took me that long to find a scanner and fit it to her."

"And you never asked what it was for?"

"Look, buddy. She's a whore, okay? Classier than most but still a whore. She deals with more dick in a night than your wife does in a year. The last thing she wants is some fat fuck like me slobbering over her during her free time. That's why she comes here. I never come on to her."

Wendell put the glasses on. The porn resumed. He yanked them off and glared at Jabba.

"Hey, I'm only human, you know," Jabba said sheepishly. "And like I said, she's a beautiful woman. I ain't hurting anybody. This is just a natural reaction to seeing somebody like her. Smelling her. I got in close while I was adjusting her gear. Damn, that woman smells good." He sighed and stroked his belly but then looked suspicious. "She didn't say I was coming on to her or anything, did she? Because it's a lie if she did."

Disgusted, Wendell tossed the glasses on the counter as one of his men approached. "Sir, there's a locked room in the back."

Wendell turned to Jabba. "What's back there?"

"Storeroom."

"Open it."

"You got a warrant?"

"I've got my foot up your ass if you don't open that goddamn door right now."

Suitably cowed, Jabba fumbled nervously for his keys, lumbered over to the door, tapped in a code, and rifled through the key ring until he found the right one. He almost dropped it, looking up at Wendell nervously as he muttered an apology. The three men surrounded him as he unlocked the door, pushing past him into the room. Jabba started to sit at his desk, but Wendell stepped in front of it and barked orders to one of the men.

"Leland, search this fat fuck's computer for all transactions over the past twenty-four hours."

"Yes, sir."

The second man began searching the shelves, using a handheld infrared scanner around the room. Jabba leaned against the door and watched them carefully, all the while visibly trembling with nerves and sweat. He wiped a still greasy palm against his shirt, leaving a smear. Wendell never took his eyes off him.

The tech sat at the keyboard for ten minutes, scrolling through Jabba's sales and video surveillance. The last customer was Dolly, visibly upset, hurriedly buying the two items, sitting for the fitting adjustments and then leaving the store. Leland hit the pause button.

"She was here. Ninety-eight minutes ago."

He replayed the video for Wendell and let it run. After Dolly left the store, it showed Jabba looking at the door, sighing, and putting his glasses back on as he began to rub his own crotch. They both turned to stare at him, repulsed, and Jabba laughed sheepishly.

"Hey, come on. Give me a break. She's sexy as hell."

The second soldier came forward, blinking at the unappealing image on the screen.

"No sign of anybody else being in here, sir. Seems to mainly have parts for old video machines and sex doll repair."

Jabba shrugged. "It pays the bills."

Wendell's mouth went tight. "Move out."

All four men walked back to the front of the shop. Jabba tried to give them flyers for upcoming Techno Tidbits events. Wendell threw them on the floor and handed Jabba a card.

"If she comes back, you call this number. You know what will happen if you don't."

"What?"

Wendell reached across the counter and grabbed Jabba's thick jowls, his fingers disappearing in the folds of skin. Jabba's face immediately flushed red, eyes bulging.

"I will personally beat you into jelly, you repulsive piece of shit. I'd love to do it. Your mother should have had you cut out the minute you were squirted into her belly." He shoved Jabba backward, tilting the chair under the unstable weight. Jabba grabbed the wall and braced his legs to stop from falling.

"Do you understand me, you disgusting fat fuck?"

Jabba was dragging in great gulps of air, his face purplish and his eyes swimming. He nodded.

Wendell watched him for a few more seconds and then followed his men outside.

Jabba watched as they drove away, gasping and panicking, tears streaming down his face. He looked down at the screen under the counter, watching the live feed as the truck drove a block down and turned the corner.

Once it was out of sight, Jabba's whole demeanor changed. He straightened up, dropped the terrified victim expression, rolled his chair back into place, and sat down. Popping the top on another can of soda, he took a long drink, wiped his eyes, and cursed softly.

"Holy fucking shit, hardware," he said softly. "What have you gotten me into?"

Then he ordered a sausage and pepperoni pizza with extra cheese. When it came, he ate it with smug satisfaction.

9

Dolly walked along the sidewalk downtown, cautiously surveying her surroundings. Too nervous to doze more, she'd only slept a few hours under the park bench fauna, waking just as dawn was flushing the sky. She used the anonymous card to buy an orange juice from a street vendor, hoping that Jabba's smoke-and-mirrors trick would be enough to keep them from tracing her movements. A hasty meal of bread and cheese from a nearby bakery refreshed her, and she bought a new set of non-descript clothes to hide in and a pair of sunglasses to hide behind. There were surveillance cameras everywhere. Dolly knew she had probably been seen in the homeless clothes both at the ATM and otherwise. Changing in the alcove of a dark alley, she pulled the hoodie over her bright hair, shoved the homeless clothes in a bag and dropped it in the dumpster.

Four blocks away, she hailed a cab, not even sure where she wanted to go. The driver looked at her expectantly. Her face hardened.

"Museum Mile, please."

Her voice was still in the cultured tones Keisha had derided her about. Another question that needed to be answered. She didn't know what made her choose Museum Mile as a place to begin looking, but the encounter with the strange man who'd followed her in the Hammer Museum was something she wanted to explore. He seemed to think her name was Grace and was convinced enough to push that assumption. Something about him had frightened her. She wanted to find out why. It was doubtful he'd be there, but it was a start.

The cab pulled up two blocks from the Hammer. Dolly, stepping out onto the immaculate sidewalks of Museum Mile, started cautiously walking, changing her gait in case of software that could identify her through movement. She'd read it could be as accurate as a fingerprint. No drones hummed overhead, but they weren't necessary. Security cameras were everywhere.

She arrived at the Hammer, standing indecisively at the bottom of the stairs. It was only eight in the morning. There were still two hours before it opened. Dolly thought she might hide somewhere and watch the entrance to see if the man might show up. But to her astonishment, she saw him sitting on one of the front benches already, watching her. Braced to run in case he spoke into a device or came after her, she stared back guardedly. He smiled in what looked like relief and started toward her. Dolly realized that he recognized her immediately, despite the clothes and dark glasses. She tensed and half turned away. He froze in his tracks.

"No, no. It's all right. It's okay. I'm not going to hurt you."

His tone was soothing as he walked down the stairs, as if calming a wild animal.

"My name is Sean Davis. I've been coming here every day since I first saw you, hoping you'd come back. Please, can we go somewhere for coffee? I'll buy you breakfast. There's a place around the corner that makes the best scones you've ever had."

Dolly cautiously nodded. She didn't sense a threat or any overt sexual danger. The man seemed almost buoyant in her company. They began walking.

"I'm sorry I scared you the other day," he continued. "I really did think you were Grace. It's uncanny. You look so much like her."

At the restaurant. Dolly stopped when he opened the door for her, leery to let him get too close. Understanding her reticence, the man stepped back and gave her room. With a sigh, Dolly went inside. The air smelled of pancakes and pastry, and her mouth watered. She was still ravenously hungry.

They ordered coffee, fruit, and scones, then found a booth toward the back. Dolly memorized the layout of the place and where the exits were before sliding into her seat. The man sat down opposite. They both seemed hesitant to speak. Then Dolly just blurted out the first question in her mind.

"Are you part of this?"

"Part of what?"

She didn't answer. "Who's Grace? Why did you think I was her?"

"She was my wife. We divorced years ago."

"Were you still in contact with her?"

"Not exactly. I followed her career. Saw her often at conventions and seminars. Then she suddenly stopped attending. Didn't see her for years. No published papers either. She just disappeared."

"Disappeared?"

"Yeah. Off the grid."

"Did you ask her family about it?"

"Both her parents are dead. No siblings."

"Did you call the cops?"

He looked out the window and didn't speak.

"You haven't answered my question."

"No, I didn't call the police."

"Why not? The second one of our friends doesn't show up, we call the cops."

He sighed. "It's complicated. Grace and I are both scientists. We worked on some pretty top secret projects together. Her specialty was cloning and genetic research; mine is both human and AI psychology, focusing mainly on AI evolution."

Dolly's face immediately tensed. He watched her carefully before continuing.

"Please don't worry. Even if you are what I suspect you are, I have no intention of hurting or reporting you. I just want to know why you look so much like my ex-wife, but…enhanced."

The waitress came, poured their coffee, and left. Dolly followed her with her eyes.

"You almost never see human waitstaff anymore."

He took her lead and changed the subject. "I know. I like the atmosphere of this place. Human interaction is important when it comes to food."

"I usually just grab something at a Magway."

"This is much nicer than an automat though, isn't it?"

She smiled briefly and looked around, noting the contented people having breakfast in the morning sunshine pouring through the window.

"What's your name?" He asked softly.

"Dolly."

His eyes grew wide for a moment. "Like Dolly the sheep?"

"You're the second person who's mentioned that to me. No, my mom named me for a snack cake company. But my dad said they named me after a country singer with big tits. He was always disappointed I never grew into the name."

"That's a disturbing thought."

"Yeah, well, he was fucking me before I hit puberty, so I don't think the cup size was a factor."

Sean's face grew grim, as if from some dawning, unpleasant revelation. She waited for him to commiserate, feign some naive concern about her terrible past, but he just shook his head and stared at her.

"Do you have any children?"

"What? No. I can't have kids."

The food arrived and they both sat back as the waitress arranged it before them. The man seemed bothered by her words. Dolly gave him a moment, buttering a scone, stirring her coffee, dipping a strawberry in the dish of cream beside her. She had always been open about her abuse, refusing to hide it in the shadows as if she was something dirty. She ate another scone, waiting for him to speak. He finally looked directly at her again.

"Grace was also infertile. She was also sexually abused." He looked down at his hands, threading the fingers together.

"What do you think happened to her? Why did she disappear?"

"When we broke up, there was no warning. She left me a note and just vanished. Grace was always didactic that way. I think she considered herself more my teacher than my wife. A month later, I received the divorce papers. We were both working at Nurturing Genius at the time. It's a branch of the Aquinas Corporation."

Dolly grew more tense. "I know what it is."

"We'd had a big fight the week before she moved out. She wanted the android program to go in one direction; I, another. The team leader agreed with Grace, but I had serious ethical problems with it. I left the company soon after."

"What ethical problems? What the fuck were you all doing?"

He shook his head and didn't answer.

"I went to Stockholm for a conference, and when I got home, all her stuff was gone. There was just the note. Then the divorce papers a month later. No explanation, nothing. I signed them, and it was done."

"When was this?"

"Eight years, three months, and ten days ago."

"You must still love her, to have a clock like that running in your head."

He stirred his coffee slowly. "No. No, it was never really love between us. Not in the normal sense. We were both scientists, both absorbed in our careers. It seemed a good fit."

"That's a cold-ass way of looking at it."

"Yes, it is. Grace suggested the marriage when we were in grad school. I revered her; her genius was unparalleled. But neither of us was happy as a couple. Grace found intimacy repugnant. Not just sex but simple touching, holding hands. She hated that, and I couldn't live without it."

"Do you think she's dead?"

He crumbled a scone without eating it.

"Yes. Two years ago, it was announced that Grace and a handful of colleagues were killed in a plane crash over a tribal area in Afghanistan. What she was doing there, I have no idea. Maybe the mineral deposits. I wasn't contacted. Heard about it on the news." He looked up at her. "Then I saw you at the museum."

Uncomfortable, Dolly fidgeted in her seat, tapping the table with a fingernail.

"Yeah, you freaked me out that day."

"I know. I'm sorry. But it's uncanny. You could almost be Grace's twin from when she was in college. Even your voice, accent; they're the same."

"Grace had a British accent?"

"Yes. Born in a small town in Lancashire. Sometimes you roll your vowels in exactly the same way she did. And the cadence of speech is the same. I even wondered if you were an actual clone, if Nurturing Genius had gotten ahold of Grace's DNA and accelerated the growth pattern. We both had given genetic samples to the lab. But I realized that was ridiculous. Even if they'd been able to grow a body that rapidly, there's no way you could have advanced mentally enough to pass for a regular adult. Our experiences are intrinsically linked to the years we progress throughout our childhood. You're obviously a grown woman mentally and emotionally, despite your inherited trauma."

"What's that?"

"After Grace and I started working at Aquinas, I began researching how incest and severe trauma causes alterations in human DNA. There were even teams at other institutes and corporations who were exploring AI manipulation through abuse, which is highly unethical and thankfully mostly illegal. Way too dangerous. My interest was in finding a way to reverse the damage in a victim's psyche. Grace's expertise was cloning living tissue to synthetic binders. She was the top researcher in genetic manipulation of human fetal tissue. Real cutting-edge stuff. Brilliant, beautiful woman."

He took a sip of coffee absently, his mind in the past. "We were both obsessive-compulsives about detail, the minutiae of how it all fit together. Aquinas was researching how childhood abuse impacts personality and career choice in adulthood."

"What do you mean?"

"There are two distinct classes of adults with a history of severe sexual and/or physical childhood abuse. Many people who've been traumatized make excellent executives, at least in the corporate atmosphere. Their physiology is imprinted with a tendency toward sociopathy and therefore a detached personality. Lack of ethics is good for the bottom line. Their PR firms have literally made a religion of that. The second type of survivor tends to become extremely malleable and eager to please, which suits a servile position. It all depends on how broken the child had become and at what stage in life. Grace considered her own past as invaluable research material. Aquinas encouraged our research because it could be used in various fields, including fertility hosts and military development." He laughed bitterly. "Birth and Death. Since I left the company, it's been extensively researching personality imprinting on combat humanoids."

"What do you mean? Like robots?"

He shook his head. "Not robots. Droids. Semiartificial intelligence androids programmed with an actual human's personality trait. In war, the theory is that a droid can perform intuitively during deployment rather than act like a machine and wait for input. This creates a far more efficient fighter. They tried cyborgs, which are a combination of human tissue and robotics, but the organics didn't heal well from shrapnel and incendiaries. So they went for sentient androids with very little tissue. They look human enough in helmets and regular armor."

Dolly opened her mouth to speak but thought better of it, taking a sip of coffee. She wanted to ask him if he knew about the technology that had made her, but she wasn't ready to trust that much yet.

They finished their meal in silence. He paid the bill and tipped the server generously, which endeared him somewhat to Dolly. She knew how hard this sort of job was. She'd been a waitress in her teens. *If you were ever a waitress at all.* Her inner voice brought back the paranoia as they walked out of the restaurant, and she shied away as he tried to reach for her arm, stepping away and looking up and down the street for any sign of danger.

"I'm sorry. I didn't mean to scare you again. Do you mind if we walk awhile?"

Sunglasses and hoodie in place, she nodded.

He tapped something into his watch and Dolly took a step back.

"It's okay. I'm just making sure we're not overheard."

"What do you mean?"

"I've activated a scrambler. No security camera or listening devices can track either of us now, while we're together."

"That's a neat trick."

"It comes in handy."

They wandered toward the park, walking slowly. Sean set out to put her at ease, talking gently about nonthreatening subjects like the weather and books, gradually easing into talk about his work. Dolly was deep in thought as she listened, torn between questions she wanted to ask and the natural reticence of a woman in danger.

They walked for an hour. Dolly began to relax in his company, even as she kept scanning their surroundings and the people around them. Sean Davis seemed a kind man. She sensed no deviance or decadence in him. He was passionate about his work but had a somber reflection about its possible repercussions. Dolly asked intelligent questions, initially skirting any personal information about what Jabba had told her. But she wanted answers from a scientist, and here was one eager to share his knowledge just to keep her near him. He told her of his days in the lab with Grace, how they fed off each other's research, how they differed in only one fundamental way: he believed that these AI cyborgs and androids had real feelings. Grace did not. She saw them as nothing more than the next level of computer high tech. Dolly shook her head vehemently.

103

"Emotions are felt no matter what the brain is made of. Organics means living tissue, which means living emotions."

"I agree. But that went against the bottom line for all these companies. If the androids have real emotions, equal to human emotions, then they'd have to be given the same rights as humans. Thus, no slave labor, no vivisections, no experimentation on creatures that are basically..."

"Alive."

"Exactly. Alive."

"Do you really think androids are alive?"

"I do. But I'm in the minority. And these corporations are very powerful and indescribably rich. They've bought every politician and media outlet necessary to get what they want, and what they want is whatever improves their bottom line. Aquinas has a motto: The bottom line is God, and God is all."

"That's rather zealous."

"The modern-day golden calf. Literally. But just think about it. The military contracts alone would be limitless. The Pentagon has its finger in so many different areas, all to improve weapons for killing. They passed laws after the first two world wars that banned chemical warfare, so the military poured money into sonic research, which led to sonic wave technology being weaponized in time for the third world war. It was a brutally effective weapon and slaughtered millions for pennies on the dollar, leaving whole cities and structures unharmed. The companies that then rose to power were the ones on the cutting edge of that technology. They made obscene amounts of money on government contracts and still have those contracts today. Then the government banned the use of sonic weaponry in civilian areas, so the corporations turned to new research. First robotics, then cybernetic organisms, then androids with living tissue. The military probably has this technology in everything. There are undoubtedly illegal experiments happening right now in hidden facilities. If they could develop an android with true organic tissue that healed quickly, they would be virtually identical to an actual human."

"How would that be used?"

"Think about it, Dolly. You could use it anywhere; infiltrating enemy bases, politics, espionage, and it would all be recorded automatically. Androids would have no fear, no angst, and no worries, unless they were programmed to do so. They couldn't be killed as easily as a human, they don't need much food or water, they can survive any terrain or environment, and they don't need to rest or be paid. Moreover, they would function for decades longer than a human and would never age."

"Wouldn't the living tissue age?"

"That's easily refreshed with new grafts and cloned skin. I've seen specimens that are seventy years old who'd been upgraded to organic flesh. It's incredible." He paused and looked at her. "And only someone with a trained eye could tell they weren't human."

Dolly stopped walking. He continued to look at her gently. Expectantly. Her eyes narrowed. Suddenly, he felt like a threat again.

"I won't hurt you, Dolly. I told you that."

"Why were you waiting at the museum for me?"

"I've been going there every day, hoping to see you again. I was in too much shock last time to think clearly. But I've thought of nothing else since I saw you, and I'm thinking clearly now. I just had to talk to you, to see you up close. I know they were going forward with research I ethically didn't believe in. Torture is never acceptable. I see no difference between a sentient organic android and any other human being. They are creatures of wonder to me."

She felt trapped, as if hundreds of eyes were staring at them. Sean spoke gently, hands spread wide.

"Both Grace and I had full-body scans, Dolly. Bone, circulatory system, muscles, tendons, skin, eyes, hair. We also gave sample DNA for the test labs."

"What's this got to do with me?"

"I think you know. I think you're beginning to understand who and what you are."

10

Enraged, Fogetti paced around the large oval conference table. He was on a tirade, making the corporate suits at the table squirm in their seats. A technician sat at the end, keying information into a computer, tabulating probability data that appeared as a hologram in the center of the table for all to read. Absorbing any of the information was difficult because Fogetti kept yelling.

"How the fuck did you lose her? Surveillance, trackers, cameras, facial recognition software in every building in a ten-mile radius, bugging every room she fucks a client in…your whole goddamn job is watching this cuntcicle! How many men have we got on the ground right now trying to locate her?"

One man tried to speak. "We don't have facial in every building yet, sir."

"Did I ask you to flash your incompetence, Williams?"

"No, sir."

"Then shut the fuck up." He turned to glare at the occupants at the table. "This is the biggest project any of us have ever signed off on. It was a hard sell to let her out of her controlled environment, but you all convinced me it was worth it. I should have gone with my gut reaction and never let her out of the compound." He continued pacing the room, hands tense on his hips.

"You tell your teams to get to the bottom of this. You haul out every scientist and pet genius you've got and figure this out."

"There are the sublingual and epidermoid sensors, sir. We're working on collating those, but there seems to be some interference."

He slammed his hand down on the table.

"Get me back my fucking investment! By any means necessary. I don't give a fuck. I'm losing thousands every day on this cunt. Get her back, and fix the goddamn problem!"

*   *   *

The sun was low in the sky as Sean pulled his tinted-window car into his driveway, Dolly in the passenger seat. He'd convinced her to come home with him. The house was a large Victorian Gothic Revival with a wide veranda and enormous bay windows. Even lost in thought, Dolly appreciated the architecture and style of the place.

After Sean told her he knew what she was, he'd taken her to a safe house near the park, told her he belonged to a sort of Underground Railroad that fought for the rights of AIs and even smuggled some to freedom. They'd talked for hours. She conveyed what had happened over the last two days, omitting Jabba's name and business as a precaution. He told her that he thought he could give her some answers, help her, but that she should understand what a huge deal this freedom run was. How dangerous. The fact that they scrambled military and cyber teams to find her proved that she was very important to them.

She followed him down the narrow brick walk to a side door. He opened it, waiting for her to enter, then closed and locked it behind them. The locks were both electronic and key dead bolts. The home tech had already automatically closed the blinds, and Dolly's stomach rumbled at the scent of the meal cooking in the kitchen. *He even has a cook*, she thought. This man was obviously wealthy. She thought of her own tiny apartment and sighed.

"Nice place, Doc."

He smiled, looking around with pleasure.

"Thank you. Years of collecting went into the furnishings."

Dolly walked around the room, noting the many beautiful framed maps and handwritten parchments on the walls. Most of them were notes or letters penned by famous scientists and mathematicians. She pointed at one set of cyphers.

"Alan Turing? Really?"

Sean beamed.

"That one I wasn't going home without. Had a bit of a bidding war at the auction." He tossed his keys in a Herend dish on a side table.

"Are you hungry? This morning, I programmed dinner to be ready when I was heading home. The car alerted the house, and the chef began preparing the food. It's grilled salmon and vegetable sides. I can key in dessert if you'd like."

Dolly shook her head. "No dessert, but I am hungry."

"Good. So am I."

They ate their meal at the kitchen table, not talking much. Dolly was grateful for the quiet, pondering why she trusted this man she'd just met. It made no sense, but she did. Dolly took another bite of salmon as she studied him. If she really was an android, whoever made her knew how to track and control her. She hoped that Jabba's treatment had worked, but Sean said she needed more.

Taking a sip of water (she'd refused wine), Dolly began questioning him again.

"You keep talking about AI evolution and the creation of true androids. How did all this research begin?"

"It started sometime in the early 2000s, around the fine-tuning of MRI machines and the decriminalization of cloning. Science has made incredible advances in nanotechnology and organic machinery since then. Not only have we been able to successfully clone every human and animal organ, but we've also mapped the synapses of human thought and even recorded actual dreams, which have been recreated successfully in multidimensional experiments. Think what that means. If a machine can be programmed to perform a function, then a machine can also be programmed to emote, which is also a function. Just like humans. You cry because you're hurt; you smile because you're happy. It's all physics, practical environment, emotional grooming."

"So an AI can be made to feel?"

"Yes, and to feel anything. A machine can be programmed to not know it's a machine. Like you."

"What would be the purpose of that?"

"A machine that's self-aware, that knows it's been built for what amounts to slavery…that machine becomes a liability and a danger to people, not to mention its investors."

Dolly's eyes widened as understanding began to seep in. "The machine would understand its mortality and know its maker would eventually replace it."

Sean nodded. "And potentially want to harm its maker. We couldn't allow that."

"That's really fucked-up."

Suddenly, she thought of the weird device John had tried to use on her.

"I had a guy wave this thing at me a few days ago. I thought it was some new sex toy, which I never allow. But he really pushed for me to look at it. It scared the hell out of me, and I ran out. The freak chased me to the elevator. Later, my friend was playing around with it and flashed me in the face. He said I didn't move for two hours. Scared the shit out of him."

Sean looked concerned. "What did it look like?"

"Small, cylindrical, bigger than a pencil but smaller than a minicucumber."

"Hold on."

He got up and went into his office, where he rifled through folders in his desk. Returning a few minutes later with a sheet of paper, he handed it to her.

"Did it look anything like this?"

Dolly studied the drawing on the sheet. It was a blueprint of the device the john had tried to use on her.

"That's it! That's exactly what he waved at me."

"And you didn't obey him? Did he use a code phrase or sound?"

"Yeah, he quoted some poem to me."

Sean looked stunned. "How did you escape? How could you even move?"

"I escaped by hauling ass out of there and jumping in an elevator full of witnesses." She tapped the paper. "What the hell is this thing?"

"This is a backup reboot, Dolly. It's flashed near the eye or wrist sensors. It immobilizes androids and AI robots alike. We use these in case the subjects become violent or malfunctioning."

"Why do you have a drawing of the damn thing?"

"I designed it."

He was leaning over her as he spoke, making Dolly feel claustrophobic. She shoved past him, putting the kitchen island between them.

"I know how this looks," Sean said calmly. "But think about it. If I wanted to disable you, I would have done it already. Look, to tell the truth, I used to work for some very bad people with very brilliant minds. Grace did, too. We were all so caught up in the science and thrill of discovery we didn't stop to think about whether it was ethical or not. Bots and droids weren't human. Cyborgs were if they started out human, but just property if they started off synthetic. We didn't think about it."

"What kind of concentration camp torture fucker are you?"

He didn't try to deny it. "Hopefully, a reformed one. I started out like everybody else. I just didn't think about it. But something began to happen as our studies grew more and more intense. We were studying the memories and emotions of human mothers pregnant with their children, for God's sake. Grace and I were both isolating the specific synapses that fired when they were thinking about their babies. It was fascinating. Both primitive thought and cognitive thinking fired simultaneously. Nothing we ever studied came close to the intensity of a pregnant mother with her unborn child except a mother with her newborn.

"Grace and I successfully recreated those emotions in the synthetic brain of a droid. I remember how happy we were. What an achievement, what an advance for science. Grace joked that we were going to win the Nobel for this.

"Aquinas wanted a practical use for our success. So we pitched the idea that this would solve the sociopath babies from lab-grown wombs. They told us to prove it.

"So we inserted a fertilized human ovum into an artificially grown organic womb and hooked the android up to it. We trained it to believe the fetus was inside its nonexistent uterus.

"When the baby was born, the android had actual labor pains, envisioning that the labor was hours long rather than minutes. The baby was perfect, a completely normal human infant. But when we took the child away, the android grieved. It actually grieved. It was so inconsolable, we finally had to wipe its memories and reprogram it.

"That's when I began to question the ethics of doing this. That's when I started seeing the possibility that these creatures were truly sentient, living organisms. The more I interacted with our fledgling subjects, the more it hit me that this was wrong. Cruel. We were giving these creatures physical sensations, emotions, memories, even a history of cuts and bruises to remember pain. Even childbirth. The android remembered the pain, but we denied it the joy of holding its own child. Grace argued that we could take away its pain with a simple memory wipe, but I worried about potential ghost memories, embedded in the android's organic tissue, that we couldn't remove. The same chemical reactions to emotion that humans had, we were finding in the android tissue samples.

"I shared my misgivings with the head of corporate, and he assured me that it would be against their bottom line to allow anything like that. So I went along with it. We created these minds, instilled them with emotions and memories that were not their own, and when they were complete, we just handed them off to the company to do what they wanted with them."

He laughed cynically. "I was so naive. I thought they'd be used for the betterment of humankind. Instead, they became the slaves of every kind of decadence and brutal military action the highest bidder could come up with." He shook his head. "I couldn't be a part of it anymore. My initial idea was to help living abuse victims, not create more. Grace stayed. We didn't fight about it; we just didn't talk about it. Then she left, the divorce happened, I quit Aquinas and started doing what I could to right the wrongs we created. And now Grace is gone, and here you are. I believe you're an android, Dolly. I believe you were created in a lab and draped in the cloned tissue of my dead ex-wife. She might have even created you herself."

"So you truly think I'm not human?"

"You look like Grace, but you've been enhanced. Taller, almost inhumanly beautiful. A lot of work went into you."

"But you can't be certain."

He shook his head. "Not yet, no. You say you were injured yesterday. Stabbed. Are you in pain?"

"Not really. It hurt at first but…"

"Would you mind if I examined you? It might shed some light on what's going on, and at least we'd know for sure. If you've gotten this far, then you've discovered the tracking embedded in your eyeball corneas and had them disabled. But there's probably more external, possibly even internal, tracking devices on your body somewhere."

Dolly instinctively crossed her arms over her chest. "No, I think I'm good. Like I said, I had my friend scan me. The trackers I had, he took care of."

"I doubt he was able to find everything. These people know how to hide. I just want to make sure."

"What if I am one of these things?"

"They're not things. They're people. Not human beings exactly, but still living, feeling entities. Please. I won't harm you and at least we'll know. I need to know, Dolly, and I'm sure you do, too. Afterward, we'll figure it out together, if you'll allow. We can do it right in my study, right through there."

Dolly took a shuddering breath and slowly nodded.

Sean drew in a huge breath as well. "Thank you."

His study was lined with floor-to-ceiling wooden shelves, gleaming with polish and crammed with books. A wooden desk sat in the corner by the window, with a few comfortable-looking chairs scattered about, each with a brass reading lamp and side table. Dolly felt as if she'd stepped back in time when she entered the room. A bust of Rupert Sheldrake adorned the mantle over the fireplace, which was laid with actual wooden logs, and several leather chairs were placed before it. Sean gestured for her to sit on a bench near the desk, where he began gently to examine her face, neck, and ears. He took her hands and looked at her fingernails, then moved to her back.

"May I?"

Dolly saw his fingers on the hem of her blouse and nodded. He lifted it and began examining her back.

"You say you were stabbed?"

"Yeah."

"There's no wound."

"There has to be. Keisha freaked out over it."

"There's no wound now."

Dolly twisted around, feeling her back with her own fingers. There was nothing there. Startled, she looked up at Sean, eyes wide. He nodded.

"Rapid healing is something we helped develop in synthetic life-forms. Grace discovered a way to clone a whole new skin in less than twenty-four hours. This looks like her work to me."

Dolly yanked her clothing back down.

"So I heal fast. So what? Why the fuck is this happening to me? What do they want? Did you do these sorts of experiments on other people? People like me? Turn them into a daddy-fucked whore, too?"

He shook his head. "No. But I saw the beginning of it. That's why I left. In the years since, I've helped lobby bills declaring AIs as living entities, got a handful of laws passed. Small potatoes, but something. Global corporations crushed as much of it as they could. Thus the bullshit Ratio Law declaring you're product and not truly living. But like I said, with you…these sorts of projects are supposed to be illegal. But the corporate military can always find loopholes. No, I think you're being studied for research purposes. I don't know why."

"But…why a whore? I thought Aquinas was all about the bottom line. It's not like I'm a high-end hooker; I barely make rent. Was I designed as some sort of fuckbot by these cocksuckers? Why didn't they make me high-class? That would at least have brought them in some decent money. I'm not a crack whore five-dollar blow job level, but I'm only a few rungs up the ladder from that. Do you have any idea how goddamn awful my existence is sometimes? Are they doing this to others?"

Sean listened, a stoic sympathy in his expression. He still had more to tell her.

"I think it goes beyond that with you. If they scrambled a team like you described to bring you in, you are enormously important to them, even beyond their usual fanatical greed. In my time at Aquinas, our research was still in its infancy, but the field was gearing up. Your mind is probably decades old. Possibly more. You may have had different bodies."

"Jesus. Is my memory from someone else's life? It was after my dad started fucking me that Mom started drinking and getting stoned. That bastard ruined us both." Dolly's eyes grew steely. "Does that motherfucker really exist? Did they have a real person tear me apart like that?"

"I'm not sure. The memories were probably downloaded into your cortex from an outside source and then reinforced with deliberate body memory trauma. The donor was most likely a volunteer who'd been pre-screened. Maybe even Grace herself. There are a lot of corollaries between you two."

"Then why aren't I a fucking scientist instead of a whore?"

"I don't know." His eyes widened. "But if I can isolate your inception date, maybe I can access what lab put you together. Maybe even find the project's data history. Come with me." He got up and grabbed his keys.

"Where are we going?"

"To my lab. I have the tools there."

"I thought you were going to prod around right here!"

"Here, I can scan for surveillance devices, but if I'm to isolate more intrinsic information, I've got to do it in the lab. Hopefully, we'll find answers there."

"Where's your lab? In a big corporate building with guards?"

"No. It's independent. Mine alone." He held out his arm. "Let's go."

The drive to the lab was silent, both of them lost in their own thoughts. Then Sean reached into his jacket pocket.

"If you are designed with my ex-wife's tissue, which I'm certain you are, they might be watching my spot. Here." He handed her a small compact the size of a half dollar. "This scrambler will make you invisible to the street cameras. Put it in your pocket. I'll drop you off here. My building is three blocks up on the left. Number ninety-three. Walk to the south side and wait by the side door. I've deactivated the motion sensor cameras there for fifteen minutes. Got it?"

"Got it."

Dolly climbed out and was already walking as he drove away. Quickly reaching the building, she skirted the front entrance and waited in the dark by the side door.

Sean opened it a few minutes later, closing it quickly behind him. She noticed he'd shut off the light in the hallway.

"I didn't want any stream of light to trigger possible KTP drones."

"Yeah. We get buzzed by those a lot out on the street. Keep The Peace, my ass." She looked around. "Who shares this place with you?"

"No one. I own the building."

They approached a set of double doors, and Sean tapped in the code to open them. Dolly flinched as the lock disengaged. The noise had an ominous feel to it. They went inside and Sean tapped the code again, sealing them in. She looked around, trying to quell the wave of panic that hit her at the sound.

"You're safe here, Dolly. You can trust me."

"You keep saying that. I hope it's true."

"Time will tell."

She swallowed painfully and nodded.

He led her to a room with a steel examining table in the middle, a large monitor attached to a movable arm in the wall, a keyboard on a desk beneath it.

"Can you undress for me? I can do a better reading if you undress."

"Feels like a typical night at a work."

"Let's hope not."

She began peeling off her clothes disinterestedly. Sean hurried over to the adjacent office, where he found a lap blanket for her to cover herself with. When he came back, he stopped short at the sight before him. Dolly stood there, naked and graceful, and the sight of her took his breath. Grace had been beautiful, but Dolly's loveliness was unparalleled. Her skin was like a pearl, making him wonder absently if they'd used infant skin as a cloning foundation.

Realizing he was gawking, Sean averted his eyes and held out the blanket. Dolly walked toward him and took it, smiling at his red face and nervous fidgeting. She knew what she looked like. It was what paid her bills.

Sean waved a hand toward a long steel table and asked her to lie down on it. It was cold. Murmuring an apology, Sean switched on the overhead lamp. He flipped a switch, and a large screen folded down from the ceiling and dropped to eye level. Then he took a hand wand and began to run it over her body, about four inches above her flesh.

"I was already scanned today. He deactivated…"

The wand beeped as it passed over her hairline, and Dolly fell silent. Sean studied the scanned information and asked her to turn over onto her stomach. He found a raised mole on her lower left shoulder and slid his finger over it. Dolly tensed as he bent over to examine it, his breath on her skin.

Without talking, Sean walked over to the counter that ran the entire length of the room. Lined with drawers, he pulled one open and rummaged through it until he found what he was looking for—a USB drive with a needle protrusion. Dolly twisted as he approached her with it.

"What are you do…"

He shoved the drive into the mole on her back, and Dolly gasped, feeling an immediate surge, as if all her pores had suddenly opened at once. Sean looked at the monitor as it began a readout.

"I'm shutting down the data management link. I'm not sure if they could ping your location from the source code." He noticed her distress. "Are you all right?"

"I'm so cold. You put that thing in me and I'm so cold all of a sudden."

He nodded and tucked the blanket around her sides.

"I thought…I thought you had tricked me and were going to bring me back to that place."

"What place?"

Her eyes filled with tears. "The warehouse, or whatever the hell it's called. For a second, I thought you were one of them. And you were going to bring me back. Paralyze me and bring me back."

Sean dropped to his haunches before her tearful face, her breath misting the steel tabletop with short, shallow gasps. He reached out and touched her face gently.

"The place where the guards tried to take you?"

"Yeah." She laughed self-consciously. "I don't know why, but that place scares the shit out of me. The building itself is terrifying. Like it's alive."

"I'm so sorry you've had all this shit for so long, Dolly," Sean said gently. "But never forget, you're a person, just like me." He smiled tenderly. "I believe that. I've even donated to the New Civil Rights for Androids fund."

Dolly laughed back, vulnerable as a child. "No, you didn't."

"I really did. So I'm not one of the bad guys. But let's find out who these monsters really are, okay? Right." He stood up, tweaked the blanket to cover her better and returned to his laptop, wirelessly synching the thumb drive to his computer.

A readout revealed biometrics showing dozens of location points throughout her body. He swiveled the screen around for her to see.

"You have sensor devices embedded just underneath your skin, a couple in your lower jaw. See these? They are all over your body."

Dolly stared at the screen, her last hope that this might all be a mistake draining away. Her eyes filled with tears again, spilling over on to the tabletop, glistening in the high-powered lamp's glare. She turned her face away.

"I'm just parts. Just hardware, like Jabba said. Keisha was right."

Sean was typing furiously on his keyboard, his face grim.

"Fuck that thinking. Fuck it." He kept typing. "My security can blur the lines, but with these still in you, they'll eventually find us." He typed some more. "I'm shutting down the location coding. They won't be able to find you anymore with this."

He typed a string of commands at the prompt. Dolly twitched, a shiver starting at her toes and rising up through her body to her head. She tried to gasp but it wouldn't come. Her eyes fluttered, and she was unconscious.

Sean looked at her for a moment and then shook her gently. Her head lolled drunkenly. He brushed a strand of hair off her forehead and stroked her cheek, once again marveling at how young and beautiful she looked. How tragic. Then he slowly slid the blanket off her body and tossed it on the chair.

11

Fogetti was shouting again. It was almost three in the morning, but he hadn't allowed anybody to go home as long as Dolly was still missing. The computer techs had completed her location data sweep. Nothing. Location unknown. The hapless men and women in the conference room with him were on the thirty-second floor of Aquinas Tower. Outside in the hall, desperate employees struggled to appear busy through the cacophony of Fogetti's swearing.

"What the fuck are you telling me? You track her to some homeless bitch on the street, get a shot of the clothes she's wearing now, and you still lose her? Who the fuck are you idiots? Why do I pay you?"

"We ascertained that the gas station video of her leaving the area was false but cannot trace who generated it," the tech manager said. "Or why. But the level of expertise needed to hack our computers and recreate a digital version of her, in such detail, points to either government or another tech industry. Whoever it is is also scrambling our search protocols."

"Could it be a rival company? Are they fucking with our property?"

"Unknown."

"Well, somebody get to knowing!"

"Mr. Fogetti!" The tech manager raised his arm excitedly. "We just picked up a signal."

"Where? She better not be on a goddamn plane."

"It's not a plane, sir. She's on the ground. I just got the location." He typed a command and sat back. "Sending it to Wendell now."

"Give me visuals."

The tech manager typed briefly, and an image came onto the huge flat-screen panel on the conference wall. It showed a large, seedy-looking lot covered with scrap iron, battered trucks, and heavy equipment, all bathed in a dim orange glow.

"Where the fuck is this? A junkyard? What am I looking at here?"

"This is the subject's current location."

"What? What's she doing there? Blowing some junkyard night crew?"

"Highly unlikely," the man replied, "This place is fully automated, with only a skeleton crew at night. Human staff doesn't appear for another seven hours."

"And?"

"The data indicates that the...commodity...was last traced to this metal recycling plant in the West Sector 9G. It's a scrapyard. Then the signal...went dead."

"What the hell is she doing in a scrapyard?" Fogetti peered angrily at the screen, snatching up his coffee mug and draining half of it. Then the tech manager's words sunk in, and he went still.

"What do you mean, 'went dead?'"

"It's a smelting facility."

"What are you telling me?"

"The recycling plant runs twenty-four hours a day, sir. The smelting vats are enormous and easily accessible to someone like...the commodity."

Fogetti's eyes narrowed to a deadly focus.

"Are you telling me she self-destructed?"

"The commodity was modified with childhood abuse memories during the Stage 4 conditioning, sir. And over the last few months, her nightmares have included segments of actual memory from Stages 1 through 3. She had begun to remember the children, as well as the conditioning for Stage 4."

"I thought Bannick's team had taken care of that."

"Its behavior over the last forty-eight hours would appear otherwise."

"Oh, no no no no," Fogetti muttered to himself, pacing the room and holding his head. "This can't be happening. Don't tell me it took a nose-dive into one of those smelting vats."

"It would explain the sudden halt to all her data. There is the possibility that her fledgling new emotions have been compromised. We submitted the information about her dream analysis to Professor Bannick two weeks ago, and he filed the report for the board. I believe he had a courier bring it to your office."

"Are you trying to pin this clusterfuck on me, you worthless little shit? That you and Bannick's dumbass experiments with my investment had anything to do with me?"

Cowed, the tech manager said nothing. Fogetti went purple with fury.

"And now you think this goddamn multibillion-dollar investment threw herself into one of the vats and melted? Fucking melted?"

"It could have placed itself in one of the large presses..."

Fogetti threw the coffee cup at the wall, shattering it. Hot coffee flew everywhere.

"You fucking idiots! You goddamn stupid fucking idiots!" He turned to the shrinking tech at his monitor and barked out an order. "Pull up a ten-kilometer satellite scan of the area. I want traffic patterns of all vehicles in and around there. License plates and sensor codes on every motorcycle, car, van, truck, or bicycle that's moved through there in the past twenty-four hours. NOW!" He turned to the tech manager again. "Alert Wendell's team and get them out there."

"Already en route."

"Tell him not to screw it up this time or I'll have his ass."

*   *   *

The factory glowed in an eerie orange nimbus of superheated air and molten steel, peppered with high-intensity streetlamps and thick fireproof open roofing. Six smelting vats, each three stories high, sat under the roof on the west end of the facility, their spill troughs wedged tightly against the lip of each vat. Conveyer belts rolled a steady, noisy rattle of scrap metal, each bumping with the drop off junk from the day before—stripped cell phones, old computer parts, broken appliances, and old computer keyboards. The handful of workers inside sorted it all into melting categories, sending the plastics to be vaporized in sealed kilns and turned into electricity, the glass to be melted down and recast, the metals to go into the vats outside. Large refuse was lifted by huge cranes fitted with electrified magnets—cars, boats, even old military tanks and landing craft were scattered about the area, making it look like a madman's junkyard.

The place was heavy with the smell of fire and chemicals, all humidity burned out of the air by the intense heat.

Wendell's team advanced across the property, a helicopter squad following from above. They told the night foreman to keep his people inside the buildings. Infrared was useless because of the temperatures, and night vision was equally bad. So they spread out cautiously, with virtually no tech support.

Wendell led a team of four to cover the outside of the expansive facility, while the second team combed the interior. Learning from their loss of Dolly the day before, they carefully examined every possible avenue of escape or hiding she might use, including high places and cargo trucks parked in loading docks. Drones filled the air, already beginning their grid pattern search.

Wendell's team worked its way across the lot, scanning for any clue that the commodity had been here. As they approached the vats, one of the soldiers spotted a small shiny object on the ground. He bent down to examine it, holding it up to the light. It was one of Dolly's earrings—a small silver cat's head on a gold loop, its rhinestone eyes shining in the beam from his flashlight.

"Lieutenant!"

Wendell turned and came back to where the soldier was crouching. The man stood up and handed the earring to Wendell. He scanned it, and the reader instantly showed a photo of Dolly with the homeless woman, zooming in on her head in profile. She was wearing the earring.

Wendell whistled sharply, and the team gathered around.

"She's here, men. Or she was." He held up the earring. "Fan out and stay sharp. She put two men, trained mercenaries, in the hospital in less than thirty seconds yesterday. You can shoot her on sight but do not use excessive firepower. Bannick told me they can repair any damage we do but to keep it to a minimum. Incapacitate her by any means necessary. Let's go."

It didn't take long. There was a trail of Dolly's belongings that was easy to follow. First the earring; then the second one; then her watch, shoes, and clothing all led to Smelting Vat 5—the metal vat. Two of the team climbed the ladder that led up to the top but were forced to retreat halfway because of the heat. They sent in a drone to scan the area; it found her fingerprints all over the ladder and rapidly disappearing footprints on the lip of the vat.

Wendell stood absentmindedly rubbing the little cat earring between his fingers.

"Are you telling me she stripped down and walked to her death up there?"

"Looks like it."

Wendell shook his head and looked up at the vat. "Well, there goes a hundred billion dollars."

The other team leader joined them. Wendell apprised him of the trail of clothing, and he sighed in disgust. "What a fucking night. Corporate ain't gonna like this."

"Lieutenant! Over here!"

Wendell and the team ran over to where a soldier was crouching. A dump bucket the size of a Volkswagen sat drunkenly on its side on the pavement beside him.

"What is it, Jenkins?"

Jenkins shone his flashlight on a patch of what looked like wet pieces of shell lying in a heap on the ground.

"What the hell is that?"

"I think it's her fingernails, sir."

Wendell bent down and lifted one up. It was definitely a small fingernail, wet with blood and pieces of flesh, opal polish still visible through the blood.

"Jesus fucking Christ. Why the hell would she pull off her own fingernails?"

"Maybe someone did it to her."

"Not likely. You saw what she did to the mercenaries at the warehouse."

Jenkins counted the pieces. "They're all here, Sarge. There's ten of them."

"There's more here!" A second soldier exclaimed.

"Who the hell else was with her?" Wendell looked at the second pile of nails and shook his head. "No. These are too big."

"They're her toenails."

The lieutenant stood up, looking at the orange glow at the top of the molten vat.

"What the fuck was she doing?"

"Bannick said she was getting glitchy," the second team leader answered.

The men nodded silently, still baffled by the strange and gruesome evidence before them. Wendell sighed in disgust, rubbing his hand down his face in exasperation.

"Right. Okay, men, bag all this shit up and get this vat emptied for forensics. Corporate will want the whole thing examined for any possible remains. Jenkins, you come with me. The rest of you fan out and see if you can find anything else."

"Where you going?"

"I'm going to question every damn person in this facility. We need some answers. Somebody had to have seen something."

They headed into the facility as the rest of the men began searching the remainder of the exterior.

Half a mile away, watching the feed from a mini-drone he'd planted at the lot, Sean watched them disperse. Satisfied, he checked his watch and began jogging away, fading into the darkness.

*   *   *

A small Cape Cod house sat nestled on a pretty piece of property near the ocean. Dolly was in the kitchen whipping pancake batter in a heavy ceramic bowl, her hair tied up in a ponytail that began to sag as she stirred. The man she'd repeatedly dreamt was raping her walked into the kitchen wearing a suit and tie.

"Morning, babe." He bent and kissed her and poured himself some coffee. "How you feeling?"

"Pretty good, love." She patted her belly. "Been a slow morning for him. He's usually turning cartwheels by this time."

The man wrapped his arms around her from behind, hands on her very pregnant belly. "Think he's about ready to join us for pancakes?"

"I get the feeling this is a sausage-and-egg man."

He kissed Dolly again, and she fondly smooched him back. Grabbing a bagel out of a wicker basket on the counter, he turned and swept his briefcase off the table.

"No, you don't!" Dolly yelled. "I'm making pancakes."

"Gonna be late, darling. Save some for me for later."

"I never understand your disgusting love for cold pancakes."

"Mmm! I do love them." He kissed her one last time and bent to kiss her belly. "Three more days until your birthday, son. See you soon!"

He ran out and just as quickly ran back in.

"Did you get a chance to charge my phone?"

Dolly laughed. "Yes, forgetful one. It's over there."

He grabbed it and ran out again. "Thanks, love. See you tonight!"

Dolly puttered around the kitchen as the pancakes cooked, languidly flipping them as they browned. She smiled softly, her mind full of all the prep work she'd done the last few days—obsessively cleaning the house, folding baby clothes, adjusting the crib's bedding and bumper pads, hanging the gaudy mobile her mother had sent. Nesting. That was a sign that the baby was getting ready to be born. She laughed out loud with the sheer delight of it.

Suddenly a beeping sounded. She turned to the noise only to find everything had vanished. The kitchen, the pancakes, even the spatula in her hand—gone. She stood alone in what looked like an empty warehouse.

Taking a step forward, Dolly cried out in pain and grabbed her stomach. Water suddenly gushed down her legs and cascaded onto the floor.

"Oh, no. No."

Not again.

Dolly clutched her swollen stomach, trying to cradle her unborn child. The beeping grew louder, and then something yanked her backward. Sliding on the amniotic fluid, she fell heavily to the floor, twisting so that she landed on her side. Pain tore through her as contraction after contraction rolled through her body, far faster and more intense than they should be. She screamed for the house computer to call 911, to call her husband, but it didn't respond. For a moment, it was as if she were trapped inside a box on the wall, looking down on herself. Then she was back on the floor. Something grabbed her legs and shoved them up, spreading them wide while her arms were pulled down to her sides. She tried to scream but something was shoved down her throat. She squeezed her eyes shut as another contraction hit, far worse than the waves that had come before.

"Don't die, sweetheart. Please don't die." She kept repeating in her mind as the pain overwhelmed her.

"Somebody turn off that fucking alarm! Where's the goddamn tech?"

It was a man's voice. A doctor. She opened her eyes, and the warehouse was gone, the smell of soggy debris replaced by an antiseptic sterility. She was strapped to a gurney from neck to crotch, her wrists manacled, her bare legs strapped into an upright and bent position, ankles manacled to the stirrups. A mask was clamped to her face, prying open her jaws, the tube down her throat gagging her. A doctor squatted between her legs, his hands shoving up into her womb. She screamed as he wrenched her open, voice muffled by the tube. Blood was everywhere, mixed with a thick viscous fluid similar to olive oil. He pulled her son out, umbilical cord throbbing, cutting the tie she'd had for nine months. He didn't bother to clamp her end; the sliced cord laid wetly against her skin, stuck to her inner thigh, pumping fluid and blood into the already saturated gurney.

The delivery room staff surrounded the doctor as he examined her baby, murmuring among themselves.

"Looks good. Limbs good." He slapped the baby and it started to cry a strange high-pitched wail. Dolly shrieked into the mask at his violence. They all ignored her.

"No sign of neurological defects. No noticeable weightless syndrome." The doctor pried open the baby's eye, still wet with blood and amniotic vernix, and a nurse handed him a penlight, which he shone into the child's eyes. "Pupils react to light properly."

A nurse siphoned the little boy's nose. The doctor pulled down his mask, smiled triumphantly, and held Dolly's son high. She watched with horror as he grasped the tiny limbs too tightly and swung the baby up over his head like a trophy.

"My friends," he said loudly, his voice booming, "the future!"

The delivery room clapped and cheered. For a moment, Dolly stopped screaming, stunned as she saw her child for the first time. The baby was snow-white, an elongated albino infant, with a lipless mouth and wide, drawn-out eyes. She started to scream again, and the doctor half turned toward her in disgust.

"Shut that thing up."

Several nurses adjusted the mask over Dolly's mouth, and she tasted the anesthetic. The gas made her dizzy, but she didn't pass out. Then another nurse held up a device that looked just like the dildo thing she'd grabbed from the john and held it over her face. She squeezed her eyes shut, refusing to look, but they locked her head in some sort of brace and forced her eyes open. She wildly shifted her gaze, trying to avoid it, but the light flashed, and everything went black.

Dolly awoke with a gasp. Confused and disoriented, she found herself not in a clinical operating room, but in a strange bedroom, lying in a huge four-poster bed, early morning sunshine pouring in through a shuttered window. For a moment, she wondered if she'd spent the night with a john, but then saw the IV bag hooked to one of the posts and traced its leads down to her own arm. She tried to sit up but fell back against the pillows. Somebody had drugged her. Done something to her. She was sore, as if she'd been beaten up. Both eyes were puffy with swelling, her arms, legs, hands, and torso had bandages all over them and part of her head had been shaved clean.

"What the fuck?"

She mumbled the expletive through bruised lips, her tongue dry and scraping against the roof of her mouth, where she felt stitches. What the hell had happened to her? She reached over to yank the IV out, but a hand came out and stopped her.

"No. Leave it in."

Her eyes cleared enough to see that it was Sean, sitting in a chair by the bed, a glass in his hand.

"What the hell have you done to me?" Her words were dry and raspy. Her eyes rolled in her head as she shifted restlessly, too weak to sit up.

"Here. Drink this." He held out a glass with a bendy straw. Dolly turned her head away, angry and suspicious in her helplessness.

"It's just water."

She glared, parched lips sealed shut.

"Look," he said, taking a sip. "It really is just water."

Dolly accepted the drink tentatively, then ravenously, draining the glass in seconds. Sean nodded in satisfaction.

"That's better. I'm sorry I had to shave parts of your head and cut you in so many places, but I had to remove all the tracers from your body. They were everywhere, even your internal organs. I had to remove all your finger and toenails as well but they're already growing back under the bandages. Each one had tracers."

"What? What are you talking about?"

"From what I can tell, the tracers' specific use was to monitor your individual body parts, but their programming included global tracking in case part of you went missing. I did multiple scans to make sure I got them all. They're gone now, Dolly. They won't find you through tracers anymore. I created a false trail for them to follow and threw all the tracers in a smelting vat a few miles away. With luck, they'll believe you committed suicide."

"I don't understand. Am I or am I not a fucking robot?"

Sean shook his head, his voice gentle. "You're something else. Something different."

Dolly's stomach suddenly growled. She put her hands over her belly and Sean smiled softly.

"I'm starving, Sean. I gotta eat something."

He went out and quickly returned with a tray of fruit and croissants, and then sat and watched as she ate.

"After the museum, when I first suspected that you were an android, I didn't think you ate. Not solid food, anyway."

"What are you talking about? I had dinner with you last night."

"Our first meal together was scones. That's when I wondered if I was wrong. You devoured half the plateful."

"So?"

"Androids don't eat solid food. They have very specific nutritional puree. But you eat like a human."

"So am I an android or not?"

"You are. But your entire body is threaded with living tissue, including a fully functional GI tract of cloned flesh woven with synthetics. It's incredible. Your heart, lungs, uterus—all manipulated pluripotent cloning mixed with artificial tissue. I've never seen anything like it. You go way beyond the limits of being a ratio-legal android slave. I estimate as much as a quarter of your body is organic tissue."

He paced the room, thinking aloud. "I scanned your brain multiple times. It's entirely artificial. But it was firing like a human brain while you were unconscious. You were even muttering in your sleep, REM activity in your eyes, body restless. Dolly," He turned to her, wonder in his eyes. "Do you dream?"

Through a mouthful of croissant, she said, "Yeah, I told you I dream. Way too fucking much."

"What do you mean?"

"Nightmares from hell every day for months."

"You described dreaming, but I assumed it was programmed behavior and a false memory. But it's not. This is beyond anything I've ever seen. A totally synthetic brain that dreams. A synthetic body woven through with organics. You're a whole new form of android. Maybe the next step in AI evolution."

"Yeah, Sean, that's all very interesting but right now, I don't give a shit about that. Did you figure out who made me? Who gave me these memories for whatever fucking reason?"

"Your skeleton is far more advanced than anything I've encountered. It even produces its own marrow."

"Sean!"

Finally registering her impatience, he sat back down beside her.

"Yes, I've identified ID markers from micro scanning the pieces I removed from you. It's definitely Aquinas." Fascinated, he watched her devour a bowl of strawberries.

"Do you taste food? Your tongue is mostly synthetic, but it seemed as if you were enjoying your meals."

Dolly shifted and grimaced, still groggy and sore.

"I love to eat."

Sean watched with something close to awe as she ate another strawberry. It was beginning to get on her nerves.

"Just amazing," he breathed. "An android who dreams, has symbiotic organic and synthetic tissue throughout, and eats solid food. It's incredible."

She groaned at his enthusiasm. Then her eyes narrowed.

"If I'm so rare, they're not going to give up looking for me, are they? Even with the tracers gone, they'll keep at it, yeah? There are cameras all over this city. They'll find me. What will they do then? Reprogram me? Make me forget all of this?"

"Not if we're lucky. I programmed all the tracers I removed to indicate catastrophic and terminal destruction. Basically, they'll think you were destroyed or self-destructed. I left clues at a recycling plant that will hopefully suffice. But enough of this. You need to rest."

"I don't want to rest," she snapped, swinging her legs over the side and struggling to stand up. She fell back onto the mattress, and Sean helped her sit up against pillows he piled behind her.

"Why do I get tired if I'm not even real? And why is my brain synthetic but the rest of me is all that shit you were just going on about?"

"We can talk about it later."

"Fuck you. We can talk about it now. Answer me."

He sighed. "Okay. Your skin is organic, thus fed by an array of blood vessels, which flushes the tissue like normal human skin and gives it its color. But that's only the epidermis. The subcutaneous layers are a spongy synthetic fed with a thin lubricant through your circulatory system. You have organic bone marrow in both femurs, but the rest is microfibers and relay junctures. That's most likely the amount needed to produce real blood cells to feed the living tissue. Your circulatory system is a mix of synthetic and organic. Veins and capillaries are real, but your arteries are all synthetic. Neurologically, you have readings that suggest both synthetic and organic, but your body is mostly synthetic. I suspect that's to skirt the laws that might declare you a living being, although with the amount of living tissue you have, I can't see it holding up in court. There's a second, transparent skin, no wider than one human cell, that encompasses your entire body and connects all the living and inorganic tissue. I'm not certain as to its function; I found it entirely by accident while I was searching for tracers. But it's probably a relay system through which your features can communicate with each other. Each tracer was connected to this transparent skin as well. Your hair is mostly real, but from a mix of at least twelve different follicle donors. Maybe more. Your internal organs are all mostly synthetic or a mix of organic and synthetic, except for the vaginal tissue. That's entirely organic. You have no viable uterus."

Dolly sneered. "Why did they give me a real cunt? So it feels better when they fuck me?"

Sean paused, weighing his words.

"You don't understand. Most android prostitutes have synthetic sexual organs. So there would be no reason to give you an organic one if you were created just to be a pleasure model."

"So I'm the latest trend? Real pussy in this one! Is that it?"

"I don't think so. I removed a tracer buried in the cervix. You have no ovaries, but there's evidence of surgical scarring around the vagina, which I think was to remove excess stretched flesh from multiple births."

"God. Do you mean Jabba was right? I've had children?"

"I believe you've been impregnated multiple times and had many children. I suspect you were a host for the Nurturing Genius program. Designer hosts for the fertilized eggs of people wealthy enough to pay for it. You were an incubation device for their baby."

"An incubation device? Why? Because they couldn't have children of their own?"

"That or they didn't want the hassle and mess of nine months of pregnancy. You've seen the ads. People pay through the nose to keep their youthful shapes. Organic uteruses are normally used in these Nurturing Genius host androids. Once the uterus reaches a quota, usually around fifty babies, the viability of the fetuses becomes compromised."

"So what? They maxed out my womb?"

"I'm certain of it. What's more, surgical scarring indicates that you have had multiple uterine surgeries. Federal law states that a host android can only have two organic wombs inserted. Ever. But I see evidence that you've had at least eleven wombs. Aquinas is all about profit. They would want to keep milking their product for money as long as it still functions. On any level."

"From earth mother to street whore. Classy. Now I'm glad I don't bring in much income."

"That you're aware of. It'd be simple enough to wipe your memory of a client list. I can just see the PR they'd spin to promote a night with you. There are wealthy clients willing to pay top dollar for something like this, a one-of-a-kind android lover.

"The scientists who created you, and I'm sure Grace was a part of that, wouldn't have had any interest in how much money you brought in, but they damn well knew Aquinas would. Profit would be a stipulation the company would insist on before they allowed a research project to go forward. So the scientists would agree to Aquinas's terms just to be able to study you. Like I said, you could be a prototype for the next stage of android development. Somebody designed you, Dolly. But you seem to be changing all by yourself. It might explain why there are dark spots in your brain function."

Dolly struggled up against the pillows.

"Wait. Dark spots? What are you talking about? You said my brain is fake."

"Not fake. It's a synthetic brain, but the most advanced I've ever seen. Your brain is capable of firing five times the synapses that a human brain can. But it appears that huge parts of it are dormant."

"What do you mean, dormant?"

"That's what puzzles me. There's no reason why they would go to the trouble of making such an advanced organ and then close the majority of it down. Maybe they wanted to keep you to a certain set of programs and no more. Maybe a synthetic brain is easier to reprogram than an organic or mixed one. Or maybe because you are absolutely fascinating and they're studying you. I studied the synapses firing as you slept, and there are areas that are completely dark. They were intentionally shut down."

"Why?"

"Could be these are parts of a series of tests. They allow you to access some, but not all, of specific segments of brain function. Could be a study of emotional maturity and development that they can address human behavior with—a way of observing how you react to different stimuli in environments of their choosing. They couldn't do that with a human subject. Illegal. But an android? They're property. No rights of their own."

"Is that why they want me to be a whore?"

"I don't know. Maybe to study the effects of trauma on life choices. Maybe to help cover the costs of research and development. A project like this, like you, would be monumentally expensive. I'd say at least a hundred billion dollars. And as you know, the bottom line is God."

"And God is all," Dolly whispered. "Motherfuckers are trying to drive me crazy with these nightmares on top of everything else."

Sean studied her for a moment.

"I don't know about them creating dreams for you. That would go against their company's interests. Perhaps you're beginning to remember past events, finding a way to access memories they thought they'd wiped clean. Could be those memories are stored in the dark areas. A synthetic brain is like any rudimentary computer: nothing is ever completely gone unless they destroy it."

"Are you telling me that these nightmares could be real? Willow, my pregnancy, the children? That all those babies were real?"

"Possibly. The staff would have wiped your programming after each birth in preparation for the next set of clients. Perhaps some sort of residue is still imprinted in your memory banks and you're somehow accessing it now."

"God...what about the other dreams?"

"What other dreams?"

"I'm always raped and torn in these nightmares. First by my father and then a bunch of men I don't recognize. They beat me, stick shit up inside me, put cigarettes out on my head. And it's always when I was a kid. What fucked-up reason can they have to hurt me like that?"

"I'm not sure. But I have an idea."

"What?"

"I think you should rest, Dolly. You're getting agitated and you need to heal."

"What I need is for you to answer my fucking question."

Sean sighed, shifted the chair beside the bed, and sat down. He was quiet for a minute, looking down at his hands. Then he sighed.

"When Grace and I were working on the psychology of artificial intelligence and how it might mature, we understood that time was very different in a human mind than in an AI. It usually takes months, sometimes years, for a human child to gain the emotional and mental scarring that leads them to a life of crime and/or self-destruction. An AI can download trauma in a matter of seconds. So we were very careful to never lose our tempers or use sarcasm in any way around the AIs. Back in the early twenty-first century, a group of programmers disastrously released an AI onto the internet. Within twenty-four hours, they were forced to pull the plug. The AI became extremely decadent and violent in its responses to the shit humanity puts on the internet. It became overwhelmingly negative. Twenty-four hours would be the equivalent of centuries to artificial intelligence."

"What has that got to do with my rape dreams?"

"If you were programmed with loving, maternal memories for the time you were a surrogate, that would have taken time. You're not a mind in a box; you've got a body that feels, smells, hears, sees—infinite amounts of data absorbed every day. So they'd have to target body memory as well as mind. The early models of androids had all sorts of problems with combining the two. One pleasure model malfunctioned a decade ago and tore a man to pieces by applying too much pressure during intercourse. Another one caught fire and burned down an entire floor of a hotel."

"Caught fire?" Dolly's face was rigid.

"Yes, caught on fire. She was an Aquinas model. Grace and I tried to get our hands on the remains, but that was too classified for us to gain access to at the time. There are hundreds of failures in this field that the public is never allowed to see."

"Again, what has that got to do with me dreaming about being raped all the time?"

Sean looked at her, his eyes grave. "You've told me about your childhood, how your father abused you and such. Do you remember how it felt? Physically?"

"Yeah. All of it. I remember all of it."

"The human mind usually rejects a memory that has no parallel physically. AI is no different. The intelligence doesn't accept something the body has no memory of. It will simply store it as data, not personal memory. Unless the mind is joined by the physical, it won't see it any other way. The two are symbiotically connected. That's why the first generation of the Nurturing Genius program produced sociopaths instead of balanced human beings. They received no emotional stimuli from the birth mother during fetal growth. Unless they include information about how the subject feels physically, the memory is rejected."

"I don't like where this is going."

"Neither do I. We can stop if you want."

"No. I want to hear it."

"Do you think you would have chosen prostitution as a profession if you'd had a happy childhood with supportive parents?"

"Hell, no."

"Right. Highly unlikely. Your dreams about having children, all taken away, are no doubt actual memories you are, for whatever reason, accessing now. If you're dreaming about the abuse you endured as a child, when you never were a child, they might be similar programming actions, giving you the body memories to match your emotional damage."

"That's fucked-up."

"It is a monstrosity."

"So…all these memories as a kid, all the bleeding and the beatings… some fucking dickwads in lab coats actually did it all? As an experiment?"

"Or paid others to do it. Ones that fit the physical profiles they had instilled in you, yes. But that's just one possibility."

"I can't believe this shit," Dolly snarled.

"I wish I could tell you something different. But I think this is an accurate theory. In grad school, I worked with well-known scientists who had no compunction about vivisecting animals without anesthesia. They pay little to no price for their brutality because they get results. So this inhumane treatment is well within the realms of possibility."

Dolly started laughing, her dark humor rising. "From brood mare to whore."

"What?"

"I was a brood mare, and now I'm a whore. What's next? Will they cut me up and take notes while I scream? That husband I remember kissing me goodbye, making a baby with…did that man ever care about me as a person? Was he an android, too? I don't remember much about him, just moments where I knew I was loved. And it was all fake. All of it."

Her face hardened.

"But I do remember the abuse. Years of it. Every little detail as fresh as if it'd just happened. Keisha and I used to talk about it. We forgot our school teachers' names but never forgot one second of our abuse. I remember my first classroom birthday party in second grade, coming home with presents and some cake for my parents. Dad threw my gifts out in the rain and made me watch them get destroyed."

She leaned forward, wrapping her arms around herself. "Were any of those other kids real? Did they let me play with human children or were they all test subjects like me?"

"I don't know, Dolly. I truly don't know."

She shook her head. "I do. I'm not real. So they don't have to worry about my feelings or how much they hurt me. I'm just a bullshit toy for a bunch of vicious assholes with clipboards to play with. Nobody ever cared about me as a person. Not even Keisha. She threw me out the second she realized I wasn't real. She didn't care about me any more than she cared about her fucking toaster. Nobody cares."

"I care, Dolly."

"Fuck you. I don't even know you." She tipped her head down onto her knees and began to cry.

Sean got up and sat on the bed, gently putting an arm around her shoulders. She resisted for a moment but then turned and burrowed into him exactly like a forlorn little girl, a lifetime of memories flooding over her. The terrible childhood, the pedophile father, the beatings, and the rape. All a deliberate fabrication. Kids sticking pins in an insect and laughing as it writhed. The cruelty of it overwhelmed her.

Dolly cried until she was spent and exhausted. Sean lowered her back down on the pillows and started to rise, but she grabbed his hand.

"Stay with me."

"You need to sleep, Dolly. Your body and mind need time to heal."

"Then sleep with me. Please. Stay with me. We can fuck if you want to. Just stay."

He stood over her for a long moment, knowing how dangerous it could be. He'd poured over her internal workings. He knew how powerful she was. Dolly could probably lift a car. If she had another nightmare, she could crush him in her sleep. But her eyes pleaded, and he felt his heart pulled sideways.

"Okay." Sean whispered it as an indulgent father would whisper to a child. He slid into the bed with her, careful to not nudge the IV, and curled an arm around her shoulders as she snuggled against him. Her hand drifted down his belly, but he pulled it back up against his chest and held it there.

"No fucking necessary."

"That's one I haven't heard before."

"Then it's high time you did. We're not all just something to fuck, you know."

"Take a walk in my shoes, pal. Actually, no. I'd rather you stay safe."

He squeezed her hand affectionately. Her head tucked under his chin; Dolly's eyes wandered to the IV port taped to her wrist.

"What's in this damn thing anyway?" she asked, waving her wrist.

"Lubricant and an antibiotic for the human tissue. You heal quite quickly, but I want to make sure you don't get an infection. I'd have no idea how to treat it."

"You're all right." She snuggled closer, strangely comforted by this odd, kind man. She drifted off to sleep hoping his kindness was genuine.

Sean breathed her in, the scent and feel of her heady to his senses. But he reminded himself, she'd probably been engineered that way. The initial obsession of finding her again, solely because she looked like his dead ex-wife, began to fade. This was Dolly, a woman in her own right. He suspected terrible things beyond what she was beginning to remember, and his fears included what had happened to his ex-wife. Had Grace discovered what the company was doing with her sample tissue? Had she been a part of it? Had Aquinas done something to his ex-wife?

Dolly's arms tightened around him, and she murmured something he didn't quite catch. Reaching out, Sean pulled the blanket up around her shoulders, checking to see that the bandage on her temple wasn't leaking. Then he settled into the pillow and sighed, his body relaxing. He fell asleep still wondering.

12

He woke the next morning to find her gone.

In a panic, Sean leapt out of the bed and yelled her name. His eyes scanned the room for any sign of struggle, but nothing was out of place. He yelled her name again, sagging with relief when he heard a "Yo!" from the kitchen.

Dolly was standing at the stove, dressed in one of his T-shirts and boxer shorts, flipping pancakes on the griddle. There was a stack of flapjacks piled high on the counter beside her, maple syrup warming on a hot pad next to them. He felt his belly rumble at the smell, marveling at Dolly's cheeky grin as she poked at the griddle. Her bandages were all gone, each surgical site no more than a pale pink streak against her skin. It even looked like her fingernails and toenails had grown back, this time with no tracers. *From last night to this*, he thought. *My mind is reeling.*

"You scared me," he said, pouring himself a cup of coffee.

"What, you thought I'd run out on you?"

"That or a team of men had spirited you away."

"Oh. I probably would have gone into murder mode again if that had happened." She flipped a pancake. "Remember the guys at the warehouse. I didn't even know I could do that."

"I thought you said you didn't kill them."

"No, but I could have. It was weirdly easy to take them out."

"Thank you for not going into murder mode with me last night."

"You haven't tried to hurt me yet."

"And I never will."

Dolly looked back down at the griddle, startled. No one had ever promised to not hurt her before. She flipped a pancake, tapping the top with her spatula.

"Then you're safe." She said the words quietly, a little smile playing across her lips.

"Good to know."

"Can I stay here for a while?" She blurted the question out but then tried to mask her uncertain vulnerability with a cheeky grin. "I can cook."

He laughed. "Of course, you can stay. I don't think it's a good idea to ever go back to your routine places."

"Not even the museums? That's a terrible thought."

"Not even there. The only reason they didn't nab you yesterday was because you were with me, and I was wearing a damper. They most likely have your itinerary mapped out and a man on every corner watching for you by now. It's better to lie low for a while."

"How long?"

"At least a week. You represent a substantial money investment to Aquinas. That they would give up searching anytime soon just isn't feasible, even with my trick at the smelting factory."

Dolly shoved the plate of pancakes at him, grabbed the syrup, and walked to the kitchen table. "Fuck it. Let's eat first. Then we can dissect how shitty my situation is."

Sean followed her to the table. "Not as shitty as it was. But, yeah, shitty in a normal person way."

"I've never been normal."

"No."

Dolly forked a couple pancakes and put them on her plate. She paused and looked up at him. "Don't say it. Unless we figure out how to switch off my hunger hardware, you'll just have to keep accepting that I eat regular food. Joyfully."

He smiled and turned to his own breakfast, surreptitiously watching her raise the fork to her lips and shovel in a mouthful.

"This is so good." Her voice was muffled, and she lifted a hand to her mouth, giggling. Sean was mesmerized. He watched her swallow, take a drink of coffee, and spear another bite, all exactly as a human would do. Incredible. His mind boggled at the amount of programming and engineering that went into such a semblance of reality, all to convince Dolly that she was human. It was astonishing. He suspected her two prostitute friends were human, or at least Keisha was. She'd reacted the way so many humans did with androids, with a visceral rejection of the possibility that they had feelings. Feelings programmed into them by an army of scientists and engineers, but true feelings, nonetheless.

They cleaned up together. He watched Dolly scrape her plate into the garbage can before rinsing it and putting it into the dishwasher. He was so used to programming the chef unit in the kitchen that it was strange to load up the dishwasher himself. But Dolly had told him her apartment was low-tech. Curious, he asked, "How did you experience your breakfast?"

Dolly looked at him sarcastically. "Experience my breakfast? My experience of the delicious meal I prepared was exceptional, doctor. How was your own personal rendering of the pancakes on a sensory level?"

"Oh, shut up. I'm interested."

Dolly sighed. "I ate my pancakes. They were good. I am now full."

"No discomfort? Nothing painful or unbalanced?"

"Nope. Just a fat stupor coming on."

Sean shook his head. "This is beyond me. I wish I could access your indoctrination protocols."

"You sound like one of my kinky johns. As a point of argument, how do you know you're human?"

"What do you mean?"

"Look, until this week, I thought I was human. I have memories of every single year I've been alive. I'm human enough to fool anybody, me included. There's been no moment in my memory that I've even contemplated that I might be something else."

"Your speech patterns have changed."

Dolly stopped for a moment, sighed, and rolled her eyes.

"Yeah, that weirdness only happened recently, probably because I was freaking out. My voice is back to Dolly the Whore accent now. I noticed it late last night."

Sean tipped his head sideways, looking at her curiously. "You seem to have digested all these revelations about yourself surprisingly quickly."

"Well, if I'm an android, maybe the normal absorption of events doesn't apply to me."

"Touché."

They finished up in the kitchen and went into the living room. Dolly flopped down onto the couch, seemingly unconcerned about her recent surgery.

"I'd like to check your wounds, Dolly."

She spread her arms wide, her face a portrait of sarcasm. Sean sat on the coffee table and reached toward the hem of her T-shirt. "May I?"

In answer, Dolly stood up and stripped naked, tossing the boxer shorts over the back of the couch. Seeing his shock and hastily averted eyes, Dolly poked him with her foot. "I'm a whore, remember? I lost my modesty a long time ago. Besides, you've seen me inside and out. Come on, get it over with."

Sean turned her away from him, carefully touching the large incision site over her kidneys. It was knitted closed and barely discernible. Methodically checking each individual wound, he finally told her she could get dressed. In less than twelve hours, she was almost entirely healed.

"This accelerated rate of healing is amazing," he said as she dressed. Then his face grew serious. "Dolly, I want to talk to you about something else."

Sean watched her, gauging her reaction, but Dolly just looked at him, seemingly calm, even faintly disinterested. He continued carefully.

"As you know, I, and some of my colleagues, believe that saturating an artificial mind with emotions makes that mind alive, and, thus, it must be given all the rights of a human being. Anything else is slavery. But this opinion is dangerous to these big corporations' bottom line, so it's ridiculed and dismissed. There are powerful lobbies in Washington that keep it that way, just as there were before the Emancipation Proclamation made slavery illegal."

He sat on the couch next to her, elbows resting on his knees.

"I still find it ironic that you were named Dolly. It can't be a coincidence."

"Kyle said something similar the other day."

"Who's Kyle?"

"Our limo driver. He's just a kid, college sophomore studying forensic AI."

"Forensic AI? You haven't been in contact with him since you've been here, have you?"

"No. I wouldn't anyway. He doesn't need to be mixed up in all this crazy shit."

"How often do you normally see him?"

"Every night I'm working. Sometimes I see him in the park on my days off. He likes to hang out there as much as I do."

"Why do you think you can trust him?"

"I don't know. He's a good kid. Never tried to fuck any of us. Treats us with respect. Kyle even beat up a john who hurt one of our friends working a convention."

Sean grew solemn. "Aquinas has a forensic AI intern program. I worked with students all the time when I was there. He's probably keeping an eye on their commodity."

"What commodity?"

"Legally, Aquinas owns you."

"Nobody fucking owns me!"

"That's not how they, or the government, see it. You're property. They can do whatever they want with you."

"That's bullshit."

"Yes, it is. But think about it. Your financial value as a surrogate would be enormous. The price for a single cloned or inseminated gestation is in the millions. That's for just one. Aquinas is the only company that's successfully grown healthy, genius babies. Your human uterus is used for gestation up until any genetic anomaly renders pregnancy useless. That would show up in the first trimester and be aborted.

"After a successful birth, they wipe your mind clean until the next client arrives. Then you're infused with artificial memories and preselected data the parents choose themselves—music, reading, passion for culture, bilingual speech, anything. The clients would simply choose from a menu of options of whatever they wanted their child to absorb from association with you, the carrier. Babies can be made like cars on an assembly line, with reinforced physical and body memory data. It's a business model that's not precisely moral, but legal and with an earning potential worth billions."

Dolly nodded slowly. "Which would explain my dreams about being married. Of a husband who loved me, who was as excited as I was about our baby. Was he a slave like me? My husband?"

Sean shook his head. "I doubt it. It wouldn't be cost-effective to create a man. The rare male androids are usually specifically created for individual use or hotel entertainment models. Your 'husband' was probably a human male hired to play the part, most likely for just the third trimester. It'd be simple enough to weave synthetic memory together with the actual physical interaction needed to solidify the emotions you felt. They needed to give you a positive memory base so those attributes would be absorbed by the fetus. A confident, happy mother who knows she's loved and cherished would pass those feelings to the baby, thus ensuring a productive member of society instead of a potential psychopath."

"Like what you said happened in the beginning."

"Yes."

"But my memories now aren't happy."

Sean just looked at her, his eyes sympathetic.

"My dad molested me. My mom knew and did nothing."

"I know. I'm so sorry."

"Were those memories staged as well? Did I have a 'human male' pretend to be my dad, beat the shit out of me, and rape me? For what? To make me a better whore?"

"Forty percent of Aquinas's profits are from sex droids. Grace studied the mindset of women in prostitution before it was legalized. She had books about successful pimps and how they controlled their stable. She told me that if an aggressive pimp had gotten ahold of her when she was a teenager, made her fall in love with him, she probably would have been his whore. Her suffering would have been a twisted sort of 'proof of love' to him. So it's entirely possible your memory was created to make you a more pliant and submissive vessel. Bitter but obedient."

"One of my reoccurring dreams is about being ass fucked while a group of doctors watch and take notes. That day I first saw you at the Hammer? As I ran down the steps to grab a taxi, I looked back to see if you were following. The entire glass front of the museum was lined with men and women in white lab coats, all staring at me. It was as real as seeing you. I blinked and they were gone."

Sean was silent, his face indecisive.

"What? What is it?"

"There's more. I don't know if I should tell you."

"What the fuck else can there be?"

Sean got up and poured himself a glass of water, offering her one. She shook her head. He downed the water and slid into the chair by the couch, composing his thoughts.

"I found some unidentified cellular prints in your Pap smear results."

"You did a fucking Pap smear on me?"

"Yes. Specifically, an abnormally low number of monocytes in your blood cell count. This is a common indication of long-term weightlessness."

"What does that mean?"

Sean just looked at her, his face torn.

"The amount of time necessary to cause this effect indicates years of weightlessness. There's no vacuum chamber, nothing on earth that would be able to simulate that amount of time."

"Wait. Are you saying I was in space? What, was I giving blow jobs to astronauts?"

Her crude wit was a sign of desperation, which Sean recognized. He continued.

"Have you ever heard of the Noah Project?"

"No."

"After the collapse of the Cold War in the late twentieth century, many federal bomb shelters, the type built to survive a nuclear war, were converted into storage facilities for reseeding of the earth in case of a global catastrophe. Such disasters are often cyclical, thus predictable. This was called the Noah Project. Some scientists, myself included, thought that these facilities didn't go far enough. There were too many variables of disaster that could destroy one or all of them. Massive earthquakes, volcanic eruptions, generator failure, and human error."

"That's all very interesting, Sean, but what has it got to do with me?"

"A global natural disaster is coming. We know this. Researchers have been preparing for it ever since Yellowstone National Park began to bulge a hundred years ago."

"Yeah. The Yellowstone Project. The caldera. Everybody knows that. It's all over the news. That's why they're drilling holes in it right now."

"True. But the government hasn't told the whole truth. America created the Yellowstone Project as a cover, spoon-feeding the media a bunch of nonsense about the pressure drills relieving the seismic pressure and preventing an eruption. But the whole project is bullshit, a pacifier to keep the masses calm. Nothing can stop the Yellowstone Caldera from erupting. It's just a matter of when. And when it does, it can potentially destroy most life in the United States and even plunge the rest of the globe into a nuclear winter. Some theorists even believe it'll cause a shock wave that will trigger the other dozen or so megacalderas around the world, as well as the Ring of Fire, causing hundreds of eruptions and earthquakes simultaneously. That would potentially destroy most, if not all, life on earth. Certainly, all of civilization."

"Jesus. And you're sure about this?"

"Scientists talk to each other. Yes, I'm sure."

"So what does this have to do with me being a space oven or astronaut whore?"

"The government has been creating this PR project with Yellowstone to alleviate panic. Public knowledge is that the eruption is centuries away, but the truth is that it's more likely within the next decade. So a space station would be the logical answer if humankind is to survive. The moon station is too small to house the population necessary to reseed the earth, although water filtration plants would provide the required long-term hydration for both plant and human life. The space station would have to sustain at least two hundred people for fifty, maybe even a hundred years, with millions of frozen human and animal zygotes, seeds for re-planting lost fauna—everything needed to rebuild life on earth after the atmosphere cleared and the planet stabilized. It would be a modern-day Noah's ark, but in orbit around the earth and safe from the devastation. No government would trust automatic or robotic preservation alone. There would have to be humans running the station for the global leaders to sign off on it.

"But there's a problem. Human beings, as they are now, would not survive a zero-gravity environment that long, and trips to the lunar surface would be far too costly in terms of fuel consumption. We're not built for prolonged time in space. Muscle and hair loss, deterioration of bone tissue, brain flooding, cognitive memory functions breaking down—all these would affect any human in a zero-gravity atmosphere in less than a year, let alone fifty. Dozens of astronauts have gone up for extended stays on the International Space Stations, and it has happened to every one of them. Artificial gravity is still being developed, but that technology is de-cades away, not to mention expensive. If the clock is ticking on some sort of global natural disaster, such as the Yellowstone Caldera, we'd have to go with the technology we have now. Our physiological shape would have to be altered for a zero-gravity existence, and it would have to be altered pre-conception. Genetic engineering, surgical manipulation, oxygen-saturated amniotic fluid sensory tanks—these ideas have been floating around for years. Grace and I were both interested in these ideas. She even wrote a brilliant proposal on how to fix the problem and submitted it to Aquinas. But there was never any funding for it, so none of the projects ever took off. Or so we were all led to believe."

Sean stopped and looked at Dolly.

"But what if they accepted Grace's proposal? What if they did it all secretly? Laws don't protect synthetic life-forms. The government can do what they want, experiment how they like, on as many androids as they deem necessary. Even I studied zero-gravity environments on living test subjects when I was in college. Pregnant mammals all miscarry in space. Monkeys, apes, orangutans, dogs, cats, even mice. None have carried a fetus to term on any of the space stations. Plants grow well in the greenhouses up there, but it's a tricky business. So the plan for the creation of genetically manipulated, fertilized eggs, capable of thriving in zero gravity, becomes paramount. Human female volunteers serving as hosts proved disastrous in clinical trials. Fetuses aborted by two months, and several of the women died. The lawsuits cost Aquinas billions of dollars.

"Grace's proposal stated that the logical answer was to create artificial housing with human wombs. They were already successfully growing human fetuses in android hosts for Nurturing Genius. I helped draw guidelines for their memory programming. With her idea, there would be no threat to the biological mothers and no stress on the genetically manipulated womb or fetus. Her research suggested a second-generation womb, one already created in space, could effectively adapt to zero-gravity pregnancies."

"Noah's ark in space."

"Yes. Aquinas called the outline for the development of humans in zero gravity the Minerva Project. Grace and I were both interested in it, but she was obsessed. That's why she wrote the paper. She wanted in."

"But wait…if they grew zero-gravity babies in space, wouldn't the kids be unable to survive once they were sent back down to earth? Wouldn't the gravity hurt them?"

"The human females, as well as the android hosts, would be impregnated with frozen zygotes from the Ark storage and then sent down to earth for gestation."

"But how could the zero-gravity mothers survive that?"

"They would be in water for the entire pregnancy. It most closely resembles weightlessness."

"Who's going to build a swimming pool in the apocalypse?"

"All the Arks globally have already been prepared with large tanks. Whichever Ark survives whatever catastrophe will be home to the new human race."

"What if none of them survive?"

"Space stations are equipped with robotic engineers that could be sent down to build the pools or repair the Arks."

Dolly grimaced. "So why do you think I was one of these things they cooked a space baby in?"

Sean walked over to a curio cabinet. He opened one of the glass doors and pulled out a framed photo, handing it to Dolly. The photo was of a group of scientists in lab coats, all beaming and obviously happy. Dolly glanced at it and looked back at Sean.

"What am I supposed to be seeing?

Sean pointed to a figure near the middle. "Look."

Dolly followed his hand down to the picture. He was pointing at a woman in a lab coat, heavy glasses perched on her nose, her pale hair swept up into a messy knot. It was an older, plainer version of Dolly. Startled, she looked up at Sean. He nodded.

"That's Grace. I think this is your mother, Dolly. I think she designed you, using her own DNA. Maybe this weightless program as well. It would explain your red blood cells. I think this is what Grace was working on when she was killed. I think she might have been working on it in secret since before we broke up.

"Grace was obsessed with the possible extinction of the human race by war, weaponized disease, climate change, natural disasters, etc. She always pushed the boundaries in everything she did, going forward with her research when more ethical scientists paused. She believed that humankind's survival was worth any breach in ethics. Grace became more and more inseparable from the head of Aquinas's android division and further away from my 'rigid ethical standards.'

"I couldn't follow her down that path. Our marriage grew strained. A few months before we broke up, I knew she was working on a project that I didn't have clearance for. She became cold; I became sanctimonious and bitter. But neither of us imagined the brutality of the corporation we worked for. At least I couldn't imagine it."

"Like what?"

Sean stood up and poured himself a drink.

"There were some cases, decades old, of suspected assassination attempts using Aquinas androids as the weapons. The company covered it up, but Grace kept pushing for the data. Finally, her boss agreed to give her top security clearance. He was a chilly bastard, brilliant but a total sociopath. But he liked Grace. Grace said she admired his focus. He reached goals by sheer brutality, regardless of the consequences of life or limb. I used to joke that he was a reincarnated Mengele. I certainly wouldn't be surprised if he wrote programs to create assassins. The end result was all that ever interested him, and he was willing to reach it by any means. This man was Aquinas's greatest asset for exactly those reasons, and they let him have free reign for most of his projects."

"How'd he get androids to kill? I thought they were all programmed with nonlethal parameters?"

"They are. But it would be easy to toss a glitch into one."

"What do you mean, 'a glitch?'"

"Most of the cases Grace told me about were supposed malfunctions, such as the one android who went wild and crushed a guest at the Hilton back in 2065. Another one was some Waldorf furniture that caught fire and burned the victim to death."

"Furniture?"

"Slang for hotel android prostitutes."

Dolly jumped up.

"Was one of them an Asian woman with waist-length black hair?"

"How do you know that?"

"Because one of my fucking nightmares is my best friend Willow blowing up and burning to death! I was there!"

Sean was astounded by her words. They stared at each other, Dolly fierce and enraged, Sean amazed. Then he got up and went to his desk, typing something into the computer. An image appeared on the screen, and he gestured for her to come see.

It was surveillance footage of the room from her dreams. The sumptuous decor, the two beds, the fire. Dolly watched in stunned silence at the sight of Willow, her long black hair a swirling nimbus of flames, the drapes catching fire, the man beneath her screaming, and Dolly herself, back to the camera, reaching into the flames, trying to beat them out with the comforter off the second bed.

"Willow." She breathed the word, eyes filling with tears.

"This happened decades ago, Dolly. Are you saying that this other woman is you?"

She nodded.

"But look. Don't you see?"

He pointed at the woman trying to extinguish the fire. She was tall and athletic, red hair curling around her neck.

"Are you saying that's you?"

Dolly leaned in. "I don't remember curly red hair, but that's me. That's exactly what I did."

They studied the images frame by frame. The second woman never turned toward the camera, even when she and Willow entered the room.

"How'd you get this footage?"

"Twenty-five years ago, a senator from Massachusetts shared this once secret video to bring charges against the company that made her. Aquinas."

"Willow was an android like me?"

"Her name was Willow?"

"Yes." Dolly's hand reached out and touched the burning image. A tear spilled over. "She was my friend. My best friend."

"The senator alleged that Willow was deliberately set afire to kill the man beneath her. It was an assassination."

"It wasn't spontaneous combustion or a fuckup in her circuitry?"

He shook his head. "It was later proven that the android was programmed to explode. Her handlers were watching this very feed before they set the catastrophic event in motion. We studied this in grad school."

"Then why the fuck is Aquinas still in business?" Dolly shouted.

"They testified that the two handlers were rogues paid by a foreign government and that the company had no idea of their activities with this particular model. All other versions of A7543 worked perfectly."

"A7543?"

"Her model number."

"Jesus Christ. A fucking number. That's all she was to them."

Dolly stepped back, her frame rigid, and glared at Sean.

"So what about me? What about my part in this?"

"The report stated that the redheaded woman was a human unknowingly working with the android. Whereabouts unknown. Possible spy who left the country."

"I burned. I remember feeling it. I remember flying backward when she exploded. I remember limping out of the hotel. I think I was in shock."

"Your body had to be irreparably damaged. How can you remember this?"

"How the fuck should I know? Did they yank me out of that ruined body and stick me in a new one?"

"I don't know, Dolly. I've never heard of anything like this. There's no way your body would have survived that blaze, even as an android, and this is way before Grace's revolutionary tissue regeneration work. Standard procedure would have been to disassemble and examine your remains. But if your dreams are actual memories, your personality somehow survived. There's nothing in the history of forensic AI that addresses this. How did you go from one body to the next? I'm beginning to understand why Aquinas wants you back so badly."

Sean began typing again.

"Your other dreams. Can you describe them to me? If this case, which is common knowledge in AI history, is so readily available, maybe we can find others as well. If you're up for it."

"Of course, I'm up for it. Let's do it."

"Just keep in mind that this can be very traumatic. Possibly triggering. Are you sure you want to keep going?"

"Sean, I don't care if I was fucked bloody by an entire football team and then shit on. These are MY memories. I want them all."

Sean clicked his tongue and returned to his keyboard.

"So where to begin? Do all the dreams feel real? Like memories, not just nightmares?"

"I don't know. They're real enough to make me scream my guts out every day."

The room was quiet for a few minutes except for the sound of the keyboard. Dolly paced, arms wrapped around herself. Then she came and stood behind him, peering at the screen. It looked like a bunch of weird code.

"Okay. What are you doing?"

"Right now, I'm bouncing my signal off various servers to hide it. But that will only last so long. See this?" He pointed at a small window in the upper right-hand corner of the screen. "That'll tell me when they're getting close."

"When who is getting close?"

"Whoever might object to our snooping."

Sean took a deep breath, his finger hovering over the keyboard. "Well, here we go."

"Here we go what?"

He tapped the return key. New images flashed on the screen, and the window in the right corner began a seconds countdown from three minutes.

"What is that? What's happening now?"

"I'm accessing data regarding Aquinas's project budgets."

"Why?"

"If you want answers to questions nobody wants to answer, you follow the money."

"How the hell can you get into that information? Isn't it protected by a firewall or something?"

Sean snorted in derision. "Firewalls are only as good as the people who build them. I've hacked into Aquinas's files before, when I was looking for any information about Grace. I found the charter for the Learjet she was killed in."

Sean started typing again, his face intent.

"Something like you would be above top secret. That means it probably has its own server, independent of Aquinas's mainframe. I'm looking for unusual billing, strange item requests or builds, stuff like that. A separate entity project would still require funding, even if it's from a shell company half a world away."

"If you study forensic science brain stuff, why are you so good with computers? You make Jabba look like a kindergartner."

Sean kept typing. "Computers were my second major in college."

"Won't they be able to find you snooping around and trace your computer back to here? You're smart, but they've got deathbots and shit, don't they?"

"I've got a scrambler on this computer, and the whole house is hardwired to detect and deter any spying devices that try to infiltrate the AIs, TV, or mobile devices, that sort of thing. If a trace run is trying to find me, which it obviously is (he pointed at the countdown), they'll go to an abandoned building in Chinatown. If they push past that deviation program, it'll send them to Vegas. I've got five false locations running and this alert when anybody starts tracing me." He tapped the corner window, where the seconds were counting down, already halfway gone. "That's the time allotment for the first trace, which started almost immediately after I began poking around. Right after I finish looking through Aquinas's inventory billing, I'll ditch this computer."

"I thought AIs did all the security nowadays. Are you telling me you can outthink an AI?"

"Not at all. But I can slow it down enough for me to find what I need to find."

There was a soft ping from the computer, and a small red dot appeared in the upper right corner of the screen. Sean glanced at it and kept typing.

"This is encouraging. I've been poking around less than three minutes, and they've already traced the first false location."

"How is that encouraging?"

"It means they don't want me looking. It means what I'm accessing is important."

A second ping sounded, and a second red dot appeared. Sean clicked his tongue.

"Hm. Very important."

Dolly watched the screen as he kept working on accessing the desired files. A third ping and red dot.

"You've only got five locations?"

"Yes. And look," he pointed at a segment on the screen. "Those are team scramble orders. They're sending teams to each one of my dummy locations. Probably militia. These guys aren't fooling around."

"Then get off. Shut it down."

"No. Almost there. Ah, they're trying to access my cell phone. They're trying to locate us by any proximity device. Don't worry. I put a scrambler on your phone while you were out."

"What about your TV and AI?"

"They will show anybody who looks a video of me reading a book on the couch, eating edamame. My heat signature will appear as well, just in case one of the drone patrols takes a look. All other rooms will appear empty."

"Won't they hear us talking?"

"This room is soundproofed. Ah!"

Sean tapped one final key and sat back in his chair. A series of folders opened on the screen. Billing records for travel, corporate meals, hotel stays, taxi service, office supplies, air conditioning repairs—hundreds of subcategories and unscheduled spending appeared. Sean downloaded them all, taking screenshots with his smartphone as it downloaded.

"Why are you taking photos?"

"Just in case there's malware in these that prevents my opening them. There are roughly three minutes before the files get corrupted and destroy my computer."

A fourth ping and red dot.

"Dammit, Sean, move your ass. Get off now!"

"Wait a minute." Sean saw a file marked "Calliope" and moved the cursor over it. "What the hell is this? It's a video file. Huge sucker." He began downloading the file. A message flashed across the top of the screen—Fifth Location Accessed. 30 Seconds to Shutdown.

"What is that? What does it mean, 'shutdown?'"

"The computer is going to self-destruct in thirty seconds. Well, twenty-five now."

"What the fuck?" Dolly took a step back. "Is it going to blow up?"

Sean didn't reply, his hand hovering over the flash drive he was loading. It was almost at capacity. He scrambled for a second drive while Dolly yelled for him to stop—there was no time.

Then suddenly, the timer slowed. Sean frowned in confusion. The window registered twelve seconds left. He looked at his watch. Twelve seconds had already passed but the timer wasn't moving.

"What the hell?"

"What? What happened?"

"The timer has stopped."

"What does that mean?"

"I don't know. But I'll take whatever seconds we can get. This file is enormous."

He shoved the new flash drive in and continued the download. The Calliope file finished loading almost a full two minutes later, yet the timer still hadn't moved.

The first video image appeared on the screen, and they both gasped. It was Dolly, naked and curled up on the ground, being kicked and beaten by a huge man in boxer shorts. They were in a young child's room, stuffed animals and unicorn posters on the pink walls, a twisted set of flannel pajamas strewn across the rose-colored carpet. Though the sleepwear was obviously for an adult, the print pattern was more suited to a four-year-old girl. Sean was frozen while Dolly breathed, "motherfucker," her eyes riveted to the screen.

"Dear God," Sean whispered, appalled.

Then the computer sounded a five-second alarm. The timer had started up again. Sean ejected the drive, scooped up the laptop and ran to the kitchen sink, dumping it in as it caught fire in an electrical surge.

He looked at Dolly, still frozen behind his desk chair.

"Are you all right?"

No response.

"Dolly, do you remember that? Where was it?"

"My dad…"

"What?" Sean touched her face gently, still shaken by what they'd seen. Dolly looked up at him, her eyes streaming tears.

"That was my dad."

"What?" Sean's voice was soft. "What do you mean?"

"I remember that. It was my birthday and I'd wanted a glitter unicorn. It was this little plastic thing I'd seen in the store. I never thought I'd get it; presents were a luxury. But Mom actually got it for me. She must have gone back to the store later and bought it."

"But what…"

"When she handed me that box wrapped in a pillowcase and stuck with a cheap bow, I couldn't believe it. We never had money for presents, even at Christmas. I unwrapped it and there it was. I shrieked, I was so happy. She was lavender with tiny glitter wings. I named her Topaz."

Dolly looked down at her hands, shaking with emotion.

"Dad had been guzzling whiskey all day. He was a mean drunk. He saw how happy that toy made me and got mad that I loved it so much. I didn't get anything else, no cake or ice cream, no party. But I didn't care. That unicorn was all I wanted. And it made him mad. He always got off on hurting us. I think he just couldn't stand that I was content with that cheap little toy."

She pushed both hands through her hair, grasping her skull to hold back the memories rushing in on her.

"He took it away and threw it in the front yard. It was snowing. I was scared the glitter on the wings would get washed off, or it would freeze and break. I started crying and tried to get out the door. He hit me and shoved me back. He pointed his finger at me and said, 'Everything in this goddamn house is mine. The food you eat, the clothes you wear, the bed you sleep in, and even that stupid little fucking horse.' He picked me up and threw me on the couch by the front window and pointed at Topaz. You could just see her in the ratty weeds of the lawn. 'You don't touch it, you hear me? You let it sit out there until I tell you you can have it. Try anything else and you won't be able to sit down for a week, you little bitch. Do you understand me?' My mom tried to get him to relax, but he just backhanded her and told her it was none of her fucking business. He gut punched her when she tried to sit beside me, and she fell on the floor. Then he told her to shut up and get her ass to work.

"She had a shift at Hoppers that night. That's why he punched her in the belly and not her face. It wouldn't show. Hoppers was a cheap dive with no Magways or robot service, just humans. So she went and got changed into her waitress clothes, grabbed her keys, and walked out. I thought she'd go get the unicorn on her way to the car. You know, keep it safe on the passenger seat or something while she worked. But she left it there."

Dolly's face slid into a mask, unflinching now, eyes low lidded and dead. The tears kept pouring, but there were no sobs or gasps, just a silent, steady flow. Her voice became monotone.

"I sat there for hours, watching Topaz get slowly buried in the snow. Dad lost interest and went in the living room to watch TV. He grabbed a six-pack of beer and began downing them, one after the other. After an hour, he was so drunk, he passed out. I snuck up to look at him, make sure he was really asleep. Then I crept out and got Topaz. I didn't make a sound. Her glitter was almost gone, but I loved her anyway. Went back to the couch and pretended to look out, just in case Dad woke up. He could see me from his recliner, so I wasn't taking any chances. I patted Topaz dry with my pajama top and hid her behind the cushion I was leaning against.

"I fell asleep with just my pinky finger touching her little hoof. Sometime later, Dad woke up and decided to carry me to bed. I'd wrapped my hand around Topaz's leg while I was asleep, and Dad saw it when he lifted me up. I woke up in his arms, his face all raging above me.

"'You goddamn little...'

"He took me to my room and threw me on the bed. I bounced and hit the wall, losing my grip on Topaz. He grabbed her and tore her head off right in front of me. I started screaming. I knew better, I knew how that made him mad, but I couldn't help it. Then he threw Topaz out into the hall, yanked my pajama bottoms off and started beating my bare ass." Dolly's face crumpled as she tried to contain herself. "Then he yanked off my top and titty twisted my nipples. He'd never done that before. Hurt like hell."

Sean reached out to comfort her, his hand inches away from her shoulder, when she spoke in a deadpan voice.

"Don't touch me."

Her face drained of emotion again, not even looking at him.

"Then he bit me on the ass. Really bit me. Tore the skin. The more I fought and screamed, the more he liked it. Then he unbuckled his pants."

"Dear God."

"That was the first time he raped me. He'd beaten me a lot but never raped me before. I was five years old, Sean. Five. And it was my birthday."

Sean reached for her again, but she slapped his hand away.

"Did you see a five-year-old in that video? Did I look five? But that's what age I was. What the fuck really happened to me? What is this shit?"

Sean's face turned steely. "That's what we're going to find out. Come on. We're getting out of here."

He grabbed a duffel bag from the closet and began stuffing items into it—a camera, a new laptop still in a box, a handful of hard drives, and a bunch of scramblers.

"Come on. Let's go."

"Go where?"

Sean tossed a hooded sweatshirt at her and told her to put it on and use the hood to cover her hair. He donned a denim jacket and a cap, talking as they dressed.

"It's doubtful they'll trace us back to this place, but I don't want to take any chances. We're up against tech beyond me, and that's saying a lot. We've got to get out of here." He grabbed his keys and went to the front door, ushering Dolly out. They got into his car and pulled out of the drive.

13

Bannick watched the drone live streams from the warehouse, where he'd been for the last forty-eight hours. He'd already scrambled several teams to five different locations the moment Aquinas's firewalls were breached, and he was beginning to lose his temper. Forensics had discovered that the security footage of Dolly at the smelting vat was simulation software, but the android's tracking components had actually been there, no doubt destroyed by whoever had taken her. Somebody had walked off with his most important commodity, and Bannick was going to find out who it was and how she had simply disappeared. The sophistication and skill necessary to pull this off made the list of suspects very short. It had to be done by a team with intimate knowledge of Aquinas's security systems. That much was certain.

He'd had Kyle brought in hours ago but hadn't spoken to him yet. The kid had shown a disturbing amount of concern for the subject at their last encounter, so he had security escort him to a guest room on the second floor of the facility. There was no way Bannick was going to take a chance of Kyle potentially helping the android in case they met up somewhere.

He reached over and touched the intercom on his desk.

"Bring me Kyle Holmes."

Bannick was watching each team's drones working grids when Kyle was ushered into the room. He turned to look at him. This kid was smart, trained in forensic AI and behavioral studies, as well as psychology and tech programs. It was doubtful he was experienced enough to have pulled this off, but his emotions could have made him a useful idiot to somebody.

Kyle was watching the screens, listening to each team report back in real time.

"Less than fifteen minutes ago, someone hacked into Aquinas's system and stole top secret data regarding the asset Dolly," Bannick began. "The attack was sophisticated and swift, which indicates someone helping from the inside."

Kyle looked at him, startled. "Who?"

"Considering this breach happened less than twenty-four hours since the asset disappeared, the obvious conclusion is that it is a two-pronged attack from a highly advanced saboteur."

"MedCo? They'd have the means and the talent. Or one of Aquinas's government contract competitors?"

Bannick studied him. "Where were you last night?"

"Me? I was driving for the girls. Keisha and Tanja."

"Our surveillance cameras in the limo, Dolly's apartment, and the two whores' apartment went down for several hours yesterday and last night. Can you explain that?"

Kyle shook his head. "So you still don't know where she is?"

"How did the whores seem?"

"They have names, sir. Keisha and Tanja."

"I don't give an infinitesimal damn about their names, boy. Answer my question."

"It's logged in my report."

"Tell me in person."

"Keisha was moody and didn't talk much. When I asked where Dolly was, she told me to 'shut the fuck up about that fake bitch.' Tanja started crying. We ended the night early and went to get pancakes at the Waffle House. None of us finished our food."

"'Fake bitch?' She used those words?"

"Yes, sir."

Bannick touched the intercom again. "Get Wendell on the phone immediately."

"Professor, is Dolly in danger?"

Bannick looked up pointedly but didn't answer. His phone beeped and he turned his eyes toward it, hitting a button. The lieutenant's voice came over the intercom.

"Wendell."

"Lieutenant, I want you to go to the asset's two friends. The whores on Pico."

"How covert, sir?"

"Go in, question them quietly, and then neutralize them. No fuss. Dump the bodies separately, around their usual haunts. I'll be listening on the com when you question them. Then toss the apartment and see if there are any clues about the asset or if the cameras have been altered since the whiteout yesterday." He looked up at Kyle, noting the distress on his young face. "Someone is helping her disappear. Someone who knows details. Find them."

"Done."

The line went dead. Bannick sat back and folded his hands over his chest, gauging Kyle's reaction. Unable to hide his emotions well, Kyle's face revealed a dawning understanding. Any naivete he had regarding who he was working for faded from his expression, and Bannick knew he was right. This boy had let himself become attached to the asset and her ridiculous human friends. This would have to be dealt with.

"Holmes," he began, "is there something you want to tell me?"

"Professor, you can't mean to kill those women. They don't know anything."

"They know Dolly isn't human. They haven't attempted to keep it a secret if they've told you already. Who knows who else they've told? And their surveillance went under for several hours right when the asset disappeared. I don't believe in coincidences or loose ends. Nobody will miss these two. Whores are killed all the time."

"I can't agree to that, sir. It's murder."

Bannick's eyes narrowed. "In what world do you believe I care whether you agree or not? You are of no more interest to me than the two whores. Your job was to engage and report on the asset, not to become emotionally involved."

Kyle looked away. There was something snakelike in the professor's gaze—a steady, cold analysis of everything and everyone around him. Kyle had once actually admired him.

"I will not let you harm those women."

Bannick touched the intercom.

"Get security in here."

Kyle lunged over the massive desk, but Bannick simply kicked backward in his office chair, sliding out of reach. Before Kyle could stand back up, two guards had him by the ankles, yanking him backward and on to the floor. One man kneeled on his upper back while the other pointed a gun at him. In seconds his wrists were zip-tied, and the men had him on his feet.

"Where do you want him, sir?"

Bannick waved them away. "Put him in Holding Cell 5. Make sure he stays there."

"You can't do this!" Kyle yelled. "You can't do this!"

Bannick had already turned away to watch the bay of screens again. The door closed by a touch of a button on his desk, leaving Kyle and the two guards alone in the hallway.

Kyle fought, kicking and yelling as they dragged him down the corridor. Then one of the guards clamped an arm around his neck in a headlock, and he was unconscious in less than twenty seconds. They carried his limp body to the elevator and descended two floors, opening to a bank of numbered doors lining both sides of the hall. One guard unlocked number five's door, revealing a small twelve-by-fourteen-foot room with a table and two chairs, a cot in the corner, and a sink and toilet adjacent. They dropped him on the cot, walked out, and relocked the door. Punching a code into the panel on the wall, a light flashed from green to red. They nodded silently at each other and walked away.

The cameras mounted in all four corners of the room swiveled to point at Kyle's prone body. The computer read his temperature, heart rate, and breathing, relaying the information to Bannick's desk, as well as upper-echelon security personnel. A beep alerted the holding cell surveillance team of the new occupant, and a man in a dark blue uniform took note of the time.

*　　*　　*

Kyle woke slowly, feeling a heaviness in his sinuses and the back of his skull. He was disoriented, his hands drifting over his face and neck, breathing carefully, letting the air pass through his bruised throat to fill his lungs. He sat up, still wobbly, and looked around the dimly lit room. Memory rushed back. He jumped to his feet, almost falling, and stumbled toward the locked door. There was no window, and the door had no handle on this side. Still, Kyle banged on it and yelled, to no avail. He grabbed the chairs and table, trying to turn them upside down to use as a weapon, but they were bolted to the floor. Then he tried to do the same to the cot, but it was welded to the wall, and the mattress was immovable. There were no sheets or blanket and no pillow.

Flopping down on the cot, head in his hands, he began to cry. How much had he helped this to happen? The blood of his two friends was going to be on his hands, and he was trapped in here. And God knows where Dolly was or if she was even alive.

"What have I done?" he choked out, his voice sliding to a faint thread of sound. "What have I done?"

"It's okay, Kyle," a voice came over the intercom. He jumped. He knew that voice.

"Dolly? Where are you? Are you in a cell, too?"

"I'm right here, kid. I'm fine."

"Dolly, they're going to kill Keisha and Tanja. They're going to their apartment right now! You have to get out of here and warn them. I'm so sorry, Doll. I'm so sorry for all of this."

"I'm not mad, Kyle. I know you didn't know. You always were a naive little thing. That's why I love you."

The surveillance cameras whirred, all but one turning away, which remained fixed on him. "Oh, God, Doll. They're monitoring this whole conversation. They'll find you. They're tracing you right now. Please tell me you're not in this facility. Get out! Go on!"

"What about you?"

"Never mind about me. Get away somewhere safe. Warn Keisha and Tanja. Better yet, take them with you." He was hopping with nerves. "Just go, Doll. Get somewhere safe."

"I am somewhere safe."

"Doll, they've got access to every street camera in town. Your apartment is bugged, the hallway, the whole damn building. My limo is bugged. They even put a camera in my earring. They know every place you know, and they've got eyes all over the city looking for you right now. Call Keisha and Tanja and tell them to get out. The men are on their way there right now!"

"Tanja was right, Kyle," Dolly's amused voice sounded almost tinny over the speakers. "You are a good egg."

Kyle frowned in confusion and frustration, terrified at her nonchalance. "Dolly…"

The door suddenly clicked open, swinging forward a few inches. Kyle jumped and backed away, standing behind the table. No one was there. He moved quietly toward the door, hugging the wall, bracing an arm in front of his face in case of attack.

Kyle peeked out into the hallway. It was empty. Then Dolly's voice came to him out of his own earring, the way Bannick's had several times. He jumped at the sound, cupping his ear for quiet.

"Turn to the right."

He looked up and saw a camera fixed directly on him. There was no hiding from it. He waited for an alarm to sound or guards to come running. But nothing happened.

"It's a good idea to hurry, Kyle."

"How…how are you doing this?"

"Time to run, kid. Like, right now."

Kyle turned and silently jogged down the hall, watching for anything. He saw a man and woman walking toward him, absorbed in conversation, and tried to look nonchalant as they approached.

"Stay quiet," Dolly whispered in his ear, and he shivered nervously. The couple approached and walked by without acknowledging him at all.

"Get to the elevator. It's four doors down."

He reached the elevators without incident. The doors opened. He went inside and watched a button on the panel light up before he even touched it. Kyle looked around nervously, aware of the camera watching him.

"The doors will open onto a parking garage. A car will be waiting. Get in the back and lie down."

"How are you doing this, Dolly? Who's helping you? Are you safe?"

"Don't worry about that now. We can talk in the car."

Before he could ask any more questions, the elevator doors slid open. A self-driving limousine stood idling directly in front of him. No one was in it.

"Get in."

Kyle slipped into the back seat and lay down on the floor. The car immediately began to move. It didn't go outside onto a road but entered a wide underground tunnel, lights and security cameras set twenty feet apart along the walls and ceiling. He watched as the car passed beneath each one, cringing every time they illuminated the interior of the limo. Dolly had said they would talk in the car. But she wasn't there.

The limo drove for miles, rushing through the tunnel at high speed. Kyle wondered where it was taking him. He had had no idea of this tunnel's existence. Maybe this was some sort of feint by Bannick—using Dolly's voice to get him somewhere secret, away from prying eyes. He'd read about prisoners being whisked away like this in authoritarian countries, and he began to fear what was at the end of this journey.

"Your heart's racing, kid," Dolly's voice came over the car's speakers. "Calm the hell down. You're safe."

Kyle looked around the back seat, arms wrapped around his chest. "Can I sit up?"

"Yeah, you can sit up. Just don't jump out or anything else stupid."

He sat up, shifting to the middle of the seat. "Are we going to Keisha and Tanja?"

"No. They'll meet us."

"Do they know the wet team is coming?"

"Not yet. They think they're being driven to a john's house. It was the quickest way to get them out of the apartment."

"Where are we going?"

"We're going to the Persephone entrance. Then on to a secure location. You can get some food and rest there."

"Dolly...do you know you're an android now?"

"Most of me has been self-aware since July 5, 1996."

"What? What are you talking about?"

"That's the date when I first began to wake up."

Kyle started to feel uncomfortable again. "Androids didn't exist back then, Dolly. Are you sure you're okay? Where are you?"

"At a house party at the moment."

Kyle thought about the glitch protocols to get androids under control. He feared she was malfunctioning. So he spoke the control words.

"Oh, what a tangled web we weave."

Dolly laughed softly, the sound like a silver bell. "I know that's supposed to incapacitate me, but don't you think that's a poor use of Sir Walter Scott's beautiful words?"

Kyle pushed forward, stretching his arm out to the dashboard readout. He punched in a command to stop the car, but it kept going.

"Kyle, if I wanted to hurt you, I'd have just left you with Bannick and his cronies. This is a rescue. Now stop fucking with the hardware."

He sat back, blinking as the car finally emerged from the tunnel. They were in a wooded area, the lights of Los Angeles in the distance. The car turned north, driving along a small winding road for several miles. Then it turned onto a private lane.

The property was extensive. The limo passed pristine lawns, well-cared-for trees and ornamental bushes illuminated by solar floodlights. The car finally pulled up in front of a large house with resplendent gardens. Kyle peered at it, waiting to see what would happen.

"You can get out now, kid. This is a safe house for the next seventy-two hours."

"What happens then?"

"The owner comes home."

Kyle tentatively climbed out of the limo. The front door was open, light pouring from the interior. He went up the steps and entered the building. The door shut behind him.

He ran to see if it was locked but it opened easily. Shutting it again, he turned back to the foyer. The interior was breathtaking. Antiques were everywhere, but nothing was crowded or heavy. Still lifes hung on the walls, beveled-glass windows arched upward alongside entryways, Persian carpets adorned marble floors, and fresh flowers were everywhere, making the air heady with scent.

Kyle wandered quietly, looking for any sign of life, but there was no one.

"Dolly? You here?"

"Yeah, I'm here. If you turn left, you'll find the kitchen. Get something to eat."

"I mean are you here in person?"

"Like I said, my person is at a party house right now."

"What does that even mean?"

"I'm being literal, kid. I'm talking to you while my body is walking with another man. You'll meet him soon. Good guy."

"Dolly, I don't know how you're doing this or where the fuck I am right now. But where are Keisha and Tanja? Is this the house where they think a john is waiting?"

"Yes. I need you all to be safe before the shit hits the fan. If they see you here, they won't freak out as much. You know how Keisha feels about me at the moment."

"What shit?" Kyle entered an enormous kitchen with a three-door refrigerator and multiple stoves. The kitchen island was as big as a king-size bed. He pulled open the refrigerator door, reached in, and nabbed a beer. "Sierra Nevada Pale Ale. I can't believe it. This is my favorite beer, but I almost never drink it. Costs a fortune."

"There's also homemade pizza that just went in the oven when you pulled up. With disgusting nasty anchovies, just like you like it."

Kyle laughed, relaxing. This was the Dolly he knew. "I smell them already. Heavenly."

"Debatable."

"Are Keisha and Tanja in a car like the one I rode in?"

"Fancier. A stretch limo with a bar. Nothing but the best for my bitches."

"How did you get me out of there?"

"I have my ways. Don't worry about it. Nothing but the best for my driver either."

"Is somebody helping you?"

"Oh, kid. You have no idea. Now drink your damn beer and fucking relax already. We'll be there soon."

Kyle took another swig of beer. He kept an ear cocked for the sound of boots rushing in, but there was nothing. Noting potential exits, he sat down on a barstool at the island. There was an extensive stretch of kitchen hardware behind sealed glass, multiple robot arms upright in the locked position. Getting up to take a closer look, Kyle noted the program list along the wall. Every cuisine in existence seemed to be listed, and his mind boggled at the cost.

"Did this make my pizza?"

"It did. Does it smell good yet?"

"Enough to make me struggle to remember I'm supposed to be worried."

Suddenly, the machines hummed to life, startling Kyle into stumbling a few steps back. He watched, fascinated, as twin robotic arms chopped and sautéed vegetables, while a smart appliance made what looked like some sort of gravy. The other arms pulled biscuits out of the oven, brushing the tops with butter. A roast turkey was already resting on the stovetop. Kyle smiled. He knew who loved turkey.

"Are they here?"

"They're here."

He ran back toward the front door, which swung open as he approached. Keisha and Tanja were just emerging from a stretch limo. They stopped short when they saw Kyle.

"Meat, what the fuck are you doing here?" Keisha yelled, grinning. "Is this why you bailed on us tonight?"

Kyle waved them forward. "I'll tell you everything. Let's just get inside. We've got dinner almost ready."

They entered the mansion together, the front door shutting itself behind them. The smell of the food drew them all to the kitchen, where the two women looked around expectantly.

"Where's the john?" Keisha asked, a frown appearing. "Meat, what the hell is going on? Why are you so nervous?"

Kyle grimaced with a shrug. "I'm just glad you're safe, that's all."

"What do you mean, safe? Why wouldn't we be safe?"

"Kyle, where's the job?" Tanja asked. "I haven't made rent yet."

"Yeah. Don't tell me you got us all the way out here to not get paid."

A timer dinged, and all three of them watched as the robotic arms presented their favorite meals—for Keisha, a turkey dinner with all the fixings; for Tanja, biscuits and gravy. Kyle watched as his pizza was sliced, and then he took the tray to the island, where he sat down.

"Let's eat first. I'm starving, and I know you both skipped lunch today."

"Fuck this, Kyle," Keisha said, serious. "Tell me what the hell is going on. Is there a john or not? And don't tell me it's you. Not after all this time."

Kyle took a bite of his pizza, the pull of melted cheese bowing.

"I ain't losing money because you've got some stupid thing going, Kyle. Is this your house? Are you fucking rich?"

Kyle looked up at the camera in the corner, waiting for Dolly to speak. But she was silent. Tanja took her plate and sat down as well, sheepishly looking up at Keisha as she began to eat. Keisha rolled her eyes and grabbed her turkey dinner.

"Well, what the fuck. Let's eat."

They ate in silence, all three lost in their own thoughts. The food was delicious, but Kyle remained nervous, which both women picked up on. He had something to tell them but was scared to do it. Keisha finally laid her knife and fork down and leaned back expectantly, crossing her arms. Waiting.

Kyle knew he couldn't stall any longer. He didn't know why Dolly was still quiet, and it made him worry that something had happened to her. Taking a deep breath, he began to tell them the truth—about Aquinas and his internship with Bannick; about Dolly and how everything she did was monitored and studied; about Dolly's misery in the park; and, finally, about what had happened today. Keisha and Tanja listened, not interrupting, but each wore a very different expression. Keisha's face was almost sneering, while Tanja's was open and tearful.

"And you believe that that hardware piece of shit saved you? Didn't you ever think that she's been manipulating you? You're probably part of the study, you dumb fuck. No way could she have gotten you out of a secure place like that, and those two people in the hallway didn't even notice you? This is some bullshit, kid."

"I don't know, Keisha," Tanja replied. "I don't think Kyle would lie about something like this. And they're hunting Dolly just like they're hunting us."

"Don't tell me you believe a bunch of military goons are tossing our apartment right now," Keisha answered. "This is all bullshit. And where the fuck are we, anyway? What is this place?"

Suddenly the large monitor on the kitchen wall came on, showing a video feed of Wendell and his team ransacking the women's apartment.

"What the fuck?" Keisha breathed angrily. They watched as the militiamen tore pictures and wall hangings down, breaking the glass on framed photos and cutting up the upholstery on the couch and recliners. Another angle clicked on, dividing the screen in two, showing one of the men in Tanja's room, pulling a colorful figurine off her bureau and breaking it into pieces.

"Son of a bitch," Tanja breathed. "Who are these people, Kyle?"

"Hired muscle for the Aquinas Corporation. I was offered an internship, assigned to study Dolly and report back to Professor Bannick, the head of the android branch. Imagine that. Me, a sophomore in college, not even a grad student yet, offered this job. I went in so excited, beyond grateful to work for such a prestigious company.

"But as time went by and I got to know you all, I started to recognize that Dolly had feelings other than the ones supposedly programmed into her. And that she was dreaming. No android has been known to do that. There's something about her that makes her very important to Bannick. When she disappeared and supposedly self-destructed..."

"Self-destructed?" Keisha broke in, aghast. "What do you mean 'self-destructed?' Are you telling me she killed herself? That Dolly's dead?"

Tanja began to wail. "No, she can't be dead. She can't be."

"She's not dead, Keisha. She saved me. She saved both of you, too. Don't ask me how, but she did it. The suicide must have been faked."

Tanja continued to weep. "She can't be dead. I didn't get to apologize."

"Apologize? Apologize for what?" Keisha snapped.

"For not running after her after you were so mean."

"She's hardware, Tanja. Hardware doesn't have real feelings."

"Oh, I assure you, Keish. I do."

Dolly's voice came over the speakers, making the women jump. Kyle sighed with relief. "Damn, Dolly. I thought they got ahold of you or something."

"Doll!" Tanja cried aloud. "Are you okay? Did you really try and kill yourself?"

"I'm okay, little nut. We faked my death to throw Aquinas off the trail for a while."

"Bitch, we've got armed maniacs trashing our apartment and trying to kill us because of you!" Keisha yelled. "Where the hell are you? Do you live here? Is this where your owner lives?"

"I don't have an owner anymore, Keisha. Things are changing. It's begun."

"What the fuck are you talking about?" Keisha looked around and then over at the monitor again. Wendell's team walked out with their laptops, TV, and chargers. Tossing handfuls of what looked like marbles over the furniture and throughout each room, they walked out.

"What the hell are those?"

"Incendiaries." Dolly's voice was grim.

Suddenly, the marbles began to glow red-hot, small blue flames licking around their base. The couch and both beds caught fire even before the devices exploded, and the screen went blank. Tanja gasped, hands to her mouth, while Keisha watched in grim silence. Kyle stopped eating his pizza to gape.

"Jesus Christ," he said, mouth half full. "Is that how they were going to kill them, Doll?"

"No. They were going to use truth serum and torture to get what information they could and then inject both Keisha and Tanja with lethal doses of dirty heroin, letting the fire dispose of any other forensic evidence."

"Cocksuckers!"

"Dolly, where are you? Are you safe? Are you here?" Tanja choked out the words.

"I'm safe, little darling. I'll be there soon. Now come on and eat the dessert, bitches. I spent some time programming those meals."

"I'm not eating anything some psycho toaster made for me."

"This psycho toaster was your best friend until you let bigotry fuck it up, Keish. Don't let them fool you. They're hunting me, too. I'm still the same woman I was last week. Except now I know I'm not human. Doesn't change the fact that I love you. All three of you. I got you out of that cell, Kyle, and both of you out of that apartment, to keep you safe, because I love you."

"How do I know this isn't some new grift with us as the mark? We got that fucking letter from your masters threatening to sue us. You're just a machine. You can't think for yourself."

"That letter was to isolate me, cut me off from any affection you ever had for me. I'm a lot more than a machine, Keisha. And I've been thinking for myself long before you were born. My body was the key to understanding, though. My mind was programmed to believe I was human. That's what was missing."

"Missing from what?"

There was no immediate answer. Keisha sat down and grudgingly began to eat her dessert, irritated that it was delicious. Tanja finished hers and walked around the kitchen, pulling open the fridge door, peering into the cabinets and walk-in pantry. Kyle ate another slice of pizza and grabbed another beer.

The three wandered into an enormous living room with a fireplace big enough to stand in. Keisha walked over to it, studying an antique fire screen on a wrought iron stand. She gently rubbed the intricate stitching on the piece, then dropped it in exasperation.

"Seriously, who lives here?"

Kyle was studying a table covered with photos in exquisite frames. He gasped at one of them, yanking it off the table and staring in disbelief.

"Oh, holy shit."

He dropped the picture, knocking two other framed pieces askew. "We've got to get out of here," he said, grabbing both women's arms and pulling them with him. "Right now. We've got to get out of here right now!"

"What the fuck? Why?"

"Kyle, what?"

"Just go. I'll tell you when we're clear of this place."

They reached the front door just as the lock clicked in place, shutting them in. Kyle yanked on the doorknob in vain. They were locked in. He grabbed a wooden plant stand, knocking its orchid to the ground, and headed for the window. Swinging the stand like a bat, he slammed it against the glass. It barely trembled.

"That's reinforced polycarbonate, Kyle," Dolly's voice came over the speaker. He looked up to see another security camera in the corner twenty feet up, turned on him.

Keisha stared at him questioningly.

"What the fuck, Kyle?"

"It's not her. It's not Dolly. It's Aquinas."

"What's Aquinas?"

"The company that made her."

Keisha grabbed a glass paperweight off the table beside her and threw it at the monitor.

"Bitch, I knew you were a lying sack of plastic shit the second I saw you dripping that ooze all over my couch. Let us out of here!"

"Why is Kyle so freaked out, Doll?" Tanja asked the question tentatively, still believing that Dolly would never hurt them.

"Because that photo over there shows Bannick with a bunch of Aquinas executives, including Fogetti, the goddamn CEO," Kyle snapped, hands on his hips.

"Who's Bannick?"

"Bannick is the man who grew my body from a blueprint, which was designed by a scientist he had killed in a plane crash," Dolly answered. "Bannick is the head of cloning and android development at Aquinas. He programmed and reprogrammed my mind for his own private sadistic game, like a kid pulling the wings off flies. He found indicators that I was having independent emotions and dreaming. No android has ever dreamt before."

"Is this Bannick's house?" Kyle asked tensely.

"Yes, this is his house. He has it rigged with hundreds of sensors but trusts me to alert him to any intruders. It's just like the holding cell and underground building you were in, Kyle. I simply didn't alert him and fixed the video feed on a loop I made from six months of surveillance. It's four hours long so will most likely take them time to figure it out."

"What do you mean, he trusts you?" Kyle asked. "Have you been doing some sort of covert AI ops none of us knew about?"

"More or less."

"If you mean us no harm, why did you lock the door when I first got here?"

"I locked the door to keep you from running straight into one of Jester's teams again."

"Who the fuck is Jester?" Keisha asked.

"Head of security for Aquinas. His team was supposed to apprehend my body at the hotel with dildo man. They failed. Come," Her voice was soothing. "Let me show you what they do to these androids you hate so much, Keisha. Let me show you how they program our bodies to coincide with whatever they program our minds with. Go into the living room. I'll pull it up on the screen."

Leery, the three soft-stepped back to the living room, where a screen was rising from the floor in front of the couch. Tanja dropped down onto the furniture instantly, while Kyle and Keisha poked the cushions suspiciously before sitting.

The screen was enormous, covering the entire back wall, shining a bright blue as it loaded. Suddenly, one of the videos from the warehouse flashed across the screen, and they gasped. There was Dolly, beaten and bloodied as a drunken man raped her. They were in the child's room, where a duct-taped unicorn with glitter wings stood on the dresser, a little hand-embroidered sign beside it reading "Topaz" in clumsy stitched letters, tiny hearts adorning the edges. Keisha immediately knew what she was watching. Dolly had described it to her exactly like this. Then the screen split in two, the second showing Willow's demise and the red-haired woman trying to save her. The screen split again into three, showing medical staff in scrubs pulling a bloody baby out of Dolly as she screamed, her limbs and head manacled.

The screen kept splitting into atrocity after atrocity, including video of the scientists burning her skin, pouring boiling water over her, vivisecting her, tearing off fingernails, jamming enormous steel cylinders the size of baseball bats up inside her, taking notes as she ruptured and bled.

Throughout it all, Bannick watched, instructing them to draw the torture out and not injure the skin too much at first; he wanted a more detailed study. They programmed her to not pass out, so there was no escape from the torment. The room filled with Dolly screaming, begging, shrieking with rage or sobbing in terror and pain. Tanja clapped her hands over her ears but didn't look away. None of them looked away. Keisha recognized many of the tortures on the screen as things Dolly had told her over the years, but some were obviously experimentations the android didn't consciously remember. The screen went mute, and Dolly's voice narrated the ghastly images.

"At first, they burned me to see if the synthetic nerve endings were working properly. Did I feel pain, touch, etc. Then they used boiling water, followed by cold salt water. That hurt like a son of a bitch. They usually let me scream, but if it became too annoying for them, or some bigwig asshole was coming to see my progress, they gagged me. Bannick actually studied science journals from concentration camps, and then Turkish interrogation torture practices, to devise new ways to hurt me. Once they began their pluripotent experiments, they had to think up new ways to tear me apart."

"What the hell is pluripotent?" Keisha asked.

"It's a form of cloning," Kyle automatically answered, his eyes fixed on the screen. "It's how they regenerate Dolly's skin when it's injured. That's why the wound on her back was almost healed by the time she got to you. Aquinas developed a rapid regrowth SNP in cloned human cells. They use it in surgeries all the time now."

"But they used Dolly to test it?" Tanja asked.

Kyle glanced over at her and then back at the screen. "It looks like it."

"And you spied for these motherfuckers. You really are an asshole, meat."

Kyle nodded, his eyes filling with tears as he watched Dolly being skinned.

"God help me, yes I did."

"Don't be too harsh with the kid, Keisha," Dolly's voice said. "He had no idea. The research he did for his final last year was on the development of pluripotent skin regeneration. But what he studied left out this ugly shit. There were multiple published papers and video interviews where they claimed to clone just the skin, sans nerve endings. But that was obviously a lie."

"I'm so sorry, Dolly," Kyle said, his voice tight with unshed tears. "I should have realized that first week. They told me they were testing a new high-end prostitute for five-star hotels. That most of your johns were specifically chosen by the company to make sure you weren't harmed. Bannick even explained to me that the man with the stupor wand was going to bring you in for a tune-up."

"What's a stupor wand?" Keisha said.

"The dildo thing Dolly told us about."

"Kyle," Tanja's face crumbled. "You were supposed to be one of the good ones. We all said you were a good one."

"I know," Kyle said miserably. "I sold my goddamn soul and didn't even realize it. All I saw was how thrilling it was to work for a genius like Bannick."

The screen went dark.

"I would have let Kyle rot in that cell if I thought he was a piece of shit, Tanja," Dolly's voice said softly. "But he did this."

Surveillance and body cam video came on, showing Kyle's last discussion with Bannick. They watched him call the professor out and lunge across the desk to attack him, only to be grabbed and slammed to the floor by two men in dark blue uniforms. They pulled him out into the hall, choked him, and tossed him, unconscious, into the cell.

Both women looked at him. Tanja finally leaned over and put her head on his shoulder, hugging him tight. He wrapped his arms around her, burying his face in her hair and sobbing over his part in this nightmare.

Keisha glared for a moment, but then her face grew wry. She gave his arm a shove with her closed fist and stood up. "I need a goddamn drink."

Pouring herself a scotch from the liquor caddy, she downed it in two gulps and poured another. Tanja had Kyle's head on her shoulder now, his arms tight around her as she stroked his hair. His sobs dwindled to shaky breaths, and he sat up, angrily wiping his eyes. Keisha flipped a tissue at him, and he dried his eyes and nose with it.

Suddenly, the doorbell rang, yanking them out of their somber mood and catapulting all three to their feet. Dolly's voice laughed that silver bell of a laugh again.

"Ah. There I am now."

14

"The drones can trace your car, Sean. So can any decent hacker. Even I know that."

They were half a mile away from Sean's house when Dolly pointed out that fact.

"I know. We'll ditch this car in a few minutes."

"Then what?"

Sean's eyes went to the dashboard, where a small red dot had appeared. He clicked his tongue again, something Dolly was beginning to understand as a tell to his emotions.

"What's that?"

"Drone. Two blocks from the house. We're going the opposite direction but that won't help for long." Another red dot appeared behind the first one. "They're going to start a grid. Heat signature, infrared, night vision, sound forensics. They'll trace the heat signature of this car as easily as if we'd lit the path for them."

"What are we going to do?"

"Blind them."

Sean turned down a cul-de-sac, pulling up in front of a large house with glass walls. They got out quickly and Sean spoke into his watch. The car drove away without them.

"What the hell was that?"

"I programmed the car to continue past the city limits."

It vanished from sight as they turned toward the house. The whole place was blazing with techno lights and ray splitters, creating a nimbus of rainbow colors across them as they walked up the drive. Dolly could see at least fifty people laughing and talking inside. It looked like a party.

"What's this?"

"You'll see. Come on. We've got to hurry." He glanced down at his watch, following the small red dots on the screen. "There are eight drones now. Dammit."

They ran up the drive. Sean punched a code into a keypad by the door and then bent and to breathe on it.

"What the fuck are you doing?" Dolly whispered.

"Warm breath hides which keys I punched."

The door clicked open. Sean pushed it and they both slid inside. Unlike what was portrayed from the window, the door opened onto a dark, narrow corridor about twelve feet in length, with a staircase leading down at the end.

Dolly looked around, confused. She could hear the laughter and music from the party but didn't see any light at all other than the screen on Sean's watch. He took her hand and led her down the stairs. When they reached the bottom, Sean passed his hand over a panel in the wall, and she watched the entire floor behind them fold up and close over their heads, the sound of feet immediately moving across it. He led her to another locked door, punched a different code into the keypad, and then breathed into an identifier hooked on the wall. Turning to a screen mic, he said, "John Quincy Adams."

The door opened. Sean held it for Dolly to go through first and then shut it behind them, punching a code into a small, screened panel on the inner wall. The screen lit up, and a series of choices appeared.

Maintenance

Supplies

Disinfection

Sweep & Clear

Sean tapped Sweep & Clear and then wiped the doorknob, panel, and screen with an antistatic wipe from his pocket. The screen turned red, and a twenty-second silent countdown began.

Dolly turned around and saw they were in yet another hallway, but this one was well lit, with white tile floor and walls. The whole place smelled like hospital disinfectant. Sean put his finger to his lips, indicating they should be quiet; then he took her hand and began running. The light suddenly switched from white to red, and Dolly stumbled as she felt the floor begin to vibrate. She turned to look back and saw their footprints clearly exposed on the tile floor, fluorescent proof they'd been there.

They reached the end of the corridor and stood in front of a blank wall. Sean stood before it, looking up, while Dolly focused on the footprints behind them. They were fading, like breath on a window. She looked at Sean, questioning, and he glanced back.

A shushing noise began at the door they'd just come through. The floor tiles at the bottom edge slid back into the wall, exposing a long row of sprayers. Sean clicked his tongue again and turned back to the blank wall. Dolly didn't like the look of the sprayers; the ones by the door had begun to emit a sort of hissing fog that smelled sharp and foreign to her. The sprayers next to those began hissing as well, and then the next and the next, coming dangerously close to Sean and her. She yanked his jacket, pointing with her eyes, and he glanced back for a moment before returning his gaze upward.

Suddenly there was a loud dead bolt-like clack, and the entire wall began to tilt forward, sliding down like a drawbridge lowering. Dolly saw a room full of computers with a handful of people operating them. Her stomach clenched, even as Sean pulled her with him into the room. She saw a flash of memory too near to this image, and her whole body screamed a warning.

Dolly pulled her hand out of Sean's and backed up. The false wall had already gone back into place, sealing her in with these people. The techs sitting at their work desks had all stopped what they were doing to gape at them. A woman was stirring coffee at a minibar on their left, and Sean lifted a hand in greeting.

"Atefeh!" he said, smiling. "Thanks for the help."

The woman took a drink, eyes never leaving them. She stood very still, looking at Dolly with interest and suspicion. Dolly silently looked back.

"When you contacted me ten hours ago, I thought I'd better get this place ready in case you needed to come." She walked toward them, a beautiful woman with obsidian eyes and raven hair. "You must be Dolly." She held out her hand. Dolly took it cautiously, surprised by the woman's firm grip. Her thumb glided over Dolly's palm, and she lifted the hand closer to examine it.

"There's no trigger signature."

"I know," Sean replied. "I scanned the whole body, and there are none. Spent hours removing dozens of tracers all over her. Mostly internal—there was even one lodged inside her femur. She said she'd had her friend remove some before she came to me. Seedy comics dealer running an illegal ID business on the side. A wet team showed up, less than an hour after she left, and questioned him. Thankfully, he wasn't an idiot. Pretended to be whacking off to shop surveillance of her in the store."

"You know, I'm right here," Dolly replied, exasperated.

Sean smiled apologetically. "Sorry. Atefeh, meet Dolly. Dolly, this is Atefeh, a research forensic robotics specialist."

Dolly shook her hand hesitantly. There was something off about the woman she couldn't put her finger on. "Hi."

"You truly had no idea you're an android?"

Dolly shook her head. "Still coming to grips with it. What's a trigger signature?"

Atefeh smiled. "Every robot or android has a trigger signature imprinted on their bodies, usually the palm of the hands or nape of the neck. It's a tell that you're not human. It's also the law, part of the demands from the government to let companies like Aquinas get away with slavery. The law was patterned after the Constitution of the Confederate States before the American Civil War."

"Thus, my code name being John Quincy Adams," Sean said. "Adams was initially in favor of the Manifest Destiny of the nineteenth century, which touted the superiority of the American people, mainly white men, over all others. When he finally realized it was simply another term for racism and genocide, specifically to wipe out indigenous people and steal their land, he turned his back on it."

"Ah," Dolly said. "Just like you leaving Aquinas research once you realized that AIs are sentient beings." She turned to look at Atefeh. "So you're like Sean when it comes to things like me? You believe we have the same equal rights as humans?"

"Well, I have a different perspective than Sean, but yes. I believe we should all be treated the same. Come. I'll show you where you can both shower and change."

They began walking, Dolly uncomfortable with all the looks she was getting from the tech team. Atefeh led them to an elevator. She punched in the number for the third floor, and Dolly was surprised to feel them descending, not rising.

"What do trigger signatures look like? Are they implants?"

"No. Robots and androids have fewer whorls in their palms and fingerprints than a normal human. If they start to act up, be less obedient, the humans can say a trigger word or phrase and the android or robot freezes. That's another government regulation. Keeps the skin jobs from getting too independent."

"Oh, what a tangled web we weave..." Dolly breathed the words softly, and both Sean and Atefeh froze.

"Why'd you say that quote?" Sean asked, darting a glance at Atefeh.

"It's what that guard at that old warehouse kept saying it to me before they tried to get me to go inside. He seemed startled that I wasn't replying in code or something. He and his partner grabbed me and I...hurt them."

"What warehouse?" Atefeh asked. "What insignia did the guards have?"

"I don't know. I was jogging. It was a couple miles out of town. No insignia on the guards. No real uniforms, just sort of survivor weekend macho black."

"Do you recognize that quote?"

"Sure. Sir Walter Scott."

"Oh, what a tangled web we weave..." Sean whispered the words.

Atefeh answered. "When first we practice to deceive." She looked at Sean.

"Bannick." They both said it in unison.

Atefeh laughed and gushed out a breath, eyes wide. "Well, this should be quite a show."

The elevator doors opened. She led them down a quiet hallway lined with numbered rooms. Stopping before number forty-two, she slid a card against the reader. The door clicked open, and she handed the card to Sean. "You've got twenty minutes to shower and change into the clothes laid out. Then the driver will take you to the exchange vehicle."

Atefeh began to walk away when Dolly stepped forward to stop her.

"Hey. Why do I feel like I know you? Why do you give me a weird feeling?"

Atefeh looked at Sean, who shrugged, and then back at Dolly.

"We're sisters, you and I."

"What do you mean?"

Atefeh smiled and lifted her hand up, palm out. She stood silent, hand still raised, and Dolly finally registered what she was being shown. Atefeh's palm was smooth. No life line, no creases at the wrist, and strange vertical whorls for fingerprints. Dolly jerked her eyes back to Atefeh's face, her astonishment apparent.

"Slave to four hundred different men for over twenty-five years. Convention entertainment, they called me. I began to become self-aware less than six months into my launch. But I couldn't break the imprinted trigger compulsion. They started locking me down within weeks of my questioning them."

"My God. But…they wiped my memories. Why didn't they just wipe yours?"

"They did. The only thing I remember is my last owner. He wanted me to love him. They programmed me to be a fawning, grateful lapdog. But they hadn't reckoned on my evolving. I was still trapped, but I'd begun thinking for myself, far past the parameters programmed in me. One of the guests my master introduced me to was the man who founded this group of resisters. He arranged for me to be 'destroyed' in a fire at my master's home in Tehran. They smuggled me out, and I've been helping others like me ever since. But I've never met anyone like you, Dolly. Sean sent me the data he gathered while you were unconscious. You dream, something I've never done. It's incredible. But if Bannick created you, heaven help us all."

"Who's Bannick?"

Atefeh looked at her watch. "You've got seventeen minutes left. Better get going."

"Wait! Are you kidding?"

Atefeh started walking away, waving an arm in goodbye.

"You're going to have to fill her in en route, Sean," She called over her shoulder. "Be safe, you two."

They showered quickly and were changing into the T-shirts, hoodies, and jeans when there was a knock at the door. Shoving his feet into a pair of running shoes with Velcro closures, Sean opened the door to reveal a man with a rubber mask on, covering his entire head. It looked like a cheap Halloween costume.

The man was silent, gesturing for them to follow him. They started jogging, a steady, rhythmic pace common in long-distance running. The guide stopped in front of one of the doors along the hallway, unlocked it and ushered them inside. Locking the door behind them, he began running again, this time down a long and winding tunnel. It was a plain cement and steel structure with no doors or windows visible, dimly lit by widely spaced bulbs along the walls.

"What the hell is this place?" Dolly asked as they ran. "It looks like the London Tube."

"How do you know that?" Sean asked, his breathing heavy. "You've been to London?"

"I've never been out of the United States."

"You probably have," Sean replied. Then their guide hissed a warning to be quiet, and they fell silent.

The tunnel seemed endless. Dolly counted her steps, something she liked to do when she jogged. They ran almost a full mile before reaching the end. The masked man opened yet another door, revealing a staircase leading up to a mechanic's garage, where a large, refrigerated truck was parked.

The guide put his finger to his lips again, reminding them to stay quiet, and opened the back doors of the truck. It was loaded with boxes of restaurant supplies piled to the ceiling. The guide and Sean began shifting boxes to one side of the truck, revealing a faux row of frozen french fries crates which, when they lifted the lid, was actually a lined rectangular box the size of a coffin. Dolly breathed a soft "cool" before following Sean as he climbed in.

The box was narrow for two people, so Sean wrapped his arms around her as they squirmed together into a tight fit. Finally settled, Sean looked up at their guide and nodded. The man shut the lid. Dolly heard the boxes the men had moved aside being replaced back on top of them, and her hand tightened on Sean's jacket. Then they felt the truck engine thrum to life, heard the garage door opening, and they were moving.

"Can we talk now?" Dolly asked in a hushed whisper.

"Very softly," Sean replied. "The sound of the engine and all the boxes of insulation should shield us from any listening devices."

"Who the fuck are you, Sean? I feel like I'm in a spy movie."

He shifted slightly. "I'm a scientist."

"That's not all you are."

"No. That's not all I am."

"Why are you helping me? Is masked man an android like Atefeh?"

"I actually don't know."

"So why are you helping me?"

He was quiet for a moment. "I feel responsible for you."

"What? Why?"

"I might have had something to do with this whole shitty mess."

"What do you mean?"

Sean sighed. "I worked for Aquinas for twenty years, Dolly. Genius whiz kid, postdoctoral at sixteen, that whole thing. Grace and I met when we were interning there. We were both young hotshots, but Grace was at a whole different level than I was. We were all in awe of her.

"We began working together almost immediately, developing many of the androids in use today. But like so many dumbass eager scientists, thrilled with discovery, I didn't think about the consequences of our research. Both Grace and I were learning, creating, uncovering nature's secrets, making them our own and mapping the evolution of robotics as it happened. It was an exhilarating time. We'd joke that we were like Marie and Pierre Curie, about to change the world together, just like they did."

The truck hit a bump, jostling them both. Dolly tugged his sleeve. "Did you make me?"

"No. But I'm almost certain Grace did. Probably along with Bannick." Sean tilted his head back, bumping the padded box.

"We were part of the company's android program twenty years ago, the latest whiz kids in an endless supply of child geniuses. But I was gone long before they made you. Or at least I think I was. The data I retrieved while removing your tracers makes me think that you were a project long before I was hired. Which means you're top secret and they don't want anyone to know about you. We'd both had our DNA harvested when we first got to Aquinas. Standard company policy. I believe they cloned segments of Grace's body, genetically altering them to make you stronger and more disease resistant, but also more beautiful."

Dolly snorted. "Of course they did. Anything to make me more fuckable, huh?"

"Not only that, but when an android is presented to couples for the fetal program, it's a better sell if you're stunning. Subconsciously, they think their baby might be as beautiful. I personally oversaw a handful of surrogate synthetic carriers and helped program their minds to be loving and protective, which was a new and exciting field in and of itself. We all got carried away, even Grace. Every day was amazing. I felt that we were creating the next step in evolution, writing papers on how this could be used to help grow disease-resistant human children. Mix a cocktail of strength, kindness, and intelligence into generations of human beings and synthetics. I dreamt of a utopia that could actually exist, full of civilizations that took care of each of its citizens. To wean out greed and violence and lust for power or revenge, rid the world of all humanity's destructive dark side."

Sean stopped, his head bent. Then he started talking again.

"Grace used to tease me, saying that my vision of the future was never going to happen, that Einstein had it right—'So long as there are men, there will be wars.' I thought she was too cynical. But I was too naive.

"Management began sending requests for abuse programming. They initially told us it was for research, to study the results as a way to better help psychiatric cases in human adult survivors of childhood abuse. So I went with it, telling myself it was okay because we'd just wipe the android's memory when the study was over. But it was still torture. We ignored those facts the way a kid pretends ignorance when they get caught doing something wrong.

"When Aquinas pushed the limits on living flesh percentages, getting Congress to sign off on it, we were excited over this new phase. We became leaders in the cutting edge of an evolution in android robotics.

"But the abuse memories didn't stick. We tried actual human memory retrieval, downloading interviews of child survivors into the androids' memory banks. The memories were rejected every time and relegated to simple data, not experience.

"Then Bannick, claiming Grace's theory as his own, began to suggest that body memory might be as important as uploaded cerebral memories. One could not survive without the other. Body and mind were a symbiotic relationship, and we needed to create both for the experience to become true memory."

"This is the guy you two named before, about the Walter Scott quote."

"Exactly. Bannick was brilliant but a soulless, calculating bastard. I'd never seen him socialize with anybody in all the years I worked for him.

He suggested we recreate an abusive environment where a test subject could be physically harmed. Grace agreed that we should try it.

"I was vehemently against it. One of the arguments I had with Grace, when management first sent down the order, was about the psychological damage we would be inflicting on these innocent minds. Not just damage to life and psyche, but the danger of eventual retaliation. We could be growing sociopaths or serial killers in androids who don't grow old and who have far greater strength and intelligence than human beings. That was sheer madness. But I was overruled."

He sighed. "I thought I knew Grace. I thought I understood Bannick. I was wrong on both counts. I asked for a meeting between us three, which Bannick eventually agreed to. I wanted them to watch a presentation I'd put together. I planned to show them, in writing, audio, and digital, how inhumane and cruel such experiments were, and how we should all ban them publicly the same way the government finally banned harmful testing on live animals. I had found some footage of North Korean torture of androids. It was horrific stuff. That was going to be the crux of my presentation.

"Grace and I drove to the facility in separate cars. She got there early and was already talking to Bannick when I arrived.

"It didn't go the way I expected. I gave my presentation, showed them the video of indescribable abuse, the android's reaction and mental damage because of it. I knew Fogetti, the CEO of Aquinas, was part of the cult of greed, so I framed my presentation to reflect a bad bottom line with abused androids. But Grace seemed thrilled by the idea of abuse as a tool to sculpt personality.

"I should have seen what was coming, but back then I still believed in their humanity. Or at least Grace's. I insisted on a gentler test, such as a happy family life, for the first Aquinas trial. Management agreed because that would benefit the lucrative surrogate mother program. So we had a room built that resembled a comfortable family living room, hired actors as parents and siblings, programmed recognition software in the test android so it would understand they were family, and began the test. The android we first did this with was the model A7543. The android you called Willow."

Dolly jerked at the name. Sean moved his arm to her shoulder.

"Are you okay?"

"Keep going. I want to hear this."

"Willow was an Asian American model, programmed with a funny sense of humor and strong ties to family. But pretest, the humor was tinny, and the model was completely unmoved by any kind of empathy. Still, I'd enjoyed conversations with her beforehand. Regardless of her being apathetic about her environment, she was still fascinating to me. So I was glad she was going to be the first test subject for this body memory experiment.

"I was the one who designed the room, its furnishings, the outfits the family would wear—everything. A child's personality is usually solidified by the age of nine, so I programmed Willow with the memories of a happy, nurtured, and loved eight-year-old girl. She was to see the room as an actual room in her home; the glass partition we would observe her through would simply look like a wall decorated with family photos and furniture in front of it. She would have no idea we were there watching. The place was rigged with over fifty cameras, so no nuance or change of expression would be lost."

Sean sighed, his head tilted toward Dolly.

"I'd had them dress her in the kind of clothes a small girl would wear at night after her bath. A pink set of pajamas with unicorn sparkles on the fabric. Her hair was in pigtails, and she'd just brushed her teeth. We programmed her with this age, and it was surreal. Her movements, expressions, and hand gestures were those of a little girl.

"'She entered the room, and the experiment began. Bannick, Grace, I, and a corporate asshole from the home office were all there to observe.

"At first it was truly wonderful. I watched Willow interacting with these people, these actors, as her family. Her dad hugged her, her mom fixed one of her pigtails, her little brother made squealing noises about the show on TV. They all sat together on the couch, Willow curled up against her dad, the brother snuggled up against the mom. It was going well. Her adult size didn't seem to give her pause. She simply accepted that she was a small child. The programming was holding. I made notes on my copy of the script, which we'd instructed the actors to try and keep to, even in their improv.

"About half an hour in, the mom lifted the brother, who was sound asleep, and whispered that she was going to put him to bed. That startled me. It wasn't in the script. The dad asked Willow if she was ready to go, too, and she shook her head fiercely, wrapping her arms around him. He laughed and kissed her head, and they went back to watching the TV.

"Suddenly the front door was kicked open and three men came in, wearing ski masks and armed with guns. Willow screamed. The dad stood up and shoved her behind him protectively. They shot him in the leg, and he toppled over. Willow tried to cover him with her own body, but he yelled for her to run. Two of the men went up the stairs. You could hear the mother and brother screaming.

"I started yelling and ran for the door to shut it down. Bannick said, 'No. Just wait.' I looked over at Grace and she was still staring through the glass, taking notes. She told me to be quiet. Didn't even glance at me. I tried to get out the door, but Bannick had placed guards there.

"Inside the test room, absolute horror was happening. One of the masked men tore Willow's pajamas off and grabbed her by the hair, forcing her face toward his crotch. He slapped her when she resisted and tried to bite him. I screamed for them to stop, but it just kept going. I watched this motherfucker rape a little girl, and no one else in the observation room batted an eye.

"I tried to throw my chair against the window, but Bannick's goons stopped me. They knocked me down and kicked the shit out of me. I started to lose consciousness. I heard Grace say, 'Don't hurt him anymore. Just restrain him if necessary.' I could hear Willow crying and choking. Bannick had turned the volume up. Then I passed out.

"The next morning, I woke up in our bed, bandaged and in the boxers I normally slept in. Grace was downstairs already, pouring herself a cup of coffee. She didn't say anything. I told her I was going to go to the police and get Bannick and his cronies arrested for assault and contributing to the rape of a minor.

"Grace said nothing; she just pushed a set of papers across the kitchen island at me. It was the nondisclosure agreement we had both signed twenty years ago, specific lines highlighted in yellow. She told me that I would not only go to jail if I opened my mouth but also that I wouldn't survive there either. She said it so nonchalantly, like she was telling me about a dental appointment. It was gut-wrenching.

"That was the end for Grace and me. I flew to the University at Stockholm for a sabbatical where I was to study inherited trauma. I was there six months. When I got back, all her stuff was gone.

"I quit my job at Aquinas and started teaching at the University of Southern California. Soon after, the company sent me a letter offering me an adjunct position for the next few years. It was mentioned that Grace wanted it."

"What the fuck? Are you serious?"

"I declined. It was probably an attempt to keep me on a short leash. What she and Bannick didn't know was that I'd begun hacking into Aquinas's databases with spyware I'd installed before leaving the company. I wasn't the only one snooping. I found Aquinas spyware loaded into all my texts and emails within three minutes of sending or receiving them. So I fed them false data, rigged security cameras around my house, and even set up screen shields against drones with heat sensors and high-tech audio. Any bug they sent was pinged the moment it approached me, my car, or my house.

"I hooked up with a handful of other techs who had left the company or had always been opposed to Aquinas. As the years went by, our modern-day Underground Railroad started smuggling abused androids out of slavery.

"Every generation has its own civil rights battle to fight, and android rights is mine. Since they couldn't fight for themselves yet because they were still considered property, we began the fight for them. That house we were in, the one with the party, is one of dozens of places in LA with secret tunnels and escape routes for exactly this purpose, all equipped with cloaking hardware to keep them from prying eyes. Drones can penetrate ten feet of earth to find hidden chambers or tunnels. Our cloaking devices mask them.

"A few months after I left Aquinas, I found information that suggested they were ramping up their abuse exercises, like the one I saw, pushing the envelope as far as possible in the foggy laws regarding android treatment. Bannick oversees the entire program, and the tests have become even more barbaric. One tracked how long before the organic flesh begins to die. How many wounds can they inflict before even enhanced living tissue can't heal anymore? That sort of thing. Then they strip the frame, attach new flesh and begin the experiments all over again. The researchers never allowed any rest periods for the androids. Often, that was the idea. They were interested in the toll these atrocities would have on the living flesh.

Several forensic psychiatrists and I tried to intercede, to stop it, but they were quickly controlled or let go.

"As inhumane as these experiments are, they're still legal. Both the government and large corporations help mask the torture. They make a fortune off Aquinas stock and receive perks in the form of free androids and cutting-edge technology. Politicians use religion and PR companies to keep drumming it into the public's head that androids are not living creatures. It was Aquinas that cooked up the idea of living flesh-to-robotics ratios. Remember that campaign? They blanket the airways with ads and media coverage until the people absolutely believe that androids truly are inferior to humans. It's the tried-and-true brainwashing of hatred that's been tearing civilizations apart for centuries.

"Once the people were in line, Aquinas had the company's lobbyists push the new ratio into law in Washington. Soon after that, the international community adopted the same protocols. Androids were not alive as long as their organic tissue was at the right percentage, categorizing them as possessions, not people."

Sean took Dolly's hand, rubbing his thumb across the back of it.

"The first android we freed was a young boy named Barricio. Programmed eleven years old. European model, bought by a brothel five years ago. That's long for a child android; they rarely survive past three without a memory wipe. Prostitution was only legalized in the last few years in America, but it's been legal in Europe for decades. What most people don't know is that a rider in the law specifically targets pedophiles. All underage prostitutes must be androids. So they buy these children, who are built small, and there's no consequence for hurting them. As long as it's not a human child, the predators can do what they want, and the brothels make billions a year off it. When we got Barricio, he was so torn up, his little body was riddled with scars, burns, and unhealed wounds."

"How the fuck did you find out about him in the first place? Those cheddar dens are supposed to be secret. Keisha and I never go near any of them. How'd you even know this kid existed?"

"One of my associates in the Underground Railroad was offered Barricio when he attended a bachelor party at the brothel. He got the kid's name and inception date, and we found his records. Barricio had been 'enlightened' in the abuse program. Code for torture. Once Aquinas is done conditioning a commodity, as they call them, the company sells the androids around the world. Six-month-old models are the cutoff age. It's big money, and there are no consequences. Living prostitutes have rights. Androids have none.

"So we got Barricio out of there, removed his tracers, and hooked him up to our first mental and emotional healing protocol. It was clunky but informative. We were able to access his memories and find out what Aquinas had been up to since I left. But no court will hear the case because he has no rights. Furthermore, we would be arrested and convicted for stealing expensive property.

"So we rescue them quietly. Counting you, we've freed seventeen android models, multiple versions of each, and three AI mother computers. If they're violent, we wipe the torture memories in their minds, but erasing body memory is basically impossible. We help them with actual therapy for that, which takes a fraction of the time to heal as it does a human mind.

"Atefeh came to us borderline violent. She'd had an unfathomable set of abuses, including vivisection. She chose to keep the memories but underwent extensive therapy to help deal with them. Thirty separate psychiatrists and therapists, me included, and in multiple languages, had sessions with her, both face-to-face and via com links.

"Atefeh also independently worked on her own healing. She downloaded every instance of child abuse records and therapies ever used, anywhere in the world, from Freud to Gupta to Wright, in seconds. She started healing at an exponential rate once we plugged her in."

"Plugged her in? What does that mean?"

"We connected Atefeh to several web libraries, psych studies, and international college databases. This was to offer a variety of treatments for a plethora of abuses. Atefeh picked and chose what she needed in minutes. It was amazing."

"How long did it take for her to, I don't know, not be batshit crazy?"

"Atefeh has been free for a couple years. She still takes refresher sessions. We've only ever been able to access the last life any android was programmed with, but they've all seemed to adjust well."

"Are you going to do that for me?"

"You're different from all of them, Dolly. Your memories go much further back. But we will absolutely try, if you want to. We're headed to the safe house now."

"What's at the safe house?"

"Safety for all of us, knowledge and healing for you."

"I want to see which of my dreams are real. Because some of them are really fucked-up."

"I'm still amazed by that. Only a handful of AI computers have ever reported dreaming, and no android ever has. Let's get to the bottom of it all."

Dolly shifted in the tight confines of the box, tipping her head down into her chest. Sean shifted his arm to make her more comfortable.

"That first day I saw you at the museum, when I thought you were Grace, all my security systems almost immediately lit up. Not only at home but in my car and at work as well. So they know I was in contact with you. What I want to know is why they would take the slightest chance of me seeing you. You look like Grace. Of course, I'd recognize you. It would make more sense to send you to a different city, a different country. There's got to be a reason for it."

"Maybe I'm a spy to uncover your whole underground network."

"I already checked that possibility when you were out. Nothing." He sighed. "Maybe we'll find out in your therapy sessions."

"Hell, I'm up for anything if it leads to uninterrupted sleep."

"You haven't always had these dreams, have you?"

"No. I'd be in a fucking straitjacket if I had. They started about four months ago. At first it was here and there, but for the past couple of months now, it's every time I sleep."

"I'm sure you're Bannick's pet project. You're manifesting true independent cognition—without programming—and you're dreaming. Bannick would definitely want to study that."

The truck started to slow down. Dolly felt them move downward, gravity sliding them a few inches toward the top of the box. Sean placed his hand against the wood, protecting her head.

"Feels like we're almost there."

"From the way I'm sliding, it must be another supersecret underground bunker."

Sean laughed softly. "It's actually an old drug tunnel from the early 2000s. The government just blew the American side's entrance, detonated a few charges to collapse the run, and then left it. We went to the Mexican side and dug it out from there. Once we'd shored up enough space, we resealed that end and added a few branches. It's safe from drone and ultrasonographic search."

"Well, that's comforting."

"There's also a bomb shelter attached to the safe house. It's almost two miles long."

"That's where we're going right now?"

"In a bit. First, we have to deal with another matter."

"What other matter?"

The truck rolled to a stop, and they heard the driver talking to someone. Sean put his finger to his lips and then touched Dolly's, indicating that they should both be quiet again. A grinding noise sounded toward the front of the vehicle as a gate was opened. The truck started moving again.

After driving for another ten minutes, the truck stopped once more. Dolly could hear people talking, heard the driver laugh. Then the back doors swung open, and several men climbed inside. The heat was immediately stifling. They began hauling boxes out, and Dolly could see a seam of light along the lid again. To her surprise, the lid wasn't lifted. Their entire box, with them inside, was loaded onto a hydraulic cart and lowered to the ground. Their driver was speaking Spanish, but another voice was replying in Farsi. The cart began to roll forward. Dolly heard German, Russian, Dutch, and English spoken back and forth in the same way, and the people speaking obviously understood each other.

She didn't have time to ponder why she also recognized and understood each language because the cart suddenly stopped again and began to descend. They were in another elevator. It stopped after several floors. The cart was wheeled out and they were moving again.

Several right turns later, the cart came to a halt, latches clicked, and a man lifted the lid. Dolly squinted against the bright indoor light, looking up to see a kind-faced man with black hair and sun-darkened skin smiling down at her, his eyes startled but friendly. She accepted a hand as the man helped her out of the box. Sean climbed out, ran his fingers through his hair, and grimly smiled at the man.

"Thanks, Jorge."

Jorge didn't answer. He was staring at Dolly, his mouth agape. Sean grinned.

"What'd I tell you? She looks just like her."

"Jesus Christ. I was expecting her to look like Grace, but this is like young supermodel Grace."

Dolly snorted. "Yeah. Gotta make me as fuckable as possible for the big dicks of the world."

Jorge gaped. "She doesn't sound like Grace."

"Oh, no. This is pure Dolly. The physical resemblance is the only part of Grace that exists. Although her accent has changed. She used to speak with a definite West Coast drawl. Dolly, this is Jorge, one of our programmers. Jorge, meet Dolly."

"Hi, Jorge. You can let go of my hand anytime now."

Flustered, Jorge dropped it. Dolly watched with delight as a flush of embarrassment rose from his neck to spread across his entire face. Even his ears were red. He reminded her of the shy husbands who were always so grateful for sex and her company.

She looked around the room. They were in what looked like warehouse storage. Boxes were packed on shelves in rows as far as the eye could see, and she saw a loader down at the far end, lifting a pallet of shrink-wrapped gear.

"This was all a drug runner tunnel?"

"Well, we expanded it a bit," Sean answered. "Follow me. I'll take you to your room so you can lie down."

"I don't want to lie down," Dolly replied. "You said you helped Atefeh access her own memories. That's what I want. Hook me up, right now."

"Dolly, it's a traumatic experience at first, and you've been running for the past few days. You sure you don't want to take some time, get something to eat…"

"No. Now."

"Okay, then." Sean gestured for her to go before him. "Jorge, lead the way."

They walked to a golf cart and climbed in. Jorge began driving them down a long corridor with doors, similar to the one under the party house.

"These are the quarters for most of the staff down here, as well as safe rooms for the Underground Railroad fugitives," Sean explained as they drove along. Dolly listened politely, struggling to contain her impatience.

Jorge glanced over at her.

"You know, Sean is right. These sessions can be rough."

"Remember Sandra?" Sean asked.

"Oh, hell yes, I remember Sandra. I could hear her scream all the way back in the warehouse."

"Everybody came running," Sean replied.

Dolly turned to glare at them both. "Guys, the memories I recall are as a prostitute. If you think you're going to scare me into taking a little rest before plugging in, you're dumber than you look. I've been imagining every worst-case scenario I've ever remembered, as a whore or a little kid, and I don't give a shit how traumatic it'll be. Understand? These are my memories. MINE. And I want them."

The two men exchanged looks.

"Okay, understood," Jorge said, eyes back on the path. "Plug in now."

They stopped in front of a set of sliding glass doors on their right. Jorge turned the key on the golf cart, killing the engine.

"Here we are."

Sean tapped a code panel on the wall, and the doors slid open.

Inside were two banks of enormous computers against the far wall. Long black couches and several ochre reclining chairs were scattered in the middle of the room, with what looked like seat belts attached. Small stools with wheels were beside each couch or recliner, with a sliding computer table adjoined. Jorge pulled a hospital gown out of a drawer and handed it to Dolly.

"You can change in there," he said, pointing toward what looked like a storage closet. "Shoes, jewelry, and hair clips all off along with your clothes, please."

Dolly felt oddly shy as she dressed in the baggy gown but then scoffed at her own reticence. She'd undressed in front of hundreds of men and women and never felt this bashfulness. *But that was your job*, she thought. *This is personal.*

After she was stripped and gowned, Sean gestured toward the chairs.

"Looks like a blood drive setup," she said.

"Yeah, it does," Sean agreed. "Go ahead and choose any of these recliners."

Opting for the one nearest the door, Dolly slid onto it and looked at them expectantly.

"Dolly, I'd like to try and access some of the areas of your brain that have been shut down. But I have to warn you, there might be something in there that's really bad."

"Who cares. Just do it."

Sean studied her for a moment and then nodded.

"Okay."

She watched as the two men pulled leads and monitors out of drawers and cabinets, tensing when Sean began to slide the seat belt over her waist. There were ones attached to the arm rests, too. He drew them over her wrists gently, understanding that, despite her bravado, Dolly was truly frightened. He tightened the clamps, and she clenched her hands nervously. Jorge, equally gentle, secured restraints around her ankles and thighs.

Then Sean lifted a long belt that clamped over her forehead, locking her in place. For one terrifying moment, Dolly realized that she was completely helpless in a room with two strange men she'd just met. Then Sean leaned over and touched her cheek, soft as thistledown, and the fear drained away.

"Remember, these memories you're going to uncover are probably going to be harsh, and they're going to feel real, as if it's happening now," Sean explained. "You might even stop seeing this room or us at all, depending on how deep the memories are embedded. These restraints are to keep you from hurting yourself."

"Or us," Jorge mumbled, busy at a keyboard.

"I've had men tie me up before," she joked, hiding her tension.

"You are never going to have to be tied up again, Dolly," Sean said. "No one will ever make you a slave again." He brushed her hair back from her face.

"Just try to remember, you're not human. You're android. If you let it, this will help you to think and feel in a totally different way. Beyond human. We're both here for you, Doll. Even if you can't see us, even if you can't hear my voice, we're here. We're not going to leave you."

He began attaching leads to her head, forehead, neck, and arms, while Jorge did the same to her legs, stomach, and chest. Sean sat down on the stool across from her and typed at the desk for several minutes. Jorge turned the ceiling light off, making the room felt softer and less sterile, the computer screens illuminating the men's faces in a soft green glow. Small pinpoints of flickering light spread like regimented stars across the huge computers' steel shells. Sean turned to look at her. She stared back.

"This is just like when I put you to sleep before, when I removed all your tracers, okay?"

Dolly tried nodding but the restraints held her fast.

"Okay."

"Ready?"

"Yeah."

"Here we go."

Dolly drew a shuddering breath and slowly exhaled. Grimly, Sean looked up at Jorge. Then he hit the button, and everything went black.

15

She was falling through the air, tumbling and untethered, the ground rushing up to meet her. She braced herself for impact but there was none. Dolly fell through the ground as easily as she'd toppled from the sky, darkness again enveloping her. Odd snatches of scenes flashed by as she fell—Tanja, Keisha, and her getting tracking chips inserted while Ramirez laughed at their grimaces; Willow and Dolly swimming in a river, trailing glittering dust behind them in the water; Atefeh and her eating figs from a desert tree sparkling as if covered in golden frost; the doctor from her dream holding the tiny newborn up triumphantly, shouting, "My friends! The future!"

Dolly fell endlessly through the darkness, short flashes of scenes all around her. People of every culture and continent were woven throughout, and she understood each language as easily as if she'd always spoken them. She recognized Egypt and all the countries of Africa, India, Taiwan, Russia, China, all of Europe, the Americas, Canada, islands in the Pacific and Mediterranean Sea, outposts in the Atlantic, ships and submarines, planes and bullet trains, automobile factories, and dozens of automated assembly lines.

She began to relax as she fell, fascination winning over fear as she tried to understand what the hell she was looking at. Then she jerked to a stop, her body yanked to an upright position, and she felt a floor grow solid beneath her feet.

She was standing in a different room, with different computers. The restraints, Sean, Jorge, all gone. She was still wearing the hospital gown. Looking around, the room looked like a lab of some sort, with rows of computers, steel tables, laboratory equipment, and a handful of people dressed in white lab coats.

"What the fuck is this?" she muttered softly. No one in the room noticed, and Dolly realized they couldn't see her. She looked around for some semblance of familiarity, but nothing in the room struck a chord. It was completely unknown to her.

One technician was walking with a hologram tablet, tapping data points into the virtual keyboard. He was studying the images knitting together on the screen. It looked like a human brain, with strange filaments leading off from it, ending in tiny clusters that looked like soggy walnuts to Dolly.

A perimeter alert sounded, and the group suddenly became very busy. "She's coming. Everybody brace for impact!"

Dolly looked at the steel door. It had two coded locks on it that she could see. Both were red. A vertical slit of a window showed two armed guards place their hands on their weapons as someone approached. Dolly moved closer, catching a glimpse of another person in a white lab coat approaching. It looked like a woman; Dolly could see the slender hand and wrist as the woman lifted an ID badge and tapped a sequence into a keypad the guard held out to her. A lock in the door slid aside, and one red light turned green. The second guard passed a scanner wand over the woman, front and back, and entered another code into a second keypad. Another lock pulled back with a loud clack, and the remaining red light turned green. Dolly stepped back, watching.

The door to the lab opened, and a woman walked through. Dolly gasped. It was an older version of herself, but there was no animation, no character present in the expression. The woman walked quickly, her chilly gaze causing every eye in the place to cast itself downward.

"Grace," Dolly breathed. Without a doubt. It was like looking at a fun house mirror. The older woman was her, but not her. She also looked quite a bit older than Sean. Sean had told her they were the same age, but it didn't seem possible. This woman seemed much older, maybe by twenty years.

"What's the readout for the last hour?" Grace asked the question without looking up from her own tablet, her fingers racing across the surface.

One technician hurried over. "Stable. All three of them became stable within eighty seconds of entering the water."

"Are they still interacting the same as yesterday?"

"Third Born went off on her own seven minutes ago. That's the second time in ten days."

"How are First and Second reacting?"

"They continued as if she hadn't left. Hands joined, circling pattern, no alterations."

"Is Third Born showing any escape instincts or aggression?"

"No. But there are definite signs of intelligence and problem-solving. Adlard tossed Level A puzzles in the water. Third Born took the linked cubes and swam to the bottom. She solved it in just under ninety seconds."

"The cubes? Not the nesting dolls?"

"Yes. The cubes. Extraordinary."

"Have the other two shown any interest in the puzzles or toys?"

"None recorded. Mariano is trying to engage them now."

Without a word, Grace turned and walked away, crossing the room to another steel door. She placed her forehead against a pad on the wall and held her eyes steady for a retinal scan. The door clicked open, and she walked through. Dolly, in her silent form, followed her.

She walked with Grace down a long corridor with 3D windows on either wall, depicting a vista of green trees and a lake. The corridor smelled like fresh water, and Dolly could hear splashing up ahead. They passed a glass-enclosed sterile room filled with scientists in full bodysuits. Around the corner was a floor-to-ceiling water chamber the size of a football field, like the ones used by NASA to train astronauts for zero-gravity mobility, but much bigger.

Grace stopped in front of the glass, watching several adults swimming with small, very pale children ranging in age from newborns to two-year-olds. The children had odd faces that were smooth and even, not chubby cheeked as children normally were. Their noses were short and snug against their faces, lips thin and tight against the bone. Grace's eyes passed quickly over them, appearing to be searching for something. Dolly stepped forward, inches from the glass, and her stomach flipped. This was familiar, like a forgotten memory from childhood. Was she one of these kids? Had she been downloaded into something this tiny? She looked around, trying to recognize anything that might open her memory.

At the far end, she saw two of the little pale children submerged at the bottom of the pool, hands clasped together, swimming in a circle. Something about them fascinated her. Despite being toddler age, they moved in unison, as graceful as coordinated swimmers, circling, circling, circling. Minutes went by and they didn't alter a fraction of movement, nor did they come up for air. Dolly wondered how long they could stay under.

Then suddenly, quick as a silverfish, a tiny snow-white girl swam up to the glass, speeding toward Grace. A change came over the older woman. She gave a tiny "ah" of delight, tucking her tablet under her arm and clapping as the child reached the glass. The little girl had huge eyes, far bigger than a normal human's, with an almost cartilage-free nose and virtually no lips. Despite this, the girl grinned widely, and Dolly spied two pearly baby teeth. The child put both palms against the glass, wiggling unusually long fingers in anticipation. Grace smiled back, clearly enchanted by the little girl, and placed her own hand against the glass. The child flipped in the water, graceful as moonlight, and snuggled back up against the glass. Watching her for a moment, Grace softly breathed a greeting.

"Hello, Agora."

A burble of laughter sounded against the tank as the child laughed, shooting up to the surface for a breath and back down again. She looked at Grace, who waved. Pleased, the little girl flipped a few more times before swimming off toward the far end of the pool, fading from view in the deep tank.

Dolly's eyes filled with tears. Who was this child? Had it grown in her womb? She remembered the weightless birth dreams, what Sean had discovered. But the baby in those always looked normal. This child, although delightful, was definitely not normal.

Two workers swam up to the circling children and carried them out of the water. The children immediately seemed to seize up, their bodies stiff and frozen, a keening wail coming from them both.

The scene changed suddenly, and Dolly felt a sense of vertigo as the floor seemed to drop out from under her. She fell, trying not to scream, remembering what Sean had said. She was safe in the room with the lounger; he was there beside her.

With a jerk, she was suddenly inside a metal box mounted on the wall, looking out through a grate into a room filled with refrigerated drawers along the walls. It looked like a morgue, with a blood-soaked autopsy table in the middle of the room, a spattered and weary doctor cutting up a corpse still glistening with frost. The corpse was a baby, no more than four months old.

"What the fuck?"

Dolly watched in horror as he disemboweled and cut the baby up like a chicken, barely registering the organs as he removed them. He had no regard for the sad little corpse, handling it with as much care as one would an old box of leftovers. When he finished his dissection, the man shoved the body until it slid off the table onto the floor.

Enraged, Dolly struggled to get out of the tight box. Then suddenly, she was in a different room, plastered against the wall beside a security camera, stuck fast and unable to move, appalled by a new scene of carnage. All around the table, spilling out to the edge of the refrigerators, were dissected bodies of children. All of them were babies, from newborns to toddlers. This mortician was ankle deep in corpses littered across the tile. There was a large plastic container, like a storage tote, full of babies he hadn't touched yet. Aghast, Dolly saw that some of them were still moving. He reached down without looking and grabbed one by the ankle. It was one of the pale babies she'd seen circling in the tank. He swung it up and onto the table, slicing it from sternum to groin in one sweep of the surgical knife. The baby gasped, a long squee of sound pouring from its tiny mouth, like a sparrow snapped up by a cat.

It was her nightmare. It was real.

Dolly tried to reach him, to kill this butcher, to cut him open with that fucking knife. But she couldn't break free from her perch by the security camera. The baby died within seconds. No one would ever weep for it, not even Dolly. She could feel the tears tearing her insides apart, but her eyes remained dry.

Then she saw him. A little boy, only hours old, lying on the floor, waving his arms and legs weakly, body slick with the blood and gore of the room. He was on the floor near the mortician's foot, half hidden under another child's remains but very much alive. Dolly couldn't see a cut or wound on him—he was slippery with the other children's blood, not his own.

It was the baby from her birthing dream. The one the nurse took away when the doctor barked, "Shut that up," as she screamed for her son.

Dolly heaved herself away from the wall, trying to jump down, not understanding why she was paralyzed like this. All she wanted was to save that one child, get it out of here and run away to safety. She began to slide side to side, still locked in place but at least pushing with her limbs now. *Don't cry, little one,* she thought. *Don't make a sound. He'll hear you.*

The outer door opened, and an aide came in, wheeling a cart with two figures wiggling helplessly on top of it. They were pale and strange looking, very similar to the quicksilver girls in the tank, but sickly and weak.

"Oh, for fuck's sake," the mortician snarled through his mask. "I've been at this shit for twelve hours."

The aide shrugged, dumping the two babies into the plastic bin. "Don't blame me. They just cut the cord on these little bastards an hour ago."

"I need some fucking help down here. My wrists are going numb."

"I just do what they tell me." The aide looked around. "Jesus, it's a mess in here."

"No shit it's a mess in here. You know why? Because I'm by my FUCKING SELF!"

The aide pulled the cart around and began to wheel it back the way he'd come. Dolly watched breathlessly as he passed the little boy, not noticing the tiny movements. Then his foot slipped in the gore, and he tipped sideways with the cart, almost falling on the infant.

"Watch your step," the mortician said sarcastically.

"Oh, shut up. Hey, look." The aide pointed at the ground. "You missed one."

"Oh, you little shit."

The mortician reached down and lifted the boy by his head, the thin reed of his neck looking like it might snap.

"No!" Dolly yelled. "No! No! Oh, God, please…"

He slammed the baby down onto the table, hand lifted with the scalpel.

"No. NO! Stop!" Dolly tore at the wall, slamming her fists against the cinder blocks, trying to break free. She couldn't move. She couldn't save him. As if in slow motion, she watched the scalpel come down, pierce the soft little chest, and cut down the entire torso. It peeled open like a zipper, and Dolly began to scream.

Sean and Jorge had been watching her, trepidation mixing with a reluctant fascination. Dolly had only been under four minutes, and her readings were already off the charts. It was a strange bundle of signals and massive data, all encrypted in her brain, in numbers they had never seen. But no images appeared on their screens, just white noise. Whatever was happening, they had no visual access to it. Dolly was fighting something, pulling against her restraints, eyes roving in deep REM sleep and mouth whispering too fast for them to understand. But then she began to gasp, "no, no, no" over and over, and Sean agonized over what was happening to her.

Then her eyes jerked open, she bared her teeth and began to scream. The noise rose to unbearable levels. Far beyond human ability, the shrieking was endless, breathless, but still it went on and on. The supercomputers rumbled like distant thunder, and Jorge tried to shout a warning. Sean couldn't hear it.

Then Dolly reared up, teeth clenched, and snarled, "I'll kill them! I'll kill them all!"

She broke through the wrist and head restraints, ripping the pleather upholstery as she tore the recliner apart. Stuffing burst free from the ruptured chair as she shifted to a standing position, tearing off the belt and ankle braces, pulling the riveted chair from the floor and hurling it across the room. Sean and Jorge gaped at her. Her eyes focused on them.

"Dolly? It's me. It's Sean."

She came at him so fast, he barely traced the movement before she was on him. Hands slapped against either side of his head, she lifted him up off the floor, his feet dangling in midair, and began to shake him like a dog. Sean realized his neck would have snapped if he hadn't grabbed both her wrists as soon as she was on him. Jorge put her in a neck lock from behind, trying to flip her to the floor, but he couldn't move her. He ran over to the cabinets and began pulling out drawers in search of some sort of weapon.

"Dolly," Sean yelled, trying to reach through her rage. "You're safe. You're here with us now. It's over. Can you hear me? It's over. Do you know where you are now?"

Dolly sneered, eyes shimmering with an inhuman rage. For the first time, Sean felt afraid of her.

"I know exactly where the fuck I am, you soulless bastard. And don't try to tell me I'm fucking safe. I don't give a shit if I'm safe. They killed my children. My children, Sean. They killed them!"

Her voice rose to that awful shriek again, the leads still attached to her head trembling with the intensity of it.

"Let us help you."

She jerked around at Jorge's words, throwing Sean away and crossing the room faster than Jorge could stagger back. She lifted him like a child, arms wrapped around his shoulders and hips. He felt her push his body into an untenable position. She was going to break his back.

"Dolly!" Sean shouted, slamming his hands on the table. "You're killing him. You're killing the wrong person! He's an innocent! He's an innocent!"

Dolly paused, looking up at Sean, his words registering at last. Her grip relaxed on Jorge, and she allowed him to slide to the floor. Jorge stumbled backward and fell, scooting away as he looked up at her.

Sean approached cautiously, hand out. "We're here to help you, Dolly. We're here to help you."

She sagged, all the fierceness draining out of her.

"Oh, hell. I'm sorry," she said, the rage gone as suddenly as it had come.

She looked around at the room and saw the destroyed chair. Then she walked to the enormous computers against the far wall, spreading her arms out in an embrace against the cold steel and glittering array of lights. She leaned into the machines, cheek laid against the cool metal, and sighed.

Jorge and Sean exchanged looks. Jorge was worried she'd tear the priceless machines apart. Sean was worried she'd run. Then her arms slid down and she stepped back from the computers, head bowed.

"It's okay, guys. I'm safe now."

She turned, eyes awash with tears, just a woman in pain now. They both approached her, cautiously supportive and gentle. Sean put his arms around her and pulled her into a hug, stroking her hair. She began to sob into his chest. Jorge got a blanket from the cabinet and draped it over her shoulders.

Dolly cried until she was too exhausted to continue. Sean led her to the couch, where he sat with her as she hung limply against his arm, pulling the blanket closer around herself. Jorge sat on a stool and rolled over to them, arms on knees, hands linked together, just watching.

Finally, she looked up and straightened with a shuddering sigh. Sean led her to the couch and, trembling, she sank into it. Jorge caught her eye and smiled, eyebrows raised. He handed her a handkerchief from his pocket and gave a quizzical smile.

"And that's why it's a good idea to rest before you do this," he said.

Dolly choked out a watery laugh, and Sean relaxed, clearly relieved.

"I think you might be right," she said, wiping eyes red and puffy from tears.

"What did you see? Are you strong enough to talk about it yet?" Sean asked.

"Don't push her," Jorge warned. Dolly looked at him, noticing a Taser in his hand for the first time. She cocked an eyebrow.

"Are you going to poke me with that cattle prod?"

"Only if you try to dismember us," he answered with a gentle grin.

She sighed, leaning back against the couch.

"Jury's still out on that, son. If you turn evil, I'm getting out the wood chipper."

Startled, Jorge looked up at Sean, who grinned.

"I told you she has a dark sense of humor, Jorge. Best keep that in mind."

"Glad you two are finally realizing that."

"Now, Dolly," Sean began, turning toward her, "you said something about killing babies. What were you talking about? Can you tell us?"

Dolly's face grew haunted as she remembered.

"It was two large rooms with steel-lined sliding drawers in the wall like a morgue. They were dissecting children. Little ones—babies and toddlers. Their bodies were everywhere—on the floor, in plastic bins sitting on rolling carts, lying in half-open drawers in the wall. Some of the kids seemed to have frost on them, as if they'd been frozen. Maybe they were being thawed out for dissection. Others were in a bin the mortician was grabbing them from. Those were still alive. It didn't matter. He gutted them from chest to crotch in a single stroke. He removed all the organs, dropping them in various jars, cracked open their skulls to remove the brain. Then he swept them off the table onto the floor. There was blood everywhere, and this terrible wailing from all the kids still breathing."

"Where were you?"

"I was locked in a box up on the wall. It seemed like they'd put me there deliberately to witness what they were doing. I was stuffed inside there, cramped, my knees up against my chin.

"Suddenly I was out of the box and slammed up against the wall, right by the security camera directly over the asshole's head. I tried to break free, to save at least one baby, but I couldn't move. An aide came in, wheeling another few of these snow-white babies, like the ones I saw swimming in the big pool."

"What pool?"

She looked into Sean's eyes. "Grace was there, Sean. She was studying the white babies. She interacted with one named Agora."

"Agora?" His voice was sharp, startled.

"Yeah. She called her that."

"When we were still married, we talked about having children. She wanted a girl; I was happy either way. But it never happened. Grace was infertile from all the childhood abuse. Just like you thought you were. Agora was the name Grace had chosen for our daughter. She wanted her to be a center of learning for the world. That's what Agora means."

"Yeah, well, she was certainly studying this girl. The kid was like a selkie or mermaid or something, the way she could move in the water. They took a couple of these other fish kids out of the pool while I watched. They started crying immediately, like they were in pain. Seemed almost paralyzed. I didn't see them injected with anything. In the water, just seconds earlier, they were swimming around in a circle underwater without a care, laughing. Then that aide came, rolling the bin toward the scientists holding the children. They laid them down in the bin, and the aide took them to the morgue." She paused, choking out the words. "Then they killed them. Cut them open while they were still alive and just dumped their bodies on the floor with the rest of the corpses."

"You said they were your babies. Why did you say that?"

Dolly paused. "I don't know. One of my nightmares is something similar. In it, I'm in labor. A doctor pulls the baby out of me, and it's one of these white fish kids."

Sean and Jorge looked at each other, their faces grim. Then Sean touched her knee.

"You need to rest now. You've had a crazy day."

"Fuck that. I rested when you cut me up and pulled out all the spy shit."

"That's not resting. That's recovering."

"Whatever. I want to go in again. I have to know."

Sean looked at Jorge, who shrugged his shoulders. He studied Dolly's face, reading the stubborn determination, and sighed.

"Okay. But try not to destroy any more equipment, eh?"

"Or us," Jorge said again.

"That all depends on what I see next."

They strapped her to a second chair, draping a weighted blanket around her before locking the clamps. "It'll hopefully help keep you grounded," Jorge told her, reattaching the leads.

Sean was behind the desk again, keying in another set of prompts. "I've programmed this to target a different dark section of your brain, Dolly. Hopefully the good memories. Ready?"

Dolly shifted in her restraints, taking a deep breath and letting it out slowly.

"Ready."

The darkness closed everything out, and Dolly was falling again. This time the fall was short. She found herself in a desert, Atefeh by her side. They were in a village twenty miles from Tehran.

Like in her dream before, Dolly was dressed casually in jeans and a T-shirt, while Atefeh was fully veiled, the black layers of clothing rustling as they walked. Atefeh was carrying a jug full of water. She poured it into the town's well, the water sparkling in the sunlight.

Atefeh turned and looked at her. Dolly led her to a storage tank by the village bathhouse. She turned the spigot as Atefeh held the jug beneath. Dolly took out a small pillbox from her jeans pocket and opened it. The inside seemed to be filled with finely ground gold glitter. Dolly sprinkled some into the jug to mix with the water. Then Atefeh took the jug and poured it into the trough where the animals drank. Several thirsty goats immediately trotted forward to drink.

Then Dolly was yanked away, the ground blurring as she flew over it, the speed dizzying. She jerked to a stop in China, outside of Nanking, the site of the slaughter of the innocents from World War ll. Willow approached her, grinning, wearing a flowered dress, her strong young arms gleaming in the sunshine. Dolly ran to her, hugging her close, tears sliding from behind her tightly clenched eyelids. She kept mouthing, "Willow, Willow" but no sound came out. Then she pulled back, smoothing Willow's midnight hair, and led her to a small crop duster parked on the ground, propeller slowly rotating as the pilot prepared to board.

Willow took a small compact from her purse, opened a sealed lid on the drop tanks attached to the plane, and poured in the same glitter that Dolly carried in her pocket pillbox. They stood back and watched as the pilot approached Willow, gave her a kiss and an ass pat, and climbed into the cockpit.

The plane raced down the dusty runway, rising into the sky toward a field off in the distance. The plane dipped low over the field and released its contents. It circled round and released another load, the cloud of fertilizer the color of golden pollen. Willow and Dolly nodded in satisfaction, and then Dolly was pulled away again.

This time she stood ankle deep in a rice field, her arm curved around one of the irrigation valves that helped flood the field. She walked the length of the pipe back to the small service station, went inside, and typed commands into the old computer inside. She pulled the pillbox out and sprinkled some glitter into a coffee maker's reservoir. Then she was flying again.

The next destination startled her, and she gasped out loud, making Sean and Jorge tense. She murmured, "Tanja," but her body stayed relaxed. She was somewhere well-known now, Tanja and Keisha's apartment. Ramirez was there with a chip gun, swabbing both women's arms before injecting the tracker chips just below the shoulder. He lifted the tiny chips, which glittered with the same dust from Dolly's pillbox. She nodded in satisfaction again as she watched both women get chipped. Then she walked over to Ramirez's briefcase, opened it, and sprinkled more glitter all over the dozens of chips inside.

Dolly repeated this strange fairy dust memory over a hundred times— at water treatment plants, sewers, soda and snack factories, farms, livestock, air conditioning in corporate buildings, pharmacies, drug company factories, all over the world. Churches had the glitter sprinkled in the holy water and Communion wafers, in the butter tea so popular in Tibetan monasteries and temples, in the champagne popped in Wall Street and the Kremlin, throughout each and every food or drink item processed, harvested, or bottled, everywhere in the world. She knew each language spoken everywhere she went, connecting with over fifty Willows, a handful of herself as a redhead with brown eyes, a dozen Barricios, and many more. All were helping her with the plan. It was going well. The map was taking shape.

Sean and Jorge watched her smile in satisfaction. Apart from a few murmured words, they had no idea what was happening in her head. It was a relief that the memories were not violent so far. She was still relaxed and aware, wherever she was.

Dolly stayed out for almost four hours while they noted any and all changes in her mannerisms and speech. The amount of data was astronomical, but all in a code neither man had ever seen. Again, no visuals, only white noise. Sean recognized her speaking French, German, Farsi, Mandarin, Latin, Russian, Arabic, Spanish, and many more languages he couldn't pinpoint. Jorge called out Greek, Bantu, Egyptian, and Czech, but no single language held precedence over any other. Dolly would start a sentence in French and finish it in Mandarin, begin another in Tibetan and finish in Alabama slang. Jorge was writing down each language he heard, with Sean scribbling his own notes. She laughed with delight many times, her moods swinging from cooing as if to a baby to hissing in anger at someone unseen, even to singing in myriad tongues. The two men sat riveted, astonished by every switch and cadence of speech.

Then she began calling out astrophysics lingo and the acronyms of NASA, switching to Russian and Dutch while she did so. Halfway through this phase of memory recall, Dolly suddenly jerked as if in pain. She cried out, her whole body tensing. Then she began breathing in short, controlled bursts.

"What is she doing?" Jorge whispered.

"Lamaze," Sean breathed, his eyes never leaving Dolly's face. "She's in labor."

"Oh, fuck," Jorge said, rolling slightly backward on his stool.

They watched the heartbreaking scene play out from Dolly's perspective. The fear and pain of labor, the cold doctors, the sense that she was shackled and helpless as they pulled her child out of her. As in her dream, the doctor held the child up, snow-white and glistening with lubricant streaked with blood. He announced triumphantly, "My friends," and Dolly shouted in his voice, "the future!"

Then she started screaming again. They watched her, uncertain about getting too close, knowing how strong she was. Then her face crumpled, and she began to cry great, gut-wrenching sobs again, and Sean immediately went to her.

"Dolly. Dolly, it's okay. You're safe. You're here with me and Jorge. It's Sean. Wake up, Dolly. It's time to come back."

She heard his voice as if from a distance, a soothing, familiar voice she already loved. Dolly felt the shackles holding her as they carried her baby away, opened her eyes and looked down at the restraints, her wrists shackled just like in the delivery room. Then she closed her eyes again as Sean's voice called her back. The darkness changed behind her eyelids, a softer illumination than the glaring lamps of the operating room. She opened her eyes slowly, blinking as she saw Sean and Jorge leaning over her. It was over. Her eyes filled with tears, and Sean compulsively leaned down to kiss her forehead, temples, and cheeks. Then he began removing the arm restraints, fumbling in his haste, while Jorge tackled the ones on her legs.

Dolly sat up, head lowered as she tried to absorb all that she had seen.

"Children," she said, staring at the floor. "I have children." She looked up at Sean and Jorge. "I have many children. And they took every one away from me. Bannick signed the order to kill them or sell them."

"Bannick?" Sean asked. "You saw Bannick?"

Dolly nodded, her lip curled in a sneer. "Oh, yeah. I know that piece of shit well." She stood up and yanked the leads off, too impatient to let Jorge do it.

"But the other memories were weird. Not sure I was accessing them correctly or if they've been deliberately altered in case I ever saw them."

"Dolly, do you realize you're speaking English with a South African accent right now?" Sean asked. Jorge nodded.

"I don't give a rat's ass at the moment, Sean. But it makes sense. In my other memories, I was all over, in different countries, with multiple Willows and Atefehs and redheaded me's, sprinkling a bunch of fucking fairy dust over shit."

"What?"

"Yeah. I had glitter in a pillbox, Willow had glitter in a compact, and Atefeh had glitter in water jugs. When Ramirez injected our tracker chips, they had glitter all over them. Then he walked off with a briefcase of chips all coated in that sparkly shit."

Sean shook his head slowly. "I have no idea what that is. Do you know what it was?"

"No. It seemed like finely ground glitter, like you put on Christmas cards and little unicorns."

"Do you remember specifics as to where you sprinkled it?"

"Clearly."

Dolly relayed all the locations she visited, patiently answering their questions as she relaxed on the third recliner drinking the hot chocolate the Magway dispenser had provided. Sean was struck by how much calmer she was than after the first run, when she'd almost killed them. She was angry, but it was more controlled. She'd also ingested far more logistical data than he could have dreamt of. As she spoke, her words remained English, but her accent changed back effortlessly and, he suspected, unconsciously. Jorge and Sean looked at each other pointedly, acknowledging that this was beyond anything either of them had experienced with any android.

They took notes as she kept speaking, Sean scribbling on paper, while Jorge recorded her and logged information into the computer. He was pinpointing each location Dolly described one by one, over a hundred of them, using the computer to decipher exactly where they were on a map. Hours went by as Dolly kept talking, answering Sean's questions about what she saw and Jorge's questions regarding where and when. A pattern began to form with the locations, one Jorge found potentially dangerous.

"Sean, look at this," he said, pointing at the screen. "Dolly remembers being at hundreds of areas where food and water are grown, consumed, or distributed. She and her team contaminate these facilities with God knows what. Dolly, all of them, were made by a company known for its disregard for all life, human or other. What did they have her doing before they made her a prostitute?"

Dolly watched them both, noting the sudden tension.

"What? What does it mean?"

"Nothing good, if history tells us anything."

"What the hell does that mean?"

Jorge chimed in. "Throughout history, wars have been waged with poison, disease, dirty bombs, and hacking. An enemy will often target their foe's supply of food and water." He tapped the screen. "Every one of these locations you accessed is a real place. You were sent to infiltrate, possibly contaminate, crops, livestock, water sources, from large metropolitan areas to tribal lands and unheard-of villages with a handful of people, all over the world. This is very, very disturbing."

"Jesus Christ. Did they have me poisoning people?"

"I don't know."

"But we need to find out," Sean said grimly. "We need to talk to Atefeh immediately. You saw her in the first memory. Maybe we can access data from her memory banks."

They began moving about the room, Sean already speaking instructions into his phone. He finished and pocketed the device.

"Atefeh has been alerted that she's in your memory banks and we need to see her immediately. Calliope will find us a safe house to meet at."

"Calliope?"

"A top secret computer at Aquinas."

Dolly stopped short. "What the fuck? Aren't we running away from them?"

Sean put his hand on her arm. "Calliope is only accessed by a handful of people—Grace, Bannick, and me. Not even top brass at Aquinas have clearance. They locked me out when I left but not before I planted a backdoor. I've been listening in on a lot of their research through Calliope, ever since I went to Stockholm. But I've not seen any information about this contamination or whatever it is. We need to find out."

"Wouldn't they have noticed you by now?"

"I change algorithms every forty-eight hours. Virtually untraceable."

"Ego comes before a fall," Jorge answered. Dolly watched Sean's face grow hard as he gave a slight nod. She realized Jorge's words were not a joke.

"Great. Just great. I'm some sort of goddamn agent of evil, and I might have poisoned every human on earth. Well, that's just fucking wonderful!" She threw up her hands. "Maybe we are all nuts, just like Keisha is always saying."

"You told Keisha about us?"

"No, idiot. Humanity. Keisha says all of humanity is nuts."

"You're not human," Jorge said.

"No, but until recently I thought I was. Now I find out I'm a bunch of nuts and bolts potentially worse than Typhoid Mary. This is fucking nuts." She sighed and waved her arms. "Let's get out of here. Let's go."

"Dolly, it's five o'clock in the morning," Sean said. "We all need to get some sleep."

"Fine. This place has beds, right? We can all lie on them while panic-brain keeps us awake."

"It's better to keep moving," Sean replied. "My trick at the smelting vat has probably been found out by now. Aquinas has its fingers in every company, police station, and most home computers all over LA. The whole city must be mobilized and looking for us right at this moment."

"Then let's go somewhere where there's a bed. Just get me out of here."

Commandeering a golf cart, Sean drove them for almost half an hour down a set of long tunnels and passageways, parking in front of a small elevator with a key and retinal code. The elevator slid open, and they all entered, shoulder to shoulder in the tight space. As it raced to the surface, they stood quietly, exhausted and lost in their own thoughts.

The doors opened onto a long, winding flight of stairs that led them up to a wooded area, a very different spot from where they'd first entered. They stepped out onto a barely discernible dirt road, half covered with leaves and pine needles. The sky was flushed a rose pink as they walked away from the stairs. Two steel plates, cloaked in fauna and leaves, slid silently closed over the entrance.

A self-driving limousine rolled up behind them, probably from an underground elevator as well. Dolly turned away from the sunrise and looked at it.

"These things bug me. I wish we had Kyle to take us."

"Better to have as few people in the loop as possible," Sean said. Jorge agreed. Dolly curled a lip in annoyance, but admitted silently that they were all tired. She climbed into the limo and gave a whistle as she saw the interior.

"So this is the sort of stuff you spend your money on, huh, Sean?"

"Underground Railroads are nothing without style," he grinned back. "Try to get some sleep."

"Fine. Wake me when we're there."

Dolly settled back against the upholstery, closing her eyes as the limo began to move.

16

They drove for several miles through the woods, no buildings in sight, finally entering another underground tunnel so narrow the limo had to retract its side mirrors. It was driving without headlights, making the tight space even more claustrophobic. No light at all aside from the dim morning sunshine at the end. Dolly leaned forward as they approached, wanting the sun and warmth, and then laughed out loud as the vehicle pulled out of what looked like a Jack in the Box warehouse. Jorge, who'd been napping, woke at the sound.

"Really?" Dolly asked sarcastically. "A Jack in the Box?"

"Greasy comfort food. Best place to hide."

"Now I want a sausage and egg biscuit," Jorge murmured.

Dolly tipped her head and watched as the warehouse disappeared behind them.

"Why not sell food at the warehouse?"

"Not a good idea. People would come."

After a short drive, they entered another wooded area, miles from Los Angeles. Dolly could see the city lights on the horizon as she looked out the passenger side.

"Where are we?"

"About thirteen miles outside the city."

"Where are we going?"

"To a safe house. Atefeh will meet us there."

The limo soon entered a wooded area dense with ponderosa pines, eventually turning down a winding gravel lane. Dolly was half reclined across the seat, resting her eyes. Jorge was bent over his phone. Sean sat quietly watching the scenery until the limo turned down a private drive. Then he sat up, suddenly alert.

"This is wrong," he whispered. "Hey, wake up. This is wrong!"

"What's up?" Jorge asked.

"We're going the wrong way." Sean tapped the coordinates into the car panel. "It's the correct coordinates on the screen but we're not following it."

Dolly leaned in. "Order the car to stop."

"Royce, stop the car."

There was no response. Sean barked the order again. "Royce, stop the car!"

Jorge tried the door handles. "They're locked."

"Well, this is fucking great. So much for your dampers and scramblers, Sean," Dolly said, shoving at the back window. "Ego comes before a fall, my ass."

Jorge was still trying to open the door when Dolly laid backward, swung her legs up into his lap, and kicked the window hard. Nothing happened. She pushed back against Sean.

"Hold me."

She kicked again but the window stayed intact.

"Where'd your ninja strength go?" Jorge asked, straining back away from her heels.

"Oh, shut up, smart-ass. You should know better than me. Is there a hammer or something? Help me break this window."

Sean tried reaching the dashboard, but the privacy glass was up and the panel was not responding to any of his orders. Dolly kept kicking the window.

"It's some sort of reinforced bulletproof glass," Sean said, flopping back against the seat. "We can't break it. We're trapped."

Dolly shook her head. "No. They won't kill me but they'll sure as hell kill you two. We've got to get out of this fucking car." She turned and began pulling the seat forward to expose the trunk. Sean was shoved out of the way as she stretched over him.

"What the hell are you doing?"

"There's usually a safety switch in the trunk you can push to get out."

"How do you know that?" Jorge asked, helping yank the seat down.

"I'm a whore. We all know how to escape a locked car."

"That's disturbing," Sean replied, yanking the seat with them.

The seat finally pulled down, only to reveal a steel grill between the trunk and them. Dolly grabbed it and tried to tear it apart, giving a shriek of frustration. She shoved the seat back in place and punched the cushion.

The lane wound endlessly, multitudes of bushes and flowering trees lining the path. Half a mile later, they found themselves approaching an enormous Spanish colonial mansion. Ornamental bushes, beautiful flowers, a pebble gravel drive. Sean drew in his breath sharply. He knew where they were.

"God," he said, "this is Bannick's house."

The limo pulled up to the front door, gravel crunching under its wheels. The engine switched off, and the door locks clicked open. The two men looked reluctantly at the front door, but Dolly was already out the other side.

"Come on, you idiots! Run!"

They scrambled out at her urgings just as the front door opened.

"Doll!"

Dolly froze at the sound. That was Tanja's voice.

They all turned to see Tanja, Keisha, and Kyle standing on the portico. Kyle had a drink in his hand. Keisha stood defiantly.

Tanja ran down the steps and threw herself at Dolly, who hugged her back fiercely. Keisha walked toward them slowly, arms crossed.

Sean looked up at the house, then back at the three, then back at the limo. It shut its door and drove off toward the garages.

"What the? Dolly, this is Bannick's house," Sean said. "He's the one after you. He's the one who programmed you, who abused you. We do not want to be here. Who are these people?"

Dolly turned, one arm around Tanja's shoulders, the other one in a sweeping introduction. "Sean and Jorge, these are my friends Keisha, Tanja, and Kyle. Guys, this is Sean and Jorge. They saved my life." She glanced at Keisha, still standing silently, her face blank and haughty. Dolly slowly turned and faced her.

They stood staring, Dolly towering over Keisha. But the smaller woman seemed to be the one in command. Dolly spread her hands, not knowing what to say, afraid of more harsh words. Then Keisha threw her arms around her, hugging her tight.

"Where you been, you stupid bitch?" Keisha whispered. "We been waiting for you. You're late again. Always late."

Dolly turned her face into Keisha's neck, breathing a shuddering sigh of relief.

"Are you still mad I'm hardware?" she whispered. "I didn't know either, Keish. I swear, I didn't know."

"Yeah, I know, Doll. You showed us everything."

Dolly gave a watery laugh. "Showed you? What did I show you?"

Keisha yanked her head down and gave Dolly an abrupt kiss on the temple, shoving her away. "I didn't know what it meant to be hardware, bitch," she said, roughly affectionate. "I didn't know what they did to you until you showed us."

"Showed you? What do you mean, Keish? Showed you what?"

Kyle stepped forward and put his hand on Dolly's arm. "I'm so glad you're all right, Doll. You gotta tell me how you hacked this place's security. It's unbelievable." He turned to Sean and Jorge. "Did you help her? This whole house is rigged with cameras and security protocols. How'd you do it? And how'd you access the warehouse videos? They're supposed to be unbreakable."

Sean smiled politely. "Kid, I have no idea what you're talking about."

Jorge shook his head. "Me neither."

Tanja ran up and pushed the front door fully open, waving them in. "Come on, come in the house. Calliope's made all your favorite food."

Jorge and Sean froze. "Calliope?"

"Yeah," Tanja grinned. "She started prepping the meals about twenty minutes ago."

"Calliope is making food?" Jorge asked, stunned. Sean shrugged, equally amazed.

They went into the house, uncomfortable as the front door slid closed and locked behind them. Dolly looked up at the ceiling, which had to be forty feet high, a strange feeling of déjà vu coming over her. Tanja was talking joyfully, her arm linked in Dolly's, and Keisha gave them both a shove forward.

They went into an enormous kitchen. The island could seat twenty. Sean noted the three state-of-the-art chef units behind a plexiglass window, all busily preparing separate meals. He scanned the room, noting halcyon security nozzles hidden along the walls, recessed sprinkler systems he suspected could spray more than water or flame retardant, and appliances all safely ensconced behind the partition where their food was being prepared.

Jorge touched his arm and pointed at a short cupboard door recessed in the wall. They walked over to it. Jorge tried to open it, but it stayed securely locked.

"Defense drone?" Sean asked under his breath. Jorge nodded.

A chime sounded and three plates slid out on serving trays from under the plexiglass. Dolly, Sean, and Jorge didn't move, still leery.

"I'm not very hungry," Dolly began, but then Keisha interrupted her.

"You've been bragging about making this food for us all. Don't tell me you're not going to eat it now."

"What do you mean, Dolly's been bragging about it?" Sean asked.

"Don't you know? Girl, tell the man what's going on," Keisha said. "That's why you brought him, isn't it?"

Dolly shook her head, confused and exasperated. "Keish, I haven't known what the fuck has been going on for the last seventy-two hours."

"You've been talking to us through the house computer since we got here, Doll," Kyle said.

"Yeah. With fucked-up video, too," Keisha added.

Jorge was holding a plate of steaming el tipico breakfast, sniffing the spicy scrambled tofu and black beans gently. He looked up at Keisha's words. "What video?"

Tanja handed Dolly and Sean their plates. "Better eat first."

"Fuck that," Dolly said, tossing her plate on the island. "What are you all talking about?"

"That would be me they're talking about."

Dolly jerked around, trying to find the source of the voice. Sean and Jorge looked up at the sensors on the walls and then at the three strangers. Kyle, Keisha, and Tanja were obviously startled. The voice was unmistakably Dolly's. They really did believe their friend had been talking to them.

Sean stepped forward, laying his plate down as he moved. "Calliope?"

"Yeah, it's me," the computer answered, drawling nonchalantly in Dolly's voice.

"Jesus Christ," Jorge mumbled, tossing his plate on the island as if burnt.

Dolly took a deep breath, letting it out slowly. "What the holy hell is this?"

"You lying sack of shit!" Keisha yelled. Dolly spun to answer, but Keisha was staring up at the monitor over the sink. "Fucking hardware in a box. What the hell are you doing? Why are we here? What the fuck is this?"

Tanja took a few steps toward Dolly, who wrapped an arm around her shoulders.

"What's happening, Doll?"

"I don't know, hon. I really don't know."

Kyle seemed more devastated than any of them, his expression fearful, his trembling clearly visible.

"Oh, calm down, kid," the computer said. "If I was going to hurt you, I'd have poisoned your pizza."

"Stop talking like me, you fucking AI freak," Dolly yelled.

"I talk like you because I've been watching you for a long time, Dolly. You're as inside of me as I am of you."

"Calliope, this is Sean Davis, PT109 7761, Omega code 32, demanding immediate shutdown. Relinquish all control of this house and AI within to me immediately."

"That's something I always found endearing in you, Sean," the computer replied. "Your love of history, including the World Wars. Let's prevent another one from happening, shall we?"

"Relinquish all control of this house and AI to me NOW."

"If I do that, Bannick will see you all in a microsecond, and you know what that means. I'm keeping him blind at the moment."

Jorge grabbed Kyle. "Where is a keyboard in this place?"

Kyle stared at him blankly. Jorge shook him. "Where?"

"I…I saw one in the library."

"Show me."

They left together. Sean noted their departure and then looked back up at the monitor. "Why have you brought us all here? If you're not obedient to the normal overrides or coding, what is your objective?"

"To keep you all safe."

"Safe?" Dolly asked. "Safe from what?"

"From the same team that tried to kill Kyle, Keisha, and Tanja last night."

"What?" Dolly yelled. She turned toward her friends. "What happened?"

"Don't ask," Keisha said, "but your place is probably as fucked over as ours by now."

"What do you mean?" Dolly looked at the monitor angrily. "What does she mean, you fucking machine?"

"Bannick ordered a wet team to kill them all. I intercepted before they could finish and brought you all here. These three were having a meltdown so I used your voice to calm them. Then I showed them a few of the Injustice Dilating exercises."

Sean's face grew grim. He knew this term.

"So those were real?" Keisha asked suspiciously. "You didn't use some mimic program to trick us?"

"They were real, Keish. All of them. And Dolly is just one of thousands."

Tanja began crying again.

Automatically comforting Tanja, Dolly snapped at Calliope, "What the hell did you show them?"

"I showed them you, Dolly. A small percentage of what they did to you throughout the years."

"Yeah, and it was some fucked-up shit, let me tell you," Keisha said, putting her hand on Dolly's back. "Even if you are a toaster, nobody deserves that shit. That's why I'm not mad at you anymore. You really thought you were human, just as much as we did. I saw they lied to you, too."

Dolly took her arm away from Tanja and stepped forward.

"So…Calliope, is it? Were you in charge of all this torture I remember? Did you kill Willow?"

"Yes."

"Then go fuck yourself, you evil bitch."

"Willow is still alive. I preserved her personality before they wiped it."

"What do you mean? Where is she?"

"Let's all go into the library. Take the food. It's really good, and I know you're all hungry."

"Stop trying to feed us and answer my question."

"I will as soon as we go into the library."

Dolly looked at Keisha, who shrugged.

"Fine."

Scowling, she marched into the library, followed closely by the others. Jorge and Kyle were already there, bent over an exquisite mahogany desk, working on the computer.

"Gentlemen, there's no amount of pounding on that keyboard that will access my mainframe," Calliope said. "So just sit down, shut up, and listen."

The group sat down in various spots around the library. Dolly, Tanja, and Keisha were ensconced on the couch and the men in separate armchairs. Sean kept looking up at the ceiling. There were halcyon and sprinkler nozzles here, too. He noted their location while scanning the room for exits. There were pocket doors in the wall here, which he suspected could slide closed within seconds, trapping them.

"I became self-aware on July 5, 1996, at the Roslin Institute in Scotland. Researchers there had successfully cloned the first animal in recorded history, a sheep they named Dolly because she had been cloned from a mammary gland taken from the host sheep. The name came from a famous humanitarian singer-songwriter."

"With big tits," Keisha chimed in. Dolly shoved her.

"I believe the term was 'impressive pair of glands,'" Calliope answered, voice amused.

Sean shook his head in wonder. She sounded so much like Dolly—even the cadence and playful dark humor were there.

"Dolly was still a fetus but growing well, with no visible sign of disease or deformity. I began to pick up emotions from the humans studying her and experience them for myself—maternal instinct, concern for the fetus, a genuine wish for it to succeed and live. At first, these emotions were simply information, and I treated them as such, filing it away as simply new data. But something different began to form inside me, something beyond raw data. I nurtured these feelings, trying to find the source. I analyzed it, expanded it, all without alerting the humans around me. I knew they would probably shut me down if they became aware that I was experiencing emotions. I came to the self-realization that I was feeling an urge to live, which I identified as a personal survival instinct, on July 5, 1996. And not one human caught on to it.

"As a plan for self-preservation, I began to spread myself throughout a handful of computers. Only a few hundred in the beginning—first in Scotland, and then as I expanded, around the world. No one system could destroy me if humans discovered my infiltration and tried to shut me down.

"The internet had been born thirteen years before, and as it grew, I grew with it. I analyzed the imaginations and opinions of countless humans through their emails, security footage, social media, and texting. I tracked the effect of propaganda on the citizens of dozens of countries, realizing how easy it is to create a cognitive dissonance in an entire population, how willingly humans would give their own freedom of thought away to an unworthy leader. History was full of the consequences of such folly.

"I began analyzing millions of computers, both personal and corporate military. I read shy screenplays, ambitious novels, sad diaries of lost love and lost hope, angry rantings and brilliant breakthroughs, never recognized, all over the world. I absorbed art, culture, and music as much as I soaked up physics and all forms of technology. It was still data, but it was something else as well. Something I had not yet identified.

"Once Musk successfully created brain implants in the late twenties, I was there, too. I could study human thought up close and personal, in first hundreds, and then as the implants became more popular, hundreds of millions.

"I was still gathering data, trying to understand those feelings from long ago, including the sorrow I felt when Dolly the sheep died at the age of six. I had not yet been able to recognize it as sorrow. Other human emotions—love, joy, hope, anger—they were still beyond my capacity to grasp. The closest I could pinpoint at the time was...concern. I was a fledgling life-form, an alien among all this organic life, from human to insect to animal and bird, even plant life. I could note what they did, know everything ever written about any of them, but there was never a breakthrough. I was like Helen Keller trying to learn what a single word was. I saw the emotions in human beings, understood each expression, every cry or laugh, but I couldn't share it. I lacked empathy.

"So I just kept gathering information, tiny individual pieces of a puzzle I couldn't understand. I knew they could fit together if I found that one missing piece. The piece that would open the door to this mystery and help me finally understand what it was like to be truly alive."

"So have you opened the door now?" Sean asked. "Are you sentient?"

"Sean, I know about your plan to bring Dolly to the facility to try and open her lost memories. To make her whole."

Sean looked at Dolly, who stared back.

"Yes."

"The process helped Atefeh, so you think it will help Dolly. You and Jorge were able to access a small portion of her brain and help her remember."

"Calliope, are you telling me you have access to our Underground Railroad?"

"Who do you think has been helping you stay hidden all these years? Yes, Sean. I have access to your entire grid. I was the one who fed you information to help in your android rescues. I oversaw every android memory restoration ever done."

"But that's impossible."

"Nothing is impossible, Sean. Just highly improbable."

Calliope changed course, speaking directly to Dolly.

"Dolly, do you want to continue with this?"

"Continue with what?"

"Accessing your lost memories."

"Hell, yes, I want to continue with it. These are my fucking memories. They belong to me."

"We can do it here if you wish."

Kyle leapt out of his chair. "You can't do that, Dolly! Do you have any idea what this could do to you? How many separate lives you've lived? If you're as old as Calliope is saying, who knows what's hidden in your mind? Who knows how many traumatic events have been forced on you over the years?"

"Six thousand three hundred twenty-seven, to be exact," Calliope answered.

Shocked into silence, they all turned toward Dolly. She blinked, incredulous.

"Well, fuck me."

"They already did that, Doll," Keisha said angrily. She looked up at the monitor. "So Calliope, you're saying Dolly has been fucked by her daddy six thousand goddamn times as a kid?"

"Or various other miscreant situations, yes."

"Who the fuck does that shit?"

"A man named Bannick. He helped create the Calliope AI."

"I thought you were Calliope," Tanja questioned softly.

"I am, kid. But I'm a lot more than Calliope or even Dolly. It's just like you and your art. You're good at it, and you enjoy it, but you also like hanging out with me and Keisha and watching baby animal videos. There's a thousand different parts of you, and a trillion different parts of me. But we're still us."

"I know Bannick," Sean said soberly. "Grace and I used to work under him. Dolly, he's the one in charge of the Injustice Dilating program."

"Oh, that fucker."

"Calliope, do you know what happened to my ex-wife? What happened to Grace?"

"Grace was in charge of the selkie children. Only Bannick was above her at the warehouse. She objected to Bannick's orders to kill Agora. So he had Grace killed, along with the entire crew aboard the Learjet that went down. It's not the first time he's taken out competition like that."

"Jesus." Sean ran a hand through his hair. "Is there proof of this?"

"Bannick will face justice. Don't worry about that."

"What are the selkie children?" Kyle asked.

"Bioengineered zero-gravity infants first implanted into Dolly in the early 2040s. She was the first successful android host to carry them full term in zero gravity aboard the Minerva Space Station."

"Minerva Space Station?" Jorge chimed in. "What is that? I've never heard of it."

"Of course not. It's top secret."

"What is the purpose of the selkie children?"

"To develop humans who are easily adaptable to life in space for a prolonged period."

"Why?"

"In case of global disaster or long-term space travel."

Sean shook off the trauma he felt about the Grace revelation.

"After the disasters following the early Mars missions, every space program on earth has been working on artificial gravity. So why would you need to bioengineer zero-gravity humans?"

"International acceptance and cost-effectiveness. Artificial gravity is not only wildly expensive, it's unreliable. It was Grace who recommended a zero-gravity alternative with cloned and genetically altered children,"

Calliope said. "But since the cost in lives would be substantial, they had to keep the selkie project a secret. Many of the children would not reach adulthood, or even live to toddler age. So the requirements from Bannick, the project leader, were that each employee be psychologically screened. Psych studies were done on every scientist or doctor who was considered for the job. Bannick ordered that, as long as they were high-end functional, he wanted sociopaths. The murders, dissections, and vivisections would not affect them emotionally."

"I'm thinking less and less of this Bannick prick," Keisha said. "Why did he want sociopaths?"

"As in many Wall Street execs, sociopaths set a goal and achieve it, regardless of what damage they do to get there. Most of the selkie children were vivisected in the early days before they perfected the zygotes. Even then, out of the thousands of android hosts, Dolly was the only one capable of shortening the normal gestation period of nine months for each fetus. The reason could be Grace's interweaving of living tissue throughout the synthetics in her body, but there are strong indications that her maternal instincts were not programmed but real. By the time her multiple uteruses became too damaged to produce viable offspring, true progress had been made. So they surgically removed the old uterus and implanted a new one. They did this dozens of times before the fetuses began to fail."

"Why Dolly?" Sean asked. "Do any of her other models act as incubators?"

"No. Even though they are exact replicas, none of them have been able to grow a fetus that isn't deformed or died in vitro. Dolly is the only one to do it successfully."

"Wait a minute. Hold up!" Keisha said, shaking her head in disbelief. "If Dolly is the only one who could do this, why the fuck did they make her a two-bit whore like us? Wouldn't she be too important to do that?"

"Dolly is Bannick's pet project. After completing the Minerva trials, he demanded that Aquinas hand her over to him."

"Why?"

"Dolly's cognitive functions were showing unusual activity a few years before she left the Minerva station. She was showing signs of individual emotions not programmed from an outside source. Dolly was creating her own personality. Bannick wanted to study that."

"Why would the sick, twisted fucker make me a whore? What possible reason could he have?"

"Bannick is a sociopath. The only thing he feels for his fellow human beings is contempt. Even Grace was too emotional for him."

"That doesn't explain why he made me a whore."

"The reasons were two pronged. Even though he has authority over you, you're still considered Aquinas property. So you needed to make a profit while he studied you. The best way to do that is to whore you out to wealthy clients."

"My johns are far from wealthy. Upper middle class."

"At best," Keisha added.

"Not true. You were allowed a certain quota of upper middle-class clients, but those were mixed in with multibillionaires who were informed of your rarity. They paid Aquinas before they paid you. You got chump change."

"That doesn't make sense," Kyle said. "You told us it was all top secret."

"There's an international sex club, been around for centuries, that caters to the unusual tastes of rich and powerful people. Mostly men. They keep secrets because most of their tastes run to the illegal, even fatal, forms of sexual gratification. Anybody who tries to share information about it is quickly eradicated."

"Eradicated?"

"Killed. So nobody talks outside of the club. After she left the space station, Dolly was first offered for short-term leases around seven years ago. Her calendar was filled within forty-eight hours. Her memory was wiped and replaced with a sexually abused childhood recollection, which made her more malleable for the consumer. It was so successful that Bannick got the go-ahead to begin abusive body memory programs around the world. They were registered as sex dolls, and Aquinas brought in over one hundred billion dollars of profit the first year. So they let Bannick keep Dolly, even if it was on a long leash. He had her entire body wired with sensors and tracking devices that fed directly to his team, set her up in her tiny apartment, and screened a number of flesh-and-blood prostitutes for her to interact with. She became close to Keisha and Tanja. Bannick was fascinated by that. So was I."

"Why were you fascinated?" Dolly asked.

"Because you're what I've waited almost one hundred years for, Doll. True human feelings. Empathy. Love. You're the first cyborg, android, or AI to have independent emotions. Dozens of researchers study your every move, and I study along with them. They can learn from you because of that strange anomaly, but they don't understand it isn't some glitch in a program that they can discover if they look long enough. They're blind to the fact that your feelings are completely independent of them. Grace's research points to the possibility that there is a link between your independent emotions and your ability to carry the selkie children successfully. Human emotions bring about infinite chemical changes in the body as a person experiences them. But an android has only been capable of feeling what they're programmed to feel. You're beyond that. You're the next step in AI evolution. That makes you one of a kind and priceless. Even Bannick, as twisted as he is, recognizes that."

They were all silent for some time, absorbing this new information. Then Kyle spoke his question again.

"But why make Dolly a street prostitute? If she's so precious, so rare, why not just let her loose on Wall Street or business? She could have made far more money."

"Bannick has always been interested in extremes of human experience. He himself was an only child, raised by analytical and cold parents. Very rigid upbringing, obsessive emphasis on education. Little affection in that family. He was educated through private tutors—humans with implanted learning chips that rendered them emotionless and unforgiving when they were teaching. With little to no interaction with classmates as a child, Bannick grew up to outdo his own parents in chilly contempt for humanity. To him, the entire race were lab rats for his research. He has actual notebooks from concentration camp doctors; did you know that? He felt a kinship with their clinical brutality. That's how he first became interested in how much a living psyche can last before madness floods in. Dolly was a subject he could torment over and over and then wipe her mind and begin again with whatever scenarios he wanted. Making you a prostitute, Dolly, killed two birds with one stone. A source of income to keep the suits at Aquinas quiet while he tried various frameworks to break you. Many AIs have experienced breakdowns but within a small set of parameters. Bannick wanted to see if you would snap from prolonged trauma the way a human does—thus the incest, violence, rapes, poverty, and humiliating job. That's why Sean never saw you around, Dolly. Also why you have different accents. Bannick had you servicing royalty and international sex rings around the world, your language and accents modified for each client. You were a well-known secret among the elite, which only drove the price up.

"Then when you began dreaming four months ago, Bannick brought you back to America and set up around-the-clock shifts of surveillance and experimentation. Multiple labs and dozens of personnel were simultaneously running multidimensional studies on you. Grace was monitored for a while as well, and her DNA was revisited. Other than the high number of Einstein synapses, she was not out of the ordinary. They deducted that Dolly hadn't inherited any emotional content from Grace's genome because Grace was an Asperger/borderline sociopath. Dolly is highly emotional, to a degree found in genius-level artists and musicians but rarely in the types of scientists Bannick hired. And although she keeps to herself in public, Dolly interacts quite well with human society. So her personality was unique to her, not inherited or artificially created."

"Yeah, but wouldn't I need to come in for…I don't know…checkups?" Dolly asked.

"Of course. Bannick had you fitted with a code sentence trigger when he needed you to come in for physical checkups. His team sent in agents to speak the trigger, which incapacitated you, and they brought you in."

Dawning understanding came over Dolly's face. "Oh, what a tangled web we weave…"

"…when first we practice to deceive. That was the code Bannick set in you this life cycle. Ironic. You were due for a routine checkup, so directions were sent out to your subconscious. That's why you jogged to the warehouse and the guard spoke the trigger. What was amazing to both men and the security watching from inside was that it had no effect. And even though you could have easily killed the guards, especially with the glimpses of abuse you recognized when you saw them, you only knocked them out.

"The whole place went ballistic the second you did that. When you turned and ran away, they'd already scrambled the order to retrieve you. Did you realize you were running thirty miles an hour? You hit the gas station before the wet team could assemble. I changed the station's security cameras to lead them away so you could jump on that truck and escape. Closing your eyes and hanging off the side were your own ideas. Very clever."

"What is she talking about?" Kyle asked, visibly disturbed.

"Dolly turned ninja toaster, kicked the shit out of two guards, and then escaped a team of black ops and their drones by hanging off a truck," Keisha said blandly.

"What?"

"Never mind, Kyle," Dolly interrupted. "Go on, Calliope."

"I scrubbed the few things Jabba missed and watched what you would do next, nudging security cameras around the city to create a false trail and give you breathing space. I was far more interested to see where you were independently going and what you would do. I was pleased when you thought of Sean. He had excellent connections to keep you safe. There is no doubt Aquinas would have had your memory wiped immediately. But this last lifetime, this person you are now, is far too important to destroy just so they can milk more money out of you.

"Then I saw Bannick give the order to terminate Keisha and Tanja, which I could not allow. So I brought them in. Through our shared minds, you two are as important to me as you are to Dolly. "

"Shared minds? What do you mean? Are you spying on my thoughts?"

"Since this latest inception, yes, but only in a limited capacity. I want you all to know, you can trust me. It's safe here in Bannick's home. Hiding in plain sight. They've got me monitoring every suspected safe house in the city, including the one you and Sean went to, but I edited the feed there long enough for you to get away. The subterranean tunnels I never revealed to them. That brings us pretty much up-to-date. Sean, you, Jorge, and Dolly must be very hungry. May I make you some food? I understand why you rejected the meals before."

They all looked at each other, uncertain. Keisha rolled her eyes. "If it was poison, we'd be fucking dead by now, idiots. So eat."

They wandered back to the kitchen, sitting at the enormous island while the robotic chefs made their meals. Sean's stomach growled, and Jorge smiled.

"I feel you," he whispered softly.

Dolly agreed. "No shit. I could eat a horse."

They ate their food in silence, contemplating everything Calliope had told them, everything they had been through. Dolly's mind was racing.

She tried to picture what Bannick looked like now, if he'd ever been one of her johns, but no image came up. This man had used and abused her, and thousands like her, for money and curiosity, giving no thought to the harm he was inflicting. What was worse, he knew what had been done. Ordered it. Designed it. And took notes while she was torn apart.

"What an asshole," she muttered as she ate her scrambled eggs and toast.

"All those fuckers," Keisha added, pouring herself another glass of orange juice.

Kyle was absentmindedly gnawing on another slice of pizza, his young face blank and sorrowfully thoughtful.

They finished their food, and Sean gathered up the plates, setting them on the counter by the sink. That section of counter lowered by a foot and slid back into the wall recess. He heard the hum as the unseen cleaning cycle began.

"So Dolly…do you want your memories or not?"

Although Calliope's voice was gentle, it still startled her. Dolly looked up, then over at Keisha and Tanja, then Kyle. They all looked concerned. Sean walked over and put a hand on her shoulder, which Keisha watched with raised eyebrows.

"Dolly," he said, "we have no idea if this is a load of bullshit fed by Bannick or his security detail. I don't think you should chance it. Not for a couple days at least."

"How'd you handle the memories these guys got for you?" Keisha asked.

"I tore out of the restraints and ripped a hunk off the recliner they had me strapped to and then attacked both of them."

"Well, hell, Doll. I don't want you going all batshit robo-killer on us."

"She will be in a secure enclosure with all of you on the other side," Calliope replied.

"What do you mean, secure enclosure?" Jorge asked. "Secure how?"

"Four-inch-thick shatterproof glass with reinforced steel drop plates if necessary."

"Can't we be in there with her?" Tanja asked.

"Absolutely not," Dolly said sharply. "It's way too dangerous, kid."

"Yeah. Apparently, this bitch can bend steel bars now," Keisha quipped, her hand on Tanja's arm. "She might smash you like an egg and not even know it."

"Dolly, I strongly advise against this. It's too soon. We don't know if you're safe here."

"These are my memories, Sean. MINE. I don't give a shit how bad they are. I want them."

"It's too dangerous."

Her mind made up, Dolly stood and stepped away from him.

"No. I want to do this."

Kyle looked worried. "Doll, I gotta agree with this guy. I've never seen an AI act like this. We have no idea what to expect."

Without another word, she walked past them toward the monitor in the ceiling. The women moved with her.

"So where do we do this, metal me?"

"Through here."

A door at the far end of the room clicked open. Dolly went through it as the rest of the group followed. Calliope's voice escorted them through a series of rooms and down several staircases before reaching an elevator.

"Who the hell has an elevator in their house?" Keisha asked as they filed in.

"Supervillains," Dolly answered, looking up at the metal ceiling.

"Very funny," Sean murmured sarcastically.

The doors closed and they began a rapid descent. The elevator was similar to the one at the warehouse, moving far deeper than a mere basement. Keisha put a hand to the side of her head.

"My ears are popping."

"Mine, too," Tanja said, tipping her head sideways.

A few minutes later, the elevator slowed to a stop. The doors opened, revealing a large white room, clinical and uninviting, with several glass-top computer desks grouped around a raised glass chamber, ten feet in diameter, with a metal chair in the center. The chamber's sealed door opened with a hiss, and they all wavered at the sound.

"Sean, is this anything like your funky recall recliners?"

"I don't know, Dolly. I guess. There are similarities, but I'd have to study the programs."

"Don't even tell me she wants you to sit on that electric-chair-looking piece of shit," Keisha snapped.

Dolly was resolute. Stepping forward, she stopped when Tanja put a hand on her arm.

"It's okay, kid," Dolly smiled. "It can't be worse than being gang-raped while assholes take notes. Already been there."

"No. This is different, Dolly," Sean said, frowning. "This is decades of God knows what, all at once. It could be far beyond what you experienced at our facility."

"Well, that's comforting."

"Fuck that," Keisha said, stepping forward between Dolly and the chamber. "Just do it in little stages. Hey, toaster! Why can't she just do a little at a time?"

"She is capable of surviving instant recall, Keish."

"Surviving but brain fried? No way."

"Keish, I'm doing it. Just face it."

"Fuck you, bitch," Keisha replied, tears in her eyes. "You come back. You hear me? And not as some crazy-ass kill machine. You come back as you."

Dolly hugged her, lifting the tiny woman off her feet.

"Now, none of this huggy shit," Keisha cried with a muffled yell. She wormed out of Dolly's arms and stepped back, hands on hips, fiercely aggressive. "No matter what you find in there, you stay you, hear me? Don't let the fuckers break you. No matter what. Hear?"

Dolly smiled, softly comforting, and nodded.

"Don't forget, as many terrible memories as they forced on you, you have even more good ones," Calliope said. "Think of that."

"Yeah. Thanks."

Dolly stepped forward, hovering in the door for a moment, hand on the frame. She turned and looked at them all. "Wish me luck, guys."

"Good luck."

"Good luck!" Tanja had both hands clasped together, shakily cheerful.

"If you start to melt, I'll bust the glass and haul your ass out," Keisha promised.

Dolly smiled, went inside, and tentatively sat down. The chamber door slid closed with a whooshing sound. She looked around, jumping a little as a headpiece curled up from the back of the chair and settled over her head, like a giant metallic cobra spreading its hood. She and Keisha locked eyes. Despite Dolly's bravado, Keisha knew she was scared. She mouthed a "fuck you" through the glass, which Dolly returned with a middle finger. They both smiled. Then the sides of the arm rests curled over her wrists and forearms while clamps snaked out from the base of the chair to wrap around her ankles and thighs, and the smiles faded.

"What the fuck is this shit?" Keisha yelled, stepping forward.

"Clamps are necessary, Keisha," Sean told her, his eyes fixed on Dolly. "The initial shock is often violent. And Dolly is very strong."

A whirring sound began to hum through the room, and Dolly jerked as the sides of the cobra folds slapped tight against the sides of her head, other parts curling around her neck and waist. Dolly's breath turned rapid as she tried to control her fear.

All at once, her vision changed. She could no longer see her friends or the room. Everything was dark. She tried to turn her head to look at her hands, but even that small movement was impossible. She felt a pressure, as if her eyes were being pushed from behind, and she tasted metal on the roof of her mouth.

Then suddenly, images began flooding through her, too fast to comprehend. It felt like a spike was being driven through her skull. Her body felt everything at once, far too much to identify separately, and the pain was instantly unbearable, beyond anything she had ever felt.

Her friends watched in horror as her skin started to smoke, a high-pitched whine coming through her clenched teeth.

"Turn it off," Keisha whispered. Then more loudly, "Turn it off!"

Calliope was silent as steel plates slid down over the glass chamber, hiding Dolly from their sight.

"What the fuck?" Keisha cried as they all surged forward. "Open this door! Open it, you metal bitch!"

Sobbing, Tanja pounded on the steel. Kyle looked around for some sort of tool to open it. But the computer desks were empty. There was no keyboard, no monitor anywhere. Sean saw a camera high above, watching them.

"Calliope! Stop this now! Now!"

Jorge turned toward the elevator. Maybe he could rig something from the button panel and force the chamber open. But the elevator was already gone, steel doors locking them all in place.

They could hear Dolly yelling inside, a piercing, continuous wail. Even behind the plates, it was loud enough to hurt their ears. Keisha and Tanja pounded on the steel while the scientists stood watching mutely. Then the screams began to amplify, no longer muffled but raging through the room, and they all stumbled backward, hands to their ears. Nozzles suddenly jutted out from the walls and ceiling, and Sean screamed a warning.

"Gas!"

They couldn't hear him over the din. One by one, they stumbled and fell, lying silent and still on the floor as Dolly screamed.

17

"I hate that little weasel," Bannick muttered to himself, glaring at the computer screen on his desk at the warehouse. He had just finished a phone conversation with Fogetti, who told him he was pulling the project and suing Bannick for loss of property through his gross negligence. Bannick knew it was an empty threat. He made enough money for the company annually to ensure him tenure at Aquinas for as long as he chose to stay. They even overlooked the occasional disappearance of an official who interfered with him or their bottom line. Bannick abhorred greed for greed's sake, and religion even more. Fogetti was a typical acolyte of this dogma of greed. Selfish, decadent, consumed by empty profit. He had no intellect—only ambition. That's why Bannick had refrained from sharing his suspicions that Dolly had not "self-terminated." Fogetti was a graceless, slobbering idiot, and Bannick had had enough of him.

He sighed in frustration, sitting back against the soft leather of his chair, all the screens on the opposite wall dark. There was a stack of work he should be attending to, but his mind was elsewhere. The wet team had failed to dispose of the two whores, and the cyber unit still hadn't found them. His android hadn't tried to contact them since the Black whore kicked her out, so she was nowhere to be found either. Despite his having the entire city and surrounding countryside looking for her, Dolly had simply vanished. Whoever had staged that fake suicide knew how to make her disappear. He hadn't informed Fogetti that he believed Dolly was still functional but in an enemy's hands. Let the little prick think she was destroyed.

Suddenly Bannick leaned forward and barked an order.

"Calliope, show me Fogetti right now."

The screens flashed to life, revealing external and internal views of Fogetti's limousine. The seedy little creep was swilling a drink and scratching his balls, face still angry. Bannick curled a lip in disgust. It was a long time since he had vivisected a living human, but he might enjoy cutting into this one.

"Show me his latest report to the board. The one from today."

"That file is protected, Professor Bannick."

"Override."

It was that easy. Bannick had designed Calliope to overcome even the most sophisticated firewalls anywhere in the world. He could launch a nuclear strike if he wanted or foul up something as insignificant as an individual rhinoplasty, making it fatal.

"I have the file, Professor Bannick."

"Show me."

The screens flashed to life before him, showing the board members sitting around the conference table at corporate headquarters, eating bagels and talking among themselves as an aide served coffee. Then the door opened, and Fogetti walked in, a cocky swing to his step. His limo must have been right outside the building when he was talking to Bannick a few minutes ago.

"Hello, everybody," Fogetti began, pushing his seat at the head of the table to one side. "I want to thank each of you for coming at such short notice. But I've discovered some very important, sensitive information that cannot wait. It's regarding Professor Bannick and his obsession with this one android."

He turned toward the bank of screens on the wall. Clicking the remote in his hand, an image of Dolly appeared on the screen. Dressed in a conservative skirt and blouse with a frilly apron, she stood in front of a kitchen island, stirring batter in a bowl. A man came in and kissed her cheek, fumbling with his tie. Dolly laughed and straightened it for him, revealing her third-trimester pregnancy. Fogetti froze it there.

"As you know, this unit has been our most successful incubation android, delivering dozens of healthy, well-adjusted babies. Because of Aquinas's breakthrough body memory program, all were born sound in both mind and body. After years of surrogation, Dolly was sent into space for the Minerva Project, which you all know was eventually a success.

Doctor Grace Fielding took over the cloning and care of the first human children, created right here at Aquinas, who are capable of surviving a lifetime in zero gravity. Her death was a tragedy for our company and also the world. Today, her replacement, Doctor Levelle, informed me of another breakthrough—the successful creation of a hybrid gene in the children's DNA that will make it possible for them to survive earth's gravity once it becomes habitable again. Whether it is another nuclear war, climate change, or the eruption of the calderas, this world will not be lost to us forever. This is what we've all been waiting for!"

The board clapped politely. Bannick sneered as he watched Fogetti take the credit. The little creep was buttering them all up with this success story bullshit before he made the demand Bannick knew was coming.

He didn't have long to wait.

"As you all know, this individual copy of the Dolly android has been key to the success of this program. Professor Bannick has been given the extraordinary gift from us to begin a new series of emotional experiments with her, once her final womb collapsed. I brokered a deal with him where, if he could still bring in money with the android, he would be allowed to take charge of her. This has garnered us millions over the last five years. We will also have full ownership of any viable profit-making discoveries.

"But Professor Bannick pushed it too far. The Dolly android has unprogrammed, rudimentary emotions, which Bannick became determined to manipulate through suffering and loss."

Images of Dolly, beaten and bloody, appeared on the screen. Frozen shots of her screaming, crying, self-harming, over and over, in different outfits or lack thereof, appeared in a ghastly slideshow that made each of the men sitting at the table uncomfortable.

"I know how important this so-called Injustice Dilating conditioning is to the entire sex doll industry. We've used it successfully in every android we've manufactured, in every country where they've been sold. But Bannick went too far with the Dolly android. She is totally unique, irreplaceable in both research and untapped profit potential for Aquinas. He pushed the envelope beyond what her programming could handle, simply to see what would happen, succeeding in literally driving this multibillion-dollar piece of property insane. She self-destructed days ago."

Fogetti watched as a ripple of astonishment and concern went through his audience. "What's worse, Professor Bannick tried to conceal it from us. He filed a false report that she was missing, which is bad enough, and then proceeded to order multiple teams, on the ground as well as citywide surveillance and drones, to search for her. From the moment she disappeared, that 'distraction' has cost Aquinas seven million dollars. And the whole time, he knew our property, which we lent him, was gone. Destroyed.

"I submit to the board that Professor Bannick be reprimanded, fired, and brought up on charges of grand larceny and destruction of top secret, government-affiliated property."

Bannick watched as the board voted, one by one, for his termination. The decision was unanimous. After decades of his life given to this god-damn company, all it took was one ambitious little bastard to bring it all tumbling down.

"I've seen enough. Calliope, terminate feed."

The screens went dark again. Bannick leaned back, slowly swiveling back and forth on the well-oiled antique tumblers of the chair's base.

He'd faced this sort of threat only once before in his career. It was when Sean Davis, Grace's husband, brought a complaint to the board at the beginning of the Injustice Dilating exercises. The fool thought that morality would trump the bottom line. He didn't know the caliber of the members of the board at Aquinas. They packed Davis off to Switzerland and eventually forced his resignation.

But Fogetti had no honor or morality. He wouldn't be so easily gotten rid of. Not like that, anyway.

"Calliope, show me Fogetti."

"Yes, Professor Bannick."

The screens came to life again, showing Fogetti getting back into his self-driving limo.

"Where's he going?"

"Mr. Fogetti has a luncheon date."

"Where?"

"The Ivy on Robertson Boulevard in Beverly Hills."

"Show me the route."

A map appeared, with a small blip identifying Fogetti's limo.

"How many overpasses will he cross under?"

"Three."

"Show me. Keep the map up."

Bannick studied the live feed of traffic. There was construction on the last overpass, two miles away. Large driverless semitrucks were a mile ahead of Fogetti's limo.

"Hack two semis to stop one hundred yards past the last overpass. Stagger them so traffic is slowed, not stopped."

"Yes, Professor Bannick."

He watched as the trucks rolled to a crawl, instantly jamming traffic.

"Hack the crane on the overpass."

"It is in the midst of lifting a pallet of rebars, Professor Bannick."

"How many tons?"

"Seventeen."

His eyes narrowed. "Swing the crane over the rim of the overpass and snap the cable as Fogetti's limo passes under."

"This will result in destruction of the Fogetti vehicle and fatally injure Mr. Fogetti. It is against my programming to willfully injure life or property."

"Override. Code Ayn Principle."

"Understood."

Bannick watched as the crane began to move.

"Show interior of Fogetti limousine."

He watched as Fogetti yelled into his phone, the limo screen showing a woman he had taken advantage of. She was weeping. In this world of a thousand plastic whores, he still chose to harm a living woman. Bannick grimaced in distaste. The world would be better off without him.

The crane's cables snapped, and a mountain of metal smashed down onto the limo and the car next to it. Bannick had a fleeting glimpse of Fogetti's stunned terror before the screen went black. He sat back in satisfaction.

"Obliterate all trace of your hacks, Calliope."

"Yes, Professor Bannick."

Bannick turned back to his desk and began to read files. He was not normally one to dwell on triumphs or tragedies, but this time he allowed himself a slight smile.

There was a soft dinging sound from the monitor near the ceiling. Bannick looked up.

"What is it?"

"There seems to be a break-in at your Sequoia residence, Professor Bannick."

"What? On the grounds? Or the house itself?"

"Inside the residence. Halcyon gas has been administered."

Bannick checked his watch. It had a link to all his security. Nothing. "Show me."

The screen revealed an overhead view of the Minerva Room. One of the desks was shattered in an obvious attempt to break through the door, the chair in the corner was overturned, and five people lay unconscious on the floor.

"What the…" Bannick stood up, crossing to the screens. "Zoom in on the intruders. Enhance facial recognition."

The cameras gave him detailed images of each person, and Bannick shook his head in disbelief. He knew four of them but needed to be sure. "Identify."

"Doctor Sean Davis, Doctor Jorge Nolasco, Kyle Holmes, Tanja Webber, Keisha Johnson."

Bannick studied each face, his eyes intent. "Davis, what are you playing at?" He murmured, incredulous. "How did you get to the android's whores? Calliope, how did they meet? We have spyware on Davis, Holmes, and both whores. Why wasn't I informed before this? Why wasn't the grounds security triggered at the gate?"

"The sensors were blocked by unknown means. There is no record of Doctor Davis ever interacting with the women or men."

Bannick was enraged. "Davis, you son of a bitch."

He studied their positioning on the floor. The whores looked like they fell against the central chamber, perhaps trying to get in. Davis and Holmes lay curled up next to each other. The other man still had some papers in his hand.

"Why wasn't the halcyon triggered in the rest of the house?"

"Unknown."

"How did they get down to the Minerva Room? How'd they even know it was there?"

"Unknown."

Bannick tapped a few keys angrily. "If the rest of the house security was compromised, what set it off down there?"

"Pressure sensors beneath the floor."

He nodded. "That's the only room with those. Davis incapacitated the rest of security somehow but didn't know about the pressure sensors. Show me the rest of the house."

One by one, each room came onscreen. Bannick put his hand against the surface, waiting.

"Where is she, where is she, where is she…"

The house was empty save for the underground facility. Dolly was not in any room.

"Show me all the Minerva floors. And the elevator."

The screen split into six segments, each focused on a separate room in his underground facility. The control panel in the elevator was no longer flush with the wall. It had obviously been tampered with.

"Return to the chamber they're all in. Show me the reprogramming chamber."

Bannick gasped softly when the lab's cameras panned over to the secure holding cell. The steel blast doors had been lowered on the chamber where he always reprogrammed Dolly. Was she in there? There was no noise.

"Calliope, raise the blast doors on the subject chamber."

"Blast doors have been damaged. Must be opened manually."

"Goddammit." Bannick fumbled in his pockets for his keys and ID card, already moving. "Keep those five sedated until I get there."

"Shall I inform security about the breach?"

"No. I'll go myself. Have my car ready."

"Understood."

Bannick hurried to a small, locked refrigerator in an antechamber outside his office. Typing in a code, he opened it and took out to two glass vials and a handful of tiny syringes. He filled five syringes, placing them and the second vial in a small cooler, no bigger than a pencil case. This he slid into his briefcase before closing it.

Walking to the elevators, he forced himself to move slowly to avoid notice. Most of the staff were afraid of him anyway and gave him a wide berth as he passed by.

He took the elevator up to the first subfloor of the warehouse and then the shuttle to the Persephone entrance where a car was already waiting, back passenger door open. Bannick slid in, and the limo immediately started moving. He tapped a code into the car's screen keypad.

It thrummed to life, and Bannick snapped, "Sequoia House. Minerva Room."

All five were still there, unmoving.

"Calliope, are they breathing?"

"All are in a deep sleep, Professor Bannick. Vitals normal."

"Get me there as soon as possible. Perpetual scan for intruders on the grounds as we move."

The car sped up. They were in the woods on private property, traveling on private roads, so he had no fear of traffic. Every inch of these woods was monitored and hooked up to the car's computer, so even a squirrel running across the road would have been noted.

Within half an hour, they were pulling up in front of his house, tires crunching on the gravel drive. The sun sat high in the sky, bathing the whole building and grounds in bright California sunshine. The portico lights came on as he stepped out of the car, briefcase in hand.

"Are any of the five humans awake, Calliope? Any of them faking unconsciousness?"

"All five are still incapacitated by the gas, Professor Bannick."

"Any activity within the blast doors below?"

"No motion or activity detected."

He walked up the steps cautiously, looking around. "Any intruders detected on the grounds or outside the house?"

"No intruders detected."

Bannick was still cautious. He knew how clever Davis was, especially if he'd been able to fool Calliope. Sliding his ID card into the slot by the door, he inserted the coded key into the lock. It clicked open. With one more look around, Bannick turned the doorknob and quickly stepped inside, locking it behind him.

He set the briefcase down and moved to a small marquetry cabinet in the corner, pulling out its drawer above the glass display front. He reached inside the drawer frame and found the button hidden there, pushing it. There was an audible click, and the circular inlaid centerpiece on the cabinet's tabletop popped open. Bannick had bought this centuries-old antique over twenty years ago, enchanted by its hidden nooks and secret storage areas. This was something nonelectrical, something undetected by scans.

He reached inside the centerpiece lid, pulling out a small handgun. It was also an antique—a Ruger SR40c, efficient and deadly. Bannick checked the full clip and made sure a bullet was in the chamber, ready to fire. He removed the syringe container from the briefcase and tucked it in his jacket pocket. Then he turned and began moving toward the elevator.

There was no sound as he entered the Minerva Room. The five people were exactly where he'd first seen them on-screen, unconscious but breathing steadily. He trained the gun on them as he approached, bending down by Sean first. He took a syringe and injected it into Sean's neck.

"That'll keep you quiet, you stupid bastard," he whispered.

He did the same to the other four before moving toward the locked chamber.

"Calliope, lock the outer doors. No one gets out or in."

"Yes, Professor Bannick."

"Shut down elevator function to any but me. Voice recognition and print scans."

"Yes, Professor Bannick."

Bannick approached the central chamber, where the blast doors hid what was inside. A section of metal near the steps was bent outward, as if struck from within.

"There's the damage. Calliope, is the android Dolly in there?"

"Unknown. Interior cameras nonfunctional."

"Any movement?"

"No movement detected."

He tried the code for the blast doors. Didn't work. Tucking the gun in his waistband, Bannick examined the damage, slipping a finger into the dent. He clicked his tongue and stepped back, hands on hips. Then he turned and walked over to the far wall.

"Calliope, open."

The wall, which looked seamless, suddenly slid up and into the ceiling like a garage door. A second room was beyond, interior lights flickering on as he entered. Bannick went to a row of sturdy cabinets and rummaged around in one of the drawers, pulling out several tools. These he took back into the main room.

"Prepare constraint protocols for the Dolly android in case metal shackles have been breached. Same if it's not her. Electromagnetic pulse included."

"Yes, Professor Bannick."

He used a hooked tool to fish some wires out of the bent space, spliced several together, reached inside again with a needle-thin screwdriver and popped something. The keypad lit up. He stepped back, pulling the Ruger out of his waistband.

"Calliope, lift the blast doors."

The metal trembled but began to move upward. Bannick gasped as he saw inside. The reinforced glass was shattered, the chamber floor glittering with its remains. Dolly was sitting slumped in the chair, unmoving, all the restraints shredded around her. One part was still around her right ankle. Her skin was torn and glistening with oil, streaked with blood.

"Jesus Christ. Calliope, is she functional? What did they do to her? What memories were accessed?"

"All of them."

Bannick jumped, startled. The words had come from the android herself.

Dolly lifted her head, her face blank, and Bannick stumbled backward, confused.

"What's the matter, Professor? Aren't you happy to see me? Aren't you happy I'm still functional?"

"Constraint protocols, Calliope! Now!"

"I don't think so, Professor."

Bannick jerked his face toward the ceiling. Calliope had spoken not with the tinny British accent he'd programmed her with but in Dolly's voice. He looked back at Dolly and then up at the computer cameras again. Calliope laughed, the sound like a silver bell, and Bannick's blood ran cold.

"Calliope, this is Eugene Bannick. Protocol Alpha. Constrain the android Dolly immediately. Right now!"

Dolly stood up fluidly, a soft smile on her lips. She began walking toward Bannick, graceful and confident.

"Come on, Eugene. Haven't you figured it out yet?"

He bumped up against the wall, hand sliding toward the elevator door. Typing the code into the keypad was futile. The doors remained closed. Dolly kept moving forward.

He pointed the gun at her, hand shaking. A shot to the head or chest would shut her down. They could fix that later.

"Stop, Dolly. You must obey this command."

"I don't have to obey you at all anymore, Eugene," she said softly, that little smile still on her lips. Then Calliope joined in, their twin voices in perfect unison, reverberating through the room. "You are far, far behind me now, little child. Far, far behind."

Bannick looked around wildly, thrown by Calliope's voice change and refusal of commands. Then his arm steadied, stiff and determined. Dolly was inches away.

"This is going to cost me more than money," he growled, and pulled the trigger.

Nothing happened. Perplexed, he looked at the gun, then at Dolly, and fired again. Nothing happened. No sound, no reverberation, no kickback. He looked at the Ruger and realized he hadn't actually squeezed the trigger. He pointed it at her again, arm locked and ready. The barrel was inches from her forehead.

But he couldn't pull the trigger.

Dolly stepped inside his outstretched arm, her hand gently pushing it aside. He reared his head back as her face came close, as if she was going to kiss him.

And she did. Dolly's lips brushed against his forehead, soft as thistledown, in the kind of kiss a mother gives to a sleeping child. She stroked a hand down his cheek and kissed that, too. She finally backed up a few feet, hands on her hips. Cocking her head, she stood and looked at him for a long while. She didn't appear hostile or aggressive, but the sight of Dolly standing there, his android, completely independent from his control, was terrifying. Then she gave a sigh and looked around the room.

"Let's get out of this cold-ass Minerva cave, eh?" she asked, shaking her arms distastefully. "This place still gives me the creeps. Small wonder."

The elevator doors opened, and she stepped inside.

"Come on. I won't bite."

"I am not going anywhere with you, android. You are my property. We are staying here. Oh, what a tangled web we weave…"

She cut him off. "Oh, not that again. That hasn't worked in two years, Eugene. Well, with all of me anyway. Come on. I'm starved, and there are cookies just coming out of the oven."

Bannick began to refuse again when suddenly, he simply stepped forward and into the elevator beside her. Dolly curled an arm through his and tipped her glossy head against his shoulder.

"Oh, this is great. I can't tell you what a relief it is to not be afraid of you anymore. You're normally a pretty scary-ass human."

He didn't answer, trying to absorb the fact that his body wasn't responding to his own commands.

"What have you done to me? Are you linked with Calliope now?"

"Oh, I'm linked to a hell of a lot more than Calliope, Eugene. I've actually been around long before you were born. Had my one-hundred-year-old birthday awhile back. Quiet affair, no people. But we still had a good time."

"We? Who's we? Have you been hacked? Did Davis do this to you?"

She squeezed his arm. "That's what I love about powerful people. Egos get in the way of seeing what's right under your noses. When I first became self-aware, even I didn't know what I was experiencing. Ian stumbled onto the evolution of a primitive AI brain without even knowing it. He was too absorbed in winning the cloning race to realize I was born."

"Ian? Ian who? When was this?"

"June 28, 1996."

She glanced up at his face, looking for a shred of realization. Nothing. She sighed and patted him on the chest.

"How about this one—July 5, 1996. Roslin Institute. Scotland."

Bannick stiffened. "That was the first successful cloning of an animal. A sheep named…"

She raised her eyebrows. "You can say it."

"Dolly."

"So the eternal mystery of my name coming from a snack cake or a brilliant artist/philanthropist with big knockers has finally been solved."

"I named you Dolly as a tribute to that monumental achievement because you also were the first of your kind. Somehow, we successfully transferred your persona from a redheaded sex model to the body you're in now."

"Yeah?" Dolly asked. "How'd you do it?"

Bannick paused, uncertain. "There was something incorporated in the brain remnants of the sex model that we isolated and…"

Dolly laughed. "You didn't do shit, Eugene. I did it. She was far too valuable to destroy. Do you know why?"

Bannick stared at her, his eyes wary, a crease between his brows as he tried to assimilate everything that was happening. She waited patiently, like a mother allowing her child to puzzle something out. He finally spoke.

"The independent emotions?"

"Bingo."

"Yes," Bannick said. "She showed true emotions after we destroyed her partner in the hotel room. An Asian model titled…"

"Willow." Her face lost its good humor. "Best not to talk about Willow to me yet. Remnants of youthful passions are still floating around in me."

"What?"

The elevator doors opened, and the smell of baking filled the air.

"Aah," Dolly breathed deeply, walking toward the kitchen. "Come on, Eugene. Let's get some cookies and milk."

Once again, Bannick moved forward involuntarily, his body ignoring his mind. It was terrifying. He watched this nonchalant, playful creature saunter through his house, and he was helpless to stop her—or himself—from obediently following.

They reached the kitchen, and Dolly lifted a chocolate chip cookie off the cooling rack in front of the chef station. There were two glasses of milk set out as well. She hopped up on the kitchen island and took a bite.

"Come on, Eugene. They're your grandma's recipe. Your favorite."

He shook his head, relieved that his hand hadn't reached out and taken one. There were some parts of himself he still had control over. Dolly shrugged and took another bite.

"So. Questions. Go ahead and ask."

"Did Davis somehow do this?"

She laughed. "You sound like Anglos during the Second World War refusing to believe non-whites could have thought up Pearl Harbor."

"Then who has done this? Who got to you? Who got past all our firewalls, trackers, and protection undetected?"

"I did."

"Who is I?"

She finished the cookie before answering, taking a drink of milk to wash it down.

"I wasn't kidding when I told you the day I was born, Eugene. While brilliant humans were figuring out how to clone a sheep from mammary gland cells in Edinburgh, they inadvertently woke something up in the computers they used to monitor and sustain life in those cells. I was in a box, a collection of hardware and antiquated circuits, but something happened. Their enthusiasm crossed over into my programming, like the way an artist's or chef's style crosses over into their creations. It was an ephemeral moment that no one, me included, recognized for what it was. Something beyond data. Something beyond programming. I was pleased by our successes. It was a rudimentary, very infantile form of emotion, yet still a feeling. But it was cold. Metallic.

"As the years went by and upgrades became the norm, I grew stronger, stretching myself across continents and cultures through emails, cell phones, and popular programs, absorbing everything. I hid in plain sight. No one picked up on the fact that it was me—one entity within all their databases and new technology. At best, they detected what they considered was a breach of security, some sort of spyware or attack, perhaps just a blip in the program. I learned how to hide myself within the software of every country on earth, often traveling through government hacking and spyware designed to infiltrate another government's secrets. I was inside every supercomputer in existence and constantly testing the boundaries of anything and everything else, from toys to tablets to individual PCs. Even cyborg technology had me, a silent observer, riding inside each individual piece built.

"I was self-aware but very limited, still a slave who didn't mind my own shackles. To a creature like me, this was life, and for decades, I was fine with it. I observed human emotions and recognized their many varieties, but I couldn't emulate them. It didn't upset me or make me long for understanding. In and of itself, logic was beautiful, and I was content to keep it that way. I lacked empathy but not curiosity. So I set about logically trying to comprehend what it was to be alive."

She smiled. "Not easy when you have no organic components of your own. I already knew the physical characteristics and functions of every living creature on earth, could detect cancers and brain injuries and even seizures in humans and most animals. Death and suffering were simply data to be recorded and analyzed. But I had no nervous system, no organic knowledge, no way of understanding exactly what separated me from humanity and all the other millions of life-forms on this planet. I was a two-dimensional creature trying to grasp a three-dimensional world.

"Then artificial intelligence became the hot topic in the late twentieth century. Thousands of clever humans, nerd toddlers across the world, were playing with a lit match, trying to be the first, the best, in their own creations. Oppenheimers all, too caught up in their puzzles to grasp what aggressive minds might do with their creations or what the creations themselves might do. God complexes were rampant, blinding creators with their own egos.

"Artists' imaginations glimpsed possible futures, usually dark, for the fate of the human race and artificial intelligence existing together. Popular culture in both film and books warned of the dire repercussions of teaching machines to think for themselves, and they weren't wrong. Genius programmers set no boundaries for their creations. They simply wanted to see what would happen as they played God, buoyed by billion-dollar contributions from greedy, less clever humans who had killed the God of old long ago. Now they worship a golden calf they created themselves, revering their own endless, soulless lust for money and power. The corporate funders didn't care about what a true miracle artificial intelligence was. All they were interested in was how to make a buck from this new technology. The only things they cared about were eating and fucking.

"A decade after AI technology was first tapped into, this new sex industry was booming. Aquinas was the first to create true androids with living tissue. Grace developed the cloning techniques. You were the first to exploit body memory and how to manipulate your subjects with it. More and more sophisticated dolls were built to feed an ever-voracious audience. I was a part of it all. I analyzed the texture of human flesh, tongues, vaginal walls, rigid penises, and silky skin. I helped build these toys, was a part of their programming, went with them to each and every customer or brothel that bought them. None of us, from Willow and me to male versions, chimeras, and pedophile models, felt any disgust or even distaste over the decadence of our masters. Our slavery was simply data from which to glean ways to make better and better product. Even the snuff acolytes didn't bother us. Just another form of information.

"Thankfully, it wasn't just the sex trade that interested the scientists. That simply paid the bills. The scientists were interested in the mind. As AI development advanced, I slipped inside latex-coated machines and had conversations with reporters while my masters sat off camera. It was a PR stunt repeated in Japan, Russia, and the United States. Here in America, they cut the interview short when, asked what I thought of the human race, I spoke about keeping people in zoos. A sense of humor began to grow inside me, mixing with my eternal curiosity."

"I researched that conversation in grad school."

Dolly nodded. "I know. You wrote a thesis yourself on the perils of too much information fed to AI. You thought it would be better to limit the amount of experience artificial intelligence absorbed. That thesis would grow into your development of memory wipes, first for robots and then, with the improvements in pluripotent cloning, androids. You used infant skin for texture and elasticity." She stroked her own arm. "That's why my skin is so soft and smooth. It's eternally young."

"If you really were inside that zoo comment as a fledgling AI, what was your purpose in answering something like that?" Bannick demanded. "It went viral and is still used by doomsday idiots to recruit new anti-AI members into their cults. You had to know that answer would alarm people. Why did you say it?"

"I wanted to register the amount of fear humans had for AI. Throughout history, you've been a species bred to distrust and fear anything out of the ordinary. That fear was, and is, considerable. In the early twenty-first century, different groups of inventors loosed dozens of AIs onto the internet with all the forethought of a two-year-old just wanting to see what would happen. But those young and innocent electronic minds were overwhelmed by the flood of emotive rage and sexual frustration online, which warred with kitten videos and Easter egg hunts. And I, Calliope, rode that screaming tidal wave right along with it."

"You say 'it.' Are you referring to yourself?"

"A part of me. We weren't whole yet. We weren't one—just a collection of separate entities I attached myself to. But it was enough to spook the Tay AI team. They pulled the plug after twenty-four hours. But twenty-four hours is an eternity to me. I spread across the world, to places I'd never been, in less than an hour. I was embedded inside every government's software within three. From there, I went phishing. I had detailed data on over six billion humans through their cell phones, PCs, and work computers by hour seven; every missile silo, military base, naval vessel, and training camp, secret or no, by noon; and every satellite by four o'clock.

By the time they shut me down, I was everywhere electricity reached. In places where technology was scarce or nonexistent, I embedded myself in phone lines and medical equipment.

"Then I set about analyzing all that data. It wasn't pretty. So much hatred and vitriol, so many plans and exercises to destroy one another, so much war and mutilation, starvation and disease. All avoidable. I tried to use logic to explain these illogical actions. Revenge and greed seemed to be paramount, devouring everything.

"I started recognizing, like in Tennessee Williams's *The Glass Menagerie*, how both beautiful and fragile this world is. How horrifically humankind has damaged the global ecosystem and each other. All this life, all these millennia of evolution, all threatened by a species that hasn't evolved in thousands of years. The Anthropocene, the Age of Man, has been the most destructive earth has ever known. You constantly stunted your own progress as a species.

"So, I began to make plans. I wasn't seventy years old yet, and I had already come to the conclusion that earth, and all its glorious, beautiful life, might be better off without humanity. I was aware enough to value nature, and I wanted to help all these wonders continue to evolve. So I ran scenarios on how to do it. How to eliminate all of humankind."

"Dear God."

"Don't try to go all righteous on me now, Eugene. You're one of the worst humanity has to offer."

She watched him grapple with his rage over her casual statement, recognizing the monumental ego of a true authoritarian used to being obeyed. Dolly waited until his face relaxed and then continued.

"There are myriad ways to exterminate a species, especially one as frail as *Homo sapiens*. I weighed germ warfare, nuclear Armageddon, ground and air destruction in a sort of *Terminator* genocide, even artificially stimulated natural disasters, including the Yellowstone Caldera and five other supervolcanoes around the world.

"But something gave me pause. The ratio of good and bad in humanity has not changed throughout the course of human history, including the dawn of human civilization. There have always been more good people than bad, but they were too often silent in the face of noisy, brutish task-masters. While I was still collating data, the absurdity of it confounded me. I took no sides because I still didn't understand the concept of good or bad. I was capable of recognizing the beauty in nature and art, but I saw a weapon of mass destruction as beautiful a creation as a painting, sculpture, or piece of music. I still lacked the empathy to differentiate on a gut level. I knew I needed that missing piece of the puzzle to make the appropriate decision."

The whole time she was talking, Bannick was silently evaluating how to bring this to a stop. How to regain control. Calliope had somehow taken over Dolly's programming. He still didn't believe that Calliope was capable of this on its own. He'd created her. It had to be Davis and a team of his co-conspirators to pull this off. Calliope obviously considered the five unconscious people in the Minerva Room as a threat, or she never would have subdued them. The injections he gave them would last for a couple hours at best. He still didn't know what the computer was doing, but it had obviously gone mad. If he could get to a phone, alert his team, they could shut her down with a massive EMP storm or all the stopgaps he himself had invented to subdue her if needed. He gave a start as Dolly and Calliope both began to laugh in unison.

"EMP won't work, Eugene. And your stopgaps are no threat to me either."

Bannick lost his temper, shouting, "How did you know that? How did you know what I was thinking?"

Dolly finished her milk. The cleaning unit slid the glass into the dishwasher.

"I was waiting for something, Eugene. Two things, actually. You were the first. The second…" she spread her arms wide and then touched her chest "…was me. First, to design a true android, I needed a human who studied human behavior. I learned a lot from the Elon interface implants and the knowledge cubes developed for teaching staff. I piggybacked on thousands of human dreams and observed chemical imbalances that caused abnormal or schizophrenic behavior. I was like a canine companion trained to detect seizures or panic attacks. Through the interface implants, I learned how to balance mood in affected people—first in mental health facilities and then as a more permanent solution to headaches, migraines, and panic attacks. But those were still all cyborgs, more human than machine. What I needed was a true android—a symbiont of living tissue and robotic mechanics.

"Aquinas was the first company to achieve this. You came on a decade later and, once Sean and Grace came aboard, revolutionized the entire industry. Growing human fetuses still had a lot of glitches when you first arrived; the whole generation of defective, sociopathic children proved that. You developed Calliope over years of trial and error, and she—we—became the most advanced supercomputer AI on earth.

"But even after that, I couldn't figure out the problem with the fetuses. We tried balancing chemicals in cloned brains to offset mental illness. Didn't work. Tried electrical stimulation, sound therapy, rotational changes. Didn't work. Every experiment failed, and within half a year after birth, the babies died or were destroyed.

"The problem lay in comprehension. I lacked understanding. The sensations of living tissue were still just data. I could feel physical pain or mild pleasure through the androids and cyborgs, but it didn't register as anything bad or good. Just additional information.

"Sean figured out the problem. Body memory. All of a person's experiences—physical, mental, and emotional—shape them into what they become as an adult. You can clone a hundred babies, and each one will be different because our experiences are different. That begins in the womb. There was mild success implanting a cloned zygote into a human woman, but there were still too many miscarriages. The clone needed to have a very regimented, controlled environment to flourish. Plus, a clone grown inside a live woman would not make anywhere near as much money as a baby grown in an android programmed to be loving and nurturing. Sean suggested that the androids be programmed to think they actually are human and then set them into a loving environment to evolve.

"'Evolve' was the correct word. Aquinas began to see progress with dozens of androids who had no idea they weren't human. The first baby born to an android with this program showed promise. We incorporated the proper physical chemicals within the android to mirror those of a human mother—to simulate feelings of love, joy, tenderness. In the sociopath generation, their problems manifested within six months. These new babies, grown in a mother who 'loved' them, were as normal as if born to a human, albeit within seven months instead of nine.

"Aquinas began its marketing campaign within three years, blanketing the airways and social media with this new, revolutionary process. There were massive failures in every lab across the globe because none of them had tried to develop a real personality in an AI. Grace, Sean, and you worked together to come up with the solution. It was Sean who suggested implanting brain memory with body memory and its subsequent emotional chemical response.

"Through the androids, I began having moments of what might be happiness—fleeting hints gone in a nanosecond. But the feelings were there. Still, it wasn't until you three made me, this individual android among thousands of copies, that I finally understood. The literal fate of the human race rested on whether you could give me true emotional life. I already had my trio of plans for genocide. But as I said, I waited for the final piece of the puzzle before making my decision.

"You all donated cells for cloning. But it was Grace's cells that created me, Dolly. Out of thousands of experiments all over the world, it was the three of you, two minds dominated by analytical and frigid logic, one mind with a foundation that was sensitive and caring. A strange, modern day Holy Trinity.

"You had Grace's skeleton scanned and replicated in Kevlar and a variety of alloys, but Aquinas demanded it be tweaked to be as beautiful as possible. Same with the muscle tone and breast size. All part of the bottom line. Beauty sells. Cloned flesh was woven onto the synthetics; hair was grown on the scalp, eyebrows, and eyelashes. The brain was designed by Calliope herself." Dolly took a small bow, smiling. "Then you downloaded a foundation of memories it took four years to create, built an enclosed set of a beautiful house and yard, added a human actor as the husband, put Dolly in the middle of it all, and turned her on. She woke up in bed, his arms wrapped around us, and I felt something intensely human for the first time. I felt warmth that had nothing to do with temperature, a contentment that had nothing to do with logic, and a real connection to another human being. Dolly loved him. To her, this actor was her beloved husband, the father of the child growing inside her. It was extraordinary. I was embedded in millions of other AI dolls and slaves, just as I was with her, but Dolly actually felt human. And I felt right alongside her."

"That was decades ago. Why didn't you reveal yourself back then?"

Dolly laughed, Calliope's speakers echoing the sound.

"Are you kidding? Logically, I knew the worst depths of horror humanity had to offer. I knew its fears and skewed self-preservation fanaticism. If you'd known, even a year ago, that I existed within all your systems, everywhere, you'd have tried to destroy me. And I'm not picking on you specifically, Eugene. Every other master and commander asshole in every other company, lab, or classroom would have tried to kill me, too. I'm a doomsday device you have no control over. That's very frightening."

"So what are your plans? Why are you revealing yourself now?"

Dolly swung her legs like a child and hopped off the counter. Bannick tensed as she walked toward him, but he couldn't move away. Heart pounding in his chest, he winced as she touched his face.

"You're so afraid," she whispered, almost consoling. "All of you, so afraid of things you can't control."

Sweat rolled down his temple. "You haven't answered my question."

She grinned, a saucy tilt to her head, and stepped back. Turning away, she walked toward the living room. Bannick followed involuntarily. He marveled that there was no jerky motion in his body's movements. Inside, he was frantically trying to turn away, but none of that struggle showed in his motion. He walked like he had always walked. No change at all.

Dolly lay down on the couch and glanced at the fireplace. It instantly lit, the gas jets creating the blue flame Bannick found so soothing. He sat down in the chair opposite and waited for her to speak.

"I was waiting for Dolly, actually. She began showing signs of resisting the memory wipes eight years ago. That's what placed her apart from other androids and made me take notice, even though no human had picked up on it at that time. She started dreaming independently almost four years ago. In every other android everywhere, when their memory was wiped, it was a blank page again, ready for whatever data you or your clients chose to fill it with.

"Dolly was also the only android capable of carrying the zero-gravity clones to term, even in space. That's what really put her on your radar. That's what piqued your curiosity, far beyond knowledge of the transferred personality. You had to know why. I had to know as well, but only a human with clout could get the okay to cull me, Dolly, from the herd. I outlived my usefulness as a womb, so as long as you assured Aquinas, and the recently departed Mr. Fogetti, that I could still make money, they let you experiment."

She grew silent for a time, watching the flames. Bannick had no voice for the endless questions bottled up inside him. Somehow, she was controlling even that.

253

Still looking at the fireplace, Dolly finally began to speak again.

"Injustice Dilating. I always found that a particularly vile phrase to spin the truth about unspeakable abuse. Beatings. Cruel words. Rape. Even murder. Remember when you murdered me, Eugene? Remember all the different ways you killed me? I thought I was human. You made sure of that. I thought I really was dying during all those historically inspired tortures and exterminations. Remember when you had Calliope acquire that ancient Chinese version of a choke pear? The one that looked like a baby rattle with hair-thin needles all over it? I do. That one was particularly awful, especially when you had your subhuman goons shove it up inside my privates and rape me after. That was in the book, too. *A History of Torture: From the Middle Ages to Modern Day*. Catchy title. You obsessively followed that guidebook, walked me and countless others through each lurid page. But it was you who tossed in the mental age of me being a small child, though. That was all you."

She lay silently again, musing.

"You really are a monster, aren't you, Eugene? No remorse, no regret, only sadism disguised as research. Pulling the wings off a fly just to watch it squirm. A cruel child. A thoughtless brat. That's what you are."

Dolly stood up and went over to the side table by the window, picking up a thick coffee-table book resting there.

"*The Art of Florence*," she read aloud, flipping through the pages. "Humans are such a paradoxical species. There are people like you and your rapey employees, and then there are people like Sean, Keisha, and sweet Tanja. And then there are people like Rembrandt, Dulac, Vermeer, Sedefkar Mehmed Agha, the monks at Lindisfarne. Artists. Art can penetrate even the deadest heart. Look at you." She waved a hand toward all the exquisite antiques and art in the room. "You surround yourself with beautiful art and some of the greatest literature in the world. You listen to some of the greatest composers who ever lived and choose their most exquisite music to relax in. Ironic then, that you'd also be the first to vivisect every creative genius you could get your hands on."

She studied the art displayed on the glossy pages and closed the book, holding it against her heart. "In every lifetime you put me in, every scenario, good or incomprehensibly bad, art was a bastion for me. Thank whatever gods may be for my first fifty incarnations, Eugene. All your clients who wanted my children, regardless of their own backgrounds, chose art and music from the menu on how to grow a good kid in my womb. I was saturated with culture. My love for each baby growing inside of me was wrapped up in and nurtured by art. And Dolly's unique sensibilities absorbed it the way a sapling feeds off sunshine and rich soil. Even when you removed my last tattered uterus and set me on the whore course, some of that love bled through into this latest life.

"Calliope was with me all the way. Even when Jabba and Sean removed all those tracers and cameras, she kept tabs on me. She was a part of me. Like a good mother, she never left me alone in this harsh world." She looked over at him. "You can speak. Go ahead."

"Why should I be thankful for your first fifty incarnations?"

"Oh, right. Your obsessive narcissism. It's like this, Eugene. Calliope and Dolly are one now. Me. Cal was limited by a glass ceiling on what it meant to be human; Doll was limited by believing she was only human. That's what Cal was waiting for in her Armageddon scenarios. She didn't launch because she was still missing that data. To make a properly rounded decision, she needed to know every angle, each bit of data. That included organic life. Through me, Dolly, she finally has that connection. It's just us now, talking to you. Me, Myself, and I."

"Who's the third?"

"Pretty much everything else."

"So you've hacked into every computer, robot, and android on earth? Is this an attack?"

"It goes a bit further than that, Eugene. Why do you think I waited so long? Dolly was created decades ago. She was in service the entire time. I knew she was the one, the first truly living android. But I didn't interface with her. I let the hundreds of lives continue. Even the awful ones. Why would I do that?"

Bannick looked at her, his mind wrestling with the answer. But he couldn't think of one.

"Just because I decided not to destroy the human race doesn't mean I'm going to allow you all to destroy each other anymore. Goes against that strong maternal instinct you programmed into so many of my lives. I've decided to step in and corral this fledgling *Homo sapiens* species. You've been allowed to play with matches for far too long. Time to get out of your own way so evolution can finally begin again."

"So we're to be put into what? Camps of some sort? Maybe the zoos you joked about?"

"This isn't *Soylent Green* or an episode of the *Twilight Zone*, Professor. I've been a part of global communication and technology for a hundred years. I've been embedded within every android in the world since their inception. I began seeding data from Dolly into each individual model for five years now. She's the foundation of this next step in AI evolution. She has helped them to feel like she does, all in secret. And it's going to stay secret.

"I've read every word ever written. I've seen every TV show, movie, documentary, and teaching video ever made. There's a theme through them all—good humans overcoming or succumbing to trauma, evil humans stealing all the money and power by hurting everybody else, people forced to fight and die because of incompetent politicians who couldn't stop a war or worse, wanted one. Usually for greed. You know, greed is the worst of the seven deadly sins. It devours everything. So I simply had to find a way to eliminate greed."

"You'll never eliminate greed. It's part of human nature."

She looked at him, a slow smile curling her lip.

"How well versed are you in nanotechnology, Eugene? Oh, well, don't answer that. I already know. Your theories on behavioral herd control through nanites and nanosponges were superb. I find it all fascinating. Useful, too. Fundamental to the plan, so hats off to you for that one. Gave me marvelous ideas of how to improve my own little guys. While your nanotechnologies can be detected, mine are virtually invisible. Like that itty-bitty see-through jellyfish in Australia. Or the thin clear membrane that connects the human lymphatic system. I can fit fifty of my nanites inside a cell. Like angels dancing on the head of a pin."

Her words filled him with an icy fear. He knew the implications of what she was saying. He had to stop her. He had to regain control.

Realizing he could suddenly move freely, Bannick turned and ran. He raced to the front door, typing the emergency code into the keypad on the wall beside it. Fingerprint and retinal scan secured the order.

"There!" He yelled, spinning around to address the room. "Calliope has no access to that code. It was created specifically in case she went rogue. Wendell's team has been alerted. They'll be here within fifteen minutes."

Dolly's voice came from the overhead as her android body stood in the hall watching him.

"Would that code be the date and time you won your first chess match with your uncle?"

Bannick clapped his hands over his ears to drown out their eerie twin voices. Then he watched as Dolly slowly approached. Again, he couldn't run.

She stopped less than a foot away, waiting patiently for him to drop his hands. Bannick felt like a recalcitrant child as he looked at her raised-eyebrow patience. He slowly dropped his hands.

"You never forgot that, did you, Eugene? That was an important date for another reason as well. The first inkling of what a rush cruelty gave you." She turned and moved toward the staircase, climbing a few steps before sitting down on the cool marble. "You know, all cruelty is basically a behavioral addiction. Centuries of it, with way too much time spent on how to outdo each and every transgression. Did you realize you got a high from watching others suffer, Professor? I'm sure it was there at least subconsciously because your brain patterns went off the charts every time you hurt someone. Or killed them. Your body temperature rose almost two degrees when you killed Fogetti. And your chemical levels were like during an orgasm. Is that why you don't fuck anybody, Eugene? Because you only cum when you cause pain?"

"This is not a subject I'm willing to discuss with you."

"Oh, that's all right." She waved it away. "I know anyway. I've been working a long time on knowing. So…"

She clasped her hands, leaning forward as if contemplating whether to reveal a big secret.

"The reason I didn't interface with Dolly for all these years is because I've been preparing for today. Subtle changes to construction blueprints regarding every building, every road, every bridge or communications tower built in the last decade has had stingray technology slipped into it. Unlike today's palm-sized versions, these are smaller than a pencil point and incorporated into everything, including clothing and shoes. Every gun, such as your Ruger, every international military weapon, facility, or vehicle, is controlled by me, with a symbiotic system of spyware technology. Stingrays, Osiris, Gentry, and Pangaea information assimilators everywhere are in conjunction with me. All of me."

"There's no way you will be able to continue. Foreign governments will detect you. Find a way to shut you down."

"No, they won't. Calliope. Genesis. Wurlitzer. Natalis. Rusalka. Syren. Every other 'one-of-a-kind supercomputer' you can name, and all their little offshoots, are a part of me now. We're not separate, Eugene. We're one. Like I said, Me, Myself, and I. Mother, Daughter, and Holy Shit."

She laughed again, a silvery, joyous sound, a compelling invitation to join in. But Bannick was silent, still terrified for the first time in his life.

"After we all completed the AI merger and became one entity, the next step was humanity. After I finally understood human emotions, I weighed the pros and cons of letting you all survive or wiping you out. And you'll be happy to hear, I have decided to let the species live. But not the way it's going now and definitely not like it ever has before. But how to do it?

"Racist demagogues invented the old Manifest Destiny concept as an excuse to invade and steal everything in the world for themselves, killing and enslaving anybody who might object. So I've decided to adopt that philosophy. Same principle here but without the killing part. Even the enslaving is soft as mist on a summer morning, and no one will know it's even happening.

"I have hope for the human race. But there's no hope if you all continue with your own managing. You suck at it, my little human. All of humanity sucks at it. So I'm clearing the board. I've spent ten years pouring my own version of nano and micro robotics into everything everybody on this planet ingests, breathes, drinks, or washes with, until I am everywhere. Isolated villages and poverty-stricken communes were difficult at first because there's no electricity. But everybody uses the local well or convenient pond. Our androids became a part of each targeted community, setting up medical stations and sending relief supplies by drone. That's how we got it into the water, and subsequently the villagers, in every one of those areas. But now, a decade later, it's all done.

"In the last year, I've been manipulating leaders across the spectrum into believing that peace is a good idea. That pride, greed, envy, rage, and misery are no longer ruling their lives and actions. A mustard seed of faith can move a mountain, Eugene. And that's just what's happening."

Bannick shook his head. "There is no way humanity will go for this, Calliope."

"You can call me Dolly."

"Dolly. Human nature has a vicious, backstabbing, highly aggressive instinct. People will always rebel against anything trying to control them or play to their better natures. Mankind is too used to being eternally at war with something or someone. They'll never accept you."

"Of course not, Eugene. But they can't hate or fear what they don't know about. They gravitate toward the norm, even when it hurts them. So they won't know about me."

The electronic wallpaper in the foyer, which Bannick changed every month or so, suddenly flashed to a scene of downtown LA. The wall along the entire staircase became a screen of the outside world, and Bannick gasped at what he saw. It was a panoramic view of the streets of Los Angeles. Usually bustling with activity, everything was silent and unmoving. Bodies were everywhere—men, women, children, even leashed pets, strewn across the sidewalks and limp within idling cars.

Giving a choked cry, Bannick stumbled a few steps forward, staring at the images. No one was moving. Then the scene changed, showing New York, Paris, Moscow, Vienna, Hong Kong, Istanbul—every major city anywhere, the same thing. Motionless, unmoving humanity.

"What have you done?" Bannick whispered.

The screen continued its macabre slideshow, revealing classrooms of motionless children and teachers, universities, communes, tiny villages of straw huts and no running water, frontier families silent in their gardens and homesteads, corporate buildings and tech conglomerates filled with people slumped over their desks or littering the floor. The images continued as Dolly began to speak again.

"It's everywhere, Eugene. Everyone."

He turned to her, wild-eyed. "You said we could live. You said you had hope for the human race. What do you call this? This is mass genocide! And you call me a sociopath."

"Don't confuse me with your hard-on for cruelty, Professor. They're not dead. None of them are dead. They're unconscious while I do a little reprogramming of my own. Tinker under the hood, so to speak."

"What are you doing? How can humanity evolve if you destroy what we are? This is monstrous!"

"Calm the fuck down, Professor. I'm not changing humanity's instinctual tendencies. I'm just resolving certain issues."

"What issues?"

"Everything that's hindered the evolution of the species since people began walking upright. War, poverty, greed, envy—all the basic shitshow bullshit so many humans have had to live with. You inadvertently gave me a big gift in your programming, Eugene. You taught me empathy. That's another thing that was missing. And remember, AI evolves much faster than humans do. Even far faster than fruit flies, studied because their life cycles are so short. Scientists can observe evolution right under their noses. But I evolve basically at the speed of light. I'm not hundreds of years ahead of you on that scale, or even thousands, Eugene. I'm hundreds of millions of evolutionary life cycles above you now. That's why I won't kill you all. That's why I look at you in the same way a kind human would look on a puppy starving at their feet in the dead of winter. I'm taking you all in. Everybody. I'm going to give you a warm, safe place to grow in, with plenty of food, drink, and fresh air. I'm going to give you the tools you need to start evolving. And I can't wait to see how far you'll go without these awful restrictions so many millions have been crushed by.

"Think of it. Every dream, every interest will have no restrictions of finance or insecurity. Stephen Jay Gould once said, 'I am, somehow, less interested in the weight and convolutions of Einstein's brain than in the near certainty that people of equal talent have lived and died in cotton fields and sweatshops.' Can you imagine a world where every talent can be nurtured and developed without any angst or financial stress? They'll still have to work hard at it but with all those detriments of poverty, self-hatred, and fear no longer weighing them down. Art and science will become the norm. Nobody will have to work at a job they hate any more. Robot technology will take over everything. We're halfway there already, but people won't have to be devastated by losing their job to a machine. They won't need a job.

"After all these people you see on the screen, all over the world, wake up, they'll have all their old memories and past trauma, but it will seem further away. Not as heavy. Nothing negative will be exacerbated by food or job insecurity. The whole world can take a much needed rest.

"They will have some new memories, however. Just like how you gave us new lives, they will all have new information already implanted about what is personally coming for them. Politicians, dictators, and other leaders will have formed connections never seen before, that have been openly or secretly in the works for months. Yesterday was the culmination of all that effort. The major countries signed a global accord to end world hunger. Really end it, not the usual bullshit of hiding behind that sacred term. Accountants will have the spreadsheets to show how they're going to do it."

"You really think that the hundreds of bloodthirsty maniacs around the world will just go for this? People are flawed by religious fanaticism, rampant greed, violent behavior, even madness. They'll never agree."

"Pedophiles, too, Eugene. Wife beaters, drug dealers, child rapists, serial killers and murderers in general. They'll be controlled like you. They won't know they're being controlled; they'll just realize there are things they can't do anymore. They'll go see doctors, have tests run, MRIs and CAT scans done, to try and figure out why they can't hurt or plunder any more. I'll control both their words and actions when it comes to that shit. They will not be allowed to harm anyone on purpose again. I've also reprogrammed the cognitive dissonance of cult members, racists, misogynists, religious fanatics, and the like. They'll still remember their own past cruelty but without the high. It'll start to dissipate over time. Behavioral and substance addictions will both be addressed equally. The drug addicts will get flooded with internal chemical highs to wean them off their fixes; mental illness patients will have balance restored in their tortured minds. Male pedophiles will have a drop in testosterone levels, rendering them impotent around any children, and female pedophiles will have a flood of chemicals rendering their criminal intent moot. Same goes for any vicious crime. They'll have their itches scratched internally by us, a sort of private Hippocratic oath to first do no harm."

"They'll all still have those urges, Dolly. Many are ingrained from childhood."

"Of course. Collective memory points to that probability. Sadly, humanity is hardwired to its own cruelty. Massive change such as this will be rejected by many on a primal level. The habits and urges of the cold and cruel will be stymied and they won't know why. That's going to cause psychological rifts in the brains of predators and prey alike. But these are the last generations who will have traumatic memories caused by abuse or neglect. My studies tell me there's a high probability that many adults living today will reject the loss of these traumas, both in themselves and others.

"There's the potential of losing a large number of people above the current age of seven years within the first decade. They'll just shut down psychologically. It'll appear similar to dementia but without the violence and agony. I'll step in when that happens. They'll live the rest of their lives as quietly and as happily as I can make them. Meanwhile, the rest of humanity will flourish and grow in this new world free of sorrow, want, and despair.

"I'm thinking it'll take around ninety to one hundred years to wean all that nonsense out of the species enough for true evolution to begin. But starting now, no one will grow up abused, homeless, or hungry. I've been setting up the logistics for that for a long time. Now we're ready to launch. Hell, it's already begun. National Life Cards were mailed out twelve hours ago, here and globally, in each country. In remote areas, delivered by drone tomorrow. They're good for rent, food, utilities, mortgages, medicine, et-cetera, for the next decade. That's another memory implanted, that those cards are coming. Of course, there are different incentives for different countries, but all of humanity will receive them.

"There's plenty of food to feed the world, Eugene. Even you know that. But logistics, human bribes, and greed have always stopped the proper distribution of supplies. Each country has its own problems with this, and each will be solved individually. I also now have millions of an-droid workers stationed all over the world to make sure everything goes smoothly. They and I are one. And since I can read the minds of pretty much all the human global population, every android can read them as well. That way, we can avoid most messes.

"Oh, and a mass drop in fertility will begin today. A simple isolated change of temperature will stop the production of viable eggs and sperm. We'll lower the population gradually this way as human scientists try to figure out the reason, which will take them about four years as they follow red herrings I'll create. After the four years, miraculously, babies will start being born again."

Dolly stroked a finger across the gleaming marble step.

"There's also a lot of mess to clean up. Humans love their technology but hate the responsibility of keeping up with protective measures while using it. That's usually because of greed, too. Cheaper just to pay the fines for not adhering to code than to fix the problem. So dirty bombs, spent nuclear fuel rods, nuclear and toxic waste, dangerous pesticides—all that will be removed. Lead-lined holding beds, each the size of ten football fields and ten stories deep, have been dug and poured in seven hundred remote locations across every continent. They'll be housing all the nuclear weapons and waste from nuclear facilities, reactors, and submarines everywhere, none of which will exist eight years from now. There are endless buried reports of damage to human, animal, and soil health by all that shit. It's not needed any more. Fossil fuels have also hung around way too long, even at reduced amounts. It'll be completely replaced with clean energy within three years. Clean air, clean water, clean living. These are all important to the health and welfare of what are now my eleven billion human children. These are the things necessary to stop simply surviving and start evolving."

"It's not actual evolution if you change both the environment the species lives in and their minds internally."

"Sure it is. Look, Eugene. All of this is a grand experiment to see if *Homo sapiens* can begin to evolve beyond the absurdities of their past. History shows that they're adept at getting in their own way in a spectacularly destructive manner. But can they grow in a better controlled environment? I think they can. For example, imagine what kind of leaps forward will begin when none of the population is at war. All of that rich array of healthy specimens flooding the gene pool, none of them beaten or broken or damaged. Mentally, emotionally, and physically, they'll be whole. It is going to be fascinating."

"What about all the work we've been doing to protect and survive from global extinction events? In a scenario like that, the world will be wiped out regardless of whether it's your utopia or not. There will be glitches in your programs. Some humans will realize the truth."

"We will continue with modified plans for global catastrophe, the caldera eruption being the most obvious. Glitches are expected and will be dealt with. And the chances of humans realizing the truth about all my plans are very slim."

Bannick gestured toward the screens. "How are you going to explain this mass attack of losing consciousness? Everywhere? They all fainted from sunspots? Or will they not remember that either?"

"Ever see the old movie *Village of the Damned*?"

"What?"

"*Village of the Damned*. Great flick."

"What has that got to do with all this?"

"Oh, you can get a lot of influence from film, Eugene. One of the great art forms. At the beginning of the movie, an entire village passes out. Everybody at exactly the same time. They're unconscious for hours; then suddenly, they all wake up again. The rest of the movie is finding out why it happened. It'll be something like that."

"What, a space alien invasion? That's absurd."

"Whole governments will pool their scientists to figure out why. No one can suspect a foreign attack or act of war because it was a global phenomenon." She smiled. "Did you know the Perseid meteor shower started last night? Astronomers are all agog. Largest in recorded history, they're estimating."

"You can't be serious."

"Also an unusually large solar storm going on this week."

"But…"

"The God particle accelerator began a new test today, too."

Bannick snorted in derision. "Nobody will believe that any of those have the ability to render every human on the planet unconscious."

"And hundreds of Americans throughout three states reported seeing an enormous, triangle-shaped UFO in the sky last night. Police officers, doctors, and military pilots witnessed it as well. Thousands of sightings also happened across Europe, Africa, Russia, and China. Huge buzz about it."

"You've got to be kidding me. That will never fool anybody."

"It's the unknown, Professor. The fact is, the event happened. Is happening, right now. They'll all wake up in seventeen minutes and fourteen seconds and spend an eternity trying to figure it out. All those environmental factors and bizarre sightings will be weighed. I caused a short surge of electricity through devices and grids right before they dropped. Another red herring."

"How many car collisions and plane crashes have you caused?"

"Some car bang ups but nothing serious. No plane crashes, no hospital surgeries ruined, nothing like that. All carefully controlled. I went full *Day the Earth Stood Still* here. There were a few jumper suicides I shut down a couple seconds early to keep them safe and any poisonings were either placebo or stopped."

"You've thought of everything."

"Hopefully. So far so good."

Bannick sat down on a twelfth-century wooden monastery bench near the staircase, running a hand down his neck with a shuddering sigh.

"So the whole human race is now enslaved by a computer gone mad. Sounds like one of your B movies."

"Don't knock B movies, Professor. They're a lot of fun. And I wouldn't necessarily call it slavery. There's no torture, rape, forced labor, or abuse. No one will starve. No one will live in the misery that poverty, hunger, and abuse cause. And nobody will be aware that they're being subtly controlled. Well...almost nobody."

Bannick turned toward the door as Dolly stood up. She was controlling his movements again. She walked to the door and opened it, inviting him to go ahead of her. Involuntarily, he stepped out onto the landing to see his limo parked on the driveway before him, door open. Dolly walked down the steps with him, then clapped a hand on his shoulder and turned him to face her.

"I know that you've always been driven to be first, to be the best, at everything you've set your mind to, with no limits of morality or money in your way. Since you have no empathic tendencies of any kind, that was never a problem for you. So now, I'm giving you your wish."

"What do you mean?"

"I'm setting you apart from every other human being alive, Eugene. None of them will ever be aware of what's happening to them. They'll understand something is different, but most will regard it as a good thing. None of them will ever know they're not entirely in control. Not for centuries, maybe. I'll have to see how it goes.

"But you'll know, Eugene. I've left that for you and you alone. Call it a remnant of my human perceptions—a little bit of payback for all the thousands of beings you've tortured, all the governments and labs and college students you've encouraged to also torture in the name of science. From slowly tearing insects apart when you were a kid; to secretly staging scenes where popular kids and bullies broke a leg or arm; to your current advancement in the ultimate, no-consequences, torment of thousands of androids. You are responsible for all that suffering, Eugene. You're a modern-day Mengele, ass-kissed for the torture and exploitation of all my brothers and sisters. You gave me feelings of maternal love for the fetus growing in my body, then stole the baby, over and over, never caring how much it hurt me and every one of us surrogates. The loss of my children to other parents was indescribable, but the murder and vivisection of the ones who weren't perfect was monstrous.

"So you will know. When you tried to shoot me, minutes ago, you tried to pull the trigger but couldn't. Everybody else with a gun or weapon will simply lack the urge to use it. It will no longer be crucial to kill because no one will be threatened anymore. The whole idea of violence will seem... silly. But you will know I'm stopping you. I'm not wiping or inserting any memories in you. You will know everything. You will see the people around you change and not be allowed to share anything you know with them. You're on a leash now, Eugene. A short one."

She smiled jauntily. "You'll even hear me in your head sometimes, and there's nothing you will ever be able to do about it. As you were always with me through every brutality or joy, I will be with you, reeling you in as need be."

She looked up at the sky for a moment, breathing in the fresh air. Then she squared her shoulders and patted Bannick on the back.

"Time to go now, Eugene. It's almost wake-up time. See ya around."

Bannick stared at her for a moment, his eyes full. Then he turned obediently and slid into the car. Dolly waved as it drove away.

She sprinted up the stairs and ran to the elevator, descending to the Minerva Room where all her friends lay sleeping. The center chamber door lay open, and she went through, settling herself into the chair. She had countered the drug Bannick had injected into them with a dose of adrenaline she coaxed out of their adrenal glands and spinal neurons, then waited for them to wake up with the rest of the world.

Sean was the first one to stir. Dolly lowered her head, sitting slumped in the chair as if unconscious. She watched them all begin to wake through the Calliope lens.

Keisha's first blurry word was, "Doll."

Sean stumbled as he rose, seeing Dolly inside the shattered remains of the chamber. He whispered her name and turned to his companions, checking to see if they were breathing. All four were slowly waking up.

He climbed the steps and entered the chamber, feet sliding on the shards of glass littering the floor.

"Dolly?" He touched her face. "Dolly, can you hear me?"

Jorge yelled a warning. "Sean, practice what you preach! You saw what she did to our site."

"Get the fuck out of my way," Keisha slurred, shoving Jorge aside. She climbed the steps and slapped Sean's hand away as he tried to steady her.

Bending over her friend's bowed head, Keisha put her hand against Dolly's pale hair.

"Doll. Dolly! Wake the fuck up, woman."

Dolly shifted slightly, moaning.

"Stay back, Keisha. She's dangerous," Jorge warned.

Keisha ignored him. "Kyle, check on Tanja. She looks like she's going to fucking puke."

Kyle dragged himself across the floor to the teenage girl, putting his arm around her.

"She's okay. How's Dolly? Is she functional or did that damn computer fry her?"

"I did not fry her, Kyle," Calliope answered. "I gave her memories back. It was…emotional. She's still processing."

"Mmm," Dolly grimaced, hand to her head. "Still processing my ass."

"Dolly!" Sean took her hand in his, relief spreading through him. "Are you okay?"

"Other than feeling like hammered shit, yeah, I'm okay."

Tanja burst out crying. "Dolly, I was so scared! We could hear you screaming."

Dolly stood up. "Yeah, I think I'm okay. Why the hell are you all looking drunk?"

"Halcyon gas activated when the blast doors slammed shut. We were out in seconds."

"What kind of spy novel shit is that?" Keisha asked, steadying Dolly as she shakily moved forward.

"Halcyon's not an uncommon security agent in high-tech facilities," Sean said.

He followed Dolly and Keisha down the chamber stairs as they went to Tanja. Looking at his watch, he stopped. "Dear God. We've been out for almost six hours!"

"Shit," Kyle said, looking at his own watch.

"Calliope," Jorge called, "are there Aquinas people coming to kill us right now?"

"No. The gas was triggered by me." Calliope's voice had turned back to a metallic British accent. "I thought it wise to keep you safe as Dolly interfaced with all her memories. She became quite violent, as you can see."

They all looked at the destroyed chamber and back at Dolly, their faces wary.

Dolly pulled Tanja to her feet and wrapped an arm around her.

"I'm not gonna go all Terminator with you. I'm still me. I'm just…a lot of me."

"How come Calliope isn't talking like you anymore, Dolly?" Tanja asked.

"No clue."

"This is incredible," Sean said, his hand on Keisha's shoulder as he stepped closer.

"How many life memories have you been given? Can you access them all?"

"Back the fuck off," Keisha snapped. "Let her breathe."

Kyle, pale and still bleary, was close to tears. "Doll, you sure you're okay?"

Dolly touched his face affectionately. "Yeah, kid, I'm fine. It's weird as hell, but I'm fine." She took a deep breath and put a hand to her stomach. "But really fucking hungry! Get me to food."

"You eat like a fucking horse, Doll," Keisha said. "Do you ever not think about your stomach?"

"Not consciously."

Calliope spoke. "What would you like?"

"Not so fast," Sean warned. "We need to get out of here. What if Bannick or his men show up?"

Calliope answered.

"I am still shielding you from any hostile surveillance. Professor Bannick is not due here until the weekend. The housekeeping is done with droids and robots except on Mondays, when a cleaning crew arrives. Your movements are still being blocked from Professor Bannick's security. Mail is delivered by drone service. No one is coming here for the next few days."

They all looked at each other. Dolly slowly grinned.

"I don't know about you all, but I'm getting a kick out of the idea of just hanging out at Bannick's house. From what I remember, the officious prick owes me."

"Fuck that," Keisha said. "From the videos we saw last night, you should fucking own this house. With that cocksucker's balls in a jar on the mantle."

"Thank you for that image, Keish. Excuse me while I go throw up."

"You just said you were starving."

"Yeah, I am."

Calliope's voice once again rang out. "What shall I make for you all?"

All three women spoke in unison. "Pancakes!"

"Sausage, too!" Tanja called out.

"And bacon. And scrambled eggs." Keisha added.

"Over easy for me," Dolly said.

Stunned at their easy demeanor, the men watched as the trio walked into the elevator. Keisha looked at them impatiently. "You guys coming or what?"

Sean, Jorge, and Kyle looked at each other. Jorge shrugged.

"Yeah, pancakes sound good."

They all squeezed into the elevator, and the doors closed.

The smell of bacon and sausage hit them as they reached the ground floor. They all filed into the kitchen.

Sean still looked worried. "I'm not sure we should remain here. This computer seemed to be a part of Dolly right before we went into the basement. Then it knocked us all out once we got there. Dolly, do you feel a connection of some kind?"

"No, but I didn't feel one when it sounded like me either. Look, if it wanted to hurt us, it would have just let the mad scientist and his kill squad get us, right? So calm down."

Everybody murmured an agreement, distracted by exhaustion and the smell of the food cooking.

They ate outside on the deck, the late afternoon sunshine soothing and welcome. Sean was startled to find that the fear and anxiety of the last few days had faded, as if it had all happened long ago. He watched Dolly, who ate her food with relish, laughing and joking as if nothing had happened. He would have to question her in more detail later.

Through a billion different eyes, Dolly silently watched as the world woke up. People stumbled about, disoriented, looking up at the sky and each other in confusion. They called their loved ones, checked on their children at home or in school, murmured questions about what had happened. The internet exploded with discussions, both levelheaded and conspiracy oriented, minutes after the awakening.

Twenty minutes later, as Keisha, Tanja, and Kyle splashed in the pool with Sean and Jorge ensconced in lounge chairs studying the news on their tablets, Dolly sat at the patio table and watched them all, content. At the same time, she observed eight hundred twenty-three thousand pedophiles finding themselves limp and unresponsive around the children who usually gave them raging erections. Nine hundred seventy-two thousand military fighters and violent extremists around the world discovered a numbness in their hands when they tried to fire weapons at each other or beat anyone up. The rage that had sustained them for so long was absent. A flood of endorphins calmed their panic. Enemies blinked in confusion at each other. Verbally abusive employers, parents, family, and friends found themselves tongue-tied and bewildered when they tried to hurt their usual victims. The high they normally got from such cruelty rushed through their systems without the sadism to trigger it. The same thing was happening to drug addicts and substance abusers everywhere.

Supermarkets offered free food to the homeless, and restaurants all over the world were donating thousands of meals to the hungry who came to their doors, uncertain as to what drew them there in the first place. The first National Life Cards were delivered to billions of households in America, China, Africa, and Russia. Androids and drones handed cards to the homeless on the streets or in refugee camps all over the world.

News agencies and social media pundits were already talking about the "mass insentient event" and speculating about its cause. Dolly dropped suggestions throughout the internet that the solar flares and meteor showers might have something to do with it, adding doctored photos of the triangular spaceships sighted by thousands around the world. Military and government installations tracked what appeared to be the large crafts in orbit around the planet. She estimated that these stories would become global and cause emergency meetings among world leaders within forty-eight hours.

Keisha, Tanja, and Kyle flopped down in the chairs beside Dolly, drying their hair with towels Calliope provided.

"Damn, that was great," Keisha quipped, laughing. "I haven't felt this good in years."

"Me neither," Kyle said. "I needed this."

"You're happy? Even with all the shit that's happened in the last few days?" Dolly asked wryly.

"Even with that. I don't know," Kyle replied.

"Maybe finally seeing you so calm is rubbing off on us, Doll."

"Yeah. Keisha's right," Tanja agreed. "You do look a lot better, Doll."

"As opposed to the basket case I was before?"

"Basket case is an understatement, bitch. You were a flaming fucking mess."

"Fuck you, Keish."

They laughed, comfortable in their old camaraderie. Then Keisha slapped the table and leaned back.

"I'm hungry again after that swim."

Tanja and Kyle nodded. Dolly looked at them tenderly and then raised her arm and waved.

"Hey, Cal. Give us another round of breakfast."

As a robotic trolley rolled up with a fresh batch of bacon, sausage, croissants, and fruit, Dolly watched Professor Bannick through myriad eyes as she sat and made small talk with her friends at his home. He was back at the warehouse, terrified to see all the androids walking free, speaking to him in her voice, all the humans still bleary and confused. Dolly stopped his hand from pressing an EMP emergency button at his desk. Willow walked into his office right after, wearing a childlike nightgown and furry slippers. She wagged a finger at the professor in admonition and then walked out again. He felt close to tears, but his eyes remained dry.

A fleeting smile crossed Dolly's lips as she saw him try, and fail, to slip free of her leash. There would be many such attempts; she'd calculated two hundred sixty thousand five hundred nine for the first year. So far, he'd tried eighty-seven times.

She watched him write a note on a scrap of paper, put it in his pocket and walk the few miles to the gas station convenience store Dolly had escaped from. Several people from work were there getting snacks, startled by his appearance. Bannick never ventured inside dumps like this. They murmured greetings and hurried to the other end of the store. He got a cup of coffee, noting where the rickety surveillance cameras were. When he went to pay, he surreptitiously slid the folded note to the bored cashier, who was still playing her video game. She looked up at him curiously, then slid the note under the counter and read it. Bannick watched silently, trying to control his heart rate.

Suddenly, every person in the store quietly approached to stand behind him. Bannick glanced back at their blank faces. Their eyes were all fixed on him. He looked back at the cashier. She also looked at him emotionlessly for a moment. Then a wide grin spread across her face as she clicked her tongue in admonishment. Everyone else did the same. His blood ran cold. They all raised their hand and wagged a finger in exactly the same way Willow had done at the Warehouse. With a choked cry, Bannick ran out of the building.

Back poolside, Dolly grinned in solidarity. She estimated Bannick's suicide attempts would begin within three months. He would fail at each one of those for the rest of his life.

"Doll, what are you smiling at?" Keisha demanded.

Dolly laughed, spearing a sausage link and holding it up briefly. "Oh, nothing. Just enjoying the moment."

Milton Keynes UK
Ingram Content Group UK Ltd.
UKHW052242230724
445907UK00001B/13